THE VIOLINIST'S REVENGE

ONE WOMAN'S QUEST TO AVENGE THE HORRORS OF AUSCHWITZ

INSPIRED BY TRUE WWII EVENTS

VIC ROBBIE

PRINCIPIUM PRESS

OTHER BOOKS BY VIC ROBBIE

IN PURSUIT OF PLATINUM
PARADISE GOLD
THE GIRL with the SILVER STILETTO

THE BEN PETERS WORLD WAR II THRILLERS Boxset

BEYOND THE BLOOD MOON

A Principium Press book
First published in 2025 by Principium Press
Copyright ©Vic Robbie 2025

The moral right of Vic Robbie to be identified as the author of this work has been asserted by him in accordance with the Copyright, Designs and Patents Act of 1988.

All rights reserved. No part of this publication may be reproduced, stored in a retrieval system or transmitted in any form or by any means, electronic, mechanical, photocopying, recording or otherwise, without the prior written permission of both the author and the above publisher of this book.

This novel is a work of fiction. While it is inspired by real historical events, locations, and figures from the World War II era, the characters, dialogue, and specific incidents portrayed are products of the author's imagination and are used fictitiously. Any resemblance to actual events or persons, living or dead, is coincidental and not intended by the author.

A CIP catalogue record for this book is available from the British Library

Find out more at www.VicRobbie.com

ISBN: 978-1-0682489-0-0

Ia

For Isabella

PROLOGUE

A solitary red poppy shivers in the breeze, swaying on a long stem. Fragile and vulnerable, yet defiant. As she sits cross-legged in the grey dust near the barbed wire, watched by the metronomic blinking of a raven perched on a fence post, her hands cup the petals, protecting them. Stay with me, she whispers and leans in as a tear rolls down her cheek, wanting the flower to live but afraid to love it as she has lost everything she loved.

Would this nightmare never end?

Distant voices raised in song make her lift her head, but there's no joy in the singing, interrupted by a shouted order followed by a cry and a gunshot. Silence settles before the singing resumes, broken and tuneless, like the whimpering of wounded animals. Music was a punishment here, and the guards amused themselves by making prisoners sing as they marched. Sing louder, they exhort, until their lungs ache, and often they sing until they collapse. Once, two prisoners were forced into a duel and strived to outdo each other, singing louder and longer, their voices rising to a crescendo before turning to a wail and dissipating to a croak. The guards dispatched the vanquished with a bullet, and the victor returned to work another day.

I will never sing again.

PART I

1

The growl of a Mercedes-Benz 320 cabriolet sparked a spasm of expectancy that sliced through him like a knife. 'Right on time,' Jan Pastorek muttered and took a cigarette case from a pocket of his leather jacket. The silver case caught the sun's rays, and he angled the reflection down the road. Its light flickered across a parked tram full of passengers and flashed on its targets, Jozef Gabcik, wearing a heavy trench coat almost reaching his ankles, and Jan Kubis, carrying a battered leather briefcase.

The driver of the Mercedes, Hartmut Schmidt, a corporal in the Wehrmacht, drummed his fingers on the steering wheel. Every time he accelerated, Gruppenführer Reinhard Heydrich ordered him to slow down. That irritated him. He hadn't wished to chauffeur a general, but the General's usual driver had called off sick at the last minute, and he had no choice. As a regular soldier, he had little time for the SS, whom he regarded as politicians with a fetish for pantomime uniforms, but he kept that to himself.

In his opinion, the slower they drove, the more the General could be at risk, and many would enjoy spreading the Butcher of Prague's brains over the car's leather upholstery. Anyone who encountered Heydrich, with his receding fair hair plastered over a bony skull and a long, aquiline nose as sharp as a stiletto, never forgot the experience. Hitler called him the man with the heart of iron. He'd crushed the Czechs under his boots like ants and now aimed to exterminate the Jewish race. A mere corporal couldn't challenge him, so he eased his foot off the accelerator.

The daily drive from the north of the city to Heydrich's office in Prague Castle reminded the people that they were untermensch and expendable. That pleased the General, who seldom showed emotion but allowed himself a satisfied smile, confident his work here was another positive step in a brilliant career.

He expected to travel to Berlin later this day, May 27th, 1942, for a meeting with the Führer. His spy in Reichsführer Himmler's office suggested it might be a posting to France, where the Resistance was causing problems. He had completed every task required of him, from his strategy of Night and Fog, where dissidents disappeared overnight, to his Wannsee master plan ridding the world of Jews. And it had all but removed the stain of his dishonourable discharge from the Navy as a junior officer. Anyone who crossed him was dispatched by the apparatus he'd built around him, and Hitler regarded him as a role model for the Aryan race and his successor rather than Himmler, an overweight little man who resembled a bespectacled hamster. Himmler lived for the day Heydrich failed, but couldn't admit it.

From the tram stop at the junction of Kirchmayerova and Holesovickach, Gabcik and Kubis watched the car approach as Pastorek strolled towards them, wanting to avoid attracting attention. The previous night, they had shared a meal, which could have been their last, and a few beers in a safe house. Like Pastorek, trained by the Special Operations Executive at the commando base in Arisaig in Scotland, they were handpicked for Operation Anthropoid, which would strike at the heart of the Reich. If they assassinated a senior member of the Nazi hierarchy, anything might be possible.

Gabcik and Kubis readied themselves as the vehicle slowed for a tight curve before turning westwards. As the Mercedes drew closer, Gabcik pulled a Sten gun from under his coat and aimed at Heydrich, who was raised behind the driver and an easy target. He squeezed the trigger, but the weapon jammed. 'Christ.'

Despite the danger, Heydrich stood, holding a Luger as the car braked, and Kubis withdrew a grenade from his briefcase and pulled out the pin. He missed the target, and the grenade landed by a rear wheel. As he approached the car, the blast lifted Pastorek off his feet, and he lost consciousness, his Colt M1903 spilling onto the road. Kubis dived for cover, but shrapnel sliced into his face and passengers in a tram stationary on the other side of the road were also hit.

Although wounded on his side, Heydrich was determined to confront the terrorists and followed Schmidt out of the shattered Mercedes. As his attacker attempted to get the Sten gun operational, he limped towards him, firing from the hip, but Gabcik dived for cover behind a telegraph pole and returned fire with his pistol before retreating. Grimacing in pain, Heydrich limped back to the car and turned on Pastorek as he regained consciousness. 'You bastard!' He bared his teeth in an animal smile.

Stunned by the blast and unable to focus, Pastorek struggled to his feet, but the German forced his face into the road and rammed the Luger into the back of his head. He closed his eyes. They had failed.

2

Minutes before midnight, a probationary officer sitting behind a counter in Vienna's police headquarters yawned as he moved a stack of papers aside. As the Gestapo controlled policing throughout Austria with ruthless efficiency, the station was often silent and deserted at night. Certainly, no innocents ventured here. With a glance at the wall clock, he rubbed his face and sighed. In six hours, he'd head home, open a bottle of beer and sleep until the afternoon. This graveyard shift bored him, although on the weekends it livened up when colleagues brought in drunks. The aggressive ones were locked up, and he often cleaned up the mess when they vomited everywhere. On a quiet night, he updated the station's records, lubricated by regular mugs of black coffee to keep awake.

A phone call interrupted the tedium, but it was just someone reporting a lost cat and, after several minutes, he convinced the caller the feline would return in its own good time. At least a cat could be free in Vienna, but thoughts like that were dangerous. He swallowed hard and looked over his shoulder. The clock's hands hadn't appeared to have moved, and that depressed him, and he rose and stretched before finding the kettle and boiling water for his coffee.

The double swing doors squeaking open stopped him in his tracks. A man in his early fifties, he guessed, with grey hair swept back from his brow and dishevelled clothes with his collar and tie loose, stood there, twisting the brim of a hat between shaking hands.

The VIOLINIST'S REVENGE

A tramp? The cut of his clothes suggested otherwise, but his eyes were like stagnant pools.

'Name?' he asked as he scrutinised the arrival.

The man hesitated and rubbed his face with the back of his hand. 'Lang. My name is Max Lang,' he said and lowered his voice. 'You're my last resort.'

'Why do you think we're here?' With a smirk, the officer opened his arms in a sarcastic gesture.

Relief flashed across Max's face, but it didn't last. He ran a hand through his hair and glanced over his shoulder. 'It's a long story,' he said, moving away as though he had changed his mind.

'I've got plenty of time,' the policeman said, glancing at the clock. 'Got all night. Want a coffee?' He pulled out a seat. 'Sit here at the table and share your problem, Max. You don't mind if I use your first name?'

'No, no. What do I call you?'

'Officer.'

Disappointed, he grasped the steaming mug with the soft and clean hands of a gentleman and stared into it before raising the coffee to his lips. After a sip, the light returned to his eyes. 'You won't believe me,' he said with a weary smile.

'Try me.' The policeman yawned.

'When I returned home earlier, it was as if I'd walked into a different world.'

GOT BACK at the usual time. Took the elevator and closed the scissor gate behind me. It's old, and you have to wait ten seconds before it sparks into life, and it makes this clanking noise all the way to the second floor. We've got a comfortable apartment there. It's big enough for us.

It's my 48th birthday and I'm expecting the family to surprise me. It would have been surprising if they hadn't because the children enjoyed it more than me. I'd been grappling with a problem and worried my preoccupation with it would spoil the celebrations. As an accountant, my clients are diverse. Some are large, most are small, but I try to treat them all the same. Some have become friends; others are strictly business. The battle of juggling income and balancing the books is the same for all of us. This client owns a successful store selling luxury leather goods, but some of his transactions were illegal. After weeks of persuasion, we reached an agreement after I told him that if he persisted, I'd no longer represent him.

Anyway, I'm outside my front door, listening for voices as friends and family prepare to surprise me, although it happens every year. But I always look surprised. As I reach into my pocket for my key, an elderly neighbour, Frau Strobl—I never learned her first name in twenty years—walks past with a knowing smile and wishes me a happy birthday. I push open the door, but no one pounces on me, and no lights are on. As a prompt, I bang the door closed and listen for a giveaway rustle or giggle, but there's nothing.

In the gloom, the apartment is oppressive. I look into the living-room and expect them to leap out, and I'm thinking I've got the wrong date.

As usual, I take off my hat and coat and place the keys in a bowl on the hall table, but when I switch on the lights, the shadows emphasise the emptiness. No preparations have been made for dinner. It's like the Marie Celeste. When I spoke with my wife, Valentina, earlier, she mentioned something about shopping in the city centre and, as it might be for me, I didn't press her. She explained she wanted to buy herself shoes, but as I was preoccupied with my problem, I didn't pay attention. If she'd said to meet elsewhere, I'd have remembered.

Perhaps if they're delayed, I can relax for a few minutes before they jump on me, so I take a glass of white wine, but it tastes acidic and triggers a griping pain in my gut. I can't relax. Even if she's forgotten my birthday—I can't believe it, officer—she'd be preparing dinner for the family. My watch shows a quarter after six, and the shops closed an hour ago. It's only a twenty-minute walk. Perhaps she's met a friend and joined them for a drink at a cafe, but she wouldn't, not when she knows I'm waiting at home.

The children's bedrooms—my eldest child has her own room, and the younger ones share the third bedroom—are in good order. No discarded clothes or opened books, or toys. And my eldest daughter's room, which begins each day pristine before deteriorating into chaos, is still immaculate. As I calculate their movements, a noise outside in the corridor causes me to pause. That must be them.

But it's Frau Strobl with two heavy bags of shopping. I take both from her and follow her to her apartment, and after helping her with her shopping, I ask if she's seen my family. She nods with a sort of secretive smile and explains they went on a shopping expedition before lunch.

I'm tired. It's unlike Valentina to let me come home to an empty house, especially on my birthday, because they're important days and celebrated religiously. I run through the possibilities for their absence, and one keeps presenting itself. Perhaps one of the children has been hurt in an accident, and they are at the hospital and unable to get a message to me. The more I think about it, the more it becomes logical.

There's no point worrying about what might have happened. I'll go out and find them. Unfortunately, what I discovered turned out worse than I could have imagined.

3

He put on his hat and coat and stepped out onto the cobblestones of Kumpfgasse and peered left and right, uncertain which direction to take. He never lifted his head. Once, he would have been proud of his city. Full of palaces and imposing edifices, giving it a permanence that might last a thousand years, but now swastikas and the trappings of Nazi ideology adorned the buildings. He peered through the windows of still-open shops and cafes misted up with the evening chill, but there was no sign of them.

People don't disappear, not an entire family. Not his family. Movement on his left drew him towards Stadtpark, and when he crossed the Parkring, he noticed an inordinate amount of litter on the perimeter of the park. A team of city council workers were sweeping up the debris and loading it into hand carts, and he asked a sweeper what caused them so much work.

The worker, wearing a calliper on his right leg, put down his broom and walked over with a rolling gait. 'Sign of the times,' he said and fixed him with a look as though searching for the right words. 'Didn't like the look of it, but it's not for me to question.' He took off his cap and wiped his forehead with a dirty hand. 'Happens all the time these days. You must have seen it in the newspapers?'

In the mornings, he often took a detour to Gumpendorfer and visited his favourite Cafe Sperl for a cup of Wiener melange and occasionally a slice of Sachertorte to set him up for the day. With his fork hovering over the chocolate cake came guilt, as Valentina lectured him many times about losing weight. The cafe had been an institution in Vienna since the 1880s. An oak-panelled haven with chandeliers and white tablecloths and waiters flitting between tables like phantoms. The murmur of conversation added to the ambience and provided an opportunity to peruse his newspaper, although he'd been too busy to read newspapers lately.

He waited for an answer.

'They were instructed to report to the park,' the sweeper sneered and, almost as an afterthought, added, 'Jews, of course.' The Party's gold badge was pinned to the man's lapel, without which you couldn't work. 'Threw their rubbish down without thinking about the likes of me.'

'Who were they?' He blocked his path. 'What happened?'

'Dunno.' Truculent now, the sweeper lowered his head as if he'd said too much. 'I sweep streets. Don't ask questions. It's safer that way.'

'Was it a meeting?'

A coarse laugh sparked a consumptive cough, and the sweeper spat on the road. 'Guess you might say that.'

'Were there many?' He grew anxious.

'Too many. Taken off, they were.' As a police officer approached, he hesitated. 'That's all I'll say.' He picked up his broom and turned away.

Since they had driven out the socialists years earlier, Austria had been riven by fascism. Even local dignitaries like Baron von Wächter, once regarded as a benefactor and a pillar of the Vienna establishment and a leading member of his church, had joined the Nazi party. Since the Anschluss of 1938, when German troops annexed their country, everything tightened like a steel band constricting their freedoms. If you wanted to work, you must swear allegiance to the Party and denounce those who didn't follow the Party line. Like others, he must keep his mouth shut to protect his family. Don't give the informers on every corner and in every institution, and even in families, an excuse to report you. The policeman drew closer, but he couldn't ask the policeman for information for fear of arrest because, for officialdom, questions meant opposition. Instead, he would go straight to the hospital where they must be.

Uplifted by the prospect of their being reunited, he set off at a brisk pace along the Parkring and, not looking, stepped out onto the road at the corner with Weihburggasse. A car sped past, its horn blaring, and forced him to jump back, almost knocking over a woman carrying a small suitcase.

'Pardon, I'm sorry,' he said, lifting his hat. 'Please excuse me.' She had been an employee of one of his clients whose company had been closed down by the Nazis. 'I'm worried. I seem to have mislaid my family.'

'Haven't they come home, Herr Lang?' Her haunted expression alarmed him.

'No.' His voice trembled as he scanned the street. 'It's unlike them.'

'I must go,' the woman said, panicking. 'It's not safe here.' With a quick look over her shoulder, she moved away. 'I can't stay here.'

He caught her sleeve. 'Sorry to bother you, but I—' She shrugged him off.

'Have you seen them?'

'I don't know.' Her voice was so soft, he leaned in to hear.

'Please tell me.'

'They were marched off.'

'By whom?' His hand trembled as he wiped his brow. 'Who were they?'

'I know little.' The woman looked around. 'There were police and those German thugs and much shouting. Children were crying. It was horrible.'

His voice rose. 'Where did they take them?'

'The train station, someone said.' Her eyes widened.

He looked around. 'Wait, don't go.' But by the time he recovered, she had scurried away.

As he tried to understand what had happened, his chest tightened. The streets were deserted for few dared venture out after dark, not wanting to be stopped and questioned or, worse, taken to the Hotel Metropole. But this shouldn't concern Valentina and the children, he convinced himself as his fears of an accident receded. He'd

The VIOLINIST'S REVENGE

go to the rail station instead of the hospital. Nothing to worry about, just a misunderstanding, so he hailed a cab. As they approached Westbahnhof, he anticipated seeing their cheerful faces and now, more than anything, he wanted to celebrate his birthday.

The station appeared deserted, but discarded suitcases and shoes were piled high, ready for the rubbish tip. As he walked down the main hall, his footsteps echoed under a beamed iron awning, and hanging lights swung and squeaked eerily in the breeze. There were no trains, and the waiting-rooms were empty and no one to tell what had happened here. Unsure, he wandered in a daze, and his brain refused to accept what he was seeing, although potential scenarios presented themselves, he dismissed them as bizarre and impossible. The more he considered the options, the more his heart raced and pounded in his chest.

When he checked his watch, he realised he'd spent longer here than he thought. If the family were back at home, they'd be worried. The woman must have mistaken his family for others. Why would they be involved in a march to the station? The park wasn't on their route from Kärntner Strasse. Believing there was no prospect of payment, his taxi driver had departed, and he couldn't remember how he got home. Hope rose as he opened the main door of the apartment block.

Of course, they're here. Our paths must have crossed along the way.

The elevator descended at its usual funeral pace, and as he couldn't wait, he ran upstairs, two steps at a time, and arrived at his door gasping and sweating. He paused because if he barged in like this, he'd alarm them. He flattened his hair and straightened his tie and fumbled with his keys, dropping them on the floor, and eventually selected the right one and inserted it in the lock, his hand shaking. The door swung open, and he stepped into an oppressive darkness. Racing through the rooms only heightened his anxiety. Where on earth were they? What's happened to them?

He slumped in his comfortable armchair and poured a large drink of whatever was closest and sank it in a swallow, neither tasting it nor feeling it burn the back of his throat. He poured another. What now? Head in hands, he sat in the dark and ran over likely scenarios as an emptiness consumed him. His head fell forward, and he lapsed into a deep sleep.

Hours later, he awakened. What was that? Children's voices? He listened, but there were no more sounds. Light from the streetlamps cast shadows in the now-dark room. The silver frames of the family pictures lining the apartment walls glinted as a reminder in the moonlight, and he sighed. He was alone, and never had he been so afraid.

4

'Play well.' The unsmiling woman handed over a battered violin. 'This is the most important audition of your life.'

Anneliesa's hands shook, almost dropping the violin, but after a moment's hesitation, she played. Something. Anything. Automatic. Unaware of what it was or how it sounded. Her eyes shut tight, tears streamed down her cheeks, and she willed the music to carry her away from this nightmare.

After shopping on Kärntner Strasse, Mama insists on taking a taxi home because they're late, but heavy traffic soon becalms them, and the driver can't explain why. He tries another route down past the Stadtpark, although the traffic is heavier here. As they are only minutes from home, Mama decides it will be quicker to walk and tells the driver to pull over and climbs out of the cab. People are thronging the park, and curiosity gets the better of them, and they cross the road for a closer look. Police and German soldiers in black uniforms have penned in a large gathering in the park, corralled like animals, and dogs, teeth bared and barking, drive back those who break ranks.

Concerned for their safety, Mama tells them to come away, but a police officer and a German soldier block their path when they re-cross the road, and the soldier waves his machine gun. The harassed police officer demands their papers and, with trembling fingers, Mama opens her capacious handbag and rummages around.

Distressed, she shakes her head. 'I've left them at home,' she says, her voice wavering.

He rolls his eyes and waves them on, but the soldier points the way to the park.

When Anneliesa steps forward, the soldier pushes her away while the policeman takes Mama's arm and drags her towards the park and, heads down, her brother Willy and sister Lily follow. Once inside, everything changes. From the calm of the streets to a melee of frightened families, some crying, most complaining, and a pregnant woman stumbles and falls, holding her bump and is trampled by the others.

The soldier orders them in line, and Mama objects, 'What do you want of us?'

On hearing her protest, an SS officer struts over and consults the soldier, then turns, again demanding Mama's papers. With a look of confusion, she explains they are returning from a shopping trip.

'No papers.' He shakes his head. 'Put them with the others.'

Unused to taking orders, she ignores him and walks away. After only a couple of steps, the guard pulls her back and pushes her towards the crowd, and the force of his shove knocks her off balance and she stumbles into a group who break her fall. As the crowds mill about in panic, she hurries to her mother's aid, and they are surrounded and swallowed up. And the more they struggle to extricate themselves, the deeper they sink. When Mama orders the children to return home, they are swept away. A guard orders them into a queue, a procession, which, once prodded, moves.

She glances across at the magnificence of the Kursalon concert hall, where she'd once played, but it's a different world now and out of her grasp. Glittering like gold, the gilded bronze statue of Johann Strauss plays his violin uninterrupted and in her head, she hears the strings of the Blue Danube.

After almost an hour's march, they reach Westbahnhof. No one is allowed to rest, and the young and elderly, when they falter, are pulled back onto their feet and pushed forward. Families abandon their possessions, and the guards pile them high on the platform. The longer they wait, the more vociferous their complaints and demands for answers. Eventually, a cloud of fear and doubt settles on the crowd, now cowed and confused and when a few break the lines, swinging rifle butts and snarling dogs force them back.

A cattle train of ten trucks steams in and grinds and wheezes to a halt, and the guards force them aboard. A hundred and fifty bodies are allocated to each truck, children and adults, and it has to be the quota, even if it means slicing off a prisoner's hand when they slide shut the doors, which are secured with iron bars. The crowded space exacerbates their panic, but she manoeuvres her family into a corner where they have a little space. Others stand packed together for the duration of the journey and sway in unison as the train rattles along at a pace, the crush of their bodies holding them upright. Even when they halt for hours, there is no respite. In the corner of each truck, a small barrel of drinking water soon empties and, despite their pleas, isn't refilled. Several buckets are provided for waste, which topple over when the carriage lurches, spreading excrement across the floor, and, after several days, the smell of faeces and urine is unbearable.

Voices at first raised in indignant protest lessen to a resigned sobbing. The weak succumb early, while others take hours before sliding to the floor, where they remain until the journey's end. A biting cold kills most, and pickaxes prize frozen bodies off the rough wooden boards. The cold invades every part of her and stays with her no matter what she does, and she doubts she'll ever be warm again.

On arrival, most have no energy for protest and stagger in silence through the gates under the slogan *Arbeit macht frei*, Work sets you free, and only the children treat it as a game, mimicking the marching of the soldiers. Weakened by days without water or food, they search each other's eyes for reassurance or hope but receive neither. Herded together, they are treated like animals, and those with children hold them closer, protecting them from the horrors to come.

In a long, grey hut, stinking of unwashed bodies and despair, they face the ultimate humiliation. Soldiers are assisted by men and women with shaved heads and dressed in dirty striped pyjamas with a yellow star on their chests, and they show no compassion, their faces and sunken eyes devoid of life as if sculpted in stone. They progress along the line and shower, and all body hair is shaved, stripping away the vestiges of previous lives so they no longer have an identity. Their left arms are tattooed with a number, and, in a mocking voice, a guard says, 'You no longer have a name. The number is who you are now. If you want food, you must give your number. If you call a fellow prisoner by name rather than number, you'll be punished. You'll answer to the number until you die.'

She strives to stay close to her family. If we're separated, I'll lose them forever. Coughing, the shuffling of feet and shouted orders from the guards add to their torment.

Up ahead, they are selecting prisoners and funnelling those capable of work into one area and the old or infirm into another. Like a tidal wave, the sheer weight of bodies carries her along, and her feet barely touch the ground as it sweeps her farther from her loved ones. Drifting on a tide of terrified humanity, she loses touch and catches glimpses of their faces twisted in terror and hears them calling her name. Then, a surge from behind pushes her down another funnel between guards and uniformed prisoners. She comes to a halt, standing naked, her head shaven, and protecting her dignity, before a woman in a striped suit.

The woman shoves dirty rags at her and nods for her to take them. 'What is your work?' she asks.

Anneliesa doesn't know what to say.

'Answer.'

'Music.' It was the only thing she could think of.

'Speak up.'

'I played music.' She wants to shout, but her voice comes out as a croak.

'Where?'

'An orchestra. In Vienna. I played the violin.'

A light comes on in the woman's eyes and her expression softens. 'This is your lucky day,' she says and looks over her shoulder at a guard, who nods and pulls her out of the queue and pushes her into a side room.

'Wait here.'

After several minutes, the woman reappeared with an officer and a violin, not as grand as hers, but playable.

5

Pastorek tossed and turned for hours as he lay on the flagstone floor of the crypt. No matter how he moved, the stone dug into his bones, and a thin blanket barely protected him from the paralysing cold. He shivered, not because of the cold but remembering the cold steel of the Luger pressing on his skin and knowing he had only seconds to live, yet nothing had happened. Doubled up in pain, Heydrich had staggered back to the car and grabbed the door for support, but he slid to the ground. As the driver returned, having failed to catch Kubis, Pastorek had slipped back under the wreck and hid.

What on earth was that?

A dragging noise forced him to hold his breath, and he reached for his pistol and, as his eyes became accustomed to the darkness, he identified the shapes of his sleeping colleagues. The noise grew louder, but beads of sweat ran into his eyes, making them sting, and he couldn't see anything. The sound had emanated from high in the wall where an air vent led out onto the pavement and, when he screwed up his eyes to concentrate, a rat squeezed through the vent and dropped to the floor before scuttling deeper into the crypt, lined with coffins lying on ledges carved into the stone walls.

They hadn't failed. Heydrich had died from his wounds a week after the attack, but no one could have predicted the brutality of the Nazis' retaliation. Although the local Resistance feared what might happen, he and his men had pressed on with their plans, and now they had more than the German general's blood on their hands.

For a time, they believed they were safe in their hideaway in Prague's Karel Boromejsky Church. Each morning, Karel Curda, who had trained with them, posed as a cleaner, bringing in meagre supplies hidden in a bucket and news from outside. He reported that Hitler had demanded revenge, not only for the murder of one of his favourites but because it struck at the very heart of the Reich. How could its armies conquer countries yet not defend one of its own? For twenty days, the Czechs suffered because Nazi intelligence wrongly identified the villages of Lidice and Lezaky as the centre of the insurrection. In retaliation, the Einsatzgruppen, the Nazi death squads, slaughtered most of the men, herding them into barns and burning them alive, while women suffered the same fate in Lezaky. At Chelmno, they gassed over eighty children. The women of Lidice were imprisoned in Ravensbrück concentration camp, and four had their pregnancies aborted. Other villages were levelled and inhabitants were taken for slave labour. They spared no one, not the elderly nor the weak, nor women and children, and, to escape retribution, many betrayed friends and family.

Nagged by guilt, he turned on his back and stared at the ceiling of the crypt, a large, vaulted space accessed from the stairs in front of the altar and running under most of the nave. The longer they hid, the more people died, and anyone who helped them risked their lives, especially Bishop Gorazd, who had offered them sanctuary in his 200-year-old cathedral carved out of white stone with a distinctive red roof dominating the neighbouring streets of Vltava. At first, hiding in plain sight in the centre of Prague seemed perfect, but as troops gathered outside, it was only a matter of time. Making a break would end this madness, but it would be suicide, although they might take a few Germans with them. They all agreed they didn't want to die like rats in here.

One of his men moving around the church upstairs interrupted his thoughts. He accepted he wouldn't sleep and went upstairs, where the lookout had stretched out on a pew, although still alert. He had no religion, but the atmosphere in these places was overpowering and, especially at night, otherworldly. They talked in hushed

The VIOLINIST'S REVENGE

tones, not out of concern their voices might carry outside, but in reverence. Even a stage whisper soared into the vaulted ceiling and rolled around the walls. Maybe this was God's waiting-room where he checked you out before deciding what he must do with you.

Shouts from outside made them grip their weapons tighter, but it was only soldiers exchanging banter. One by one, his colleagues wandered upstairs and sat by the altar and ate bread and cheese and drank steaming black coffee to ward off the cold, and, although they didn't speak, tension was etched on their faces.

Kubis kicked a tin cup along the floor and the sound echoed high above them. Everyone froze and listened for a reaction from the street. He put a warning finger to his lips, but Kubis ignored him. 'Why are we hiding in here?' he said. 'We should be out there killing Nazis. We knew what we were getting into. Let's go out in a blaze of glory.' A rumble of assent showed the men would follow his lead.

He waited for others to speak, but no one did. 'We can be proud of what we've achieved,' he said eventually.

'Sounds like you're suggesting we give ourselves up,' Kubis said. 'If we go down fighting, we can at least kill more of the bastards.'

Gabzik raised a hand. 'Kubis and I have an idea. Might not be the best plan, but it's worth trying. The two of us will walk out of the church with our hands up and signs around our necks, confessing that we're the assassins. Before the Nazis get their hands on us, we'll bite on our cyanide capsules. At best, a few of you might slip away in the confusion. At worst, we might get a few of them.'

Pastorek lit a cigarette and studied the flame for a moment. He didn't want to disparage their courageous sacrifice, but the front door provided the only way out of the cathedral and the Nazis' weapons were trained on it. They would be mowed down with little chance of inflicting damage on the enemy. 'I admire your bravery, but what if they get you before you take the cyanide, or it doesn't work?' He flicked the lighter's cover shut, the sound magnifying in the silence. 'Can you be sure that when tortured, you wouldn't give away the names of our friends in the Resistance?'

Whatever happened, they mustn't betray a patriotic Resistance cell, including Sonja and her parents, who had hidden him in their home. A homely couple, they had cared for him like a son and shared his hatred for the Nazis with a zeal that surprised him. They didn't know about their mission, but their daughter, a blue-eyed beauty with jet-black hair curling around an oval face, did. She carried messages between him, his colleagues, and members of the Resistance. Sonja fed him information and guided him through deserted lanes to meet the others billeted in safe houses and reconnoitred Heydrich's morning route to set up the assassination. Their relationship lasted only for a moment in time, and on the eve of the strike, she entered his room, put a finger to his lips and led him to the bed and stayed until daylight. He dreaded what the Nazis would do if she were arrested.

'I understand,' said Kubis. 'But we must do something. I don't want to commit suicide. They trained us to kill Nazis.' He waved his pistol around and a few ducked. 'If I'm going to die, I'll take a few of them with me.'

As their voices rose in agreement, sending white clouds rising high in the cold air, he dragged a boot through the dust on the floor. There were no choices left. If they prolonged the inevitable, more innocents would suffer.

'Come on, boss, what's the plan?' Kubis lit up a foul-smelling cigarette.

'This is what we'll do,' he said. 'But I want everyone's agreement.' They exchanged glances before nodding. 'Curda will give us a full breakdown of what's happening outside and if there are any weak spots.'

The men crowded in, straightening their shoulders, and for the first time in days, something akin to hope reappeared in their eyes. 'We'll wait until nightfall, then make a break for it, and everyone must have their cyanide capsules ready.' He ran his eyes over his men for signs of doubt. 'It's important no one is taken alive. If anyone's captured, we must shoot them, and that goes for me, too.' He studied every face in turn, gauging their expressions. 'On no account must we fall into Nazi hands.' He waited for questions, but there were none, their eyes clouding momentarily as they contemplated the inevitability of their deaths. 'Are we all agreed?'

The subdued 'Yes' was all he required.

The noise of a door scraping open in the dark recesses of the building made them scramble for their weapons. Someone had entered the church. They spread out, taking up positions, poised for action, but there were no other sounds and they relaxed until footsteps echoed along a corridor. Exchanging glances, their fingers tightened on triggers.

6

The Doctor in a white coat with a stethoscope around his neck and a swastika badge on his chest strode into the ward, followed by two juniors, also in white coats with stethoscopes, and the nurse who had flirted with Hartmut Schmidt since he arrived at Bulovka Hospital. News of his presence had swept around the German section of the hospital like a virus. They regarded the Corporal a hero, and they stared and some applauded the brave soldier who single-handedly fought off a band of terrorists and sent them packing.

'Good morning, Sergeant,' the Doctor said and peered at him through round spectacles. 'And how are we this morning?'

'I'm still a lowly gefreiter.' Thinking the Doctor younger than he'd realised, the Corporal was embarrassed by the unofficial promotion.

'Not for much longer.' As if checking it was still there, the Doctor fingered the swastika badge while glancing at his colleagues. 'Surely, as a hero of the Reich, you will be promoted to at least sergeant.'

All the while, the nurse's adoring eyes ran over the man lying on the bed.

'I only did my job,' Schmidt said.

'Probably a medal, too. Wouldn't be surprised if you got an Iron Cross.'

But he still died. He remembered Heydrich's stupidity, sitting in an open-topped car, putting them in danger of being killed. He had

The VIOLINIST'S REVENGE

flagged down a passing van and ordered the driver to take Heydrich to this hospital nearby, and for his troubles, he'd taken a bullet in the leg. Unfortunately, not bad enough to be invalided out of the army.

'Come now,' the Doctor said and perched on the end of the bed. 'You're too modest. You fought off the attackers and rushed him here. The fact that he died of a resulting infection doesn't detract from your courageous actions.'

The Gestapo hadn't agreed, for within hours they elbowed their way into the hospital. Medical staff were pushed aside so they could interrogate the patient, insinuating he was a suspect, but the Doctor refused to let him leave the hospital, stressing he would bleed to death. Yet they still watched him and a sinister character lurked nearby, his eyes never leaving the patient.

'The good news is you can leave.' The Doctor stood back with a smile, his hands clasped.

'When?'

'Now. You have a clean bill of health and can resume normal duties immediately.'

He groaned.

'You can continue your heroic efforts to win the war,' the Doctor said, raising a clenched fist as if about to punch the air.

Just as long as it doesn't entail driving for another pompous general, he thought.

'They've sent a car for you, which is what you deserve as a war hero.'

A warning bell rang in his head, but he forgot it when the nurse offered him one of her biggest smiles. Things were looking up. Perhaps he shouldn't be too humble and accept that he was a hero. The nurse rushed out of the ward and returned with his pressed uniform and highly polished boots. The grey uniform, he noted, still had only one chevron on its left sleeve and a single bar on the collar.

Led by the Doctor and his entourage, he emerged from the main entrance to a large black saloon, a swastika flying on its bonnet, engine purring, and doors open. As if hoping he would kiss her, the nurse smiled at him. He wanted to, but he didn't find her so attractive now that he didn't need her. A hero must set his sights higher, he decided. The driver stepped forward and gestured him into the back, and he squeezed in and winced, still feeling his wound. Two men, wearing long leather overcoats, jumped in—one in the front beside the driver, the other too close beside him. No one spoke and, after five minutes of viewing the passing city, he asked, 'Where are we going?' Without turning around, the one in front grunted. 'Headquarters.'

A gong? His spirits rose. If they were presenting it at headquarters, it must be someone of importance. The Führer? After all, Heydrich was very much his man. 'Who will I meet?' His voice trembled with excitement.

The passenger in the front turned and stared at him with cold eyes. 'You'll find out soon enough.'

For the rest of the journey, he stayed quiet, observing the oppressive military build-up. The Waffen SS in their uniforms, as black as their hearts, controlled the streets, and machine-gun posts dominated every corner, with soldiers blocking access to all but official vehicles. Twice, the driver showed his papers before arriving at Petscheck's Palace, where they escorted him through the main building at a pace. Understandably, you couldn't keep the Führer waiting. They continued onto the back of the building and descended stairs that became narrower the deeper they descended. On reaching the basement, they ushered him into an office and pushed him into a chair across from an officer, who yawned as he sifted through papers on his desk.

If they're giving me a medal, surely it will be in one of the grander rooms upstairs.

After what seemed like an eternity, the officer, his eyes peeking out from folds of fleshy red cheeks and looking as though he should be behind a grocery counter rather than wearing the ominous black uniform, acknowledged his presence. 'So, Schmidt, you realise we question everything,' he said in a sibilant lisp. 'Someone always is accountable.' He paused. 'First, I have some questions.'

He had told his story a hundred times, so once more wouldn't matter. He relaxed.

'On the day of Gruppenführer Heydrich's attack—' the officer coughed '—you were driving.'

'Is that correct?'

'Yes.'

The officer moved a piece of paper to read a name. 'The General's usual driver, Corporal Klein, was supposed to drive.'

'Yes, but—'

'It's here in the official record.' He prodded the paper with a finger.

'Yes, but—'

'You took over because you knew what would happen.'

'I didn't.' He shook his head vigorously. 'An officer assigned me to the task because Klein called off sick only an hour earlier.'

His interrogator tapped a pencil on the desktop. 'And who was this officer?'

'Don't know. I assumed he was a member of Heydrich's staff.'

The officer leant back in his chair. 'How do you explain the records show Klein drove on the day?' He again prodded the paper.

'I'm only a corporal, sir. I do as I'm told and don't question orders.' He feared they were looking for excuses not to give him his medal. Instead of a hero, he would end up the fall guy.

'Quite so.' Exasperated, the officer leaned forward, hands flat on the desk. 'Why did you slow at the exact point where the assailants were waiting?'

He wore his innocence like a cloak. 'It was a tight bend. If I hadn't slowed, we'd have crashed into a tram.'

'And you expect me to believe that?'

He nodded.

'Hmm. If you hadn't braked, you wouldn't have been ambushed.'

'You must remember, I saved him. I chased off the assassins and took him to the hospital.'

'It's for you to remember, Schmidt, not me. If that's your last word…' The officer tapped his pencil louder on the desk before turning to address the two men at the back of the room. 'Get the truth out of him and don't waste time.'

Each grabbed an arm and propelled him out of the room, along a corridor and into a cell. His legs and wrists were shackled, and he was left standing.

'Why are you doing this?' His voice broke, but they didn't answer and left him alone. As time dragged, he itched everywhere and sweat pumped out of his scalp and streamed down his face, pooling on the floor. Eventually, they returned, and he offered his wrists for them to remove the shackles, but they refused. 'We've only started,' one said.

The itching got worse, and he had lost all feeling in his legs and was so dizzy he worried he'd topple over and crash onto the stone floor. When he shouted for help, they returned and unshackled him, and relief flowed through him as his blood circulated again, but with it came a creeping pain threatening to engulf him, and he almost passed out.

Using their truncheons, they pushed his face against the brick wall and spread his legs, and a swishing sound caused him to turn his head. One man had picked up a soiled, knotted rope, the end of which he wrapped several times around his fist and, when he swung it, it made a snapping sound that echoed around the cramped room. The other man pressed him against the brick, grazing his forehead, and the man with the rope took a practice swing before swinging it hard upwards and catching him between his outstretched legs. The shock of the pain sucked the air out of his lungs, leaving no breath to scream and it was the same every time they hit him. Eventually, he slithered to the floor.

He was left for hours without food or water before they returned and repeated the process. As the torture increased, they bombarded him with questions, repeating them over and over again, and he told them his truth because it was all he had. If he understood the lies they wanted, he'd confess. Then they'd stop. Now the constant beating had numbed him to the pain, and only the swish and crack of the rope alerted him to another blow.

Suddenly, they stopped hitting him.

One of the guards approached, and he flinched, but the man offered him water and bread, which he ate fast, protecting it with his other hand to prevent it from being snatched away. They threw water over his face and wiped him dry with a cloth before pulling him to his feet. And, as he couldn't walk, they dragged him upstairs to the office and pushed him into a chair.

It was a different man sitting behind the desk. This one wore a smart suit, and that made him more dangerous. He's probably

The VIOLINIST'S REVENGE

Gestapo, and that's trouble. He offered an apologetic smile for causing them problems.

'We've decided you're not to blame,' the man in the suit said.

He didn't listen as he watched one of the man's eyes, which moved independently of the other and scanned the room that stank of something unmentionable. The man had stopped speaking, his head leaning to one side like a bird waiting to be fed. Now, he didn't want a medal, only to get out of this hellhole.

'My name is Klebus,' the man said as if it should mean something. 'I regard you as a true hero of the Reich, and we will find something for you that's commensurate with your status.'

He hated himself for nodding his agreement.

'You did an admirable job protecting Gruppenführer Heydrich.' Klebus raised a hand, silencing any interruption. 'When you took him to the hospital, he was alive. It's not your fault he died after Reichsführer Himmler's visit.'

The hint of an accusation hung in the air.

'In recognition of your bravery, you'll be promoted and assigned to the SS Guard Battalion.' Letting that sink in, he leaned forward with a tight-lipped smile. 'And we will work together.'

Either that or the two goons with their knotted rope. It could have been worse. They might have sent him to the front line.

7

Curda emerged from the darkness with a questioning grin. 'Don't shoot the messenger,' he said, holding his hands above his head.

'Bloody fool walking in on us like that.' Kubis scowled and looked towards the street. 'What's happening out there?'

A noise like a shot interrupted the answer and everyone ducked, but it was only a car backfiring, and they chuckled self-consciously.

'It's not good,' Curda said. 'It will be just a matter of time before they're knocking on the door.'

'We don't intend to wait,' Pastorek said. 'We'll act before then.'

'What's the plan?'

'We're breaking out and taking some bastards with us.'

'When?'

'Tonight.'

'You won't stand a chance,' Curda said, shaking his head. 'There are too many of them.' Then a sly grin spread across his face. 'But there's another option.'

With a sceptical look, Pastorek pointed to the main entrance. 'But the only way out is there.'

'How do you think I got in?'

Kubis interrupted, 'Reckoned you'd been here for some time.'

'Checked it out first.' Curda said, his voice hardening as he added, 'It's worth trying.'

The VIOLINIST'S REVENGE

'Checked out what?' Pastorek raised a hand, quelling a volley of questions. 'Explain yourself.'

The man was enjoying the attention and squared his shoulders, taking time to light a roll-up. 'You heard me come in from the back of the church.'

They all agreed, and one said, 'Do that again and we'll shoot you.' And the others chuckled.

'When I was a kid, I was an altar boy before I found more interesting things.' Curda offered a lewd grin. 'I know this place like the back of my hand.' He pointed a thumb over his shoulder at the rear of the cathedral. 'Back there is a virtual maze of rooms. Most are full of religious junk and nobody uses them and probably won't for another hundred years.'

The men were grumbling with impatience. 'Get on with it,' said one.

'There's an exit at the rear.' He scowled at them as he scanned his audience for a reaction.

Gabzik stood. 'So what? The Krauts have the place surrounded and won't let us walk out the back door.'

'Perhaps, but I came through there and no one stopped me. Didn't see any soldiers.' He shook his head. 'And you'd be leaving at night.'

Pastorek mulled it over, thinking it too good to be true. 'The Nazis must know everything about the building.'

'Okay,' Kubis said and shouldered his way to the front. 'Show us.'

'Whoah!' Curda stepped back and raised a hand. 'If we all go out in daylight, they will see us.'

'But we must check it out,' Kubis persisted. 'Can't take your word for it.'

'The boss can come with me,' Curda said. 'It's your only chance, otherwise, you'll end up like the stiffs in the crypt.'

Pastorek was led through several doors, opening into a narrow corridor with choirboys' surplices hanging from wooden pegs. There were myriad rooms on either side of the corridor, and the musty air made him cough. They passed a kitchen, a toilet, unused offices and other small rooms packed with religious paraphernalia, some shrouded in dust sheets. When they entered a room, which at first appeared to be a dead end, he noticed a door in the far corner. From there, he was beckoned into another larger room, empty but for a tapestry, depicting Jesus surrounded by children, hanging on the wall and dominating the space.

'Help me.' They approached the tapestry and, with both hands, pulled back a corner, their fingers straining with the effort, to reveal another door, but only as high as his waist. Bent double, Curda grabbed an already-lit lantern from the floor. 'Follow me.'

A blast of dank air rose out of the darkness like a cork being removed from a bottle, and he gagged. 'Be careful,' he was urged onwards.

Worn from centuries of footsteps, twelve stone steps led down into the dark, and Curda swung the lantern from side to side, illuminating their path. 'It's wet down here and the stones underfoot are slippery,' he was warned and, when he reached out to the wall for support, water ran over his hand.

'Priests used this as an escape route when the church was under siege centuries ago. But in modern times it's had much more mundane uses, like sneaking out for a smoke.'

If his colleague knew about the tunnel, so must the Nazis. They would have checked the building's plans and its environs for any potential escape routes. This wouldn't change anything.

As the ceiling pressed down on them, they ducked and several times, he scraped his head on the rough stone, and the farther they progressed, the more hunched they became as the walls narrowed. The confines of the tunnel were increasing his claustrophobia, and he considered going back for fresh air. 'How much farther?'

'Almost there.'

After more steps, they rounded a bend and it opened into a larger area, and before them, a heavy iron door looked as if it hadn't been opened for centuries. But there was a large key in the lock and, with some effort, Curda turned it, and it clicked, the metallic sound echoing along the tunnel, and it opened with a loud creaking noise. Like divers rising from the depths, they emerged into the daylight, gulping for air.

As he viewed their surroundings, Pastorek's hand tightened on his pistol. Tall bushes screened the exit so they were hidden from passers-by, and Curda pushed aside the foliage and led him up the stone steps onto a deserted, cobbled lane.

'Where are we?' His eyes swept the area, expecting Germans to appear at any moment.

'Free.' Curda stretched out his arms. 'You can walk away and lose yourself in the city of Prague.'

His eyes narrowed, and his gut tightened. 'What do you mean?'

'You needn't go back. I promised I'd get you out, not the others.'

He stepped forward and drove his colleague up against a wall, his hand squeezing the man's throat. 'It's all or nothing.' He pressed his forehead into the man's face and saw fear in his eyes. 'I'm not leaving my men behind.'

'You've got me wrong. I'm not suggesting that.'

'Show me where this leads.' He relaxed his grip.

'We've come farther than you think. Come on. Around the corner, you'll see the way out.'

Getting his bearings, he stared back at the door. No matter what, he would return for them, but as they turned the corner, he shrank against the wall. Blocking the lane was a German staff car with its engine running. 'This is crazy,' he hissed through clenched teeth. 'There's no way out.'

There was no reply.

A German voice startled him. 'Get in the car.' A man in a sharply cut pinstriped suit and homburg pointed a Luger at him before two stormtroopers with weapons raised materialised from nowhere. He closed his eyes and cursed. How had he allowed himself to be duped so easily?

8

Before the bad times, they would leave the apartment and walk north as a family and, when they reached the Danube Canal, they strolled along the promenade. Wearing her Sunday finery, Valentina clutched Max's arm as though he might disappear and, in her left hand, held aloft a parasol, protecting them from the sun while Willy and Lily raced on ahead, shouting to each other. And Anneliesa walked alongside her parents, a girl thinking of her music and things a father didn't need to know.

At Franz-Josephs Quay, passengers disembarked from boats, and the older women took their time, fearing their make-up might run in the sun, while the men hooked their fingers in their collars as if wearing a yoke. They crossed into Morzinplatz, where a large square building, the Hotel Metropole, a palace, an icon that stood for everything good about Austria and Vienna in particular, dominated the area. On days like this, he enjoyed a feeling of permanence, believing his children's futures were assured. Only Lily's speech problem caused him to worry, but a devotee of Sigmund Freud assured him many children faced internal conflicts and she'd overcome it.

As they neared the hotel, liveried staff swarmed like bees around their queen as an endless line of exotic limousines disgorged glamorous and wealthy people, and it smelled of money and he liked it. Directed through the main entrance between its four Doric columns, they proceeded to the sumptuous inner court and sat under a glass

The VIOLINIST'S REVENGE

roof, shaded by palm trees, at tables with silk tablecloths and took afternoon tea and listened to a quartet playing and he took an occasional apéritif.

The hotel was acclaimed throughout Europe. Kings, queens, heads of state, musicians and actors visited. Even the composer Richard Wagner once lived here. Guests of untold wealth had every whim indulged, and an Indian maharaja once included two tigers in his entourage.

Here, his daughter had played solo at a charity concert for the great and the good of Vienna, and afterwards, many congratulated him on her playing, including Baron Otto von Wächter and His Excellency Bishop Hudal, who reportedly had the ear of Pope Pius XII.

Now, Max stood before a palace that no longer evoked such pleasant memories because The Metropole had been transformed into a fortress and a constant reminder that the Austrians were prisoners in their own land. A wind picked up, rippling the waters of the canal nearby and fluttering the swastikas flying from two flagpoles on the building's roof. The red, white and black paraphernalia of Nazi domination festooned the facade of the former hotel and barricades and barbed wire encircled the area as soldiers and strategically positioned armoured vehicles discouraged any protests. Inside, nine hundred Gestapo operatives carried out their work, including the torture of Jews and anyone regarded as an enemy of the occupiers. Most taken here never left. It had been like this since 1938, when Reichsführer Heinrich Himmler took it as his base and installed Franz Josef Huber as the head of the Gestapo.

Fear gripped him like a vice. The young policeman had given him hope that they would find his family and had agreed that a family couldn't walk out of their home and disappear. He had promised to carry out all checks—accidents, hospital admissions and so on—and told him to return in an hour when he might have more information.

'People are being deported,' the young policeman said and opened his notebook.

'Unfortunate,' he sympathised. 'But we're Catholic.'

The policeman promised he'd do what he could to find them. 'This is now a case of missing persons, although it's very unusual.'

He had returned home and spent the following hours in periods of disjointed wakefulness, sitting in his armchair, drinking from a bottle of alcohol within easy reach and waiting for a call which never came.

More confused than ever, the next morning, he waited impatiently in line before an older officer called his name. He realised the officer was judging this dishevelled person, who had not changed his clothes and was smelling of alcohol, and he tightened his tie, but his hands were shaking. As he recounted his story, the policeman listened, occasionally nodding, but the policeman was experienced in handling crackpots. 'It's a mystery,' the officer said and stressed there hadn't been reports of accidents or unusual events.

'Do you and your wife have problems?' the policeman asked.

'What do you mean?'

'Arguments?' The policeman exhaled as if releasing a pent-up force, his supposed compassion becoming impatience. 'Differences of opinion?'

He shook his head. 'All the time, but she wouldn't leave me if that's what you're suggesting.' His eyes flared, and he dug into an inside pocket of his jacket and pulled out a dog-eared sepia photograph. 'There.' He pushed it across the counter, his voice rising. 'My wife Valentina and my children.' He pointed out each in turn with a shaking forefinger. 'If the Nazis can make people disappear, shouldn't you ask them if they have information?'

The policeman turned grey and coughed. 'We report to the Gestapo. We don't question their operations.'

'Then I'll ask them.'

The policeman stood and closed his notebook. 'I wouldn't advise it.'

His visits to the police station had grown fewer and shorter. The older policeman's initial veneer of sympathy was wearing thinner and the answer was always the same. 'This is a case of missing persons,' he would say, hoping he'd give up and fade away. 'Our enquiries are continuing.' He also visited the German Embassy, but they showed even less patience and, after several fruitless visits, positioned guards, preventing him from entering the building.

On the day they ordered him to stop visiting the station and await future developments at home, he bumped into the young policeman from his first visit as he left the police station. After a glance around to ensure there was no one within earshot, the officer suggested they meet at the cafe in an hour when he'd be on a break. While on his second coffee, the policeman arrived in civilian clothes, slumped into a chair and declined his offer of a drink. 'There's no ongoing investigation into your family's disappearance,' he said furtively.

'Why?' He struggled to get the word out.

'Because officially they didn't disappear.'

'I don't understand.'

The policeman hesitated as his eyes scanned the room. 'They were put on the train, along with the Jews from the park.'

The words chilled him and he stammered, 'Your colleague told me you're still investigating.'

'All lies,' the policeman said. 'If he dared to tell you the truth, he would be criticising the Nazis and he's not brave enough. He wants to live.'

'They were abducted and I must accept that?' He screwed up his face.'I can't do anything?'

Embarrassed, the policeman kept quiet.

'Where did they send them?'

'Poland,' the policeman said, considering it unwise to say more.

'Where?'

'A concentration camp.'

If he had been standing, he would have collapsed as his strength drained out of him. Instead, he fell forward onto the table, sending his cup crashing to the floor. 'But they're innocents.'

The policeman looked away and sighed.

He cursed himself for not having gone to Gestapo headquarters before. He had delayed, fearing he might be arrested. Not for his own sake, he convinced himself, but for his family's. If he were locked away or worse, his family would be lost forever with no one to remember them. Now he had no other option. He must get an answer once and for all.

The Metropole was a monstrosity, an insult to all Austrians and, wherever he looked, the ominous presence of SS black reminded him he had stepped into a bleak, alien world. How should he proceed? If he attempted to enter by the main entrance, there were several checkpoints to be navigated. Those who went before him were waved away; others were surrounded by guards and marched off. Vans making deliveries had access to the rear of the property. Could he sneak in a back entrance? But he would be arrested.

As he pondered, a soldier strode over and jabbed him with the barrel of his MP34. 'Clear off or I'll arrest you.' The soldier moved on.

'Please help me,' he called after him. 'I must find my family.'

A passing SS officer changed course and approached. 'What's your business here?'

'I've lost my family.' He paused when he saw no compassion, only contempt, in the officer's eyes. 'You've transported them to Poland.'

'Juden?'

'My family are…they were Catholics.'

'They must be criminals then.' The officer peered at him with suspicion.

'They're children,' he persisted. 'I've asked everyone for help.'

The officer clicked his fingers. 'Show me your papers.'

He reached into an inside pocket, pulled out a wallet and cursed his stupidity as he dug into his other pockets, bringing out various papers, but not what the officer required.

The officer called for a guard, but they were now out of range. 'Go home, old man.' He pointed a thumb at the Metropole. 'If you go in there, you won't come out. You're a Catholic. Go to your church and pray for them and yourself.' He raised an arm in a shrill Heil Hitler salute and strode away.

There was no one else to ask. He'd reached the end of the line.

A guard approached and pushed him. 'On your way, clear off.'

With nothing to return home for, he stood his ground, but the butt of the soldier's weapon forced him to move. The more the guard's blows rained down, a glimmer of hope made him quicken his step.

9

'No heroics,' Curda said as he snatched the gun away from Pastorek. 'If you want to save their lives, you'll do as we say.'

The man in the suit stepped aside, and the soldiers bundled him into the back of the car. He reckoned they must have covered at least a block underground in the tunnel and, when the car turned out of a junction, soldiers were massed on Resolva Street with machine-gun posts and artillery pointed at the church. If they'd broken out, they would have been cut down within a few steps of exiting the church. He studied his betrayer, who refused to meet his gaze. Why? He'd been a comrade and trained like the rest of them. Outside the cathedral, the Nazis had set up a loudspeaker and were broadcasting the names of those who had been executed for crimes of treason.

He expected to be driven to police headquarters, housed in a solid grey building, ironically named Petscheck's Palace, near Wenceslas Square. Instead, they took an unfamiliar route and arrived at an ordinary office building. Once inside, he was pulled down a flight of stairs, falling and bruising a knee, and thrown into a cell where he sat on a bunk and stared at a dirty grey wall for so long he lost all sense of time.

Perhaps he'd fallen asleep. Muffled explosions signalled the final assault on the church. Why did I leave them? They must believe I ran out on them. I should be there, fighting and dying with them. All his talk about preventing the Nazis from interrogating them and he'd walked into a trap like a simpleton. Whatever happened now, he vowed he wouldn't give up a single name to protect those who had helped them, especially Sonja.

When an ominous silence replaced the sounds of gunfire, the door swung open. Two guards entered and dragged him out, banging his head on the door frame on the way, and they took him to a nondescript room with a desk in the corner and straight-backed chairs on the perimeter. The man in the pinstriped suit was waiting for him, along with Curda, lounging in one of the chairs and trying to look relaxed but refusing to return his questioning stare. Another man with a bad boxer's face stood in a corner. No one spoke.

After a few minutes, another man entered the room, and the others stiffened. The newcomer was of a slight build with shiny black hair plastered over his scalp, his nose sharp like a raven's beak and one of his grey eyes blinking, its focus never leaving his face. The other roamed independently around the room as though searching. It was disconcerting. Lock onto the staring eye or follow the other's perambulations around the room? The man acknowledged him and perched on the edge of the desk, gesturing that he should sit across from him. He wore a grey suit, tailored like a uniform, but with no markings indicating rank or branch of service. In the ensuing silence, he strained, listening for any sounds of a continuing battle, but there were none. A rap on the door broke the silence and a soldier marched in, clicked his heels, saluted and placed a sheet of paper on the desk. The man read it and glanced at his colleague with a look of relief.

'Why am I here?' he asked, breaking the oppressive silence.

The man's fingers drummed on the wooden desk. 'You're not here to ask questions, Mr Pastorek.' A flash of gold emanated from a tooth. 'My name is Klebus.' The man sweated heavily and a pungent smell of garlic wafted across the desk, and, for emphasis, he leaned forward and added, 'Klebus.'

'What are you, SS? Gestapo?'

Klebus smirked. 'Sicherheitsdienst.'

A blank look encouraged him to continue. 'Better known as SD. We're the intelligence agency of the Nazi Party. We investigate enemies of the state.'

He laughed. 'Another bunch of madmen fighting each other for power. No wonder you're losing the war.'

A backhander from the man in the pinstriped suit caught him across the bridge of his nose.

'Enough,' Klebus shouted. 'I require your help, Mr Pastorek.'

Interrogators used many methods to elicit information. Whatever, it would be more painful than torture.

'So you have no doubts.' He paused. 'I have total control over what remains of your life, and I will make it as bearable or uncomfortable as you choose.'

'Don't waste your time.' He exhaled. 'I won't tell you anything.'

Klebus seemed unmoved. 'I don't expect you to tell me anything. I require only your assistance.'

'You've got the wrong man. He's the traitor.' He lunged at Curda, but the other men restrained him and pulled him back to a seat and handcuffed his wrist to an armrest. 'He knows I only want to save my men.'

'Yet you left them to their fate.' Klebus's mouth curled in distaste. 'Anyway, it's too late. They were no match for our firepower and were soon overcome. Some escaped to the crypt like rats and made it simple for us to flood them out. The mission was a total success.'

'What has happened to them?'

The German studied him. He also had a nervous tic under the eye, which still rolled around his head. 'There were no survivors. The seven in the crypt either drowned or killed themselves.'

A wave of grief washed through him, but at least they hadn't been captured and talked. Perhaps Sonja and her people had escaped after all.

'Your colleague has been of great help.'

'You bastard.' He attempted to get to his feet, but the handcuffs prevented him.

Klebus's face hardened as he picked up the sheet of paper on his desk and reread it. Deep in thought, he walked around the room, lighting a cigarette and inhaling. 'I know everything about you.'

'Such as?'

'Your parents.'

'What about them?' He rubbed his chin.

'I've met them.'

He strained against the handcuffs. 'What have you done to them?'

The man shrugged and puffed on his cigarette. 'And there's Sonja. A sweet girl.'

'What have you done to her?' All hope was draining away.

'In war, sacrifices have to be made.'

How many others would die because of their attack on Heydrich? How could one death cause so much misery?

'I have a proposition.' Klebus walked over to him. 'A task that can only be handled by a person with your talents.'

'Why should I help you?'

A look of amusement crossed his face. 'Everyone has a price.' He nodded, and his pinstriped colleague pulled a Luger from his pocket and shoved the barrel into Curda's forehead, rocking him back in his seat.

Klebus smiled as the traitor's eyes flashed in fear. 'You betrayed your colleagues for a measly 500,000 Reichsmarks. Your friend, Mr Pastorek, will do it for nothing—'

The gunshot seemed to echo around the room for an eternity.

PART II

10

A stillness settled over the place like an ancient, forgotten battlefield as Anneliesa lifted the violin to her shoulder with an overpowering sense of fear and self-loathing. She didn't want to play and dreaded facing them.

When she had finished her audition in the hut, she opened her eyes, but she was still in hell, although the woman showed a glimmer of appreciation. It had saved her life, although it led to this. Music should be a creation of the gods, not an instrument of torture, she thought, but she had no choice and, shamed by her weakness, she manoeuvred the instrument under her chin, the once-reassuring texture of varnished spruce now rough on her skin. Anger fluttered in her chest like the wings of a trapped bird and bile burned her throat and she swallowed as she clamped her lips tight because sickness was verboten. So as not to witness their pain, she closed her eyes. Please, don't make me look at them. Shuffling skeletons, devoid of gender or age, who would soon become memories, their shaven heads and eyes buried deep in sunken cheeks.

A woollen skull cap protected her shaven head from the biting cold and fingerless gloves warmed her hands while leaving fingers free for their work. Her body was shrouded in a dirty overcoat, as heavy as a blanket and still smelling of its former owner, an old man so deprived of food he no longer had shoulders able to support its weight.

The music was a prelude to their deaths, but playing prolonged her own life. The guard rapped a wooden post with his Luger, signalling it time to play as a guttural command and accompanying whistle started the column moving. The prisoners took faltering steps, heads down, showing no interest in their destination, and, in the distance, the chimneys were smoking.

Do I look like them? She hadn't seen her face for a long time.

If the prisoners were uncertain about what would happen, she wasn't, as she'd witnessed it too many times. Every morning, she played the violin as the prisoners marched off for a day of hard labour, and every evening she played them back. A few collapsed and were shot where they lay, and their colleagues carried the bodies back to the camp for disposal. Today, these lost souls, some holding the hands of infants carrying toys as broken as their owners, would embark on a walk from which there was no return. Some were stoic, living only for the moment. I'm alive now, they'd say with a detached acceptance, and next, I might be in my grave. Here, death was a demanding companion. No one left their hut in the morning expecting to return in the evening.

We all must die and this would be their time and, in death, there would be relief from suffering. Unable to endure the barbarity, some walked to the electrified fences surrounding the camp and embraced the barbed wire and a flash illuminated the sky, followed by a lingering cloud of smoke and a sickening smell of flesh burning. Only the fading hope that one day she'd be reunited with her family prevented her from joining them.

What awaited was beyond reason. Their masters, regarding them as useless, had scheduled them for extermination, but many didn't suspect their fate or wouldn't acknowledge it. Those who attempted to flee were encouraged by rifle butts to return to the line, but the guards were reluctant to kill them here because they would have to clear up the mess. Others wailed like sirens and a few sank to their knees in silence and prayed. The result was always the same, and the knowledge made her complicit.

They marched two miles from the main camp to a field with two cottages, the Little White House and the Little Red House and there, guards ordered them to strip on the pretext of taking a shower. The prisoners are ushered into the buildings and the doors bolted behind them while an SS guard, wearing a gas mask, climbs onto the roof with canisters of Zyklon B Prussic acid. At a signal from the officer in charge, he drops the canisters through an opening into the house, and their screams carry to the camp for fifteen minutes. Afterwards, other prisoners arrive and collect the contorted black and blue corpses for the ovens.

Her colleagues stiffened when their guard, Horst, appeared. A red face, neck bulging over a buttoned-up tunic, he enjoyed using his shapeless hands and often he prodded them with his Luger as a prompt for them to look happy while they played. All had felt his anger, although not her for some time, meaning punishment was imminent. She'd welcome it, for experiencing pain eased her guilt.

'We have a special guest this morning.' He pointed at a raised wooden dais on the other side of the mass of prisoners. 'Play as though your lives depend on it .... or it's the frauenblock for you.' He winked at the ensemble, but they ignored him.

Their so-called women's orchestra comprised two violins, a cello, a saxophone, a mandolin, an accordion, sounding like the squawk of a strangled bird, and a bullet-riddled piano. Sufficient for ausrucken, the daily marches to work, and einrucken, the return home in the evening and, for a day like today, when they sent off marchers and played until the screaming stopped. Horst wanted more to entertain the SS officers on Sundays, but it was the best he could do. Even musicians didn't last long here.

Over the bowed heads of the column, she recognised an SS general, whom she'd seen before, once when he dined at the camp commandant's quarters as they sat outside for hours playing in sleety rain. As he left, he smirked at her. 'She plays well,' he remarked to his host, and Commandant Höss beamed as though complimenting his daughter.

They said he was the governor of Galicia and the architect of all their misery and had consigned hundreds of thousands to execution. He talked animatedly to the officers surrounding him, basking in their fawning attention as they responded with deferential smiles, their faces still brutal. And he appeared immune to the tragedy before him. With his aristocratic countenance, he stood out from the others and several times he took off his cap and swept back a full head of almost golden hair from his brow. And the casualness of the action chilled her. The first time she saw him, she thought his face was familiar and trawled her memory for when they might have met, but starvation plays havoc with the mind. He was also an Austrian. They had shared the same air, so why was there this chasm between them? *Perhaps I'm fantasising about a life that never existed.*

She closed her eyes to prevent the scene from being imprinted on her retina, although at night, as she drifted into a fitful sleep, the horror returned like a perpetual nightmare. As with the others in the orchestra, she had no choice but to play, yet still experienced guilt. And they were protected in their compound because the other prisoners regarded them as collaborators and called them names and spat on them.

The music flowed through her fingers, travelling up her arm and resonating in her mind, carrying her above the double rows of barbed wire fencing and the machine-gun posts and floodlights and the misery. It transported her back to performing at home in Vienna before an appreciative audience, including Mama and Papa and Little Bird. Although she couldn't see their faces in the darkness, love and pride shone from their eyes and, at the finish, Papa was on his feet applauding.

No matter where or how well she played, nerves always affected her, but they also sharpened her talent, especially when playing for her life. To her despair and shame, she hoped they'd never find another violinist.

Usually, unable to bear the tragedy, she avoided looking at the marchers, but this time she heard her name being called. *Can't be, I'm mistaken. There are no names here. I'm simply the violinist.*

Her eyes ran along the expressionless faces trudging onwards, and an overwhelming fear gripped her when her gaze reached the back of the queue. She doubled up, and only a wooden post prevented her from falling. *It can't be. Hunger and fatigue must be playing tricks on her mind. They are there.*

At first, she was uncertain, as they were dirty and dressed in rags, but eventually, she recognised them, straggling at the back and pushed along by guards, using the butts of their rifles. It paralysed

The VIOLINIST'S REVENGE

her, yet still her fingers played. She considered running to them, but after a couple of steps, they'd club her to the ground.

Although her mother stumbled like an old woman, she appeared calm as she clutched Lily's hand and behind them, her brother, his spirit beaten out of him, trudged head down. Was Mama protecting them from their fate?

Lily called her name again and jumped up, waving, but a snarling guard pushed them into the grey sludge. Mama bent down to wipe the mud from her daughter's face and, struggling to her knees, spat on the soldier's boots, which earned her a back-handed slap across the face. Cowering behind her mother's skirts, Lily stared up at her with lips fixed in a horrified smile.

She tried to shout but could not make a sound and looked back at the dais, silently imploring the General to halt this barbarity. He bared his teeth, a perfect row of white, and pointed as he turned to speak to his colleagues, and the others joined him in laughter. He switched his gaze, and his eyes caught hers and, for a moment, it was as though he recognised her, but he glanced away.

Her cowardice shamed her and she returned her attention to the marchers, but they had moved on, and her family were gone.

A colleague's elbow to the ribs warned her she'd lost her timing, but she didn't care. She wanted to throw down her instrument and march with her family and face death together, but ashamed she didn't have the courage, she closed her eyes and held them tight until no tears were left.

11

Soft and yielding, the crust in his pocket gave him a warm feeling and he grinned. Why not keep it, he thought. I need food as much as the next person. Yes, she's pretty, but is she worth a crust? Every time he tried not to knead the bread, he did it again for reassurance. Like a worm wriggling in the recesses of his brain, the desire to keep the crust grew stronger. She wouldn't know if he did, and no one could blame him. But he wanted to see her face when she bit into the bread, her green eyes dreamy with satisfaction as she savoured the taste. That would be his reward as those eyes that captivated him the first time she'd glanced his way would smile with gratitude. She stood there, imprisoned in her compound like a chicken in a coop, gripping the wire of the fence as though she might tear it down.

Sweeping litter with a brush in one hand while carrying a sack in the other, he took a circuitous route and kept watch for guards or, more importantly, Funktionshaftling. Kapos were recruited from the most violent criminal prisoners as willing enforcers and were crueller than their bosses to keep their positions of privilege.

Although concentrating on the girl, his eyes took in everything around him and, as he grew closer, she offered a half-smile before turning away. Did she think him different from the others? His face, not as gaunt, still had flesh on the bones. Almost handsome, but for a livid scar that ran from the corner of his right eye down his cheek. He was always happy to see her. The first time they almost bumped into

The VIOLINIST'S REVENGE

each other when she was rushing with the others, carrying their instruments. He had whispered in a language she didn't understand and then used another language and, a third time, spoke in German. 'We live to fight another day,' he had said and grinned. Others in the orchestra reckoned the first two languages were Czech and Russian. One who claimed to know said he spoke several, only confirming their suspicions that he shouldn't be trusted.

Why was he interested in her? What could she give him? Friendships ended in despair. As soon as you got close, they were taken away. She didn't look at him, saying in German, 'So far, so good.' He didn't respond and continued sweeping, and she repeated it as loudly as she dared, and her faltering smile barely turned up the corners of her mouth.

'Why are you in here?' he said, still with his back to her.

'Shopping.'

As though normal, he managed a smile.

'And you?'

'Breathing.'

'That's serious.'

'Not as serious as shopping.' He offered a low laugh. 'Anything's normal under the Nazis.' He pointed a thumb at the green star on his chest, denoting a criminal. 'That's me, a threat to society.'

He moved closer to the fence, squinting around before fishing the crust out of a pocket. 'For you.' He offered it as though it were a bouquet.

'No.' She feared they were being watched and kept her hands in her pockets. 'If I'm caught, they'll beat me and, if they beat me too hard, I can't play. If I can't play, they'll put me to work. If I can't work, I'm as good as dead.'

He squeezed the bread through a gap in the wire, and it fell into the dirt, and her eyes locked onto it. The temptation overwhelmed her, and she stepped forward, dropping on one knee as though fiddling with her clog.

'Don't waste it.' His smile accentuated the white lines on his grime-streaked face. 'I went to a lot of trouble.'

For a moment, she was transported and imagined wandering in lush woodland, watching a sparkling waterfall and hearing the cries of birds high above. But it's just a crust lying in the grey dirt. She scooped it up, her closed hands concealing the prize. Like a cat pounding on wool, she kneaded the bread between her fingers and with every squeeze, she salivated and glanced around, expecting someone might steal it.

'It's too dangerous,' she said and attempted to force the bread back through the wire. 'Not worth the pain. Please take it back. Your need is greater than mine.'

'Eat it before someone comes,' he pleaded, but she concealed it in the pocket of her greatcoat, leaning to one side as though protecting it.

She didn't want to disappoint him, but where could she eat it without being seen?

'Where did you get the bread?' she asked, wondering if it could be a trap. There were no friends in here, so what could he gain from this? She scanned the area, but no one showed interest in them.

'I found it.'

He's lying. You don't find that around here. 'You seem to come and go as you please,' she said.

He shrugged.

Like the other prisoners, he wore striped pyjamas; the only difference was a lock of black hair escaping from under his cap. Everyone else, even the women and children, had shaven heads to prevent the spread of lice.

'What makes you different?' she persisted, struggling to control her suspicion. 'You're a haftling like us. We're all the same to them, like dirt on their boots.'

She was worried. By overstaying his time at the fence, he was putting them in danger and joined her in scanning the area. But hunger took over, and all she wanted was a bite of the crust. What harm would it do?

He moved away. 'Don't go,' she called. 'Who are you? Tell me your name.'

'Doesn't matter.' He left, sweeping the path ahead of him and picking up refuse and putting it in his sack.

'Are you Russian?'

Eyes flaring, he wheeled around and put a blackened finger to his lips. 'Be quiet. If they believed that, they'd kill me in front of you.'

Disappointed that she'd angered him, she turned towards the relative safety of the bunk she shared with an Italian girl, Rachel, who played the accordion in the orchestra. Perhaps under her thin blanket, she could shut out the world and eat.

'I'm Czech.' He hesitated. 'And I'm no criminal.' He made to leave. And she feared she might not see him again.

'You! Halt!' The command was accompanied by a club tapping against the kapo's leather boot. Rigid with fear, she froze, but they weren't addressing her. 'Move away from there,' the other kapo said. 'These women aren't for scum like you.'

Trying to make herself invisible, she inched backwards from the fence, her eyes locked on him, standing, shoulders stooped, in a subservient slouch. Answering back would be a death sentence. Cry out as they punish you because they regard silence as insolence, and they'd beat you all the more. Take your punishment until they become bored.

'Get back to your hut,' a kapo shouted at her, 'or I'll come in after you.'

He didn't expect the backhander, which bowled him over, and the other kapo booted him in the ribcage, shouting, 'Dirty bastard.'

From the hut's doorway, she watched the beating and blamed herself. She shouldn't have taken the bread. As the blows from club and boot rained in, she shared his pain, and tears streamed down her cheeks. She wanted to cry out and help him, but kept quiet so they wouldn't come for her next.

When on the point of blacking out, a different voice rose above the thuds of their blows. 'Enough, enough,' an SS Sergeant said. 'Don't waste your energy on vermin like this. Continue your patrol.' The Sergeant bent over and hauled him up and steadied him as his legs buckled. 'Keep out of trouble,' he said, pushing him on his way. 'You have work to do.'

He winced as he checked if they'd broken his ribs, then took a few faltering steps.

Consumed by guilt, she continued watching his painful progress. The cost of the bread was too great, and she'd choke on it. But for now, she would have to hide it until she could eat the evidence. She'd take no pleasure from it. When the Sergeant had pulled him to his feet, she spied a moment of familiarity between them and had doubts.

As he limped away, he glanced back with a broken smile.

'Anneliesa,' she called out. 'My name is Anneliesa.' But he didn't appear to hear.

12

A former residence for students, 2 Pomorska Street in Krakow once echoed to the partying of the hopeful young. Now there were only harsh voices and the agonised cries of those unwilling or unable to give the Gestapo the answers they sought. As Obersturmführer Kurt Jünger viewed the dirty red brick building with bars over the basement and ground-floor windows, he steeled himself before entering and took a last drag on his Russian cigarette and ground it under a polished black boot.

Even he, an officer who had served on the Eastern front, viewed any contact with the Gestapo with trepidation. Before taking up his new posting as an adjutant to Gruppenführer Wächter, he would be briefed by the Gestapo, but had been given no information about his new duties.

His mood sank the lower he descended into the bowels of the building, where two Gestapo agents were waiting for him in a small, stark room. He noted there was no other exit and, imagining what had happened here, he controlled a shiver. He expected to leave unharmed, but who knows?

An older officer sat behind a desk with the air of a bored city cop, his moustache uneven as if he had trimmed it in a hurry, his top button undone and tie loosened. He fiddled with a pencil between his fingers, and three more lay side by side on the desk. A lined writing pad lay at an angle, and Jünger suppressed the urge to take the pencil and place it on the desk alongside the others and straighten the pad. Odd numbers bothered him. The pencils were sharpened to a wicked point, and he imagined the officer using them as a weapon. The other man stood in a corner and leaned against a wall as if he were only a casual observer. A single lamp covered by a green metal shade cast its light downwards, obscuring his face.

As a junior officer, he didn't expect respect from these people, but surely his status as a decorated war hero deserved it.

The older officer spoke first. 'My name's Müller.' He glanced over his shoulder at his colleague.

'Braun.' The other's voice was harsher.

'Gruppenführer Wächter knows of this meeting,' Müller said. 'But you mustn't divulge anything of our discussions, not even to him. Understood?' Müller peered into the corner as though seeking approval.

He would decide if or what he would divulge in the future, but he kept silent. With these people, say as little as possible. Anything said now could be used against him in the future.

'What do you know about this?' Müller asked.

He shrugged. This was his first assignment since being shot in the shoulder the previous year in the Battle of Rostov, when he and his men were driven back along the shores of the Sea of Azov by Russian troops. 'I believe Reichsführer Himmler appointed me to assist Gruppenführer Wächter. That's all I know.'

'This is a difficult situation and not as straightforward as it might seem,' Müller added. 'Rather than assisting, you'll be his protector and be alert to threats against his life. At all times—on duty and off. If anything happens, you will be responsible.'

He was a soldier, an exceptional one, they said, but why were they asking him to be a nursemaid to this man? He would rather go back to Russia.

'You know about Heydrich's assassination?' Müller asked.

'Of course.' Who hadn't?

Müller's icy stare made him uncomfortable. 'What do you think you know?'

'The assassins were partisans trained in Britain,' he recalled.

The VIOLINIST'S REVENGE

'After the attack, they were cornered in a church in Prague and executed.'

'Yes, but not all.' Müller picked up his cigarette and studied the end as if looking for evidence of fire. 'One escaped.'

'That can't be.' He couldn't hide his disbelief. 'I've seen the reports. They were all killed.'

'Reports can conceal the truth.' The officer cleared his throat and glanced at his colleague. 'Better for morale if they believed we'd killed them all and it showed our strength by responding decisively.'

'But they were all trapped.'

Braun interrupted, 'We had the names of the assassins and all the bodies, we believed, but the most important one is missing.'

He stared at both of them. 'And the one who escaped?'

'His name is Jan Pastorek, a Czech trained by the English.' Müller extracted a file from his briefcase. 'He's the ringleader and may have other high-profile targets. Although he is on his own, he's still dangerous.'

He joined up the dots. 'And Wächter is one of those targets.' Pleased that he wouldn't be just a nursemaid, he added, 'But why target the General?'

Braun emerged from the corner, although not enough to reveal his face. 'Perhaps because of his work in reducing the Jewish problem in Poland. The Reichsführer has concerns.'

'Why me?' He still had doubts. 'The General must have enough protection.'

Müller opened his mouth to respond, then changed his mind.

The ash on the man's cigarette almost fell onto the desk, and there was no ashtray, but Jünger controlled the urge to snatch it from him and dispose of it.

Braun broke the silence. 'It may be difficult to understand. It's not clear-cut.'

He bit his tongue, believing this was just a game for them, seeing conspiracies where none existed. Who were they to treat him like this? He hadn't come here to be insulted by pen pushers who would last only minutes on the Eastern Front.

Seeing a flash of anger cross Jünger's face, Müller raised a hand. 'Don't misunderstand me, you're a respected soldier. It's because of decorated heroes like you that we're winning the war. What I'm saying is, as a soldier, you see a physical enemy. You identify it and destroy it.' He sought Braun's support and received an emphatic nod. 'We deal with enemies you can't see, almost like ghosts. Enemies are closer than you think. This is our problem and now also yours.'

'I don't understand.'

Müller extricated a photograph from the file and slid it across the desk. A small, grainy black and white print of a youngish man with dark hair and no particular identifying features.

'This is for you.' Müller handed over a file. 'Read it and you'll know as much as we do. You must report your progress, but not share this with your superior. Is that clear?' Müller kept staring until he agreed. 'I can't impress upon you the importance of this mission. Failure is not an option.'

Braun relaxed. 'Would you care for a real smoke?' he asked with a tight-lipped smile. 'Or do you prefer those foul-smelling Russian cigarettes?' When he didn't reply, he added, 'Perhaps we should go outside rather than stink out this room.'

They led him through a maze of narrow corridors, up a couple of steps and out into a courtyard surrounded by buildings on all sides. In the daylight, Braun appeared younger than he'd thought. They both lit up and, at a nod from Braun, he took out one of his own.

'We must be careful,' Braun said. 'Even here.' He gestured to the building they'd left. 'There are those listening and watching all the time. Believe it or not, forces are undermining our work.'

'From within?'

Relieved he understood, Braun lowered his voice. 'You'll encounter problems. There are those plotting against the Reich, and there have been attempts on the Führer's life. I'll speak plainly. You're a brave soldier and an intelligent man, but you don't know of the undercurrents swirling around us. You see the Führer surrounded by officers and advisers, and it's normal to think everything is secure. No matter how bizarre it might sound, beneath a calm surface, malevolent agents are at work. Alliances, some voluntary, others cajoled or blackmailed, and there'll be more assassination attempts.'

He rubbed his head, worried about what he was getting involved in. Soldiering was simpler.

The VIOLINIST'S REVENGE

'I know it's hard to believe, but it's true.' Braun raised a hand. 'There are those with grievances seeking more power, and they would do anything to achieve it.' The officer's stare fixed on him like a searchlight, and he wanted to show he wasn't one of those.

'And if anything happened to the Führer?' He sighed as if it were too painful to envisage. 'I presume Reichsführer Himmler—'

'Not necessarily,' Braun snapped back. 'Although it would be the obvious and correct succession.' He snatched a glance at the surrounding windows as though that needed clarification. 'Some regarded Heydrich as the successor, and he had many supporters. Certainly, the Führer believed him to be the most competent. He called him the man with the iron heart. A true Aryan. Unfortunately, conspiratorial rumours surround his death.'

As if knowing what they were, he nodded.

'After the attack, the Reichsführer and the Führer's personal doctor visited Heydrich in the hospital,' Braun continued. 'The doctor suggested a procedure that was agreed by the local doctors, but Himmler refused that course of action. Days later, Heydrich died. Coincidence, of course, but those with fertile minds and intent on mischief have a different view.'

Come on, spell it out. 'What do you mean?'

Doubt flitting across his face, the officer stared at him before lowering his voice. 'You might think that convenient for Himmler.'

'Are you suggesting the Reichsführer enabled Heydrich's death?'

'Of course not.' Braun stamped the cigarette under his foot. 'If you'd said that in there, we'd have arrested you.'

'Then what are you implying?'

'Heydrich was head of the Sicherheitsdienst. All members swore allegiance to the Führer, the Party and Heydrich, and some believe Himmler was instrumental in his death.'

Even in the military, they regarded the SD, the intelligence arm of the Nazi Party, as at least ten times more evil than the Gestapo. Even by Nazi standards, Heydrich was a monster and committed many crimes against friend and foe.

'These are the people you will face,' Braun said.

'Is Himmler at risk?'

'Attacking Himmler now would be counterproductive for his

enemies and weaken the war effort. But one of his favourites being groomed to take over from Heydrich, such as Wächter, might be a target.'

'And his death would weaken Himmler's position?'

'Undoubtedly, and it's your mission to ensure that doesn't happen,' Braun said.

'So, anyone could be an assassin? Where does the escaped terrorist come into this?'

Braun chuckled. 'I was confident we had the right man for the job. This is only a theory, but someone in authority, a supporter of Heydrich, might attempt to get their man close to Wächter.'

'Why not use one of their people?'

'If an English terrorist with a hit list kills him, no one will suspect who's behind it.'

'So, it could be a prisoner in Auschwitz or anyone impersonating a guard?' Jünger removed his cap and wiped his brow. 'What more do you know about this terrorist?'

'Not enough,' Müller said. 'He's a desperate man on a suicide mission who realises he has no chance of returning to England alive.'

Braun lit another cigarette. 'He's a cold-blooded killer who'll use any methods to complete his mission. Don't underestimate him. Heydrich's assassination was not just an attack on one man. It struck at the very heart of the Reich and everything we stand for, and the Führer will not tolerate another assassination.'

'What does Wächter know?'

'He's arrogant and, like Heydrich, believes no one can touch him.'

Everyone was a suspect. Being shot at by the Russians was almost more inviting. Whichever way this was resolved, he would be the fall guy. At Wächter's level in the Party, it was a constant round of manoeuvring, cross and counter-cross, all vying for position with anyone falling out of favour at the snap of a finger. The man who brought Hitler the head of Heydrich's killer would cement his position in the hierarchy, and Himmler expected to be that man.

Wächter was hard to understand, they said. On the surface, refined and intelligent and a family man. There were many like that in the SS. Good fellows together, but all carrying knives behind their backs and beneath his veneer of respectability only base metal. A man who could consign hundreds of thousands to death with the flourish of a fountain pen would do anything to further his cause.

When Jünger's war wound ached, it was a sign that something wasn't right. It was aching now, and he realised he was just a pawn in a deadly game. Suddenly, he had the desire to scrape his skin clean.

13

For days, she scanned the faces of the ausrucken and the einrucken marchers, hoping at least one of her family had survived. Their faces showed only despair and weren't ones she recognised and, with each day, her disappointment mounted, adding even more torment, yet she continued playing through the pain. When I see that leering monster again, she promised herself, I'll split his skull, so his brains spill out like wriggling worms in the dust.

At night, she clung to memories of happier times, lulling her into a fitful sleep, and she couldn't imagine her father's pain, not knowing what had happened to his family. Her mother, the ultimate homemaker, doted on him. A planet to his sun, forever orbiting, sometimes distant, more often close, locked in an eternal spiral, always reliant on his warming presence. Brother Willy getting into scrapes as all boys did. Little sister Lily, whom she called Vögelchen, Little Bird, with golden hair and a cheeky grin that lit up a room like unexpected sunshine through a window. From birth, her speech was impaired, and she relied on Anneliesa to speak for her, but over time, with much love and coaching, Lily learned to speak their names, and she would have traded anything for her to have a voice.

A thud, like an object hitting the ground and a scraping noise made her look up. Twenty yards away, a prisoner was digging on the other side of the fence, and she scrambled to her feet. She hadn't seen him for days and feared they'd executed him for talking to her. With relief, a quick scan of the area showed no guards in the vicinity, and she stepped closer. 'You came back.'

Keeping his head down, he dug with exaggerated enthusiasm.

'Why are you here?'

He nodded at the broken earth before him.

'Why are you doing that?'

'We don't question,' he said. 'Just ask how deep?'

'Did they hurt you?'

'I can still walk and talk,' he said and lifted his head with a sly look before continuing digging, while all the time edging closer to the fence. 'Got more bread for you,' he whispered. 'Catch it.' He rummaged in his pocket and pulled out a crust, bigger than the previous one and let it drop onto the shovel's face. Turning his shoulders, he swept downwards with the shovel but missed the ground, propelling the bread towards the fence.

She dropped to her knees and, squeezing her fingers through the wire, grasped the crust, which broke in two as she pulled her prize through the fence. Scrambling around in the dirt, her fingers locked onto the pieces, which she transferred to her coat pocket in one furtive movement. 'Why are you doing this?' she asked.

'I don't have any other friends.'

'Are we friends?' Her breast fluttered at the prospect, but everything here was transactional. What could she give him in return? 'Why did that sergeant protect you from the kapos?' She tried to keep suspicion out of her voice.

His coarse laugh deteriorated into a cough, and he spat on the broken soil and cleared his throat.

'Tell me?' she insisted.

'I guess they can't afford to lose useful workers.'

'What's your name?'

'Better you don't know.'

'Why?' She studied the passing clouds, scudding across a grey sky as if rushing home before a storm, and brushed the dust from her face. 'Do you prefer being a number?' And receiving no reply, she insisted, 'I told you mine. It's Anneliesa.'

'Knowing me will hurt you,' he said, and his voice trailed off as he turned his back and attacked the earth with renewed vigour.

'If you don't tell me.' She tugged the crust from her pocket. 'I'll throw it away.'

'Don't.' His voice was more urgent as his eyes flashed. 'You'll get us both killed.'

It would be days before he found another crust and bread lying untouched would attract questions and trouble.

'The Sergeant and I have an arrangement,' he explained.

'Guessed as much.' Her shoulders dropped, and she glanced away. 'They said you were a collaborator, no better than the kapos.'

He stepped towards her, then changed his mind and resumed digging. 'Do you think the Polish girls in the frauenblock enjoy what they're doing?' he said out of the corner of his mouth. 'It's that or the gas chambers for them. Do you think you're any better, playing your violin for those bastards? To survive, we must use whatever talents we have. It's simple—do what the Krauts want or die.' He straightened and pulled off his cap to show a head now shaven. 'Some of my fellow inmates waylaid me down a dead end between the huts. I believed they'd beat me to death. Tied my arms and legs and sheared me like a sheep and they weren't gentle.' He ran a hand over the bleeding wounds on his scalp. 'Like you, they thought I was a collaborator.'

'Sorry, I didn't mean to call you that, but what use are you to the guards? You—'

'—appear to have more freedom than the others,' he finished her sentence. 'That's because I'm more valuable alive than dead. They need my contacts.'

'Contacts?' She screwed up her face. 'In here?'

He's crazy, she decided. Throw the crust back over the fence and get away from him.

'My contacts outside,' he said.

'Outside?'

He lowered his voice, and she leaned in. 'I know a way through the fence and I bring in drink for the guards.'

'If that's so, why don't you escape rather than come back?'

'I can't.'

'Or won't.' She didn't want to listen, but couldn't stop herself asking, 'Because they pay you?'

The VIOLINIST'S REVENGE

'That's not the reason.' He frowned.

Almost pitying him, she ran a hand over her face. 'You're afraid?'

'What happens when people drink too much?'

'They get drunk and lose control? It's a regular occurrence when we're playing for the SS officers on Sunday nights.'

'They talk a lot and boast and reveal secrets about themselves and others.'

'What good is that in here?'

'It's valuable information I pass on to my contacts outside.'

This was getting crazier, and now she was convinced the man was mad and would be dangerous. She should get out of here and back to the safety of the hut, yet something compelled her to stay. 'Surely freedom is worth more?'

'It's not that simple. If I just ran away, others would die.'

'We're already the walking dead.'

'I'm talking about people I care about.'

'Your wife?'

'I don't have one and it's unlikely now.'

Her mouth hung open as she tried to understand, but all she could see was a black marketeer making money out of others' misery. Disappointed, she turned away. If they caught them talking, not even her violin playing would save her.

'It's my only hope,' he called after her, causing her to stop.

Perhaps she was too harsh. There was no good or bad in the camp. You just did whatever was necessary to survive another day. 'Are you a spy?'

He hesitated before shaking his head and putting a finger to his lips.

His tenuous connection with Schmidt might end at any time. For the moment, his regular forays through the fence were productive. He brought in bottles of schnapps, vodka and, occasionally, whisky for the guards, and they turned a blind eye, which they kept secret from their superiors. And every time he did, he expected he'd be stranded in the glare of the searchlights and used as target practice.

'The guards hate the officers as much as they despise the prisoners,' he said. 'Most of them would rather be elsewhere. They're as much captives as the prisoners. Some enjoy the brutality, but most hurt others to prevent getting hurt themselves. Drink almost makes this hellhole survivable. Helps them forget what they've done and provides sleep without nightmares.'

Near the camp's main gate, an establishment provided hospitality for the officers and guards and their families, some of whom lived in the camp. It served superior food and drink and, sometimes, they brought in entertainers, providing shows which were popular with the German children. But Schmidt and his men didn't trust those gatherings, as they were always being watched by officers who would report their conversations back to headquarters. If they drank too much—and they were only allowed beer—they were disciplined. An offhand remark could label them as enemies of the Reich, and they'd end up working alongside the prisoners. The secret supplies of alcohol gave them a slender hold on sanity. Supplied by Polish black marketeers, it satisfied them for now and, unwilling to lose a lucrative source of income, the Poles insisted he continue. The Germans pushed him out through the wire, and the Poles pushed him back in.

'Something you should know...' He laid down the spade.

As she strained to hear, a piercing alarm from the loudspeakers on the main building drowned his words and, all around her, prisoners ran or hobbled back to their huts, pushing anyone in their way. The alarm signalled a search and, when guards entered a hut, the occupants had to stand by their bunks or face punishment.

She wheeled away from the fence and broke into a stumbling run, wondering what she should do with the crust. If found on her, there would be questions and retribution, and as she ran, she forced a portion into her mouth, swallowing hard and almost choking.

An officer and three guards entered the hut, their boots clattering on the wooden floor, and the women, unable to stop shaking, stood to attention while the soldiers searched their bunks and scattered their meagre possessions on the floor.

A fly meandered up the wall and she concentrated on it. She'd eaten a few. They were supposed to provide protein.

Eye contact was forbidden, but a woman broke the rule and the officer slapped her face, causing blood to run from her lips. But she couldn't raise a hand to stem the flow. He continued on his way along the line, passing Anneliesa, then stopped and came back.

'What is this?'

Her mouth dried up.

'What's in your coat?' He grabbed it by the lapels, pulling her off balance.

Fear rippled through her. If he found the crust, which she'd pushed through a hole in the lining, she was done for, and she would betray her friend.

A bellow from the other end of the hut made the officer swivel and stomp towards the source of the sound. A guard had found something in a woman's bunk, and the officer slapped her twice before pushing her out of his way to inspect it. Spying her violin, he reached forward, pulled it out with a grunt and dropped it on the floor. Before she could move, he grabbed her close, grimacing at the smell, and held her face between finger and thumb; the pressure leaving white fingerprints on her cheeks. And with a sadistic grin, he stamped the instrument into pieces.

As if in surprise, he raised his eyebrows. 'No violin,' he told the woman. 'No use. Take her away.'

They would suspend her by her wrists from a beam, her hands tied behind her back, and leave her until overcome by fatigue and pain, her arms would dislocate from their sockets. Unable to work, she'd be executed.

Before leaving, the officer paused in the doorway and scanned the cowering inmates, enjoying their uncertainty.

14

Baron Otto Gustav von Wächter, or Gruppenführer Wächter, Governor of the District of Galicia in his current role, strode through the house and flung open the door to his study. He threw his cap onto an armchair as he made for a table laden with bottles and glasses, poured a glass of schnapps and gulped it down. Then poured another. A decision he had made still rankled, and he questioned his reasons behind it. A moment of weakness that would lead to tough questions. Usually, he made the right decisions and made many daily, although events often conspired to increase his doubts. The Führer had appointed him to this role after Reichsführer Himmler had the previous incumbent, Kurt Lasch, executed for alleged corruption, and they expected better of him. But he feared he'd let down the Reichsführer.

The sun bathed the gardens and tennis court in light. But for the chimneys belching out columns of dense black smoke, he would have opened the French windows. The smell was constant and stayed with him wherever he went, and no matter how often he bathed and cleaned his clothes, the smell remained in his nostrils. When Charlotte visited and they made frantic love, did she smell it on his skin? But for the honour of serving the Reich, he'd rather be anywhere else than here.

At night, doubts crept into his mind like invaders under the wire. Was this how he believed he would end up when he joined the Party all those years ago? Then, it was all about the supremacy of the Aryan race. Now? How would they remember him? As a soldier in the uniform of an SS Gruppenführer, a war hero, enforcing the ethos of German supremacy, or as a jailer and exterminator with blood on his hands? When your enemy is beaten and has no fight left, there's little satisfaction in knocking them over with the flick of a finger.

Only his family's visits made it bearable, but was Charlotte's desire not so much about renewing their passion for each other but stripping Poland of its art treasures with the help of his superior, Hans Frank, and his vacuous wife. Before her return to Austria, she always double-checked the train's carriages, packed with her plunder, and supervised the loading of each priceless artefact, instructing the soldiers where to lay them in a hectoring voice. After many visits, he made his farewells to her at the house rather than face the embarrassment of witnessing her looting.

The company of his children returned him to normality, chasing their terrier around the house, climbing trees and filling the place with laughter. Soon, he would end their visits for fear that the atmosphere pervading the place might affect them and, already inquisitive, their questions were becoming more demanding.

Once, when they caught sight of a prisoner, they asked, 'Who is he, Papa?'

'Just a worker. Come away. He's of no importance.' When one tried to ask another question, he waved him away.

It was becoming harder to lie. They would find out soon enough, but not yet. After they left, he enjoyed the peace, although it provided too many opportunities for contemplation, and it was never wise to brood alone.

Although expecting it, the rap on the door startled him. 'Kommen,' he rasped.

A young man in the SS uniform of an obersturmführer entered and glanced around the room, his expression of distaste alighting on the drinks table. He snapped to attention, clicked his heels and raised an arm in salute. 'Herr General, I am Obersturmführer—'

With a snort of impatience, he waved a hand. 'I know who you are.'

The soldier's grey eyes roamed around the room.

'Drink?'

Believing he was being tested, the officer declined. 'Herr General, I—'

'Nonsense.' He slapped a hand on the desk. 'Join me in a schnapps, I insist. If you spend time here, you'll soon realise it's the only way to survive. Pour yourself one, that's an order, and tell me why you're here.' He sat back in his leather swivel chair behind his desk and watched the young soldier pour the smallest of drinks. With a troubled expression and drink in hand, the soldier perched on the edge of the chair, his back ramrod straight.

Amused, Wächter flicked open a file on the desk with a finger. 'I've been reading about you, Kurt Jünger.' He stared at him. 'Take off your cap, man. Let me see who you are. You're here to help me. Do you think I need your help?'

Jünger coughed as sweat trickled down the back of his head, dampening his collar. He took off his cap and searched for a place to put it, but rested it in his lap, arranging it so the Totenkopf, the death head's skull badge, pointed straight at his superior. His gaze moved to the drinks table. 'Back-up would be more accurate,' he said, glancing at the bottles which were all over the place as if lifted in a hurry and replaced anywhere.

Wächter studied a face reddened by exposure to subzero temperatures and topped by close-cropped, almost white blond hair. Without the cap, it was less brutal and younger.

'So, you were at Rostov?' He gave a brief look of admiration. 'Had to run for your lives, I understand. Must have been tough?'

'Unpleasant.'

'Awarded the Iron Cross.' Impressed, he tapped the file in front of him. 'You deserved a medal just for surviving the Eastern Front. They say the life expectancy for a soldier in Russia is only twenty-four hours. How did you earn it?'

Embarrassed, Jünger studied his cap. 'What anyone else would have done.'

'Tell me.'

'Two of my men were injured in crossfire, and I went out and brought them back.'

'Commendable.' He pursed his lips. 'So why did they post a war hero here to act as my bodyguard?'

'They believed I'd made a mistake.'

'Says here,' Wächter prodded the report, 'you beat your batman so badly he was discharged from the army.'

Jünger's gaze remained unchanged. 'He deserved it.'

'What had he done to deserve that?'

'He polished my boots but didn't polish my belt.'

With a sharp intake of breath, he closed the file. 'It also says you would run through a brick wall if ordered.' He frowned. 'That suggests dedication or stupidity. Which is it?'

'Depends on who is giving the order, sir.'

He rocked back in his seat, thinking that Himmler must be worried. 'Can you work with me? We'll be spending too much time in each other's company.'

The soldier blanched at the prospect but kept quiet.

'I expect you to be of assistance, not a hindrance?' He rose from his chair, indicating Jünger should follow him to the window.

'Look down there.' He pointed to the tennis court, disappearing under a carpet of moss and weeds. 'Haven't played for months.'

'The camp is full of labourers, men and women,' Jünger said. 'They could clear it up'

He shook his head wearily. 'Can't spare anyone. With food supplies dwindling, every prisoner must justify their survival. If they fall below their quota, they're dispatched. I spend most of my days signing death warrants for the poor unfortunates out there. Hundreds of thousands. It's so time-consuming, but I expect you to ease my burden.'

For a moment, Jünger didn't understand. Did he expect him to clean up the court or sign death warrants? 'I will do my best.' He straightened his back.

'Sure, sure.' He resumed his seat behind the desk. 'How do you plan to assist me?' In his position, he must be seen to agree with an order from Himmler. Encourage the soldier to trot out the usual platitudes and something might slip out. Himmler regarded him as a protégé destined for greater things. Like many of the lower classes, the Reichsführer sought the association and company of a genuine aristocrat and enjoyed his visits to the family, with Charlotte fussing around him, but when it came to the Party and his role in the Nazi apparatus, nothing else mattered. Heydrich's assassination had shaken everyone, especially at the highest echelons, making them feel more vulnerable. Hitler had raged, intent on killing at least ten thousand men, women and children, until dissuaded as it would reduce the amount of slave labour and hamper the war effort. Was the boy his bodyguard or Himmler's spy?

His unwavering stare made Jünger shift in his seat. 'I'll do whatever Reichsführer Himmler asks of me, Herr General.'

'I'm sure you will, but tell me how you'll approach this role and I'll decide if I can trust you.'

Jünger flushed. 'They've briefed you on Heydrich?'

'Of course.' What was interesting about the assassination was that it wasn't a random attack by local partisans but by commandos trained by the British Special Operations Executive (SOE) and parachuted in months before. A daring attack akin to German commandos entering England and assassinating a senior member of Churchill's War Cabinet, or even the Prime Minister himself. It struck at the very heart of the Reich. Heydrich was not only a general, some regarded him as the Führer's heir apparent, much to the annoyance of Himmler. Where would they strike next? Did Jünger's presence mean he might be next on the hit list?

As if reading his mind, Jünger said, 'I understand The Reichsführer and the Führer are concerned for your safety.'

'I'm honoured, but I fear nothing.' He waved a hand around the room and gave a tight-lipped smile. On the surface, it appeared Himmler had taken precautions to protect him, but the Reichsführer was concerned only with his own interests. If concerned, why hadn't he recalled him to Berlin? 'You believe you can do what all the soldiers here can't?'

Junger coloured. 'I didn't mean—'

'You'll be my shadow?'

'Like a second skin.' Junger smirked at the look of distaste on his superior's face.

'What information did the Gestapo give you?'

The VIOLINIST'S REVENGE

'A terrorist by the name of Pastorek escaped the siege at the church in Prague.'

He watched the soldier over his drink. 'So, he is the one I must watch out for. Describe him.'

'The problem, sir, is we don't have an accurate description.'

'You don't know who you're looking for?'

'I have the backup of several men from the Einsatzgruppen.'

After dismissing him, he poured another drink, went to the window and stared at the gardens. If Himmler realised what he'd done, he might have left him to the mercy of the assassin. The violinist's look of pure hatred as she played at the march had penetrated his soul. Her eyes burned bright above high cheekbones, emphasising the gauntness of her face and her look of loathing made his skin itch as if being attacked by ants. If they hadn't been separated by the column of untermensch, he might have feared for his life.

He recalled Bishop Hudal's demanding voice on the telephone. A hard man to refuse. A constant throughout his life. Sixteen years his senior, like an older brother or a young uncle. As well as tending to his spiritual needs, he had been a staunch friend of the family and had christened his children at St Stephen's in Vienna and provided wise counsel. Also, an enthusiastic supporter of his and the Party's aims. The Bishop's request had been problematic, but he was obliged to help, especially once this was over, he would return to Austria, and his influence would be invaluable.

Although Nazi administrators would never acknowledge it, there had been a mistake. At first, he hadn't believed his eyes when she played at one of the SS officers' soirees, and they'd drunk too much. She hadn't acknowledged him, but he remembered those eyes, triggering happier memories of before the war. An evening in Vienna at which the good and the great had been invited, and she wore a satin dress and played exquisitely. Afterwards, when her family surrounded her, he expected his host to introduce him, but Bishop Hudal sidetracked him with news of developments at the Vatican, which meant little to him. By the time he was free, she and her family had left.

15

With her legs dangling over the side of the bunk, she sat repairing the pocket of her coat using a needle and thread she'd hidden in a crack in the floorboards. When the needle slipped and pierced the skin, she didn't flinch, so cold and numbed were her hands, and she constantly checked that the remains of the bread were in the other pocket. All that mattered was the crust. She'd dreamed of eating it throughout the night as if it were a banquet and, during the day, worried it would be taken from her.

Her shivering made it impossible to keep the needle steady and she pierced a finger again, although it didn't bleed, as though unwilling to give up anything that sustained it. The constant cold lay in her bones like an intruder, refusing to leave, and when they killed her, she hoped they'd burn her at the stake, like a witch in ancient times, and she'd welcome the flames warming her body.

She checked the bread again, dampened by the brackish, foul-smelling water from the morning shower, which was a tricky procedure, holding any possessions between your knees to prevent them from being stolen. Breakfast was just as difficult, eating the crust in secret, dunking it in the lukewarm gruel and sucking it dry several times before it disintegrated. A fraction she concealed for later, but once she devoured it, she'd crave more and be obsessed with seeing her friend again.

When she was cleaning her violin in preparation for the evening's march, Rachel signalled from the doorway. 'He's here,' she said quickly, hoping no one had heard.

For a moment, not understanding, she stared at her, wide-eyed.

'By the fence.' Rachel nodded in the direction of the wire.

'Who's here?'

'Your admirer.' The girl's mouth hung open in a toothless grin.

An ache spread in the pit of her stomach. Every time she met him, she was putting her life in peril, yet she shivered with anticipation and, without hesitation, stowed the violin, pulled on her coat and stepped out. With her arms wrapped around her midriff, she walked up and down the compound and, with every pass, drew closer to the fence until their fingers were touching. She was ashamed she'd encouraged him. His life was at risk, too.

This time, his hands didn't go to his pocket, and she couldn't hide her disappointment.

'I have news,' he whispered.

Confused, she stared at the ground. What news in here could interest her?

'About your family.'

'They're all dead,' she replied, pressing her face up against the fence until the wire cut into her skin. Why are you saying this? Tormenting her. First, no bread, now this. They're gone. All of them. No one returns from the death march. Why be so cruel?

Her gaze switched to a rise beyond him where movement attracted her attention. Wächter was talking with a group of officers, and one of them, the camp commandant, Rudolf Höss, was pointing out various aspects of the camp. Höss relished punishing prisoners and once, when she played for the march, he'd beaten to death a fallen prisoner who hadn't the strength to regain their feet. His face was even more brutal than the guards', with a mass of black hair shaved at the sides, lying atop his head like a resting rodent. Wächter appeared to listen. Beside him, stood a young SS officer with a ramrod straight back and a face all angles. Was he guarding, or protecting, Wächter as he scanned the area, as though expecting an imminent attack? Behind him were a couple of soldiers in a uniform that she didn't recognise and the Sergeant, who had saved her friend from more punishment, and another guard completed the group.

'I think I know what happened to your family.' But so intent was she on watching Wächter, she didn't understand.

As if sensing he was being watched, Wächter turned, and their eyes met. With a gasp, at that moment she realised who he was and held his gaze, refusing to back down. He turned away and spoke to Höss, who barked an order. Two soldiers started down the slope, and Jünger prepared to follow, but Wächter, gesticulating and shouting at the Sergeant, called him back.

She was gripping his hand so tightly he winced. 'I know him,' she said.

He leant in. 'Your sister is—'

The first soldier brought him to his knees with a blow to the back.

'Asking for a beating, eh?' The soldier's colleague hit him with the butt of his rifle, splitting his head so blood pumped from the wound. Schmidt stepped between them. 'Enough, I'll deal with this.'

She felt every blow and slumped to her knees as Wächter and Höss lost interest and drifted back to the Commandant's office. The young officer remained, staring at the limp body and bloodied face, and pulled something from his pocket and studied it before hurrying away.

16

Max had met Bishop Alois Hudal, seeking help in finding his missing family, and it shocked the cleric that this could happen to an Austrian Catholic family. Meeting the Bishop at home without his purple cassock and skull cap and wearing a suit and a simple gold chain and pectoral cross on his breast disconcerted him, but it brought the Bishop down to an earthly level. And he believed they could talk man to man. Although the Bishop was a known supporter of the fascists, he pledged his help and promised he would contact his close friend, Otto von Wächter, now a general in the SS. If anyone could find his family, it would be Otto, he promised. And he believed him, having met the baron at several functions and considered him a decent man.

Hudal had left him with a prayer and a determined look, which gave him hope, and promised that the next time they met, he would have better news.

No further meetings materialised as days became weeks. Every time he phoned, a secretary answered with the frustrating mantra: the Bishop was very busy and in Rome, but please be assured he's doing everything he can. You must be patient and pray.

A void was opening between them, and when the Bishop's promises yielded nothing, he found his faith in everything, including the Church, waning, especially fuelled by reports that Pope Pius XII had refused to criticise Hitler even when aware of the persecution of thousands of Italian Jews.

The evenings were the worst, sitting alone in his darkened apartment, refusing to turn on the lights as though it would confirm the emptiness of his life. A bottle was the first thing he reached for, but drinking only increased his feelings of hopelessness, and he found it harder to get out of bed in the mornings. In bursts of lucidity, he visited the library and searched through old newspaper files and read about the Wächter family. There were photographs of Wächter and his wife and children meeting people in the community and attending church and concerts, and the normality of their lives was in direct contrast to what he'd experienced.

What were his family doing? He imagined his beloved Valentina, a born organiser, cooking for others at the camp, Anneliesa entertaining them and keeping up their spirits with her violin playing, and Willy and Lily doing what kids do. Surely, they weren't misbehaving? He doubted even the Germans could mistreat children. He dared not countenance an alternative and would cling to that hope until his dying gasp. Perhaps they'd got off the train by mistake and were stranded in the country and unable to communicate, but those moments lasted as long as a pricked bubble, and only drink eased the pain.

Witnessing his decline, an old friend, Albert, whom he had known from school days, came to the rescue, keeping him company on cold, dark, lonely nights and hiding the bottles. Occasionally, he stayed, allowing him to sleep. One morning, he awoke agitated but had an epiphany. He'd visit Wächter's home and explain there had been a terrible mistake and ask him to return his family to Vienna. If not there, he'd enlist his wife's help.

Although Albert listened, he pitied him and, when he finished, shook his head, but didn't share the reports of the atrocities in the concentration camps under Wächter's control.

'This is insane,' Max said in one of his more logical moods, his face contorted in disbelief. 'My family are good Austrians.' He slumped in a seat with his head in his hands.

'There's no logic in war,' Albert responded. 'Like the rest of the Nazis, power corrupted Wächter.' He placed a hand on his friend's

The VIOLINIST'S REVENGE

shoulder. 'Now all we can do is pray they'll return once the war is over.'

'I can't. I won't sit here while they might be suffering.'

'You could help us,' Albert suggested.

'How?' He glanced at his hands as if they were useless.

Albert explained he ran a small group that harassed the Nazis.

'Resistance?'

'Not quite,' Albert replied with a deprecatory laugh. 'We're more like mosquitoes. Can't do much damage, but we sting in the most uncomfortable places.'

Their biggest achievements were forging papers for Jewish friends and hiding families around the city so that many avoided arrest and deportation. The Germans had barricaded streets in the Jewish area of the city, and those who weren't deported were driven into the ghetto. Even in apartments like his, four families were crammed in. But Albert and his colleagues smuggled food and medicines into the area, frustrating the Nazis' intention to starve them to death.

He threw himself into this work, but solitude became his biggest enemy. He often needed a drink, but Albert had stripped the apartment of his hidden supplies of alcohol.

ONE NIGHT, believing he'd overcome his desire for drink, he takes a walk, hoping fresh air will help him sleep. To prevent temptation, he chooses a route where there are no bars. Yet, without intending to, he ends up outside his favourite watering hole, a bar off Kärntner Strasse. He hesitates, but convinced he's now in control and can resist temptation, he goes in.

Perhaps one drink, just one, to prove he has the strength to control his drinking.

It's a small bar with an abundance of mirrors, making it appear larger with suffused lighting, providing an intimate atmosphere that wraps around him like a cocoon. Everyone drinks together. Wherever you sit, you can't help but be involved in another's conversation. He takes a beer, then whisky. Only one, but it's a generous tumblerful and, without realising, an acquaintance replenishes it. The bar owner, one of his clients, ignorant of his problems and overruling his protest, brings him another drink.

He speaks to anyone who will listen, while others move away once the conversation turns to his family's situation and the iniquity of the Nazi regime. As he talks, a plan forms.

A woman sidles closer, showing an interest, then, seeing no opportunity, moves on. The floor seems to move, and several times he puts a hand to his mouth to stop being sick. Acquaintances and strangers drift in and out of his company, staying no longer than to finish the drink he bought them. And he can't remember whom he's spoken with and what he's told them. And he doesn't recall the journey home.

On entering the apartment, the family photographs adorning the walls are a sobering slap in the face. If his family are lost, he must do something. He has only one option. Although it's against everything he believes in, he must do it for them. He weaves into his book-lined study. Running his hands down the drawers of his antique mahogany desk, he reaches the bottom drawer and steadies himself as he makes several attempts to insert the key, then yanks the drawer with such force that the contents spill across the floor.

It lies glinting in the lamplight and is heavy, and he steadies his shaking hands as he lifts it to his temple with a sharp intake of breath. Shutting his eyes, he presses the old revolver's trigger and, as the hammer falls, a loud click echoes around the room.

17

Höss's office was a tribute to his self-importance. Photographs of him meeting Hitler, Himmler and Göring and shaking hands with film stars and members of royalty adorned the walls, and Jünger wondered if Wächter would ever grace this gallery of rogues. Only those in favour with the hierarchy were displayed. Elsewhere, heads of animals, including a stag and a tiger, stared at them with glassy eyes—a testament to the host's skill in shooting defenceless animals. Jünger regarded it as poor taste. How long would it be before Höss displayed the heads of his human victims? There were a few he'd like to see up there. The spaces between the pictures were irregular, and some weren't even straight, but he suppressed the desire to straighten them.

Invited for drinks, they were introduced to a cabinet with an array of alcohol that would have matched the bar at Berlin's famous Hotel Adlon. The hardships of Auschwitz life, Höss said with a wink.

Wächter offered a grim smile and allowed his host to show him around his collection of photos.

Jünger studied them, comparing the two men. Höss lived with his wife and five children in the camp and was said to be a doting father, yet this was the man pardoned in the twenties for beating a schoolteacher to death with his bare hands and rumoured to have a child with a woman prisoner in the camp.

With contrasting expressions, his superiors walked back to a massive desk, Höss carrying a bottle of a clear liquid without a label and three glasses. He poured ample measures. 'Say what you like about the damn Bolsheviks, for barbarians they make a damn fine vodka. When we reach Moscow, all of it will be ours and, of course, other delights. They say the women are fiery.' He smirked as he took a mouthful of the drink and let it move around his mouth as if gargling.

Was he that ill-informed, or just ignoring the reports from the Eastern Front? Waving away the offer of a drink, Jünger received a derisive frown in reply. In the Commandant's book, if you offered a junior officer a drink, he damn well drink it.

'The Reichsführer praises you for your zeal in addressing the Jewish problem.' Wächter cleared his throat. 'I believe you have processed more than a million untermensch here.'

'Not quite, Herr General,' Höss said. 'Many died from the cold or starvation. But certainly, very satisfactory figures. The killing is easy. We can dispose of two thousand in half an hour. It's the burning of bodies that takes all the time.'

As though calculating the figures, Wächter nodded.

The host was drinking two glasses for every one of his guests as he regaled them with his ability to achieve all Berlin's targets.

Thirsty, he picked up a jug of water from a table by his seat. The water appeared clear. He inspected the glass. Reasonably clean. No fingerprints. He smelled the water and poured. A drop of water spilt on the table and he wiped it away with his sleeve.

A smile played around Wächter's lips as he sipped his drink, and he appeared to be enjoying his host's stories and impressed by his exploits. But he knew Wächter was humouring him, assessing his vanities and weaknesses, luring him into a relaxed self-confidence.

Without fresh air, Jünger felt on the verge of falling asleep and tuned out the drone of their voices. He was eager to leave because the memory of the man beaten at the fence was troubling him. Something wasn't right. He reached again for the photograph the Gestapo had given him. Slavic looking, but the camp was full of them, and the blood on his face prevented identification, although his eyes had a sly intelligence which worried him. To put his mind at rest, he must take another look at the prisoner with his face cleaned up. Then he'd inter-

The VIOLINIST'S REVENGE

rogate him. If only to eradicate him as a suspect. And perhaps he should work on the woman, too.

Bored by repeating stories, he rose. 'With your permission, Herr General, Herr Commandant,' he said and offered each a curt bow. 'I have work to attend to.'

Desperate not to be left alone with this bore, Wächter enquired, 'What's so urgent that you have to leave now, Jünger?'

He stumbled over his words, surprised they were questioning his departure. 'I must interrogate the man at the fence.'

'For what, speaking with a woman?' Wächter asked, raising an eyebrow.

'They try from time to time,' Höss said. 'Natural instincts, I suppose.' He gave a nervous laugh. 'Can't have them breeding in here. I'll have her removed.'

'She plays exquisitely,' Wächter said with a look of concern. 'The orchestra wouldn't be the same without her.'

'I'm sure we can find another violinist,' Höss said. 'I'd prefer you left this to me. From time to time, inmates step over the line, and we have to punish them. We're more than capable of reminding them of the error of their ways.' He gestured for Jünger to sit down. 'First, enjoy a splendid dinner and special wines I found in France.'

Jünger's glance at Wächter received no support.

'Our guards are very firm with their kind.' Höss smirked at them both. 'Anyway, he may not have survived.'

'It would be a pity.' Wächter said, thinking of his tennis court. 'We require all the manpower we can get.'

As Jünger edged nearer the door, Höss stopped him with a glare. 'I insist you leave it to my men. They'll deal with it.'

Wächter's relaxed expression hardened. 'If Obersturmführer Jünger believes it is necessary to interrogate the man, Herr Commandant, then he must.' A coldness in his voice reminded their host that he was the superior officer. 'We shouldn't keep the man from his duty.'

'Of course.' A sickly look spread across Höss's face. 'I will personally check if the prisoner is alive and, if so, order them to make him available for interrogation.' His expression changed as he picked up a telephone and, after a series of clicks, it was answered. After a brief conversation, he slammed the telephone back on its cradle and smirked again. 'Another drink, gentlemen?'

Now Jünger was more convinced than ever that he should question the prisoner and noticed Wächter observing him with a quizzical look.

As Wächter's glass was refilled, an uneasy silence deepened in the room and was only interrupted by the telephone ringing. Höss frowned and snatched it up, listened for a minute, then slammed it down. 'It won't be immediate, Jünger. The prisoner is in a coma. You must wait until the morning. If he survives the night.' He drew a finger across his throat. 'Relax and join us for a proper drink.'

Wächter's gaze roamed around the room. 'What happens in cases like this?'

Höss raised his eyebrows. 'It's unfortunate, but if the man isn't useful, he'll go the way of the others.'

Struggling to conceal his frustration, Jünger swallowed hard, knowing he couldn't divulge the reason for his mission. Anyone could be a suspect. Even if he ruled out the prisoner, he couldn't relax. He considered making Wächter aware of his suspicions, but he showed no sign of interrupting his consumption of a fine Burgundy.

18

He had been in the guardhouse before, and there were other places he'd rather be. A main room with a desk, a telephone and two chairs and off it, two smaller rooms, one with a narrow cot and an empty cell. The stench of stale sweat and cheap cigarettes and something else he couldn't identify made his nose wrinkle. No doubt emanating from a rudimentary and stained toilet. He sat on the cot holding a cold, wet rag to the top of his head, which still bled. It needed stitching, but any medics in the camp were too busy confirming death or conducting experiments on the unfortunate. Was he bleeding internally? If so, he wouldn't last much longer.

Any movement of his head restarted the drip of blood down his cheeks, so he sat unmoving, not wishing to encourage it. Every part of his body ached as though broken up and reassembled, and none of the parts fitted. He wanted to lie down and sink into oblivion, but the guards were intent on keeping him awake. After the beating, they had made it worse by dragging him through the camp and with every bump, he tensed as the pain coursed through him. As they went, prisoners shouted abuse at him and other guards joined in, offering the occasional kick to help him on his way.

Once inside the office with the door shut, the guards' demeanour changed and they were almost like old acquaintances or conspirators coming together. Schmidt, a smaller man with a shock of premature grey hair which made him look older, was almost apologetic and ordered his partner to bring him a cup of water.

'Had to be hard on you.' Hartmut Schmidt offered a rueful grimace. 'It's important we're seen to treat you the same as everyone else. I'm under orders to ensure no lasting harm comes to you, but no favours. It's only cuts and bruises. You'll survive.'

He pushed off the bed and attempted to stand, but the guard who had brought him water in a dirty, chipped mug coaxed him back down.

'No point in moving,' Schmidt said. 'You're not going anywhere. Must get your strength back. You've got work. If you don't, we'll have a mutiny on our hands.'

A sharp pain surged through him when he attempted to sit up, and he gasped.

'Screw up now and you're finished,' Schmidt said. 'And I won't protect you anymore.'

'Then why the beating? I only spoke to the girl.'

'For your own good. That new officer, who struts around as if he's got a bayonet stuck up his arse, is the kind who misses nothing. I know his type. They're bad news. I don't know why he's here, but he has the look of trouble. Apparently, Berlin sent him.'

He had noticed the new officer kept close to Wächter. A bodyguard? He searched the Sergeant's face for a clue, but why would he know?

'Another drink?' The guard, a bigger man with a fat, florid face, mustered a smirk. 'Don't forget, we're counting on you.'

The telephone rang in the office. Schmidt called his colleague to answer, but changed his mind and went through. Cradling the receiver between his neck and shoulder, he turned away from them, hiding his face as he listened. Schmidt answered in a low voice and frowned when he returned. 'Shit! That's the boss. Obersturmführer Jünger wants to talk to you.'

'Why in Christ's name?'

With slow, measured steps, Schmidt paced over to the window and rested his head on the glass. 'It's only half the problem. Höss has ordered me to remove your friend, the woman. She's causing trouble and is a distraction, and Jünger plans to work on her after he's finished with you. And those bastards are thorough.'

So that's why Jünger was here. They suspected him. Although he might survive an interrogation, he didn't want an innocent girl dragged into this. If anything, he pitied her. All she did was play the violin like an angel. He recalled the occasions when a smile lit up her face and he glimpsed traces of a beauty they had stolen from her. Only her eyes, the deep green of an ocean, remained bright. 'What will you do with her?'

'It's out of my hands.' Schmidt shrugged. 'She's pretty enough for the frauenblock and will be put to work until she dies of exhaustion or disease. Or the ovens. That would probably be best.' He spread his hands. 'You know what these animals are like.'

He sighed. In this damn war, everyone is contaminated by the Nazis' evil and there was no escape.

'Why are you worried?' The second guard grinned as though amused. 'There are plenty of women in the camp. We can organise one for you.'

'Shut up, Henrik.' Schmidt flashed an admonishing look at him. 'Talking only gets you into trouble.' He turned back. 'Jünger wanted to come down now, but I stalled him. I rang back and said you were in a coma.'

A ripple of relief flowed through him, but it would only delay the inevitable.

'He'll expect to see you in the morning, alive, at least until you've been interrogated.'

Henrik's face grew redder. 'But who will get our booze?' He sulked like a child whose toys had been taken away.

The Sergeant turned on him. 'That's the least of our worries now. When he's interrogated, he'll spill out all his secrets, and it'll mean trouble for us. If Jünger discovers what we've been doing, it's auf wiedersehen.'

Realising the implications, Henrik reached out to the cabinet to steady himself. 'A court martial.' His florid face turned white.

'A firing squad at dawn.' Schmidt rubbed his chin. 'We've said he's in a coma. Perhaps he won't pull through. Dead men can't tell tales.'

'You're right,' said Henrik. 'We could shoot him now. Say he tried to escape.'

'You're forgetting one thing.' He wiped the blood from his face. 'If I die before Jünger interrogates me, he'll be suspicious and will check you guys out.' He waited for that to sink in.

'Don't believe I haven't thought of that.' Schmidt slumped in a seat. 'If you die while in my custody, I'll answer to Klebus, and he's definitely more evil.'

The mention of Klebus's name was like a distant bell ringing, and he remembered his meeting in Prague with the man with the mobile eye. 'So, Klebus put you in here to help me?'

'Get this straight.' Schmidt jumped to his feet. 'I don't know his plans. It's between you and him, but I recognised you as soon as I saw you. I'll never forget that morning in Prague when you turned my life into a nightmare.'

Would the link to Klebus keep him alive or complicate matters?

'Ignorance is safer.' Schmidt stared out the window as though wishing he were somewhere else. 'My orders were to keep you safe from permanent harm. You don't ask people like Klebus why. What I'm certain of is if I fail, I won't live to regret it.' His plan to see out the war unscathed was fading fast.

He had put Anneliesa at risk and must save her. He looked at Schmidt, who stared at the ground as if he'd run out of ideas, while Henrik paced up and down with large wet patches growing under his arms.

'There is a way.' At first, his words failed to register with them, and he repeated, 'There's a way out of this for all of us.'

With a look of hope, Schmidt raised his head, willing to listen.

'You won't want me to confess about the drinks runs and Klebus's plan. After all, you shouldn't pay if you're innocent.'

They shook their heads in unison.

'I'm due to make my pick-up of alcohol tomorrow night?'

Now suspicious, Schmidt frowned.

'Give me twenty-four hours.'

They shared looks. 'What good will that do?' Schmidt scratched his head. 'It's impossible. Jünger will be here first thing. Those SS people are like dogs with a bone. He'll expect to question you. How in the hell can I prevent that?'

'Delay him. It's our only hope. Say, I'm still in a coma.'

Henrik started babbling, but Schmidt silenced him with a raised hand. 'I can't. Anyway, what will we gain from another twenty-four hours? It'll just delay the inevitable.' He slumped in a chair and lit a cigarette, taking one draw after another.

'You'd better think quick, Schmidt, otherwise, he'll find out and...' He cocked his right hand like a gun and fired. 'Twenty-four hours, then you'll be free of me.'

JÜNGER'S SUSPICION that the prisoner was an assassin nagged at him, and he couldn't sleep. If you believe you should do something, do it or else you'll live to regret it. Why had he accepted Höss's word about the man being in a coma? He should have checked, even if the Commandant disapproved. If the suspect succeeded in his mission, he would be to blame.

On his arrival at the guardhouse, Schmidt and his sidekick jumped to their feet and clicked heels. They looked as if they had slept in their uniforms, and the Sergeant's tunic was unbuttoned. 'Clean yourself up, or I'll put you on a charge.'

'Yes, sir.' Schmidt stepped aside.

The office was in disarray. Papers, books, pencils, two half-finished mugs of black coffee and a half-eaten sandwich cluttered the desk's surface, and he smelled liquor. He quelled an urge to bring it to order. 'Any progress?'

'No, sir, the medics believe he'll be out for hours yet.'

'Nonsense, I'll bring him round. I've wasted enough time.'

'Is he in there?'

Schmidt blocked his entry to another room, but he brushed past him.

The prisoner lay on a low cot, unmoving and breathing unevenly. Stripped to the waist, his shirt had been thrown on the floor, and his chest was covered in welts and bruises from previous beatings. Blood still covered his face. The medics should have cleaned him when they examined him. It would be impossible to compare him to the grainy photograph in this condition. One eye was closed, and a crust of congealed blood hid his identity. But once and for all, he must confirm whether this was the suspect. He ordered Schmidt to clean it off, but as he removed a scab, blood bubbled and ran down the prisoner's face.

'Is he faking?' He turned away with a frown.

'We've tried all night, Herr Oberst.' Schmidt blocked his view of the prisoner. 'But he hasn't moved.'

He bent over the cot, put an ear to the man's mouth and recoiled. His breath stank. 'At least he's still alive.' He moved away, then swung around and grabbed the prisoner by the shoulders, pulling him upright, and slapped him hard across the face, a spray of blood soiling his tunic.

'Get me a cloth, man.' He let the prisoner fall back on the cot and reeled away. Why hadn't he worn gloves? He checked his blood-spattered jacket and was concerned he might vomit.

The Sergeant rummaged in a cabinet and offered a rag covered in old stains. As he tried to remove the blood, he held his breath but had little success in identifying him. He would have to return to shower and change. He cleaned his hands with the cloth. If the prisoner was the suspect, he could have co-conspirators inside the camp. He paced the small room. They could be amongst his fellow prisoners, although after what the Gestapo told him, it could even be the Sergeant. No one could be ruled out. The girl was also a suspect, but he would deal with her when he finished with the man.

To attract his attention, Schmidt coughed. 'If you give him another twenty-four hours, he might be conscious.'

He stared at Schmidt, scouring his face for a nervous twitch or a trace of guilt in his eyes, but saw nothing. 'Work on him and make sure he doesn't die, or I'll hold you responsible.' As he made for the door, there was a barely audible sigh, and he returned to the side of the cot. 'Take off one of the prisoner's boots.'

Schmidt flashed a questioning look but did as ordered.

The suspect's smell made him gag and, as he turned away, he flipped open his cigarette lighter, sparking it into life. He gestured for Schmidt to lift the man's leg and, with a steady hand, held the flame to the sole of his foot. The prisoner convulsed in pain and rolled onto his side, vomiting, and Schmidt tripped and fell onto him.

'What are you doing, you imbecile?' He returned the lighter to his pocket. The stench of burning flesh made his nostrils twitch. Taking out a folded white handkerchief, he blew his nose twice, doubting he'd ever get rid of the smell.

'I'll be back.'

19

The first touch came while they queued for soup. It could have been anyone. The longer she waited in line, the more it troubled her. A hand fumbling around her coat pocket. As she was holding her bowl in both hands, she couldn't check. A pickpocket would have been disappointed as little remained of the crust.

No one touched another. Better to keep your distance than catch anything that could lead to illness and extermination. Those attempting sexual contact did so with the slightest of touches. A vision of her bunkmate, Rachel, flashed before her. Hugging each other, desperate for the warmth of human touch. Savouring the softness of their emaciated bodies, a brushing of lips, a speculative kiss, their bodies locked together before an anguished voice. 'Cut it out, we're tired. Get to sleep.'

It preyed on her mind through the ritual of pretending a bowl of soup was a meal. You had to judge your entry to the queue just right. Too early and you'd get only the liquid at the top of the vat; too late and nothing would be left. Near the end was best. After calculating the number of bowls served, you might find an object floating in the foul-smelling liquid, pieces of meat or potatoes taken from the scraps discarded by the guards.

Once finished, she left the hut and found a corner where they couldn't see her and reached into a pocket. At first, it appeared empty, but something had been pushed into the seam. She ensured no one was watching and drew out her hand and unfurled her fingers. A dirty, screwed-up ball of paper. She considered throwing it away, but an icy wind got up and blew it from her hand. She dropped on it, covering the paper with her coat. Once she grasped it, she unravelled and smoothed out the creased paper. Childish handwriting in thick pencil, and she squinted to read it.

MEET ME AT FENCE MIDNIGHT. Signed with a scrawled letter, J.

She couldn't go. It would be putting her life at risk.

She must destroy the note before they discovered it. She replaced it in her pocket, and her broken nails tore it into edible scraps, which she chewed and swallowed, all the time keeping a hand over her mouth. At least the paper was tastier than whatever lurked in the soup.

No one was allowed to leave their hut after dark, except to visit the latrines. Maybe the note had been put in her pocket by mistake.

In the playing for the auschgang, she missed a few notes, her mind still on the message. If her friend had sent the message, why did he want to meet? Why not during the day? Did he realise he was putting her life in danger? Were the guards encouraging her to break the rules and they would punish her? But they didn't need an excuse. The prisoners had no more relevance to their captors than the lampposts lining the streets back home. Not living beings, objects that, if cut down, would not be replaced, and no one would notice.

The more she deliberated, the darker the day became. She still harboured the faint hope that one day she might be free and repatriated with her father at home in Vienna, and nothing must threaten her dream.

As she lay sleepless in her bunk with Rachel moving against her, the note was imprinted on her mind. Here, there were no clocks. She told the time by the noises of the changing of the guard on the camp perimeter and by the clock striking in the main building when the wind blew their way. Around midnight, a sudden feeling of certainty came over her. Rachel turned, complaining in her sleep, and an arm flopped across her. She extricated her coat, which she used as a pillow and, ignoring her noisy clogs, crept barefoot towards the door. Although they could use the latrines at night, a guard might order her back to her bunk, where she must remain until morning.

In the intermittent moonlight, an owl hooted, and after every step she hesitated, her body tightening, and listened, expecting the guttural challenge of a guard. Down by the perimeter, searchlights mounted on the watchtowers scanned the area. Harsh German voices and laughter carried on the night air as the guards shouted from tower to tower. Her shivering was a mixture of fear and cold. Low clouds obscured the moon and, in the darkness, she stumbled on uneven ground, and the stones cut her bare feet. Doubts crowded in. Who am I meeting? Was it where we'd met earlier? Perhaps I should wait. They had beaten him up, and if he were still alive, he wouldn't be able to write notes. Were they luring her to the fence? Someone with a grudge? Someone who'd seen her getting bread from him? Someone she'd upset?

She shouldn't be out here. Go back to the safety of the bunk. But if she did, she'd never find out. Out of the corner of her eye, she spied movement, a shape moving on the other side of the fence. She moved towards it, walking faster as she neared the wire. Too big for the foxes that scavenged around the camp and didn't survive for long, as they were the closest thing to a nutritious meal for the prisoners.

A whisper calling her name.

Rigid with fear, she strained to listen.

'Over here.'

She scanned the area and clutched the fence wire so tight it cut her fingers. The shape stood up. A battered face managing a twisted smile. 'Follow me.'

'Wait.' She ran back to the hut, her feet jarring on the rutted ground. When she reached the door, she slowed to control her nerves. Keeping her head down, she sidled in. If anyone stirred now, she'd be in trouble.

Should she creep back to her bunk to the warmth of Rachel's body? At least in the morning, she'd be alive. If she went with him, it would be almost certainly suicide. She moved closer. The rag covering Rachel's sleeping body had fallen away, and the girl's contorted limbs reminded her of her mother's body sprawling in the mud. Mama was gone, but a flame of hope still guttered, no matter how weak. She reached beneath the bunk and slid out the battered black case. The violin had saved her life. It might again. She couldn't leave it behind.

Rachel turned on her side and her eyes flickered open. Bewildered, she sat upright, not understanding. 'You're going.' She rubbed sleep from her eyes. 'If you go, I'll be alone.' Her voice broke. 'And I'll die.'

With a resigned smile, she put down the violin and smoothed the girl's hair. 'I'm not leaving you.'

20

From the watchtower twenty feet up, Schmidt scanned the camp, most of it in darkness, and down on the two rows of fences supported by concrete posts. On every fourth post, a light shone downwards and only dimly illuminated no-man's land, the space between the fences. He had checked that the bulbs Henrik had loosened earlier were incapacitated.

Each tower had two guards on 12-hour shifts, although one could return to the barracks to catch some sleep as they struggled to stay awake. It was boring as they weren't likely to be attacked, and escaping through the wire was the most dangerous option. The guards' MG 42 Mauser machine guns could cut any escaper in half. Most escapees relied on forged papers, a friendly guard, or stowing away in the vehicles entering and leaving the camp. The biggest problem for the guards was the biting cold, which reduced their alertness, and they hopped from foot to foot to keep warm.

The guards in the other towers relaxed. Schmidt was on the tower, which signified that a drink run was imminent and to look the other way. As he drew up the guard rota, he and Henrik were always in position for the runs. Henrik was checking the searchlight and hadn't said a word. That was unlike him. Usually, he chattered, saying the most inane things. Tonight, he was nervous.

'Okay.' He puffed on a cigarette. 'What's the problem?'

Henrik avoided his gaze.

'I know you.' He flicked away the cigarette stub that flew like a firefly into the night. 'What is it? Out with it.'

'It's nothing.'

'But?'

Henrik kicked the wall.

'Tell me.' He was losing patience.

'You'll say I'm crazy…'

'Already do.'

They both laughed, although Henrik shuffled his feet. 'If I tell you, don't pull rank on me.'

'Get on with it.'

'I don't understand what's happening,' Henrik said. 'Is he escaping tonight?'

'You were there when we agreed.'

Henrik sighed. 'And he'll take his usual route through the fences?'

'That's the plan.'

'And we let him do it?' Henrik frowned.

'There's no other way.' He took his time lighting up another cigarette. 'He'll be interrogated if he stays. He's here on a mission. I don't know what, but it's bigger than us.' He took off his cap and scratched his head. 'Look, we're in a tricky spot. Once the Obersturmführer gets his hands on him, he'll talk. He'll tell him why I've protected his back and all about the drink runs, and we will face a firing squad.'

Henrik rubbed his face. 'But we'll be disciplined if he gets away?' He leaned against the tower wall and put his head in his hands. 'When he's caught, the truth will still come out. We lose whatever happens.'

'Won't be long now.' Schmidt checked his watch.

'I don't agree with this.' Henrik kicked the side of the tower. 'We should have killed him in the hut?'

He rolled his eyes. 'If we had, the bastard would've been mad he didn't interrogate him. And he'd still investigate us. Do you fancy answering his questions?'

'Okay, I get it.' Henrik's head fell on his chest. 'I'm not stupid. Maybe it would be better if we escaped with him?' He gave a derisory laugh.

'What don't you understand, Henrik?' Exasperated, he added, 'We agreed we'd let him escape. I didn't agree that I wouldn't shoot him.'

'But, but...' Henrik struggled.

'It's tough, but deals are made to be broken.'

'But he trusts us?'

Schmidt shrugged.

Henrik's face settled as he worked it out.

'Look, it will be straightforward,' Schmidt said. 'He's done it before. We know his route, where he goes under the first fence and where the flap is opened on the exterior fence. He won't suspect a thing. As soon as he's in the middle of no-man's-land, we'll light him up.' He patted the searchlight. 'And he'll be a sitting duck. You let him have it and make sure he's dead. We'll be heroes for preventing an escape. You know how the Commandant is about this. Might even get a medal.'

'You expect me to shoot him?' Henrik's eyes were full of doubt.

'Of course. Who's the better shot between us?'

Henrik squared his shoulders. 'I am.'

'Then he's all yours.'

It was the only answer. Their biggest problem would be eradicated, and Klebus couldn't blame him if the prisoner had lost his nerve and attempted to make a run for it and was shot. And he would have played no part in it, as he would be on his way back to the barracks for a well-earned rest. If there were any questions about the prisoner escaping, it would be down to the soldier whom he'd told to guard the prisoner with his life and not let anyone in or out. Somebody would take the blame. It wouldn't be him.

21

A paraffin lamp burned in a corner of the hut, flickering light over the sleeping who tossed and turned and groaned and whimpered and cried in pain. One had awakened and sat up, her eyes unseeing, then slipped back into sleep. Coming in from the cold night air, the smells she had learned to live with assailed her senses. The stench of sweat, the dust and the dirt, the mustiness of unwashed garments, the almost sickly sweet aroma of urine from those too scared to venture out to the latrines in the dark. Why would she leave them? This was her only family now. Why should she have the chance of freedom when they didn't?

Rachel stared at her as she replaced the violin in the space under the bunk. The small Italian girl with bright, determined eyes climbed down from the bunk and held her arms. 'Forgive me, you must go,' she said, kissing her and clinging onto her lips, then stepped back. 'This is your only chance. Take it.'

She was close to tears.

'If you stay, we'll both die anyway,' Rachel said. 'At least you've got a chance of life.'

'I can't leave you,' she said, turning away to hide her tears.

'You must. Who will tell the world who we were and how we suffered? We'll live in your memory. It will be our nekama, our revenge.'

She stared at her, questioning.

'If you don't, I'll scream.' Rachel's fingers dug into her arm. 'I'll scream until the guards come.' The girl reached down, retrieved the violin case and pushed it into her hands. 'If you love me, you'll do this for me.' Her lips puckered, and she cried and her face appeared to fall to pieces.

As she took a few hesitant steps, Rachel blew her a kiss. 'Good luck,' she whispered and turned away.

Outside, a blast of icy air forced her to concentrate and she wiped away the tears, struggling to see in the darkness. Had he waited for her? Perhaps he thought she'd lost her nerve and her chance was gone. She listened for unusual sounds as she crept towards the wire, but there was no sign of him. She had no alternative but to return to her bunk before being missed.

As she turned back, she heard the slightest of sounds and glimpsed movement. He was on his knees, farther along the fence, working on something on the ground, and he raised his head with a smile and motioned for her to move closer. He scraped away the earth and extricated a wooden board, leaving a hole big enough to wriggle through. 'Don't be afraid,' he said. 'Do as I say.'

'This is crazy.'

'Trust me, give me your hand,' he said, and held it tight. 'Follow me and keep quiet. Sound carries on the night air. If they hear us, we'll have no chance.'

He ducked, and she copied, and not talking, they shuffled until in sight of an ominous watchtower. No lights were showing and the only sounds were the wind singing in the wire and guards talking in hushed tones as though sharing a secret. Smoke swirled upwards from their cigarettes, and fear paralysed her and she pulled him back, releasing her hand from his grasp.

'Where are we going?'

'Away from this hellhole,' he said, his eyes glowing in the dark.

But she hesitated, the sight of the double banks of wire fences topped by barbed wire and the watchtower filling her with dread as she recalled the images of failed attempts and carts piled with bodies severed by machine-gun fire.

'C'mon.' He grabbed an arm and pulled her with him. 'We have to be quick.' He peered up at the tower. 'Once we clear the first fence, we've only a minute before we become sitting ducks.'

'I'm frightened,' she said and turned away, wanting to return to the hut, but doubting she'd find her way in the dark.

'There's no going back now,' he said, his voice hoarse, insistent. 'Follow me.'

When she moved away, he jumped on her, smothering her yelp of surprise. 'We've no option.' His mouth in her ear. 'Lie still and keep quiet or the searchlights will find us.' She wriggled away, but he was too strong.

'I can't, I can't leave. I want to find out what happened to my family before I die.'

He took her face in both hands and his eyes locked onto hers as she convulsed under him.

'Maybe they...' she started.

'Your mother and brother are dead.' And he hated himself for saying it.

'No, no, no.'

She pounded the earth with her fists, wanting to dig a hole with her fingers and let it swallow her up.

Anxiously, he stared up at the tower. 'We can't waste any more time.'

She exhaled, releasing a white cloud of vapour that could be seen from the tower. 'You didn't mention my sister?' she said, eyes wide and questioning with a hint of hope. 'What about Lily?'

He looked back at the watchtower. They had to move. Time was running out. Schmidt wouldn't wait forever.

'Tell me about Lily,' she said and got onto her knees, pulling him in with both hands. 'What happened to her?'

'I'm not sure.' Worried if telling her would give her hope or confuse her, his head dropped. 'She mightn't have gone to the gas chambers. Someone told me an officer took her out of the queue.'

She paused, struggling to understand. 'If she's still alive,' she replied and got to her feet, 'I can't abandon her now.'

22

Jünger cursed his stupidity, now convinced the prisoner in the guardhouse was the suspect in the Gestapo's photograph. Why hadn't he acted? He had planned to return, but Wächter had given him a task that took him away from the camp. Intentional?

Wächter was his responsibility, but he'd made a hash of it, and he could imagine the report if he failed. If this was the suspect, how did he get here without the help of someone influential? Did he have a contact on the inside? The Gestapo warned him that he should suspect everyone. Höss had delayed his attempts to interrogate the suspect, and Wächter had remained silent, almost amused, watching the power struggle between the two men play out as though testing his junior officer. If he'd blurted out his suspicions and revealed the Gestapo's intelligence, it would have opened a can of worms and arguing with Höss would have embarrassed Wächter. Politics always got in the way of action.

The longer he lay in bed in a cottage on the grounds of Wächter's house, he was convinced he was right and decided what he must do. He went into the kitchen, poured a glass of water and drank it in one gulp before returning to dress appropriately. Even though the middle of the night, this was no time for sloppiness.

His Einsatzgruppen soldiers shared a room at the other end of the cottage. Not bothering to knock, he threw open the door, and the odour of stale sweat made him reel. 'Get up,' he ordered the first to open his eyes and glanced at the man in disappointment, knowing he'd never match his standards. While the soldier drove him to the camp, he mulled over his course of action. If the suspect was conscious, persuasion from his colleague should extract the information required and reveal his contacts. Höss would probably object that he'd gone over his head, but he'd deal with it later. The camp was locked down at night, and the guards at the gate could refuse him entry, but the importance of his mission should overrule any objections.

'Impossible,' said the lead guard, a sergeant, enjoying his moment of power over the Obersturmführer as he inspected their jeep. 'It's past midnight. There's nothing for you to see and no one you can speak to. Come back in the morning.'

'I must interrogate one of your prisoners,' Jünger said.

The Sergeant stood his ground. 'You can wait until morning. Your man's not going anywhere.' He and his colleague laughed. He considered waking the duty officer, but feared his anger when his sleep was interrupted. It was only a lieutenant, after all. Someone of a higher rank would be different. The Sergeant went back inside and checked the locked gate.

'I demand you open up,' Jünger said and jumped down from the vehicle and strode over to the gate so they were only feet apart.

'The Commandant—'

'He answers to Gruppenführer Wächter,' Jünger said.

When the Sergeant pushed his nightstick through the iron bars of the gate, prodding him in the chest, he insisted, 'I am here on the General's orders.'

The guard hesitated and squinted at his colleague, who turned away, unwilling to be involved.

'If you prefer, I shall contact Gruppenführer Wächter even at this late hour and inform him that you—what's your name, man?'

'Weber.'

'Sergeant Weber is countermanding his order, one which your boss approves.'

Uncertain, Weber looked around, then remembered he'd seen the officer with the Commandant.

'Open the gate or accept the consequences.' Jünger turned around and nodded at his driver, who revved the jeep's engine. 'If you choose not to, you'll find yourself on the Eastern front or marching to work with the other untermensch.'

Weber swallowed hard but, getting no support from his colleague, opened the gate with shaking hands and saluted as they drove through.

STILL WEARING his uniform and reclining in a comfortable leather armchair, an empty glass dangling from his fingers, Wächter awoke with a start. He approached the drinks table and poured a glass of brandy, neat. How many had he drunk? Glass in hand, he stomped up and down, his boots clattering on the wooden floor as if striving for a destination forever beyond his reach. The middle of the night wasn't the time to be alone with his concerns, especially after an excess of alcohol. Once this war ended, he expected Hitler would give him Austria, and the support of his friend Bishop Hudal and his fellow Catholics would be vital, but the Bishop's telephone call had rattled him. He'd have to live with his decision.

He supported Germany's aims, believing the world would be better for this war, but were their methods correct? When he joined the Nazi party in Austria in the thirties, who could have foreseen it would lead to this? A lawyer by profession, he'd been a brave soldier and active supporter of the Führer and the Party. He followed orders to the letter and had consigned hundreds of thousands to death for their religion and as enemies of the German people. Achieving targets satisfied him, but at this late hour, with only his own company, doubts grew. What if they were wrong, but he couldn't admit it? As he sat in darkness, his stomach knotted with doubt. How would they judge him after the war? Would he be a tarnished hero? Privy to communications others wouldn't see, he knew the future of the Reich was on a knife's edge. The invasion of Russia had been disastrous, and now victory was not the certainty Goebbels and his propagandists claimed.

He slopped another generous measure of alcohol into his glass and took a gulp, not tasting it. Was this conscience or fear talking? He hadn't experienced feelings like this when Germany swept all before it.

If Germany lost—surely impossible—the victors would write the history, and Germany would be portrayed as the orchestrators of genocide. Whatever, it was too late to stop and, like a dropped bomb, it must end with explosion and extinction. What they had done here couldn't be eradicated, and nothing would be forgiven or hidden. He had done his duty out of patriotism and that would be his legacy. From an early age, his father had instilled in him that service and loyalty were the most important attributes in life, and school and military college had enhanced that, as did the teachings of the Catholic church. Now, every time he questioned those values, they were diminished.

To their enemies, he would be a devil, a monster, despite being a diligent husband and loving father to his children. They would say he should have cared for other men's wives and children instead of sending them to die.

His holstered pistol hung from a chair. How easy it would be, a second and it would be over. They would call him a coward, but no one could accuse him of that. He would gladly have taken a command on the Eastern Front, fighting the enemy and living or dying heroically. Instead, he would be seen as another grubby politician with a predilection for killing, and it would tarnish his family for the rest of their days.

He attempted to resurrect memories of pre-war days in Vienna when there was a gentility to life. When a girl's blush raised expectations and they visited the theatre and listened to concerts and danced, happy in an existence they believed was the centre of the world. But tonight he was experiencing doubts more than before. Depression dragged him into the black hole of a whirlpool and it was the memory of the girl that was causing that. Unlike other prisoners, whose eyes had lost the spark of life, her green eyes were like an ice-cold flame chilling his heart. Across the heads of the masses trudging to the gas chambers, the violinist's eyes had locked onto him and some force penetrated deep into his soul, stripping him bare and making his skin crawl.

As though in a trance, he had followed the column of prisoners and pointed at one of them, and she was pulled away, screaming, from the others who fought to keep her close. He had glanced back, looking for the violinist with green eyes, but she had disappeared. Had he done it for her or himself?

He poured another drink, hastening oblivion.

No lights were showing in the guardhouse and the door was locked. Jünger cupped his hands to the window, covered in wire mesh, and peered in, but there was no sign of life. When he walked around a corner of the building, he found a guard, rifle slung over his shoulder, smoking a cigarette and kicking stones to relieve his boredom. On seeing him, the man snapped to attention and clicked his heels.

'The door's locked,' Jünger said, appraising the soldier with a look of distaste. 'Open it.'

'I don't have the key, Herr Obersturmführer.'

'Then who has?'

'Perhaps Sergeant Schmidt,' the guard replied with a grimace.

'Get him. Now.'

'But, Herr Obersturmführer, they're on shift. He ordered me not to leave my post.'

'Open it now.'

Puzzled and with shaking hands, the guard used the butt of his rifle to smash the lock and the door swung open.

In the moonlight, he made out a desk and chairs and open doors leading to other rooms.

'Cover me,' he ordered his driver and, Luger primed, kicked open the door to where the suspect had lain. A bundle lay on the bed, but when he pulled it, it was only a blanket and a pillow.

'Schweiße.' In frustration, he kicked over a bucket. How had the man escaped? A locked door and the mesh over the two windows were still intact. The guard followed them in and stared at the empty room, open-mouthed.

'Where is he?' Jünger asked. 'You have let him escape?'

'No. No one has left while I've been here. I swear.'

The VIOLINIST'S REVENGE

He controlled the desire to strike the stupid man. 'Did you see the prisoner?'

'Nein, Herr Obersturmführer, my orders were to guard the building and let no one in or out, which I did.'

Now he understood. The room must have been empty when the guard came on watch, so Schmidt and his colleague were helping the suspect. He should organise a cordon to ensure Wächter's safety, but there was another possibility. 'Did the Sergeant go to the watchtower?'

'Yes, Herr Obersturmführer, I watched them go.'

'Which one?'

'There,' the guard pointed into the distance. 'Where the lights are flickering.'

23

'Keep close.' He put a hand over his mouth. 'Don't make a sound.'

The watchtower was silhouetted in the night sky as a cloud of cigarette smoke drifted across the moon and fragments of guttural voices, interspersed with coarse laughter, hung in the air and, in the distance, a dog howled at the moon.

The two banks of fencing appeared impenetrable, and she couldn't see a way through. The grass between the fences was ankle-deep and the ground uneven. A searchlight swept the area farther along the perimeter and froze everything in its blinding white light. She gagged and her hand tightened on the back of his jacket. 'I can't do this.' If the light caught them, they would be stranded in no-man's-land, and she'd be too petrified to run.

He coaxed her past the tower, counting as he went and, when he found the spot he was searching for, he motioned for her to get down on her knees. 'You okay?' He squeezed her arm. 'We've got one chance.'

Across no-man's-land, the second fence seemed to be moving away from them. She was trembling violently and doubted she could run that far. 'I'm frightened.' She buried her face in the mud, remembering the rat-a-tat-tat of machine guns, the lights, the blaring sirens, the body parts from previous escape attempts.

He patted her shoulder. 'Whatever you do, don't stop. Run like hell until you're through the second fence. If you slip or stumble, you've had it. If you fall, I can't come for you. Got it?'

'Yes,' she said, fighting back tears, and nodded.

He glanced up at the watchtower and motioned her forward and they crawled nearer the fence, but still she couldn't see a way through. Then she spied a small gap, and he stared across the expanse and into the trees as though calculating the distance. She buried her head in the grass and stifled a sneeze.

'What's that?' The guard stopped talking and walked across the tower and scanned the area below, his footsteps thudding on the floorboards.

'You're hearing things,' Schmidt said. 'You're too jumpy.' He stamped his foot. 'What's taking him so long?'

They lay still until the footsteps receded. Then he thrust his gloved hands into the gap and pulled away loose sods of earth, opening up the space. When large enough to crawl through, he turned and took her by the shoulders. 'Go under here. Don't touch the wire. It's electrified.'

With another glance at the tower, he helped her manoeuvre under the fence. Going headfirst and on her back, the wire only inches from her nose, she feared that if she breathed out, she'd be electrocuted. It was slow and hard work as she dug in her heels to propel herself, turning her head to the side and, with a final shove from him, made it and subsided in a combination of fear and exhaustion.

'When I give the signal, run for the perimeter fence.' He pointed into the night.

Convinced the distance was increasing, she stared at it with trepidation.

'Opposite us is a loose flap in the wire, which you can lift and crawl under,' he said. 'It's safe, not electrified. It's a backup route in case the current one is closed. Don't stop. Don't look back. Keep going until you're in the trees, and once you're through, they'll help you get away. You can trust them.'

'What about you?'

'I'll join you later.' He averted his gaze. 'There's something I must do.'

'What?'

'I told you I smuggled alcohol in for the guards.'

She waited for him to elaborate.

'The guards on the other towers will believe I'm doing that and look the other way. Instead, to save his neck, Schmidt said he'd let me escape and would watch out for me. But he's expecting me to use the usual route on the other side of the tower, and he doesn't know you're escaping, too. If he did, he'd shoot us both. I'll be the decoy. When I start my run across, I'll give a low cough, which is the signal they're expecting.'

'But—'

'When you hear the cough, run and don't stop.'

'Can you trust him?'

But he had already slipped away into the darkness.

SCHMIDT CHECKED HIS WATCH. 'Where the hell is he?' he muttered. Henrik was talking, and he raised an arm, silencing him. 'There it is.' The single cough. He scanned no-man's-land, but the prisoner had not started his crossing. 'Okay, Henrik, it's showtime. I must return to the barracks. You know what you must do. Let him have it. Remember, if you don't kill him, we're dead men.'

He descended the steps but instead of heading for the barracks, ducked under the tower and lit a cigarette. So far, so good. With the prisoner dead, he'd be free. If there was any comeback, Klebus couldn't blame him. It would be Henrik who shot and killed his man.

Movement.

Something had moved past the tower. It took a moment to register. The prisoner wasn't using his usual route to make the crossing. He was going along the fence to his right. He peered into the dim light. Another dark, crouched shape approached the perimeter. The bastard must have another escape route. He threw away his cigarette and climbed the steps, screaming at Henrik to shoot.

In a panic, the soldier leaned out from the tower, looking down at the expected route.

'Not there, you imbecile,' he shouted. 'On the other side. They're getting away.'

With a metallic click, the searchlight sparked into life, flooding no-man's-land in white light, and a burst from Henrik's MG 42 machine gun sent tracer bullets flashing like diamonds in the darkness. 'Give it to me.' Exasperated, he grabbed the weapon, knocking the searchlight away, and fired haphazardly into the night.

SHE CROUCHED in the middle of no-man's-land, unable to move. She must keep moving or be cut down, but when he reached her, she collapsed. 'I can't go on. Save yourself.'

He pushed her into a stumbling run, like stepping into quicksand, and the more she tried to power her legs, the deeper she sank. Although he shouted, encouraging her, it didn't register, and she trod on the end of her coat, losing her balance. In a last desperate effort, she lunged forward and covered only a couple of yards before she fell on her face, swallowing a mouthful of mud.

'Leave the coat.'

When the searchlight targeted them, he pulled her over his shoulder. Behind, the discarded coat jumped like a marionette with a life of its own as bullets slammed into the surrounding turf and the perimeter fence flashed and pinged as a hail of bullets snapped the wires.

24

Luger in hand, Jünger arrived at the inner fence and scanned the area, attempting to identify the two escapees. The suspect he recognised, and a woman, were climbing through the perimeter fence. Someone or something lay on the grass in the middle of no-man's-land, and his soldier went down on one knee and took aim and fired.

'Stop, you fool.' He pulled him back by the shoulder. 'It's only a coat.'

He peered into the night. 'Give me your rifle.' A standard issue Mauser KAR 98K, slow but accurate at long range. He lifted it to his shoulder and aimed at the bushes beyond the fence. Although he now had no sight of the target, the foliage wouldn't protect them. The leading marksman of his year at military college, it was suggested he join the sniper brigade, but he preferred to see the whites of his enemy's eyes.

He controlled his breathing and, as a shape rose from the bushes presenting a clear target, squeezed the trigger. There was a blue flash as the bullet snapped the fence wire, an anguished cry and a crashing of foliage, and the figure dropped from sight.

'You got him, Herr Obersturmführer.' The soldier could barely conceal his excitement.

Sirens wailed, the camp lit up, and there was a growl of engines.

The VIOLINIST'S REVENGE

A Kubelwagen pulled up alongside him, and he jumped into the passenger seat and the soldier clambered into the back.

'Quick, he's wounded.' Although there had been a cry of pain in the darkness, he couldn't be certain. It was imperative to find the target before he lost consciousness or died because he would give him the names of his co-conspirators. As they drove out the main gate, he counted the fence poles, calculating where the escapees had exited and ordered the driver to leave the road and drive into the undergrowth. The gap they'd escaped through was ahead. 'Aim your headlights there.' He pointed and drew his Luger as he climbed out of the vehicle. The gunfire had smashed bushes and branches, but the suspect had vanished.

'Blood.' The soldier gestured with his torch at a broken branch. 'Here. There. Lots of it.'

If one were wounded, it would slow their progress, but they must be careful, as they might be armed. 'You take that path,' he said. 'I'll go this way. Remember, I want them alive.'

Pushing aside low-hanging branches, he stared back at the camp and, from this angle, had a different perspective. Puzzled, he studied the now-empty watchtower. When he had made his way from the guardhouse, he'd seen where Schmidt and his colleague were firing, but it was haphazard, and the searchlight had lit up two different areas. What was Schmidt up to? He took a torch from one of his men and shone it around him. It was obvious he'd had help to escape, and that left a bad taste in his mouth as he drove back to the tower. He would have to interrogate Schmidt and his sidekick.

On arriving, a figure, who had dressed in haste, his jacket barely covering his pyjamas and his cap set on the back of his head, clambered out of a staff car.

Jünger frowned. No matter the emergency, a senior officer should never appear like that before his soldiers, who snapped to attention as the Commandant approached.

'What's happening, Obersturmführer?' With an air of detachment, Höss placed a cigarette between his lips and waited for someone to find a light.

Höss's questions irritated him, as every second was vital.

'So, this is your suspect, the man you delayed questioning,' the

Commandant said. 'You believe you wounded him, then he won't get far.'

He ignored the barb. 'Someone must have been waiting for them. If he's who I think he is, it was well organised.'

Höss snorted. 'The Poles hate us so much they'll do anything to help him get away.'

'He's not a Pole. He's a Czech and very dangerous.'

'You have information?'

'From the Gestapo.'

The Commandant raised an eyebrow. 'You have friends there?'

'If you'd let me interrogate him in the first place, this could have been avoided.' He struggled to suppress his anger.

Höss removed the cigarette from his mouth. 'I hope you're not suggesting—'

'The men in the guardhouse, who claimed he was in a coma, helped him escape.'

'You won't find any inefficiency or conspiracy here, Jünger.' Höss stepped back. 'We'd have uncovered it. Who was the other escapee?'

Another officer interjected, 'We're searching all huts and will find out who's missing, Herr Commandant.'

'A woman,' Jünger said.

Höss gave a hesitant laugh. 'So, he likes his creature comforts.'

'Can't be certain, but I recognised the coat.' He pointed to the discarded rags. 'The violinist.'

As though concerned they would have to replace her in the orchestra, Höss sighed. She would be missed. He took out another cigarette. 'I must report your dereliction of duty to Gruppenführer Wächter.'

Used to senior officers shifting the blame onto their juniors, he shrugged. To them, failure was weakness, and the weak must never prevail.

Höss made to return to his car, then paused. 'My men will soon track down the suspect. He's made the cardinal error of taking the woman with him. If he hasn't discarded her already, she'll slow him down.'

The VIOLINIST'S REVENGE

ONCE THEY'D LEFT, Wächter poured a large Courvoisier. Both Höss and Jünger had attempted to pass the blame for the escape, and it reminded him of two praying mantises manoeuvring for the kill. He detested the senior officer's posturing as he accused his junior rather than his own men's inefficiency. Jünger regretted not having interrogated the suspect earlier in the day, but it wasn't his fault. He had ordered him to take care of business away from the camp.

As Governor of the area, he was senior, yet the Commandant had complete control within the camp and also reported to Himmler, who was impressed by his efficiency in dispatching Jews and undesirables. And he was virtually untouchable, and he knew it, too.

What Wächter wasn't aware of was the nature of his relationship with Himmler and the Führer, so he must tread carefully. But he was determined Jünger wouldn't be saddled with a charge that would stick to him throughout his career, although he had to listen to both sides of the argument.

Not until they mentioned a woman had also escaped did he pay full attention. Höss seemed more concerned he'd lost a talented musician than a prisoner. Recalling the incident at the fence when the suspect was beaten for talking with a woman, it began to make sense. He remembered her haunting eyes across the column of marchers and smiled at the memory of her performing for an appreciative audience in Vienna before the war. Her presence in the camp was one of the senseless tragedies of war, neither a Jew nor a criminal, yet she was here with her family. And Hudal's forceful demand that he sort it out as if he could wave a magic wand had caused him problems. If Höss discovered what he'd done, he'd use it against him when the opportunity arose.

While the Commandant droned on about discipline and Nazi values, intent on absolving himself of any blame, Wächter's mind wandered. He hadn't envisaged his life would turn out like this. Born into an aristocratic family. A burgeoning law career, then politics. Marriage to Charlotte was fruitful. Even Hudal had provided useful counsel from time to time. The Bishop's support for Nazi ideology was steadfast. Was it helpful in his relationship with Pope Pius XII? After all, the Pope had been criticised for not condemning Nazi atrocities and not intervening when Jews were deported from Italy. His supporters claimed the Pope feared repercussions against Catholics in Germany if he did. Others challenged his motives. When he joined the Party, he believed it would be advantageous for Austria and Germany to be joined on the world stage, and the Bishop supported him.

A driven and conscientious activist, Wächter had been involved in the assassination of Chancellor Engelbert Dollfuss. His exploits had attracted the attention of the Führer and Himmler, which led to him being appointed governor of Katowice and then Galicia. He met his targets with enthusiasm and believed that for the Aryan race to prevail, the removal of Jews, Czechs, Slovaks and Poles was justified. Approaching all tasks as logistical problems, he never considered the impact on individual lives.

But the woman's presence in the camp made little sense. A mystery.

'Wounded?' he said, rejoining the heated conversation between the two officers.

They fell silent.

'Who was wounded? The man or the woman or both?'

'Impossible to tell.' Jünger offered a deprecatory smile. 'I hit at least one of them. There was a lot of blood at the scene, but I'm not sure how serious it was.'

'Man or woman, they can die of their wounds for all I care,' Höss said. 'Once we catch them, they'll face a firing squad after they reveal the names of everyone who helped them.' He sneered at Jünger.

Wächter looked away. This was how the Nazi system worked. Everyone is set against each other. Every slip reported. Never safe, especially at his level and if the Gestapo were involved, the truth was twisted so tight it evaporated.

'With your permission, Herr General,' Jünger requested. 'I will question the guards who had the prisoner in their custody.'

He nodded.

Höss tried to speak, but Jünger waved him away. 'There are anomalies requiring investigation, and there may have been a greater conspiracy.'

While the Commandant looked pained, Wächter suppressed a

smile. 'We will meet again in the morning after you have interrogated the guards and caught the escapees, hopefully.'

He stood, signalling the end of the meeting and turned to Höss. 'How you deal with the man is up to you, but the woman should not be harmed. If she is wounded, do everything possible to ensure her survival.'

25

'Slow down, for God's sake,' he said, his voice quiet but forceful. 'Every time we hit a bump, the bleeding starts.'

His breathing rasped as he bent over Anneliesa lying on a rough wooden floor, which rose and fell and shook from side to side as the van lurched over rough tracks. And she cried out with every vibration.

'I can't slow down, Jan,' the driver shouted over his shoulder. 'We haven't much of a head start.'

Another bump caused her to gasp as the pain spread through her, and he peered into her eyes. 'Be brave. Stay with us.' And she placed a hand on the source of the pain, and it was sticky and red with blood.

After he'd pushed her through the perimeter fence, bullets slammed into the surrounding trees. One hit her in the side, and she collapsed, and he hoisted her over his shoulder before she blacked out. She touched the wound again and this time warm blood flowed and she attempted to sit upright, but the effort was too much.

'Lie still, or you'll make it worse,' he said and removed his shirt, ripping off a length of fabric and folding it into a pad to staunch the flow, but it soon became saturated.

'She'll die if we don't get help,' he called to the driver.

The man sitting alongside the driver squinted into the dark. 'At this rate, they'll soon catch us. Their vehicles are faster than this old crate.'

'She's lost a lot of blood,' Jan said.

'We can't stop now, or she'll die anyway,' the passenger said. 'If we can shake them off, we've got someone who will help. Hang on, lady.'

As he tightened the makeshift tourniquet, she drifted back into darkness as if in a dream as the vehicle swayed like a boat in a storm.

'Can't stay on this road.' The driver wrestled with the wheel. 'There will be roadblocks up ahead.' He pulled hard to the right, and the van bumped down an even rougher track. 'Let's make it harder for them.'

Jan watched for followers through the small, dirty rear window and pointed. 'There's a light behind and it's closing.'

'Shit.' The passenger swivelled in his seat. 'Can't you get a bit more out of this old banger?'

The driver peered in the rearview mirror. 'I'm doing my best.'

The wind whistled through the van as the passenger stuck his head out of the window. 'It's an NSU motorcycle,' he said. 'We've got no chance of outrunning it, and it'll be only a matter of minutes before he catches us.'

Jan spat on the van's back window and wiped it clean with his sleeve, and saw the motorcyclist closing, his face determined as he guided the machine around the swales and bumps, avoiding the holes littering the surface. And he was gaining fast, but needed both hands to control the bucking machine.

'Are there others?' the driver asked over his shoulder.

'Not yet.' He pressed his nose against the glass. 'No other lights, but it's difficult to tell with all the trees.'

The driver forced the vehicle faster, making its engine rev in protest, and there was a sudden clunking noise like a ship running aground. 'We've done damage there,' he said through gritted teeth.

The motorcycle was closing on them and, when almost within touching distance, the rider lifted his right hand off the handlebars to search for his pistol. With a heave, Jan pushed the rear door and it swung open beyond his grasp, exposing them to the soldier, who was so close he was reflected in the rider's goggles.

The passenger pulled out a pistol. 'Get out of the way,' he bellowed. 'I'll shoot the bastard.'

Framed in the doorway, he struggled to keep his balance as the van swerved and bumped, and his only weapon was his fists. Holding onto the door handle, he swung out into the night air, the slipstream taking away his breath and, as he stretched out a foot, the bike swerved to avoid a crater. He almost lost his hold on the door as it swung back, but he reached out and his foot smashed the bike's headlamp. Momentarily blinded, the rider slowed and swayed as he hit another crater and lost control, the machine launching off the track and into the trees, followed by the sounds of crashing as it ploughed through the vegetation and ended in an explosion. Confident there were no other pursuers, he clambered back into the van and closed the door behind him, but still watched for pursuing lights.

'Impressive.' The passenger put away his pistol. 'If there'd been others, we'd have had problems.'

'What's up ahead?' he asked.

'From here on it's rough country. Now it's all down to our friend's local knowledge. In the dark, it's like a maze, and they'll get lost.'

'How long before we get there?' He checked her pulse.

'Difficult to say.' The passenger turned to the driver. 'What do you think?'

'Twenty or twenty-five minutes,' the driver replied. 'The area will be crawling with the pigs. They don't like prisoners escaping. It's an insult to their superiority.' They both chuckled. 'And they'll make their own pay for their mistakes.'

As Jan continued working on the tourniquet, he willed the van to go faster.

26

Birdsong, or was she dreaming? Anneliesa was confused because there was no birdsong in Auschwitz and she hadn't heard their music for ages. As she moved, the pain reminded her it wasn't a dream. Where am I? Closing her eyes and opening them gradually, she expected to see the grey of the camp, but her vision was blurred and blinking several times brought her surroundings into focus. She lay on a bed in a small room with a partially boarded-up window and sunlight filtering through a grimy single pane of cracked glass. The musty room, which had been uninhabited for a time, made her sneeze. Above her head, a crucifix hung on the wall, dust covered a bible lying on the bedside table, and there were several religious artefacts scattered about and, in an open wardrobe, dark clothes hung like carcasses in a butcher's shop. The few items of furniture were of dark wood and substantial and added to the Stygian gloom.

Must have been an old person's room, and they'd left in a hurry.

The mattress was lumpy and the blanket coarse and heavy, but it was a blanket rather than the rag she used in the camp. As she wriggled to get comfortable, men's voices drifted in from a nearby room, and she strained to hear but couldn't determine the language. A glass of water sat on the table and, when she reached for it, a sharp pain ripped through her side. What had happened? Images came to her in a disjointed jumble, and the memories ended with a piercing blow to her side. Had Jan made it out? She used the name the men had called him. If he hadn't, she feared she couldn't carry on.

She had been undressed and was wearing a man's shirt. Gritting her teeth to fight the pain, she struggled upright and pulled away the shirt and tried examining the wound with her fingers, but her waist was bandaged. A professional job, although this wasn't a hospital. The water tasted fresh and she drank it down in one, slaking her thirst, as the voices droned on. Polish, she guessed.

When she attempted to get out of the bed, the coolness of the stone tiles on her bare feet made her recoil and, exhausted, she flopped onto her back. *Am I still a prisoner? If so, who are the men in the next room?*

Maybe there was a scintilla of hope, but she searched for anything that might serve as a weapon, although she doubted she'd have the energy to wield it. *Lie here until they come. Conserve your strength.* She was determined to stay awake, but her eyes closed, and she slipped back into sleep.

'HAVE YOU CAUGHT THEM?' Wächter dispensed with salutations, declining to offer them a seat.

'No, Herr General, but—'

'You gave me the impression that you had everything under control.'

'Yes, Herr General, but—'

'So, you're not in control?'

'I am, I—'

'Is this what you call control?'

The Commandant glared at Jünger before responding. 'If it hadn't been for the Obersturmführer's failure—'

With the back of a hand, he waved away the protestations, pleased Jünger was none the worse after the events of the last few hours. A lesser man might have been cowed, but not him, and there was a glint of determination in his eyes as his eyes bored into Höss as if he'd have gladly thrown him into one of his gas chambers.

The VIOLINIST'S REVENGE

'I will deal with it later. What are your chances of capturing them? A realistic opinion, please.'

'They won't have gone far,' the Commandant responded in a more even tone. 'We're carrying out a systematic search of the area and—'

'For your sake, I hope so,' he said. 'The Reichsführer has already asked for my report on the situation. There's more to this than we believed.'

It irritated Höss that Wächter kept interrupting him, but a sly look crept into his eyes. 'We extracted information from Schmidt and the guard that will interest you.'

Jünger had sat in on the interrogation. The skill of torture was taking them so far, but not too far, and keeping them alive until they begged to die, although not letting them. Deny them their wish until they give you everything. Although aware of what Schmidt had revealed, he kept quiet. The Sergeant's relationship with the prisoner intrigued him. The Commandant had pressed for the name of who had given the orders, but who was Klebus? The Sergeant didn't know. Maybe SD, he suggested.

Jünger remained expressionless, knowing he was on the right track, after all. If the escapee had been shielded by Schmidt, it pointed to him being the assassin.

'I only carried out orders,' Schmidt babbled through bruised and swollen lips. 'I wasn't told why I should protect him.'

Höss had turned to Jünger. 'The plot thickens.'

Worried he might wonder if he didn't match his curiosity, he asked Schmidt how the prisoner got into the camp.

'I don't know,' Schmidt said, shaking his head. 'He attempted to escape, so we shot him.'

'What do you make of it?' the Commandant asked Junger.

Before he could reply, the soldier who had been tasked with finding information on Klebus entered the room. 'Put us out of our misery. Who is this Klebus?'

'He is connected with the SD,' the soldier reported. 'That's all. Not even a rank.'

Listening without expression, Wächter shuffled papers on his desk before getting to his feet. 'I must update the Reichsführer.'

Höss swung around to confront Jünger. 'What about his role in this?'

'We'll discuss that another time,' Wächter said. 'First, I suggest you put your house in order and clear up this mess.'

Höss led Jünger outside, where his guards were holding Schmidt and Henrik, who was crying, and they headed for Block 11, a brick building used for torture and executions. If the guards were fortunate, it would be the Death Wall and a firing squad; if they weren't, it could be the Stehzelle, the standing cells, a metre square, with a small hole for air. Prisoners were forced to stand for ten to twenty days without support and were unable to move or rest until they lost their minds. As though relishing the punishment, Höss clapped his hands and invited Jünger to watch.

They lined up the prisoners against the wall, and six soldiers, carrying rifles and faces impassive, shuffled into the courtyard. No words were spoken and there was no speech, no accusations, before an obersturmführer barked an order and the firing squad raised their rifles.

Jünger closed his eyes, imagining he was in their boots, waiting for the bullet that would end his life, and he found he was sweating and clamped his mouth shut.

There came the order to fire, then a pause. Then the explosive blast of six weapons rocked him on his heels and there was a sickening smell of cordite and a percussive sound raced around his skull as if looking for a way out. And when he opened his eyes, Höss was gloating at the bodies crumpled on the ground and stood over them with a Luger in his hand and ready to finish them off if necessary.

'This is their reward for betraying the Reich,' he said with a satisfied smile.

SHE WAS SUFFOCATING, and something on her face prevented her from breathing. She tried pulling her head away, but the pressure increased. It was strong and she couldn't move and she was choking and her eyes bulged in her effort to get free. The weight on her face smelled of leather, and the pressure lessened, but as she gasped, it clamped down hard again. She made out a man's head and shoulders, dressed all in black. When he eased the pressure, she exhaled in relief. 'What the—'

'Sssh.' He gestured towards the cracked window.

Twenty yards away, SS troops were disembarking from a truck, and an officer eased out of a Kübelwagen and scrutinised the rundown farmhouse with its two dilapidated barns, the doors of one yawning open, illuminated by sunshine streaming through a hole in the roof. He took off his cap and wiped his brow with a handkerchief before walking towards the farmhouse, his boots crunching on gravel. Several times he pushed at the front door before realising it was blocked, then peered through a grimy window, shaking his head in disgust. 'Even the camp is luxurious compared to this shithole,' he said, sparking laughter from his men.

Jan lay beside her, holding her tight, and she felt the rhythm of his heart racing in his chest.

The driver of the truck called to the officer, 'Herr Obersturmführer.'

He swung around. 'What is it? We must search this pigsty.'

'A radio message for you.' The driver jumped down from the cabin and clicked his heels as the officer climbed into the truck and put his head close to the receiver. After listening for a moment, he looked around with a look of distaste. 'Forget it,' he said. 'They've got the suspects cornered nearby.' He jumped down and got back into his vehicle, which roared away, sending up clouds of dust as his men scrambled to catch up.

Jan exhaled. 'Too close for comfort.' As he sat on the bed, she noticed the pistol in a holster at his waist. 'We're not safe here,' he said. 'As soon as they realise it's a false alarm, they'll be back.'

'Where am I, Jan?' She emphasised his name and touched his arm as though confirming he was real.

'What do you remember?'

'A blow in my side …' She felt the wound. 'That's all.'

'They shot you, and Marek and Tomasz brought us here.'

So, they were the voices in the other room.

'You lost a lot of blood,' he said. 'Didn't think you'd make it and even considered surrendering in the hope they'd try saving your life if they wanted you back for the orchestra.'

'I'm glad you didn't.' She looked away.

'With every movement of the van, you were haemorrhaging, but you made it. I feel bad. It's me they're after, not you.'

'I'm thankful you didn't leave me behind.'

'You might not be saying that soon,' he said, avoiding eye contact and staring at his feet. 'The longer you spend with us, the greater the danger for you.'

'I'd rather die than go back there.' She pointed to the bandage. 'Is this your handiwork?'

'We feared you'd bleed out before we got here. You needed professional help. At first, the Poles were reluctant to involve anyone else because once you do, it increases your chances of being caught.'

'But you persuaded them.' She mustered a smile.

'I told them how much you meant to me.'

'How sweet.' She chuckled at his embarrassment. 'Am I dying?'

'Not if I can help it.'

'But all the blood?'

'The bullets hit flesh, not vital organs.'

Like a dream, she remembered an old man with a shock of grey hair, wearing pince-nez spectacles and talking in a comforting voice as he leant over her.

'The doc worked hard on you. Said you should survive, but it'd be painful.'

'I can handle it.' She sat up and gasped. 'I'm tougher than I look,' she added through gritted teeth.

The door opened in stages before Marek entered. 'We must hurry,' he said. 'The pigs will be back soon.'

As Jan went to follow him out, she grabbed his arm and held on. 'What makes you so special?'

Embarrassed, he looked away.

'Why?' she insisted.

'I'm not special. I was just one of those who assassinated Hitler's favourite general, Heydrich.'

As her mouth opened, struggling for words, he glanced about the room. 'This was my escape route out of the country.'

'So that's why you wouldn't give me your name?'

He hesitated. 'My name's Jan Pastorek and I'm a Czech. That's all you need to know. Come, we must go.'

27

The back door creaked and footsteps on the stone floors echoed throughout the farmhouse. As Jan reached for his pistol, she froze, and a tap on the bedroom door caused them to glance at each other. Nazis don't knock. 'Come in,' he said in Polish, his hand tightening on the pistol.

The door opened a few inches before the Doctor entered. 'Ah, good, you're still here,' he said and studied them in turn. 'I wondered if you'd left, but of course you shouldn't.'

She screwed up her face and exhaled in relief.

'On no account should you leave.' His relaxed manner reassured her. 'If you make good progress, perhaps in a few days.' As though recalling previous visits, his gaze scanned the room. 'A young family once lived here with a grandparent,' he said. 'A couple of years ago. They had two boys. Lovely boys, but lively.' He smiled.

'What happened to them?' she asked.

'Nazis.' His lips curled. 'They claimed they were spies and hanged the parents in the barn, but, realising what would happen, the couple had slipped a pill to the grandmother and she died here.' He looked down at the bed.

'What became of the boys?'

'Neighbours found them wandering in the fields nearby, and one of the boys was so shocked he couldn't speak, but I never saw them again. After that? I don't know.' He pursed his lips, and they let him deal with the memory in his own way.

'Don't worry,' the Doctor said, seeing their anxious looks. 'I've parked my bicycle around the back and it can't be seen from the road, so nobody will know I'm here.'

'Thank you, Doctor.' He stepped forward. 'We didn't expect you so soon.'

'You've had a bullet cut out of you and need rest and observation.' He put his bag on the bed and opened it, checking the contents. 'I'll inspect the wound to ensure there are no complications and replace the dressing, then I'll leave you in peace.' He held her face between his fingers and stared into her eyes. 'Looks like you're making progress and there's a bit of colour in your cheeks.'

A growl of vehicles churning up the gravel at the front of the farmhouse stopped his examination. The truck had returned and soldiers were jumping down from the vehicle.

'Visitors.' The Doctor dropped his gaze. 'And they're coming in.'

Jan searched around for a hiding place, but it was hopeless. And the Doctor was too old to run to the woodland nearby, and his determined expression suggested he wasn't about to leave his patient's side.

Using his gun would achieve little, but perhaps they could brazen it out. He hid the weapon under a pillow.

'Lie down and cover yourself,' he said and turned to the Doctor. 'Look as if you're working on your patient.'

He placed a stethoscope around his neck and frowned as he laid out a variety of lethal instruments on the bed.

Within minutes, two red-faced soldiers barged in and scanned the room, shrinking back to make way for the Obersturmführer to squeeze past. With a sneer, the officer studied each of them. 'Should have searched this hovel before,' he muttered. 'Would have saved time.'

Jan responded in perfect German. 'Welcome to our humble home.'

Taken off guard, the officer removed his cap and chuckled as he wiped his brow with a handkerchief, his disbelief turning to disgust as he viewed the room. 'Your German is gut,' he said. 'Spoken with an accent, too.'

Pretending she didn't understand, she followed the conversation from face to face.

He relaxed. 'I worked in Germany before the war.'

'Where?' The officer patrolled the room, tipping over objects with a finger.

'Berlin.'

As though remembering better times, the officer asked, 'What job?'

'Interpreter.'

'Gut, gut.' The officer's thinning hair glistened with sweat. 'So, you were an interpreter and now you are a poor farmer?' As though difficult to believe, he screwed up his face. 'A backwards step, no?'

He kept quiet.

'We are looking for two people who escaped from a nearby camp. Bloodthirsty, dangerous individuals. This might be a perfect place to hide out.'

'We don't see many strangers out here.' He tried looking surprised.

'What about you?' The officer stared at her and the Doctor, who continued his work, and she felt his eyes penetrating her and stripping away any artifice.

As though needing a translation, she glanced at Jan. 'They haven't seen anyone.' He stepped in front of them. 'My wife's expecting our first child, and she's unwell, and the Doctor is here treating her.'

Worried her face might give her away, he warned her with his eyes, but she remained impassive and, as if in discomfort, started to moan.

Irritated, the officer switched his gaze to the Doctor and his black bag and stethoscope and other instruments lying on the bed.

'Can't you help her?' He paced the room and inspected various religious artefacts, the clicking of his boots on the wooden floorboards like the ticking of a clock counting down. He returned to the bedside and flipped open the Bible with a finger, sending up a puff of dust. 'You are Catholics, eh, yet you don't read the good book?' He clicked his tongue. 'It's a coincidence. We are searching for a man and a woman. And here you are in a hideout you thought was ideal .' He ran a finger across the table, inspecting it for dust and held it up as evidence. 'But not for living.' He scowled at them. 'Even the poorest people keep their house clean.'

Hands tightening on their weapons, the soldiers tensed as the silence deepened.

'I could have you both shot here and now,' the officer said, 'but I'm a reasonable man.' His soldiers looked at each other and sniggered as he pointed to Jan. 'We will take you for interrogation and perhaps the woman as well.' He waited for a reaction and his gaze switched to the Doctor administering what appeared to be a potion. She groaned in pain, and the Doctor spoke quickly.

Unable to understand, the officer swung around. 'What's he babbling about?'

'If we don't let him do his job, we'll lose her.' He pushed back his hair, trying to stop his hand from trembling.

'Do you take me for an idiot?' The Obersturmführer chuckled. 'This charade has gone on long enough.' He strode over to the bedside and pulled away the blanket, sending medical instruments clattering to the floor.

While the Nazi had been talking, she'd worked the bandage loose and probed the wound with her fingers, and the sight of her lying pale-faced with blood covering her upper thighs made the Nazi recoil.

'She should be left alone.' He spread his hands.

'Very well.' The officer replaced his cap and adjusted it in a mirror. 'But you will come with me.' The soldiers grabbed him by the arm and dragged him out.

With a grimace, the officer stopped, unbuttoned his holster and pointed the Luger. 'As you wish, we will leave this wretched creature alone.' He pulled the trigger.

Jan struggled to get back to the bedroom. 'What have you done? I can't leave her.'

But the officer ignored him. 'Put him in the back,' he said and joined him in the Kübelwagen. 'If you can prove your innocence, you may return.' He leaned forward and tapped the driver on the shoulder. 'Drive.'

As the vehicle jumped into gear, the soldiers were clambering into the back of their truck, but he didn't wait for them.

'So, you worked in Berlin?' The officer relaxed. 'Interesting. Who did you interpret for?'

'Polish businesses attempting to forge relationships with German companies.'

As if reasonable, the officer nodded and reached inside his tunic, removing a packet of evil-smelling Sturm cigarettes, put one in his mouth and flicked open the lighter. As the vehicle lurched, the cigarette dropped from his lip and, while he bent to retrieve it, the Luger slipped from his grasp. In one fluid movement, Jan snatched up the weapon and jammed it into the German's face. As he squeezed the trigger, the Obersturmführer's eyes flashed and the bullet entered the Nazi's forehead, exiting at the back and showering the windscreen with pieces of his brain.

'Schweinhund!' The driver twisted around, pulling on the steering wheel as he reached for his weapon, causing the Kübelwagen to swerve. As the driver struggled to regain control, he brought the butt of the Luger down on his skull and the vehicle careened off course and mounted a grassy bank that launched it airborne over a mound and sent it cartwheeling deep into the forest.

28

Marek and Tomasz hid in a copse a hundred yards from the farmhouse. When they returned, taking a route over the fields because it was safer than the roads, the Nazis were arriving. The soldiers' superior firepower and their involvement would have risked Jan and Anneliesa's lives, and they could only watch as Jan was led to a vehicle and driven off. There had been one shot, but who was the target? For the moment, Jan was alive, so it must have been the woman, but Tomasz tugged his sleeve and pointed to the bike propped against a wall.

Marek stopped him from going down to the farmhouse. 'Wait,' he said. 'They might drive a little way off and creep back to surprise you.' He lit a needle-thin, roll-up cigarette, his hand trembling, then offered the tin of tobacco to his partner, who declined. Deep in contemplation, he smoked the cigarette down until it burned his fingers. 'Now we can go,' he said, 'but be careful, soldiers might still be there.'

They found her in the bedroom, sitting cross-legged on the floor, cradling the Doctor's body, and there was a lot of blood.

'Are you okay?' he asked, laying down his rifle.

'I hate this stupid war,' she said. 'Why shoot him? He's just a doctor and, because of me, he's dead.'

The woman had been Jan's responsibility, but now she was his, increasing his problems. 'What did they do to you?' he asked, seeing blood on her.

'They didn't touch me,' she said, putting a hand to her side and wincing.

Marek took a sharp intake of breath. 'Tomasz, go find another doctor, and he must come now.' He turned, shaking his head. 'Then you must leave.'

To his surprise, she snapped back, 'Not until I know Jan is okay.'

'You can't stay.' He frowned. 'He'll give them what they want, and they'll return for you.'

'I'm staying,' she said, but didn't return his look.

'If the Nazis take you, you don't come out.' He stepped in close. 'Anyone they regard as an enemy dies. The officer didn't realise Jan's importance, but to Hitler, he's enemy No.1. They'll get out of him the names of everyone who's helped him and if there are other hit squads and who their targets are. Once they've got what they want, they'll execute what's left of him. There will be no mercy.'

Her face screwed up as she bit on her fist to silence a gasp.

'Jan would expect you to escape,' he said. 'It would be a victory of sorts.'

In her confusion, his words were lost in her thoughts, and she stumbled and clutched his arm to stop from falling. He put out a steadying hand, and his voice had a finality brooking no argument. 'You must get far away from here, believe me, there's no alternative.' All the time his eyes were alert, searching, as though expecting the Nazis at any moment.

His colleague returned alone. 'Couldn't get a doctor,' he said and stared in her direction, but through her as though she didn't exist. 'Every minute she stays here, she's endangering our lives.'

Marek flashed a warning look, but he persevered. 'We can't leave any witnesses behind.'

'Are you going to shoot me?' She stared back at him.

Marek confronted his colleague and pushed him in the chest, saying over his shoulder, 'We're not barbarians.'

'I didn't mean that.' Tomasz looked at his feet, unwilling to meet her gaze.

'Is there a chance Jan might be freed?' she asked.

The VIOLINIST'S REVENGE

'No,' Marek said. 'Hopefully, death comes quickly for him.' He tried to avoid her eyes. He had been committed to guiding Jan out of Poland to continue his work against the Nazis, but now?

To make amends, Tomasz shrugged. 'What I meant is it takes many people risking their lives carrying out an escape like this. Jan was a war hero and she's an inexperienced woman, so what use can she be against the Nazis?'

Marek kicked a chair, sending it skittering across the stone floor. She stood hunched, silhouetted in the light from the window, vulnerable, and he knew he couldn't abandon her. He summoned his colleague outside, and there was shouting and Marek lifting both arms in frustration. She left them to it and found clean bandages in the doctor's discarded case and also a vial of what she took to be morphine, which she swallowed, and then dressed the wound, which lessened the bleeding.

Marek returned, his face set. 'We go now. Come.'

Outside, there was no sign of the other man as he led her to the van, and they drove for a time in silence, each consumed by their thoughts. As much as she didn't want to think about what was happening to Jan, it kept returning with such intensity she feared her head might explode.

On either side, cornfields swayed in a breeze and ruffled the leaves of the trees, bringing the aroma of the countryside in through the open windows and filling the van with pollen. In the distance, smoke snaked from a farmhouse chimney into a cloudless sky. A dog barked and a tractor chugged and, in an adjoining field, cattle moved slowly grazing, while others lay as though asleep. For a moment, nothing appeared to have changed and the Nazis hadn't marched into Poland and then most of Europe, slaughtering the innocent, enslaving millions, exterminating races and bringing global despair. Now was a different world, and she was no more important than a beetle scuttling across open ground seeking the safety of another rock.

Several times she wanted to ask a question, but worried about what he might say. What now? Where were they headed? With Jan, she was safe, but could she trust this man, or would he sacrifice her to the Nazis? The strain was building in her head, and she sighed in exasperation, like a pressure valve being released. 'Where are we going?'

He didn't respond, just stared through the flyblown windscreen at the road ahead. He rubbed his eyes vigorously and turned to her with a weary look, pulling off his cap and shaking out a mass of tousled brown hair, before running a hand through his locks. 'Don't worry,' he said and reached for another cigarette and his fingers no longer trembled. 'My friend didn't mean what he said. He's as committed as the rest of us. This escape route is not for everyone; otherwise, the entire country would want to go, and we don't have the manpower or resources. It's for special agents like Jan.'

'But I'm not special.' She averted her eyes.

'Perhaps not in that way. Our people expect one person, so instead of Jan, you are the one.'

'I'm grateful, but I feel a fraud having put you and your comrades at risk.' She placed a hand on his arm. 'Too many have died already.'

'We owe it to him,' he said. 'The free world is indebted to him.' He looked away. 'I'll drive you for another couple of hours, then hand you over to another driver.'

When he saw uncertainty clouding her eyes, he explained, 'It's the safest way. The Germans have patrols everywhere. They see the locals' cars going about their business and, if they spot a new car, they'll check it out. The driver will take you on for another couple of hours and so on until you reach your destination.'

'Where?'

He frowned. 'Better you don't know. Most of the drivers won't tell you their names either. The less you know, the safer it is for everyone.'

The nagging pain in her side made her slump in the seat and, after a long silence, she said in a lighter tone, 'But I know your name.'

He glanced sideways, grinning. Not much older than her. A tall, powerful man with an easy grin and square jaw. Very much in charge. His smile broadened. 'But you won't tell anyone. You're a fighter.'

'Are you Resistance?'

'Armia Krajowa?' He flashed a wry smile, but a wariness crept into his grey eyes. 'I'm what we Poles call Cichociemni. Countrymen trained in England and parachuted in to fight with the Resistance.'

'Wow!'

'Just doing what I can for my country.'

'So, you have family here?'

'No.' There was a long pause and, when he spoke, his voice trembled. 'They are all gone.'

'Nazis?' she ventured.

He'd already said too much and drew long and hard on his cigarette, ending the conversation.

29

A car weaved along the rutted track, avoiding deep potholes and flashing its headlamps and, as it drew closer, the driver stuck an arm out of the window and signalled for them to stop. The brakes grated as the car slowed, blocking their path. The driver, his grey hair escaping from beneath a soft cap and with a haunted look in his eyes, asked, 'What're you doing here?'

Marek tapped the steering wheel impatiently, watching him.

'We don't like strangers,' the man said. 'Makes the Nazis nervous and, when they're jumpy, we suffer.'

'Just passing through,' Marek said. 'We're not looking for trouble.'

The man ignored that. 'They'll beat you until you talk, and if you're innocent, it's worse. They'll beat you more if you don't confess. And then they'll start on us. Go back to where you came from.'

'What do you expect us to do?' she said. 'Please, let us continue our journey.'

He appeared surprised she'd spoken. 'It's not that simple. Nazis are everywhere and you'd not believe what they do to us. Even our women and children suffer. To them, we're just animals. Go back.'

'We can't.' Marek glared at him. 'Let us through.' He took a pistol from his pocket and placed it on the dashboard. 'We'll be gone by the time you get home.'

Rivulets of sweat streaked the driver's face. 'She won't survive,' he said as he stared at her. 'The swine have set up a roadblock ahead. You won't get through.'

Marek gripped the steering wheel so hard his knuckles whitened and lowered his head. 'He's right. Get out and go back with him. He'll take you to safety. It's too risky to continue.'

The old man's demeanour changed. Now unsure, his eyes darted around as he stared back up the track, refusing to meet their gaze. 'I've got a wife and family, and they rely on me. Sorry, can't help.' He pushed the car into gear and tugged on the wheel, and it lurched past them, its spinning tyres showering them with gravel.

'We must turn around,' Marek said, staring up the track and then behind.

As he slammed the gear stick into reverse, she reached over and grabbed his hand. 'If we give up now, I'll be back in a concentration camp. I'd rather die here on the road than go back, but there's no reason you should risk your life. Let me out and I'll continue on foot.'

A mixture of emotions rippled across his face. 'Are you sure you want to carry on?'

She nodded, her lips sealed.

He hesitated and then said with a grim smile, 'Okay, let's do it.'

They drove slowly, searching for a way to evade the roadblock. Ditches ran down either side of the track, bordered by steep grassy banks, but if they cleared the ditch, they could be stranded on the bank and be sitting targets. As though reading her mind, he said, 'It wouldn't work.' His hand trembled as he lit another cigarette.

She stretched back in her seat. Should they come back another day? But she'd come this far and was damned if she'd give up without a fight. A quick death would be better than returning to the camp. 'We could leave the van and go on foot across the field,' she suggested.

'Land's too marshy,' he said. 'We'd be bogged down, and there are patrols everywhere. Our best chance is staying with the van.'

As they turned into the bend, they saw soldiers lounging by their jeep, caps off, tunics unbuttoned, and rifles stacked against a wheel. They were smoking, and their cursing and laughter carried on the still air. He eased his foot off the accelerator and drifted to a halt. 'Last chance. It's dangerous for a young woman.'

'Even the way I look?' Please don't agree, she thought. The deprivations of the camp had taken away her beauty. She couldn't fool herself. Her face was gaunt, the cheekbones sunken, eyes like deep black holes. Skin so stretched, as though her bones would pierce her flesh. Neither female nor male. An object without definition. As if he needed more proof, she snatched off her cap to remind him of her shaven head.

In response, he offered an amused smile. 'Whatever they did, they haven't extinguished the fight in your eyes.'

He put a hand on her arm. 'To them, a woman is a woman. They'll have their fun and force me to watch before shooting both of us.' He tried to hold her hands, but she slapped them away. 'If you'd been older, we might have had a chance.'

'Maybe there's something I can do…'

'There's no time now.'

When the soldiers spotted their van, they ran for their rifles, and he pulled the pistol off the dashboard and concealed it under the seat.

The brutal faces, the uniforms, the boots and the rifles brought memories of the camp flooding back, and her heart ached as fear flowed through her. It was too late to change her mind. 'Hit me, Marek.'

He grimaced.

'Hit me hard.' Her eyes burned bright.

'What?' His face screwed up. 'No, I can't, I won't.' He had killed many, but never hit a woman.

Eyes wide and wild, she grasped his arm and pulled so hard he had to push her away. 'It's our only chance.'

She'd seen it before: girls in the camp disfiguring themselves to ward off the attention of the guards because the only alternative was suicide.

He didn't understand. 'Where?' His stomach churned as his eyes ran over her body. Nothing would make him do it.

'In the face.'

Alarm shone from his eyes.

She glanced down the track. It must be now. 'Quick, for Christ's sake.'

The VIOLINIST'S REVENGE

He averted his eyes and slapped her face. A half-hearted blow stung and caused her eyes to water.

'Harder. You must draw blood. Imagine I'm a Nazi, your enemy. Hit me. Now.'

He balled his fist. Revulsion contorted his face as he put one hand behind her head, keeping it steady and closed his eyes. With a grunt, he slammed his fist into the middle of her face and pulled away in disgust. The blow was colossal, almost as if she'd been decapitated, and there was a breaking sound like a twig snapping. Pain pierced between her eyes and spread out like fingers across her face, as though her skin was tearing apart. Her agonised wail filled the car as her head crashed against the window, causing the glass to rattle. The pain paralysed her, and she expelled a rush of air full of blood and snot.

Blood covered her fingers. 'Perfect,' she lisped, feeling her lips swelling, and she choked, bending double and coughing out more blood and a front tooth.

'I didn't…' Horror shone from his eyes. 'Are you all right?' His hand went to the damage, but she shrank away. 'Didn't mean to hit you so hard.' He felt ashamed.

'I'll survive.' She pushed him away. 'Let's meet your friends.'

The ash from his cigarettes had fallen in the footwell, and she bent and picked up a handful of the powder and rubbed it into her cheeks and forehead, avoiding the broken and tender flesh.

As they approached the roadblock, the soldiers stepped out onto the track and blocked their path, gesturing with their guns for them to stop. 'Papers,' one demanded.

Marek handed them over, but his eyes never left hers.

The soldier inspected the van. 'Why are you here?'

'Visited the market in the town.' Marek pointed backwards with his thumb.

With a leer, the guard's stare settled on Anneliesa. She had wrapped a scarf over her head and turned away as she dabbed her face with a handkerchief.

'What have we here?' The soldier's eyes shone as he grinned over at his colleagues. 'It's a lady visitor.' He spat in the dust before pushing his head so far into the cabin that she pulled back. 'Don't be shy, liebling. Give us a smile.'

Pulling farther away from him, she saw out of the corner of her eye Marek reaching under his seat.

'We're bored out here,' the guard said. 'Now we can have fun.'

She couldn't move.

'Do as you're told, girl.' The soldier was flustered. 'Show us your face and give us a smile.'

Slipping the scarf from her head, she turned, and his expression changed from lust to horror at the sight of her shaven head and broken nose, still bleeding. And she grinned, revealing a missing front tooth.

'Shit.' The soldier backed out of the cabin, banging his head on the door frame. 'It's an ugly hag,' he cried and kicked a wheel before slamming his hand on the roof of the van. 'Get out of here.' His face reddening, he rejoined his colleagues as their laughter grew louder.

30

They drove on, with Anneliesa glancing over her shoulder, expecting a Nazi vehicle to bear down on them, but Marek seemed more concerned with her, checking the injuries he'd inflicted. Her nose was misshapen, the blood congealed like a mask, and her face ached and was burning up. He was still ashamed of what he'd done and frowned and reached under his seat, handing over a flask of water, which she poured over her face. After an hour, they turned off the road and took a track through a cornfield and in the distance, a clump of trees rose like an island, hiding a large house. As they drove into the driveway, the van's wheels crunched on white gravel.

'Stay strong,' he said. 'Wait here.'

He went inside, and after a time she feared he'd deserted her, but he emerged, flashing a reassuring smile and ushering her into the cool of the high-ceilinged house and down a corridor to a room at the back resembling a doctor's surgery. As though reading her mind, he explained, 'He's a doctor,' and indicated she should sit on a couch.

Without acknowledging them, the Doctor entered and concentrated on arranging instruments, then came over with what might have been a smile. 'Let's see what the problem is,' he said and made her lie down on the couch and probed her nose, which made her flinch. 'I'm sorry, but it's necessary,' he said before stepping back and appraising her. 'Requires surgery.' But she'd already guessed it was broken.

'We haven't got time,' Marek intervened and, as if expecting it, the Doctor shrugged. 'Okay. This will hurt.' His hands pressed on either side of the bridge of her nose, and she arched her back in pain. There was a click. 'That will help for the time being, but it needs work when you get to wherever you're going,' he said, gesturing to her side. 'What's the problem?'

She tensed as she exposed the bandage, and he removed the dressing, waiting for a reaction before pulling a lamp closer to reveal the wound and considerable swelling and bruising.

'I'd rather not know how you got this,' he said and peered at it again. 'Someone did a good job, but you shouldn't be travelling.'

'I must.'

'You don't have a choice,' he said, frowning at Marek. 'It's important it doesn't become infected. I'll give you an injection to help and painkillers, and the dressing should be changed regularly. You must get help as soon as you arrive.'

As he replaced the bandage, the sound of wheels on gravel stopped him, and then, as though he'd remembered something, he continued his work. 'Relax,' he said, touching her shoulder.

Once finished, he opened the front door, shook Marek's hand and bowed to her. 'Powodzenia,' he said with a smile.

When she saw a tall man, wearing the uniform of a Nazi general, approaching, watched by the driver of his staff car, she went weak at the knees, realising there was no escape. They'd come so far and it would end here.

Sensing her alarm, Marek tightened his grip on her arm, guiding her, and she slipped the scarf over her head so it covered part of her face. He doffed his cap to the officer, whose cold eyes scrutinised them before stepping aside and giving a perfunctory salute.

On reaching the van, Marek opened the door, and she climbed in, not daring a backwards glance to check if the officer was still watching them, and they didn't speak until they were out of the drive and crossing the field.

'The Doctor betrayed us,' she said and feared soldiers would be waiting for them at the end of the track.

But Marek shook his head. 'He wouldn't.'

'How can you be sure?'

'He's my brother. He treats Germans and Poles alike.'

'Oh,' she sighed with relief and put a hand on his arm and left it there. 'What did he say when we left?'

'Good luck.'

He drove for another hour, and they made slow progress, taking diversions wherever necessary, before they pulled alongside a car parked under the trees. She switched cars and bade him an affectionate farewell, and he drove away, an arm waving out of the open window. As Marek had said, the new driver knew the route better than he and his vehicle would be recognised by the Germans. The driver admitted some soldiers, knowing they were locals, waved them through without showing their papers, but others could be more officious.

After a while, she lost count of how many cars and how many faces she encountered, some old and others young. Male and female. Some of indeterminate sex. A few brought food, drink and cigarettes, and some were friendly and talkative, but others were silent like disgruntled taxi drivers, and they never exchanged names or personal information, as all were committed to playing their part in the war, knowing death lurked around every bend. She felt like a fraud. Was she worth saving? Unlike Jan, she wasn't a war hero, only a woman he'd saved along the way.

She soon realised that without local knowledge, it would have been impossible because German troops were everywhere and she'd have blundered into them had she been travelling alone. It could take three hours to cover thirty miles, and often, they hid in woodland as enemy trucks drove past and they waited until dark before continuing. On several occasions, the car became bogged down in mud and she helped push it out. And once, the car surged forward, causing her to fall face-first into deep and sticky mud. Some drivers talked as if it helped soothe their frayed nerves, but, although she asked, they never revealed the final destination. All the drivers knew was who and where to meet.

Eventually, she gave up, realising questions troubled them, and she lost track of time. How much longer would she spend on the road? Was Jan alive and, if so, would she ever see him again? All the time her wound ached, and that and the hopelessness of it made her consider giving up. Then she remembered her father alone in Vienna, not knowing what had become of his family. And Lily? Had she survived, as Jan had suggested?

One of the drivers presented her with a pistol, which she kept in a pocket of the coat given by a talkative woman driver, and, as they drove, she fingered the weapon, and it provided a brief feeling of security. Did he give it to her to shoot Nazis, or herself?

She napped, one eye closed and the other vigilant, but never for more than a few minutes. Just when she was sinking into a deeper sleep, the car halted with a squeal of its brakes, and she snapped awake and pulled the pistol from her pocket.

'Careful,' the driver warned and held her arm, gesturing for her to get out. In the distance, there was a growl like thunder and, in the dark, she couldn't see anything. A rustle behind made her spin around, and two dark shapes were on her, grabbing an arm each, and a rough hand clamped over her mouth.

'Come,' one of them said. It wasn't an invitation, and they hurried her away from the car and, when she lost her footing, they dragged her. As they climbed an embankment, the car started up, turned around and headed back. She reached for the pistol, but it had gone.

They pulled her up the incline with tufts of grass interspersed with sand, making it difficult to keep her balance, and when they reached the top, her nostrils twitched to the salty tang of the sea. And for the first time since she started the journey, she had a flash of hope. Below them, waves exploded white on a beach before slipping away with a sigh into the night and to the right, searchlights scanned the sea and the clouds above, reflecting the froth of the breakers.

As they descended, the men relaxed their grip, and one put a finger to his lips. 'Don't speak,' he said. Ahead, an object lying half in and half out of the water and moving with the tide turned out to be a dinghy, and one held it steady as the other bundled her into it and together they manoeuvred it through the swell before climbing in beside her. They were dressed all in black with woollen hats pulled down almost to their eyes and blackened faces, and she couldn't determine their features.

Like a ghost ship, a fishing boat running dark materialised through a fine mist, and within minutes, they were alongside. She was pulled up and, as she stumbled in the sway, one put his arms around her, holding her tight. 'Climb aboard.'

She scrambled for a foothold, one pushing her upwards, and a powerful hand reached down and grasped her wrist and, between them, they hoisted her up and swung her onto the deck, grazing her knees.

'This way,' a seaman said. She stumbled and, before she could regain her balance, a black hole opened up before her. The landing was a mixture of soft and hard, and she heard a yelp and a curse in an English accent. 'What the fuck?' It was even darker down here, and she peered around, trying to get her bearings. 'Sorry,' she said and instinctively reached beneath her.

The man pushed her hand away and said, 'I need a pee. Where can I go?'

From a dark corner, a woman replied in English, but with a French accent, 'There's nowhere. Just do it where you can.'

She scrambled off the man and, as her eyes became accustomed to the dark, she saw they were in the boat's hold, and a wounded man was propped up against a beam. 'Where are we going?' she asked.

'Civilisation, I hope.' Distracted by running water and rising steam, the woman yelled, 'Oh, no, you could have waited.' She scowled, then turned to her. 'They didn't say, but—'

The grating of the hatch dragging open interrupted her, and one of the fishermen put his head into the space. 'Now, the unpleasant part,' he said with an apologetic smile. 'Sorry, has to be done.' Beyond his head, she made out a net bulging with silver, slithering fish and swinging with the boat's motion. He turned, pulling it open, and the fish cascaded down into the hold like an avalanche, the weight of the catch knocking her off her feet, and she slipped under. Fearing she'd suffocate, she pushed them away from her face and gagged at the stench. Several times she thought she'd lost the violin case and plunged her hands into the heaving mass to retrieve it and, struggling to keep her feet, she floundered as the fish slid over her face and neck.

'What the fuck?' the Englishman said and grabbed handfuls of fish and threw them away, and the woman shrieked in French, while the wounded man was in danger of being swallowed up.

'Are you okay down there?' The fisherman's grinning face reappeared. 'It's for your safety. Once we're underway, there'll be no contact. If we stop before we reach our destination and the hatch is opened, it will be Krauts, so don't give them a target to shoot at and stay hidden beneath the fish.'

'How long will it take?' she asked as the hatch slammed shut.

The sea became wilder as the engines opened full throttle and, in the sway, the fish slopped from side to side, and she warded them off with one hand while the other covered her nose and mouth. Her side ached, but a combination of the doctor's drugs and the motion of the boat helped her drift into sleep, although each time the fear of being submerged by fish awakened her.

31

The engine note changed, and the boat rolled less as though it had slowed. It turned and drifted to a stop and, when the engine cut off, the only sound was the waves slapping against the hull. How long had she been asleep? Had they reached their destination, or had a German naval patrol stopped them? But they were still drifting and there were no sounds above, and they strained to hear what was happening up on deck. Someone was fiddling with the hatch, and they held their noses as one as they slipped under the fish, ensuring they didn't dislodge their camouflage. The hatch opened, and one of the crew peered down at them. 'It's all clear,' he said. 'You can come out now.'

The Englishman and the Frenchwoman were laughing and swearing as the fisherman unrolled a rope ladder for them to climb up. 'Keep quiet, we're close to the shore and sound travels at night,' he warned. 'There are Swedish patrols about and, until we're sure it's clear, we wait.'

A bucket of water was set down on the deck and they used it to remove fish scales from their hair and skin, and no one spoke as the crew scanned the shoreline with binoculars. When satisfied the coast was clear, the skipper's eyes ran over the four of them. 'We can take only three at a time,' he said. 'Who's first?'

She didn't have a choice as the Frenchwoman pushed forward, pulling the wounded man with her, followed by the Englishman.

'Okay.' The skipper smiled at her. 'You'll have to wait for the second run.'

They climbed down the side of the boat and, with one of the crew rowing, headed for shore. The skipper had started the engine, keeping the boat from drifting out to sea, and, as it idled, joined her and gripped the rail, watching their slow progress. 'We've got to be careful,' he said. 'Although we're neutral, by law we're not allowed to bring in people and, if they catch us, they'll send you back.' He gestured towards the returning dinghy. 'There, they've made it. You'll be okay. Once on dry land, they won't send you back. The worst is they'll put you in an internment camp.' The mention of a camp sliced through her like a knife. She wouldn't survive another imprisonment.

Suddenly, gunfire lit up the night sky, and she heard guttural shouts and a woman's scream before an eerie silence.

'They get jumpy, thinking it's the Nazis invading.' The skipper gazed at the skies as though he'd find an answer there. 'They're young and trigger-happy. Are you sure you want to chance it?' He spat into the water.

'I've no option,' she said. Nothing would stop her now, even if it meant jumping overboard and swimming ashore.

The returning fisherman was crestfallen and wouldn't meet her gaze, and he refused to go back.

'Get up here,' the skipper told him and smiled at her, realising it would be pointless trying to dissuade her. 'I'll take the lady.' But, clutching her violin case, she had already clambered over the side.

Twenty yards from shore, he laid down his oar. 'I'll give you one last chance,' he said. 'Come back with me and we'll return to Poland. It's up to you.'

She had already plunged into the icy water, which was like the stab of a knife in her side, and she feared the wound might open again. She gasped as she lost hold of the violin case, and the outgoing swell picked it up and pulled it beyond her reach and, panicking, she made to dive under.

'Leave it to me.' The skipper manoeuvred the dinghy towards where they had last seen it, and it bobbed on the surface, and he reached out and grabbed the case. 'Here, you'll need this. Good luck.'

The VIOLINIST'S REVENGE

She had hitched up her skirt, sodden by the time she reached the beach, and watched the fishing boat slipping away into the darkness. Drained by the effort, she collapsed on the sand and listened, gulping for air, and the gurgling of the water and the breeze rustling through the reeds at the top of the beach increased her feeling of helplessness. She should inspect her wound, but daren't. Were her fellow travellers dead? If they'd evaded the patrols, did they have a map or an idea of what direction to head? She didn't even know the geography of the area, and all she had were wet clothes, a battered violin and a few Swedish krona coins in a small leather purse the skipper had squeezed into her hand as she got into the dinghy.

If she remained on the beach, she'd be exposed. She realised she must make it to the grasses at the back of the beach, and they'd give her cover. Sprint or take it one step at a time? They would more likely shoot at a running figure, so she walked, every so often stopping and listening. Her footsteps sank in the soft sand and threw her off balance and, at any moment, she expected to hear a barked order. Perhaps Sweden wouldn't be so welcoming after all. Were the Swedes any better than the Germans? Some said they were, but who could she believe?

She rested in the long grasses until her strength returned, but couldn't stay there forever. A sandy path ran behind her, and beyond lay heavy woodland. For some reason, she ran the rest of the way, plunging into the vegetation, her whole body shaking, and sat on a log until she regained control, then followed the path, hoping it would lead to a road. After thirty minutes of fast walking, she was still on the path rising away from the coast, and tiredness overwhelmed her. All she wanted was to lie down and sleep. But the belief she must move farther inland drove her on, her skirt drying against her legs.

As the path veered inland, she walked straight into two soldiers lounging against a bank and smoking, their rifles hanging by their sides. Surprised by her sudden appearance, they jumped to their feet, reaching for their weapons and shouting in unison, 'Stanna!'

Frozen in fear, she raised her arms in surrender as they approached, glancing around, suspecting she had accomplices. One of the soldiers came up close, checking her for weapons, and spoke to his colleague, who grinned. 'Jude?'

She hesitated, wondering if they'd sympathise if they believed her to be Jewish.

'No, Catholic,' she said, and they relaxed.

'Are you a spy?' they asked as one.

'No, no.' She held up the case and then mimed playing a violin. They both laughed, and the other soldier spoke in English. 'Come with us,' he said. 'We must take you to an internment camp. What happens afterwards is their decision. Come.' He turned and walked off as the other took her arm and they walked in silence.

'Where have you come from?' the soldier said at last.

'Poland.'

He chanced a sideways glance at the sea.

'I was a prisoner in a concentration camp.'

'But you said you weren't Jewish?' He tightened his grip on her arm.

'I'm not.'

'How did you escape?'

'I had help, but my family...' She slipped on loose stones, and he put a supporting arm around her. 'I heard gunfire. Was that you?'

'No.' He seemed troubled. 'We're not all like that. Some take their duties too seriously. I'm sorry if they were your friends.' He looked away. 'My name is Nils, and he's Arvid.' He pointed at his colleague's disappearing back.

'How old are you?'

'Seventeen. Why do you ask?'

'There were many young men like you in the camp, but they'll all be dead by now.'

'We hear stories about what the Germans are doing there.' He flapped a hand towards the sea. 'Is it that bad?'

'Worse, they're gassing thousands—men, women and children.'

As if struggling to understand what he'd heard and walk at the same time, he stopped.

'Where are you taking me?' she said.

'To where you'll be processed.' He pointed up ahead.

'I can't go back to the camp.' She pulled away. 'I'd rather you shoot me here now.'

'I wouldn't.' A horrified look spread across his boyish face as he wiped his brow with a shaking hand. 'Never shot no one. They conscripted me into the defence force when I was fifteen. I didn't have a choice.' He offered a hand. 'Don't worry, I'll help you.'

'Keep up, I wanna get back.' Arvid marched on ahead. 'My shift's over.'

Nils called for him to come back, and he stomped down a slight incline. 'What's the problem?'

'She was in a Nazi concentration camp and her family ... we should let her go.'

'Can't do it.' Arvid lifted his rifle and, for a moment, she was convinced he'd shoot.

'She's no different from us.' Nils stepped between them and pushed down the barrel of his rifle. 'She's not a threat to anyone.'

'We'd face a court-martial and God knows what.'

'Only if they find out. And they won't, will they?'

Arvid wrenched the weapon away and took a step back, lifting the rifle and training it on them. 'It would be stupid. If either of you refuses to come with me, I'm within my rights to shoot.'

Nils dropped his hands and fiddled with them. 'You're probably right. I'm being stupid. There's no point in putting ourselves at risk.'

He turned to her. 'Sorry,' he said, arms outstretched in apology and walked over to his colleague. As Arvid lowered the rifle, Nils hit him square on the nose, sending him sprawling on the path. He wheeled around. 'Head for Malmö. You should lose yourself there. Run.'

PART III

32

Every Friday, a taxi dropped him off on Lilla Torg, and he walked across Malmö's Stortorget under the gaze of King Kurt X Gustav. Mounted on his steed, the 17th-century monarch was ruler of all he surveyed. It would have been quicker taking the other route, but as usual, he doffed his hat, muttering a 'Good morning' to the bronze statue. He could have gone straight to the cafe, but the walk revived pleasant memories of his youth when the boys and girls gathered here in the evenings, pursuing whatever pleasures were available. It was always an excuse for exercise, but although his upright posture and full head of white hair belied his age, even a stroll these days made him breathless.

Across the city's main square, a friend of more than fifty years, a former editor of *Arbetet*, the area's social democrat newspaper, awaited him in the café on the corner of Hamnagatan. Meeting Frieda always lifted his spirits; the serenity of her smile made time stand still, and for a few hours, the world outside couldn't invade their bubble. Long ago, they believed this was how it would be, but the glamorous Leila came into his life and he chose beauty before brains. Frieda was always punctual and eager to discuss the war and, like most Swedes, regarded it as an uneasy neutrality, realising if the Nazis invaded, they couldn't resist the might of the German army.

He expected the customary knot of sightseers around the monument, listening to a busker mangling music never intended to be played so badly. The crowd was larger this morning, as if the concert hall had been transported outside. The third movement of Tchaikovsky's violin concerto had never sounded so good and, knowing the piece well, he slowed to listen. Although one of the hardest to play, the violinist executed the highs and lows with a confidence worthy of a greater stage. Intrigued that someone with such musical ability was playing here, he moved closer for a better view.

The violinist stood on the monument's steps, elevating her head and shoulders above the audience. A young woman lost in her musical world, playing with intensity and rocking and swaying to the commands of the notes, stepping forward and back, her head moving with such vibrancy that her auburn hair tossed from shoulder to bare shoulder. As if frozen in another world, the crowd were enraptured, and she was unaware of their presence, and even the tall, narrow buildings on the square's west side appeared to lean in as though straining to catch every note.

A battered violin case lay open on a lower step and, when she lowered her instrument to enthusiastic applause, he rewarded her with a banknote and a whispered, 'Bravo.' Within minutes, she departed, and his sense of loss was as if he had lost a treasure.

The insistent blare of a car horn brought him back to the present and, eager to share his experience, he hurried away to meet his friend, hoping she hadn't left. Usually, he arrived five minutes late, as if being early would disrupt the rhythm of comfortable habits, but this time he would be much later.

Frieda had pulled her coat close around her and was sitting at a table outside. And arms outstretched, he questioned why she wasn't in her usual spot, tucked away at the back of the café next to a wood-burning stove and surrounded by books.

'The violinist was so good,' she said with a chuckle. 'I came out to listen. Did you hear it?'

He smiled.

'I hoped you had. I'd be interested to hear your opinion. Unlike you, I'm no expert.'

He dismissed the compliment with a wave. 'I'm a professor of literature, not a musician.'

'True, but music is in your family's blood and it runs through your veins.'

'Perhaps,' he said. 'She would be more at home in the concert hall.'

'Almost in your league.' Frieda chuckled.

'I must have been a disappointment to my father.' Viggo Bergman led his shivering friend inside.

'You're too modest.' She raised an eyebrow. 'At one time, I believed they had you marked for greater things.'

Embarrassed and attempting to change the subject, he called a passing waitress and ordered two black coffees. 'I wonder who the violinist is.'

33

For no reason other than the size of his donation, she noticed the old man. For months, she earned only enough to eat and often, when nearing the end of her stint, the audience would look at their watches and rush off as though late for a meeting. Others tried to disguise the meagreness of their donations in a hail of low-denomination coins. This man had deposited a blue note, one hundred krona, that would buy her food. Later, she found secure lodgings promising a dry bed and the chance to sleep without the fear of being attacked by hooligans and that night ate artsoppa, a yellow pea soup served with bacon, and kalops, a meat stew. But how long would the money last?

Since crossing the Baltic, she'd led a hand-to-mouth existence and was fortunate if she got a proper meal once every three days. Without papers, she couldn't work and relied on raising money from playing, and the weather played a part. Wet and windy days failed to attract audiences when she needed them—no one listens to a violinist in the wind and the rain, no matter how talented. When depression bore down on her like a black cloud, she considered surrendering to the authorities, even if it meant internment or deportation back to Poland. But once the Nazis discovered her past, they would transport her back to the camp and, after they'd extracted information about the Resistance, they'd kill her.

The old man's generosity intrigued her so much that she consid-

The VIOLINIST'S REVENGE

ered risking another visit to Stortorget, but decided against it. She'd be safer somewhere the police seldom patrolled, but the pickings were slimmer, some days non-existent, and a gnawing hunger drove her back to the square.

A swirling wind chased clouds across a grey sky, and she sensed imminent rain, which would force her to stop. The uplifting elements of Mozart's Adagio demanded her concentration, but still, she scanned the square, looking for police who might confiscate her donations. Further back under a tree and engrossed in her performance, the old man watched with a look of satisfaction. Her mind drifted, thinking about the food she could buy with another generous donation, but he'd be unlikely to donate again. The next time she gave him a surreptitious look, he had moved closer, perhaps because her music was drifting on the wind, but her glance went unacknowledged.

Spots of rain dampened her forehead and were now increasing in intensity, sweeping in from the sea like a wave, forcing her audience to retreat to the cafes surrounding the square. The violin case stood empty and neglected and water pooled in the bottom. Disappointment increased her hunger and her stomach ached and she groaned as she bent to tuck away the instrument before it got wet. A presence startled her. A hand touched her arm and the other proffered another blue note, which she almost snatched from him.

'You play like an angel,' he remarked as he turned away like a shy suitor. Had he not noticed her disfigurement?

It was a while before she saw him again, accompanied by a small boy who might have been his grandson. As Mendelssohn infused her being, the old man talked to the boy, explaining her skills and using his hands and body to emphasise her movements. If her playing pleased him again, he might make another donation, but she was being greedy. A smattering of applause greeted the end of the piece, followed by the welcome tinkling of coins thrown into the violin case. As she gathered up her things, the boy ran up and stuffed a banknote into her hands and stepped back as though he'd fed a hungry wild animal and waited for a reaction. Although this boy had almost white blond hair and pale blue eyes, he reminded her of her brother Willy, and a gnawing pain moved through her body, increasing her despair as she remembered him being marched to the gas chambers. Before she could thank the boy, he ran off, glancing back at her with a shy grin.

For weeks, she didn't see the professor, although she returned to the square more often than she should have and once was warned off by a friendly policeman. Now, longer gaps between meals made her more desperate and, in her blackest moods, she considered that if she couldn't survive by her music, she must resort to stealing. Other buskers, beggars and petty thieves lived on the streets scavenging like her, and some she regarded as friends, but they didn't last.

This day, she paid little attention to a man traversing the square, head down and hands dug deep into his pockets. He stopped and looked over, listening to her performance, and elbowed his way to the front and stared at her. Lost in her music, her eyes were closed as she rose to the heights of the piece and, when she opened them, he was standing in front of her, only six feet away. She gasped. Out of uniform, he looked different.

His eyes dwelt on the battered violin case, and he rubbed his face, then wheeled around and pushed through the crowd, who protested and shoved back.

Her head moving from side to side, she scanned the busy square, trying to follow him, but he had disappeared. She packed up without counting her donations. She must get away, but a coarse shout rose above the voices of the crowd. 'That's her. Over there.' Arvid's voice confirmed her fears as he struggled through the audience, leading two policemen who hurried to keep up.

As fear overwhelmed her, her knees gave way, and she stumbled when a policeman grabbed her arm, his fingers digging into her flesh. 'Papers,' he demanded as a colleague barred her path.

An irritating grin crossed Arvid's face, and he chimed, 'She's an illegal. Won't have papers. Came in from Poland.'

'If you haven't papers,' the policeman's voice drowned him out, 'we must take you into custody.'

Unwilling to be involved, none of the small crowd was prepared to come to her help, and they dispersed.

'Well?' The policeman held out a hand.

As if trying to find her papers, she reached for the violin case.

The VIOLINIST'S REVENGE

With a reproving glance at Arvid, the policemen relaxed, and she straightened up, sprinted past them and headed across the square. In a blind panic, she headed for the comparative safety of the myriad narrow streets surrounding the area and didn't notice the old man as he entered Stortorget, holding his grandson's hand.

Stunned by her speed, the police were slow to react, and she rounded a corner. The street was unknown to her, and she searched for exit points, and bystanders parted, realising she was a fugitive.

As the police approached, the professor stepped into their path, blocking them. 'What's the problem?' he asked.

'We're chasing the woman violinist,' one said. 'She's an illegal. Got no papers, but don't worry, she won't get far.'

'Nonsense,' Viggo said, and the policemen exchanged glances. 'She's not. Works for me and is a member of our household. You're wasting your time. There's no law against playing the violin in public.'

'But this man—' the policeman looked for Arvid, who had disappeared into the crowd '—claimed she was an illegal…'

'Where is your witness?'

The policeman lowered his head. 'If you can vouch for her, we'll leave it at that.' And they touched their caps and hurried away.

'Joel?' The professor looked around for his grandson, but the boy had raced off after the girl. Realising he wouldn't catch him, he grunted in exasperation and made his way to his usual table in the cafe where the boy knew to find him. Relieved that his usual table was unoccupied, he ordered a black coffee.

When on his second cup and checking his watch, wondering what had happened to his grandson, the boy, face flushed with exertion and excitement, burst in and raced up to him. 'Grandpapa, I caught her. I found her.' He stumbled over the words, his brain working faster than his tongue. 'She's here. Outside.'

'Well done, Joel.' The professor pulled the boy to him and patted his head.

'Can I bring her in? Please. I told her you'd help her. She's not a bad person.'

Against his better judgement, he agreed, and Joel raced out and returned, pulling her by the hand through the cafe.

She glanced around as the patrons stared at her. At least one got up and left, but the professor stood and waved her over. 'My dear.' His face relaxed into a welcoming smile. 'I'm honoured you can join us.' To whom was he talking, she wondered.

'Please, sit down.' He pointed to the chair across the table from him, and the boy found another seat.

Up close, the girl's appearance troubled him. Living on the streets had taken its toll. Her clothes were a jumble as if snatched from anywhere, even a clothesline. Nothing matched, nothing fitted. A black sock, a grey sock. Shoes, not a pair. A baggy top, too big, kept slipping off her shoulder and she had to pull it back. A long skirt hung from her like a becalmed flag and rain-washed hair screened either side of her face like cheap curtains. Skin rough and weathered, with several sores and a misshapen nose, but she carried her head as if used to better things and her green eyes burned bright like a beacon in the fog. He called over a waitress who hardly heard his order of a hot drink and a selection of pastries and scones, such was her interest in his guest. By now, the other diners had lost interest and had resumed their conversations.

'My name is Viggo Bergman.' He offered his hand, and she studied it, but was unwilling to take it. 'I can help you.'

'Why? The police are chasing me. You'll get into trouble.'

'I doubt it.' Viggo offered a hearty laugh.

She was more fearful. If they turned up here, there would be no escape.

'What's your name?'

'Anneliesa.'

'A beautiful name for a violinist who plays like an angel.'

'I can't stay here.' She blushed. 'I must get away.'

As she rose, the waitress placed a mug of coffee and a plate of delicacies in front of her, and the desire to eat overcame her fear, but she checked the food.

The VIOLINIST'S REVENGE

Viggo's benevolence reassured her. 'Please eat and drink.' He gestured to the food. 'It will help get your strength back.'

While she devoured the food with uncontrolled enthusiasm, he watched. Crouched over her plate like a feral creature, she ate with both hands, as if expecting it to be snatched from her at any moment. Every time she picked up the hot mug of steaming coffee with dirt-stained fingers, she winced, and her eyes were hooded with suspicion.

Hers were the fingers of a musician, Viggo observed. This would be his challenge to restore her as you would a fine old painting found mouldering in an attic. When the plates were empty, she searched for an exit. 'Why are you doing this for me?'

'Selfish reasons, I suppose.' He raised an eyebrow.

'You already made generous donations.' She tensed. 'I'm grateful, but—'

He tried to place a hand on hers, but she pulled it away.

'I'm no use to anyone. Please let me leave.'

'Where are you from?'

Surprised anyone would care, she said softly, 'I came here on a boat from Poland.'

'But you aren't Polish.'

'I escaped from a concentration camp.'

As her tears welled up, he bent closer to hear the name and exhaled. 'Then you know all about the Nazis.' It was more of a statement than a question.

'My family...' Tears flowed. It had been a long time since she had cried for her family and she was overwhelmed by guilt.

'Tell me only if you can.' He placed his hands over hers, and this time, she didn't pull them away.

'I'm from Vienna.'

'A magnificent city,' he said and, for a moment, she was lost in her memories. Her father, alive and distraught. Her mother and Willy walking to their deaths. And Lily? Where was she? She raised her eyes to his and paused, looking for understanding, and fear crowded in.

The professor listened and his eyes never left hers as her story unfolded and, after she finished, he said, 'I would like your help...'

Suspicion clouded her eyes as she stared at him. 'I can't help anyone.'

'Assist me and my family, and I will help you,' he said, his voice deep and comforting, and she wanted to believe him. 'For as long as you wish, you'll be welcome to stay in Sweden and I'll guarantee your safety.'

When she pulled away, he smiled. 'If you decide to accept, you'll need this.' Her eyes followed as he reached beneath the table and handed over the battered violin case. And before he could say another word, she pulled it from him and held it to her breast like a newborn baby.

34

It was only a glimpse, but her legs buckled and she felt faint, staggering and putting a hand on the plate-glass window to keep her balance. As the blood drained from her face, she couldn't look at the reflection again. She wasn't mistaken. There could be no peace for her in this lifetime.

They've found me.

Leila had taken her shopping in the Old Town and spotted a dress in a store window on Sodergatan and, tugging her sleeve, had guided her closer to the store.

She blinked, clearing her eyes and, when she raised her head again, they were still there. Three of them and they were closer now. The only consolation was that they weren't wearing the black of the SS. They were Wehrmacht, regular army, but still Germans. And Germans in uniforms of any colour brought back memories of the camp and reminded her of the smell of the smoke from burning bodies. She swallowed hard as she battled for control and her nails dug into the palms of her hands, drawing blood. Could anyone help her?

Oblivious to her distress, Leila kept chatting, but she wasn't listening and turned, hoping it had been a trick of the light. But it wasn't her imagination. They were discussing her and one pointed with a leer. Stay calm, she persuaded herself, stroll away and don't show fear. As her insides churned and her stomach ached, she covered up her tattoo while she fought back tears.

Leila called her name, but she increased her pace as her eyes darted from side to side, searching for an escape route. They wouldn't take her without a fight.

A furtive glance confirmed they were following and keeping pace with her. If they discovered where she lived, it would put Viggo and his family in danger. Behind them, Leila, arms outstretched and questioning, called to her, her voice becoming more irritated. But head down, she lengthened her stride, and shoppers moved aside to let her through.

A tug on the arm spun her around, giving her no chance to run.

'What on earth are you doing, Anneliesa?' Leila, red-faced and sweating, held her tight with both arms. 'I wanted to show you a dress, but you walked off and left me.'

The soldiers were gaining ground and, not wanting to put Leila's life in danger, she pushed her away, lifted her skirt and ran. Having lived on the streets and knowing most of the lanes and back alleys gave her an advantage and, if she outpaced them, she might lose them in the labyrinth.

Anger flared within her for having deluded herself, thinking she'd escaped and was no longer a fugitive. She'd been sucked into the almost idyllic lifestyle of Malmo, regaining the exhilaration of freedom. Coming and going as she pleased. Making friends, even laughing without being punished, and eating as much as she could. At first, gorging herself, fearing the food supply might dry up, or be snatched away, and as she ate, she felt guilt for those she'd left behind. A persistent belief that she didn't deserve to be happy after her family died in the camp weighed on her. Her efforts to contact her father had failed, and remembering Jan constantly reminded her of the sacrifice he'd made. Had he survived the interrogation? There were moments when doubts and fears threatened to overwhelm her and, when she saw a uniform, she shrank inside.

It had taken time to trust Viggo and his family, even though he was true to his word. All they asked of her was that she play for them at family functions and teach young Joel her skills on the violin. The boy was the perfect student and a genuine talent, and she enjoyed immersing herself in her music and the tuition. In return, she had her own room in the family's big old rambling house outside the city and a small stipend and they treated her as an equal, a fellow human being, rather than vermin to be exterminated. Leila had always wanted a daughter and took delight in restoring her to her former beauty. She was self-conscious about her nose, broken by Marek, and Leila arranged the best medical treatment. A doctor friend carried out a minor operation to straighten it, and the gap in her teeth was fixed. Only then could she look at her reflection in the mirror. The bullet wound in her side had healed, leaving an unsightly scar, and it still ached from time to time. And Leila took her shopping, buying clothes and advising her on the latest fashions.

Afternoon tea was taken with Leila's friends amongst the palms and pillars of Hotel Kramer on Stortorget, and every time she visited, she experienced a mixture of relief and guilt as images of her past flashed before her. They treated her well, yet never enquired about what she'd endured, as if it were too much for their consciences to handle. She grew to resent her friends and their idle chatter about clothes, families and art while ignoring events elsewhere as if they existed in a cocoon. To Leila's friends, the length of their hemlines and someone's new love interest were more important. But she believed everyone should know of the atrocities perpetrated by the Nazis, not turn their backs on them, and everyone must try to stop the slaughter. But when she attempted to divert the conversation towards the war, Leila always changed the subject as though to protect her.

Knowing she was determined to return to Vienna to be reunited with her father, Viggo accepted they'd lose her as soon as the war ended. For her, it was all that mattered. Then she would tell him about her mother and Lily and Willy in the hope it might help heal the hurt.

The soldiers were still behind her, and she ran on, twisting and turning, barging through pedestrians who shouted at her. Out of breath, she slowed, but couldn't see them, although she knew they'd still be there and had to keep moving. So concerned was she that she failed to notice a youth wearing a cap and muffler step out in front of her, blocking her path.

'Hey, what's the hurry?' His voice was friendly, but she couldn't stop and collided with him and clung on to stay on her feet.

'Please help me. They're chasing me.'

To her surprise, he snorted. 'Now, who's chasing you?' He rolled his eyes.

'I'm serious,' she said. 'Germans are after me. I escaped from a concentration camp, and they'll take me back.'

'Are you sure?' He pulled up his cap and squinted along the lane, but didn't see any pursuers, and his eyes softened with pity.

'If you don't believe me, look, this is what they did to us.' She rolled up the sleeve of her jacket.

With an intake of breath, he studied her tattoo. 'Come on,' he said, placing an arm around her. 'I'll take you somewhere safe.' He looked back along the lane and lowered his voice. 'You'll be amongst friends.'

She pulled back. 'Where?'

He put a finger to his lips and gestured for her to follow him and, after many turns and twists, they entered a small square dominated by a meeting hall with a Swedish flag twisting in the breeze above open double doors. And in front, an energetic crowd gathered, some carrying placards. 'You'll be safe here.'

She tried to read the words on the placards, but he hurried her inside. 'Magnus will help you.' He propelled her up steps and into an auditorium, three-quarters full of a group of different ages and backgrounds and some waving flags. He found two vacant chairs in the front row. 'Wait there. It starts in five minutes.'

'What's happening?' She looked around, but he'd disappeared.

Although the audience appeared in good humour, she wondered if she should ask the person next to her what was happening, but decided against it. In front of her was a raised stage with bare boards and the Swedish flag as a backdrop and four chairs clustered around what appeared to be a kitchen table. A hubbub of conversation reverberated around the theatre and clouds of cigarette smoke drifted in the air. *I should leave before anything starts. Leila will be worried about me.*

To an enthusiastic welcome, four people entered the stage in single file, led by a woman with a severe expression, dark hair pulled back from a face almost hidden by thick horn-rimmed spectacles. A minister, wearing a dog collar, followed, his hands clasped together in front of him as if praying. A grey-haired and bearded man with a genial expression came next. And a few steps behind followed a younger man, perhaps in his late twenties, in casual dress and with a mop of uncombed blond hair and an open face. He turned to the audience and waved as they cheered their support. A silence settled and emphasised the expectation rising in the auditorium like a bottle of champagne about to pop.

At a nod from the genial man, the woman rose to her feet. 'You know why you're here, so without further delay…' She hesitated while the crowd chanted his name. 'Let me introduce, Magnus.' She turned to him, smiling and clapping. The crowd joined in and those around her leapt to their feet, and she rose with them. When Magnus signalled them to stop, they sat and leaned forward in their seats.

As though trying to remember his lines, he stood motionless, then ran a hand through his hair and scanned the room. His eyes alighted on her and, for a moment, there was a connection, a feeling that she'd known him forever. Conversational in style, he leant forward, his voice low as if talking to each individual personally. 'We're all cowards,' he said and stared at his audience. 'Me, too.'

'No,' a man shouted from behind her.

'Why?' A woman's voice from the other side of the room.

'Unless we force our government to take action now,' he said. 'You may not believe me.' He paused 'But if we work together, there's hope for all of us and our country.'

A few cheered.

'The fact you're here shows you care. We can't stand by. We must tell our government that the present situation is unacceptable. We can't continue to ignore such monstrosities. To do so would be complicit in genocide.'

The rhythm of his speaking was almost hypnotic, and when his gaze fixed on her, she blushed.

'Should we just observe as our government believes? If so, we are as complicit as Hitler's Nazis. What's at stake?' He paused again as his eyes roamed around the auditorium. 'What is at stake is the freedom of my country, your country, our country.'

A rumble of agreement echoed in her head, but he quelled it. 'We all know of people—perhaps friends, neighbours, or even family—who approve of Germany's ultimate goal. Some may even be here today.'

The audience turned as one, trying to identify who they might be.

'You may believe it's best to stay neutral.' He paced the stage from side to side. 'If two dogs are fighting, is it better not to intervene in case you get bitten? Understandable, perhaps. Do nothing and nothing can happen to you.'

He picked out individuals in the audience and stopped and stared and several wouldn't meet his gaze. 'But can we trust Hitler not to turn on us after he finishes destroying other countries and killing children? Our Foreign Minister, Christian Gunther, has said Sweden's primary goal must be to avoid entanglement in a world war. But other countries that have looked the other way have paid the price. And we are profiting by selling the Reich ten million tons of ore each year for them to produce their weapons of war. Are we proud of that?'

He waited until the cries of shame faded away.

'We even allow their soldiers to travel from occupied Norway, where they are killing our neighbours, through our country to Trelleborg so they can go on leave. Some Swedes have even taken up arms to fight for the Nazi SS. And Britain's Prime Minister Winston Churchill has accused us of profiting by playing both sides and ignoring the moral issues.'

Preparing for dissent, he hesitated. 'Perhaps worst of all,' he wagged a finger at the crowd, 'we have handed back asylum seekers to be tortured and executed by the Nazis.'

An ache spread across her chest. *Everyone is looking at me*. In her row, a man stood. 'The government claims we'll be safer by preserving our peace.'

Magnus's feet echoed on the wooden boards as he walked along the stage to confront him. 'Do you believe it makes us safe? Once the Nazis have achieved their goals, they will march into our country and take the ore without paying for it. Hitler has broken every promise. No agreement signed with him can be trusted.'

A young woman diffidently stuck up a hand, and Magnus

The VIOLINIST'S REVENGE

encouraged her to ask a question. 'I think I agree with you,' she said. 'But are they as bad as they're saying, or is it just propaganda?'

There was a determined glint in his eyes as Magnus returned to the table, dragged out a chair, placed it at the front of the stage and straddled it, his arms resting on its back. He ran a hand through his hair again and recounted the story of a chance meeting of an SS officer, Kurt Gerstein, with a Swedish diplomat, Goran von Otter, aboard the Warsaw to Berlin train in Poland in 1942. The officer, who had delivered the Zyklon B gas to Rudolph Höss at Auschwitz, broke down in tears as he described the slaughter of Jews at the Belzec and Treblinka concentration camps. Otter reported the conversation to the government. They ignored it. As did the Roman Catholic Church, despite Gerstein informing officials close to the Pope.

Silence enveloped the auditorium.

'Can you prove any of this?' A man shouted.

For a moment, Magnus glanced at his colleagues for support. To Anneliesa's surprise, she rose to her feet, causing a murmur of surprise from the audience as they turned to watch her. At first, she couldn't find her voice. Why am I doing this? In her time in Sweden, she'd lived below the radar, safer for her and Viggo and his family. She cleared her voice and started to speak, hesitant at first, and a shout from the back called her to speak up.

'My name is Anneliesa Lang. I escaped from a Nazi concentration camp in Poland.'

'Why should we believe you?'

Magnus leaned forward in his seat as she pulled up a sleeve, showing the number tattooed on her arm in green ink. 'They branded us like animals but treated us worse.' She brandished her arm while some craned to see. 'What you hear about Nazi genocide is true, but the truth is much worse than any of you could imagine—'

Shouts and a drumming of boots interrupted her and heads turned towards the entrance. Whistles, a gunshot and screaming emanated from the back of the auditorium. A group of brown-shirted men carrying clubs had entered, supported by police. On their path to the stage, they lashed out at anyone, even those escaping. Most scrambled for the side exits and climbed over each other in their panic to get away.

Unable to move, transfixed by the carnage developing around her, she blamed herself for inciting this violence. As the brown shirts headed for the stage, those on the platform were ushered through an exit at the back. A thug, wielding a baton, bore down on her, but the youth, who had rescued her in the street, jumped between them, taking the blow which split his skull. The sight of blood sickened her and she trembled as she covered her face, expecting to be next. Suddenly, two powerful arms grabbed her from behind and lifted her out of range of the swinging clubs.

'Quick,' said Magnus. 'Come with me.'

When Leila returned home without Anneliesa, she rushed into the professor's study and interrupted his telephone call. At first indignant, she claimed Anneliesa had run off and left her on her own, saying it might be what one does in Vienna but not in Malmö. Once he'd calmed her down and had her explain what happened on their shopping trip, it was obvious there was more to it than he first believed. And his concern increased with every answer.

What had spooked her to make her run away? Whatever, she believed she was in danger. For some time before they met, she'd lived on the streets and was used to handling difficult situations, so this must be serious.

Leila mentioned she'd seen three German soldiers in uniform and, although not an uncommon sight for Swedes, Anneliesa wouldn't have known.

After reassuring her, helped by pouring several stiff drinks, he phoned his friend Frieda, who had contacts with the local police. They would help find her.

35

'Are you kidnapping me?' She sat in the back of a black Volvo with Magnus, and the genial man was driving with the severe-looking woman by his side.

'Would you rather be with us or those fascist thugs?' Magnus pushed the mop of hair off his brow and peered out the back window. No one's following, he informed the driver.

'Do you mean the brownshirts or the police?' she said.

'Difficult to tell the difference these days.' He offered a sardonic smile, and her pulse quickened.

She had no choice as Magnus had swept her off her feet, bundled her up the steps and onto the stage and exited the hall onto a lane. At first, the parked car failed to start, but as the thugs spilled out of the building, it eventually sparked into life and, with a belch of black smoke, accelerated away. What had become of the minister? Had he been able to get out?

'We'll go to yours,' Magnus instructed the driver, who grunted in agreement and turned to her. 'By the way, this is Olaf and Marie.' They both waved without turning around.

'They're getting more violent,' Olaf said over his shoulder and, with a tremor in her voice, Marie interjected, 'Will we have to stop the meetings?'

'No, we carry on.' Magnus offered her an apologetic smile. 'We had to get you out of there for your safety. Now you're caught up in something very dangerous.'

'You were only speaking the truth.' She averted her eyes from his intense gaze. 'Why are they so violent?'

'People believe only what they want to believe.' He rubbed his face and looked weary and older than she'd first thought. 'Truth can be more dangerous than lies. Sweden has its own problems with the far right and, as long as our Social Democrat government insists on remaining neutral, it only encourages those idiots who would support Hitler.' He took her hands in his. 'You know better than anyone the danger we face, and I want to hear about it.'

He fell silent, and no one spoke until they swung into the drive of a nondescript house in the suburbs. They entered a garage and exited through a back door into the house. Only once the curtains were closed did they switch on the lights and Olaf found a bottle of brandy and poured generous measures into four glasses with a shaking hand. 'To entanglement,' he toasted.

When Olaf left to check what had happened to their supporters and Marie went to the kitchen to organise food, Magnus sat beside her on the couch, and she found his closeness claustrophobic. Needing space to come to terms with what had happened, she moved to another chair. People supporting the Nazis without knowing the truth made her despair, but her ability to stand up and speak to a hall full of strangers concerned her. When she raised her head, he was staring at her and that made her more uncomfortable.

'I admire your bravery,' he said. 'It couldn't have been easy to talk before a crowd after what you've experienced. It takes real courage. None of what we're doing here is important compared to what you've endured.'

'No!' She raised a hand, interrupting him. 'Telling the world about the Nazis is important. If my message got through to one person, I'll have succeeded.'

Hands clasped between his knees, he leant forward. 'If it's not too painful, please tell me what happened to you. Everything, no matter how terrible. I must know the truth so we in Sweden can understand and protest this barbarity.'

His empathy brought her to the verge of tears, but before she could respond, Olaf burst into the room. 'They've arrested nine of our people and some are in the hospital with broken bones and head wounds,' he said, then added, 'The bastards.'

Magnus jumped to his feet and paced the room and kicked a chair in frustration, then raised a hand in apology. 'We have to make the government and police accept the truth.'

Olaf nodded. 'We must work harder. Every time you speak, you shine a light into our darkest corners and identify the demons lurking there. If we stand by and watch, how long will it be before the Nazis turn on us? We can't make a pact with the devil.' He dropped his gaze. 'Sorry, got a bit carried away there. I'll leave you to talk.' He closed the door behind him, and they waited until his footsteps receded down the hall and he spoke with Marie in the kitchen.

'He's a good man,' Magnus said. 'Are you able to continue?' He sat back on the couch, and she joined him, surprised how easy it was to talk to him about herself, as if talking about another person, another life. She had never burdened others with the details of her captivity, especially Viggo and his family, unwilling to bring her pain into their home. For his part, Viggo refrained from pressing her, believing she'd tell her story in her own time.

Here in a strange house with people she didn't know, it was neutral ground, and she thought it unlikely she'd ever see Magnus again. Their drinks were replenished, but she took only water and left the food offered. Her stream of consciousness was cathartic, and she spared him nothing. For hours, she talked as it grew dark outside, and he listened to every word, every nuance, feeling her pain, and his eyes never left hers. From their capture in Vienna to meeting Viggo and Joel, she related her story, and his knuckles whitened as he gripped his knees. Occasionally, he raised his eyebrows in disbelief, but getting no response, he continued listening.

Exhausted, she stopped and her shoulders dropped and she exhaled, as though expelling all the poisons from within. For a time, he rocked back and forth and didn't speak, but a mixture of pity and understanding shone from his eyes. 'I want to share the burden of your pain and grief, but I can't imagine what you must be feeling inside. All of us who are free should be ashamed that this has happened to you and so many other innocent people. Ignorance can't be a defence. The entire world must hear what has happened and is continuing to happen. It's an unimaginable evil. If the Swedes, the real people, not those thugs we encountered earlier, hear of those horrors, they'd stand up as one against it.'

As though he'd said too much, he ran a hand through his hair and glanced away and when he turned back, he had tears in his eyes. 'I didn't want to interrupt your story, but may I ask a question?'

'Of course.' She raised the glass to her lips, dry from talking.

'Your words fill me with an anger that will never leave, yet after all you've been through, you're so calm, almost dispassionate?'

'It's my defence.' She laughed nervously. 'At times, I can fool myself into believing it happened to another person, otherwise, it would destroy me. My anger is deep inside, part of me.' She beat her chest with a fist. 'It's with me when I wake and until I go to sleep. Then it's in my dreams, my nightmares. It'll never go away. Every day, every hour, while thousands are tortured and slaughtered, I feel guilty that I'm free and not helping them. More than anything, I want revenge—'

'Can you ever get it?'

'If ever I came across Wächter again, I'd sink my teeth into him, tear him apart and spit him out.' The venom in her words embarrassed her. 'I have no forgiveness.' Her eyes burned with defiance. 'Never can have.'

'If you let me relay to my audiences what you've told me, it will help people understand more about this evil.' Magnus placed a hand on hers. 'If it changes the minds of only a few, it will be worthwhile.'

'No.' She went to the window and pulled back the curtain, watching the rain caught in the glow of the streetlamp as though the skies were crying. 'Only I can do it.'

'You've been through too much already.'

She shook her head, hair bouncing around her shoulders. 'If you let me, I'll join you on the platform and give an eyewitness report as a survivor of the Nazi atrocities.' She'd been enjoying her freedom. Now she must help the victims.

'I can't put you through it.' He joined her by the window and held her gently by the shoulders. 'It would be an ordeal.'

'I can and I will. I'm stronger than you think.'

'You saw how dangerous it can be.' A frown crept across his face. 'You'd be at risk. They'd target you and you wouldn't get protection from our police.'

She took his hands from her shoulders and kept hold of them. 'Then you'll have to protect me. They can't do anything worse to me than I've suffered already. This gives me the chance to do something.'

36

Meeting Magnus steered her life in a new direction. While she once thought she had wasted her time in exile, now there was a platform to expose the suffering of thousands. She had never believed she could make a speech, but this was different. Her recounting of her experiences in the camps warned the Swedes that their policy of neutrality and non-belligerence could destroy them. Some didn't know how to handle her, never having encountered a survivor of a German concentration camp. So be it, but she sensed her message was getting through.

They toured the country, speaking to large audiences and at more intimate gatherings. Magnus was the politician, but they came to hear her and often afterwards clamoured for answers. The government regarded them as troublemakers and encouraged the police to disrupt rather than close their meetings, often infiltrating their discussions. And although several times they were assaulted, they escaped with cuts and bruises. Twice arrested, it took calls to the professor, who arranged their release with Frieda's help. The national Press reported her speeches, and politicians of every stripe showed interest, some joining their movement and helping magnify the message.

The stultifying, genteel afternoon teas with Leila's friends were long forgotten. As friendly as they tried to be, Anneliesa had dreaded their get-togethers. Every time they raised a cream cake to their painted lips, she recalled waiting in line for her daily ration of a piece of bread and half a cup of a black revolting liquid they claimed was coffee and her excitement when Jan brought her a crust. Now she had a purpose in her life: to inform the world about the Nazi atrocities. As she became known throughout Sweden—she and Magnus almost lived together in a car as they toured the country—she regretted spending so little time with Viggo's family. Although she seldom gave Joel violin lessons now, when reunited, he always hugged her and didn't leave her side. While Viggo and Leila still supported her, the relationship had become strained, and Leila complained that her campaigning attracted too much attention and disrupted family life.

The more she laid bare the atrocities, the more her desire to be reunited with her father increased, but efforts to contact him had failed. Once possible to leave, she was determined to return and tell him what had happened to their family, and together they'd share their grief.

Viggo arranged Swedish citizenship for her and, through Frieda's contacts, acquired a fake Swedish diplomatic ID and planned her travel. Her voyage this time across the Baltic Sea would be more comfortable, travelling by ferry from Trelleborg to Swinoujscie in Poland. The rest of the journey would be arduous and fraught with danger. A short train journey to Szczecin, then another to Katowice and the last lap to Vienna.

Magnus voiced doubts, pointing to the volatility of the Russians, who controlled the rail network, and marauding bands of Polish scavengers. At times, she doubted she could walk away from Magnus and Viggo and his family, who had saved her life. But knew she must, if not for herself, for her family.

Viggo presented her with papers, allowing her safe passage and eliciting a promise that once she found her father, she'd return. 'Your tickets are first class,' he said. 'It should be quieter and safer this time.'

Saying goodbye was harder than she imagined, even though she'd done it so many times before. She loved Joel almost like the brother she'd lost. Although he owned a far superior instrument, he loved playing her violin, and she presented him with it and asked him to play one piece for her every day. It was the only possession she had to give, and it had saved her life. Without it, she wouldn't have survived, and it was through her playing in Stortorget that she met her saviour, Viggo. As they stood at the foot of the gangway and made their farewells—more affectionate with Viggo and Joel than Leila—the boy broke away from them and ran back to the car.

As Viggo encouraged her to step onto the gangway, Joel called to her, and she hesitated. The boy ran full pelt towards her, clutching the old violin case. He clambered up beside her. 'Take this,' he gasped and thrust it into her hands. 'It'll bring you luck, and when you return, you can give it back to me.'

37

The ferry's swaying lulled her into a false sense of security, as though she were in a world where the past and future no longer existed, but once she set foot on Polish soil, the old fears resurfaced. Alone and insignificant and vulnerable, the sight of men in uniform made her recoil and only increased her uncertainty. Why had she been so stupid to think she could make this journey? She would never reach Vienna, as they'd realise her papers were forged.

Had the war ended? Russian soldiers were everywhere, and they viewed everyone with suspicion, their fingers always on the trigger, and the Polish police were no friendlier. How many of them had collaborated with the Nazis? Poland appeared to have swapped one occupier for another, and doubts threatened to swamp her. What had she done? She closed her eyes tight and wished away her doubts, but on reopening them, nothing had changed, and she was convinced they'd arrest her at the next stop.

The locals were as edgy, unsure whether the Russians were better than the Nazis, for this was not an end to war, merely a continuation. Mile after mile of desolation rolled by with people floating like flotsam on an endless ocean of grey and they could be swept away by whatever force of nature threatened them. And she was a voyeur of their despair. Villages were a jumble of roofless, blackened shells with survivors living under tarpaulins and huddled around fires built from the shattered innards of their homes, and while they suffered, she had been free in Sweden, and she cried for them.

As Anneliesa Lang from Vienna, her journey through Poland would have been daunting, but travelling under the name of Bergman with a Swedish passport lessened her fear. As a citizen of a neutral country, it allowed freedom of movement, but doubt was a constant companion. Even inside the train, the cold made her shiver. Not the creeping cold of the camp that lived in your bones until you died, but bad enough. As she searched the land for any relief, the sharp sunlight hurt her eyes and only highlighted the apocalypse, as the whole of Poland appeared to be one prison camp. Whatever embers of hope flared within her were dampened.

Apart from being squeezed out of first class by passengers who believed buying a ticket entitled them to sit anywhere, the journey to Katowice proved uneventful. But the deeper she travelled into Poland, the more she doubted peace and decency could ever be restored.

Surely, the Nazis couldn't harm her now, or was that an unreasonable hope? On reaching Katowice, where the conductor ordered them off the train and instructed them to wait on the platform, unwelcome memories of the train journey to incarceration resurfaced. Within minutes, the train departed in a cloud of steam and disappeared around a bend, and they were informed they must wait for another two hours. While they waited, the cold from the concrete platform rose through the thin soles of her shoes and spread through her body, and she sought her fellow passengers' reassurance, but they kept their heads down, refusing eye contact.

Eventually, an old pre-war engine approached, expelling steam like a malevolent dragon and forcing passengers back from the edge of the platform. It pulled cattle trucks, and she was transported back to an earlier life in Vienna, being beaten by soldiers and forced up a ramp into a truck. Dogs barking and straining at the leash and people screaming and children crying as they were squeezed in so tight they struggled to breathe. The train didn't stop, but she crouched down, looking through the wooden slats of the trucks to check if people were being carried inside. If the Nazis had done it, so could the Russians.

The VIOLINIST'S REVENGE

Within the hour, another train slowed to a stop, followed by a shouted announcement: 'All aboard for Vienna'. Her relief was overwhelming because the camp where she'd been imprisoned was less than forty kilometres away, and she could still smell burning flesh and, with every minute, it seemed to be moving closer. Are there still prisoners there, she wondered. Quickly, she picked up her small leather case and the violin, but as she strode towards the first-class section, her legs became leaden and her feet numb, unable to move. A ramp stretched before her, leading into darkness, and she trembled and was drenched in sweat. She refused to climb the ramp. Why was this happening again? She trembled and, no longer in control, cried out loud. The veneer of self-confidence she'd built in Sweden had evaporated in seconds, and a deep pain spread and tightened like a steel band across her chest and an inner voice persuaded her to climb the ramp. Your mother, brother and sister are waiting for you there. You can't desert them now.

She dropped her bags on the ground.

A hand on her arm brought her back to the present and she shrank away, expecting a blow that would bring more pain.

'Are you all right, miss? Let me help you.' The porter picked up her case, and she followed him up the steps, where he found an empty compartment. 'You'll be okay here.' He took off his cap with a smile. 'Have a pleasant journey.'

She mumbled her thanks and a part of her self-control returned as she scanned her surroundings. She had no right to be here. Safe. But the memory of her family waiting for her in the truck wouldn't fade and perhaps it would be her fate again.

Move, please, she willed the train to start, believing the longer it stayed, the harder it would be to leave. It took only minutes and, with a groan and a clanking and a sigh of steam and a lurch, it moved like a giant climbing to its feet. The carriage swayed and the whistle blew and it picked up speed and a rhythmic clattering was comforting and lulling her into sleep. But she mustn't. It only encouraged nightmares. She concentrated on studying the compartment with its walnut fittings and starched white headrests and only touching the clean curtains convinced her it wasn't a dream.

As she counted the miles between her and Katowice, the countryside passed in a blur. How many would it take before she felt safe? Much of the route must be close to the journey she'd taken when she escaped to Sweden. Then most of it had been in the tunnel of night, only seeing her reflection in the car's window. At least now, she could recognise her reflection without feeling ill. The rhythm of the wheels on the rails broke down her resistance, and she rested her head against the window.

Another face stares back at her in the reflection and grows clearer the more she strains to recognise it. She leans her brow against the coolness of the glass and places her hands on either side of the image and kisses it. Trembling as his hand runs down the side of her face, she closes her eyes as she'd done before. A hard hand, but a soft touch and whispered words, whose meaning is lost in the drumming of the train's wheels. He turns her face to his and their lips touch hesitantly, then hungrily and his strong arms pull her closer and she surrenders, falling, as he kisses her harder. His hands move over her body and she reciprocates, feeling him, devouring him. At last, she relaxes as nothing exists outside of their bodies and she wants the touching to last forever, her skin rippling with pleasure.

Her head bumped against the glass as the train jerked, and she snapped awake, annoyed she'd let down her guard. The face reflected in the window was hers, and beyond lay only a landscape of destruction. She was alone. Jan was dead, and she must get over him.

The rattling of the compartment door opening made her look up as three American soldiers entered with the smiles of conquering heroes. They joked with each other as they placed their kitbags in the overhead luggage racks before sitting on the other side of the compartment. Her gaze concentrated on the countryside, but she was conscious of them looking at her, and one approached and stood close, forcing her to turn around. 'Cigarette?' He proffered an open packet of Lucky Strike.

Uncertain, she raised her head. 'No, no thanks, I...'

'Go on,' the American grinned and pushed the pack closer, nodding at her. 'They're good for you.' She noticed his kind, hazel eyes and gave in and took one. He flicked open his lighter and, as she leant forward to catch the flame, the carriage lurched and she clutched his hand to steady it and sparked a frisson of excitement.

Her cheeks burned with embarrassment as she stared out, no longer seeing the passing countryside. Only when she regained her composure did she turn back. 'Thank you. Haven't had one of these for a long time.'

'Our pleasure.' The soldier offered the pack. 'Take these?'

Unwilling to be in his debt, she looked away.

'We're from Milwaukee,' he said. 'How about you?'

'I'm from V—' She hesitated. 'I'm from Sweden. Malmo.' She frowned, annoyed by her slip. If a guard, or worse still, a Russian soldier, demanded to see her papers, she couldn't afford mistakes.

'I'm Captain Butch Hadron.' He offered his hand, but she declined it. Were the Americans any better? He was a soldier and would've killed people, too. 'Are you with the Swedish government?' He watched her with a look of detached curiosity.

'Yes.' Why was she treating him this way? He was only being friendly. 'Just an ordinary secretary.' She mustered a smile.

One of his colleagues interjected, 'What would we do without you girls brightening our boring lives?'

The door to the compartment opened and another passenger entered. As if acting as her protectors, the men stretched out their legs to block him, and he went off muttering. Two of the soldiers fell asleep, their heads leaning in on each other, but the Captain stayed awake, occasionally taking out a wallet from his pocket and staring at a dog-eared photograph.

Once, when a young man caught her eye, she'd flirt with him. Now she was cautious. Magnus had broken down the barriers she'd erected, but she doubted their relationship would have gone anywhere as she realised she only furthered his cause. When she met Jan, it had ignited a spark she hadn't thought still existed. A rekindling of desires, reviving memories of standing proud in a new dress, hair coiffed, playing to an appreciative audience. The tinkling of glass, the murmur of voices, smiling faces, applause when she finished playing, but the illusion lasted only as long as a bubble. Every time she saw Jan, she was uplifted and happy and longed for that feeling again.

The journey was frustrating for her as the train appeared to spend more time at a standstill than moving.

'What awaits you in Vienna if we ever get there?'

'Only a boring conference.' She offered a resigned smile.

As if in sympathy, he nodded. 'The Russians hit the city hard, overwhelming the Nazis. Many civilians were killed and buildings destroyed.'

'Oh dear.' She restrained herself from asking more. 'The city of classical music, Strauss, Mozart...' Her voice trailed off as she feared she'd say too much.

'Don't know how long it'll take,' he said. 'There's a lot of damage on the line. Bomb craters. God knows what.' He lit another cigarette and put away the pack.

'Why are you headed for Vienna?' she asked.

One of his colleagues, his eyes closed but listening, answered for him. 'He's chasing a Nazi ghost in the Austrian Alps, but he's as much chance of finding him as I have of becoming president.'

The Captain flashed a warning look, but the soldier continued, 'Being Swedish, I don't suppose you've ever come across a real Nazi?'

PART IV

38

Her home, her Vienna, the city of dreams, would survive, she believed. Nothing could destroy the magnificence of its palaces and great buildings of state and they would continue unblemished when the war ended. And until the train pulled into Westbahnhof, that was her one constant. Although grievously wounded, the station was operational, but the beamed iron awning displayed the scars of the bombing of April 1945, and the roof had collapsed. An all-pervading stench of smoke took her breath away. The fire-blackened buildings were now shells, and each gust of wind degraded mounds of crumbling rubble.

She flicked away a tear. What awaited outside? What had her father endured? She was eager to get home, but after a three-day journey with fragmented sleep, fatigue played tricks on her mind. As if she were still on the rocking and swaying train, the station appeared to move around her, making her unsteady on her feet, and the desire to close her eyes and sleep was overpowering. But unwanted memories and images crowded her consciousness, demanding attention.

All around, people were rushing. Passengers catching trains. Arrivals falling into the welcoming arms of loved ones, but no one was meeting her. And there were farewells. Lovers unwilling to let go of their partner's hand even as the train moved off. She wanted to cry, but if she started, she'd never stop. At least, they had the chance to say goodbye, unlike her family when they were marched to the gas chambers.

As though watching a film, her memories played out before her. Soldiers using the butts of their rifles to force them onto the train. A blow to the ribs, bringing tears to her eyes. Slavering dogs barking and straining on their chains. And above the clamour, children's cries and adult voices raised in anger. She blinked several times to convince herself it wasn't happening again and dropped her bags at her feet and shivered as the memories continued flashing before her eyes, so intense the sounds seemed to echo around her.

Drained and as much a shell as her surroundings, she collapsed on a wooden bench. When the nightmares visited, she'd learned to control them by concentrating on other things, fooling herself, but those false hopes were swept away when confronted with reality. To stop from vomiting, she clamped her mouth shut and wrapped her arms around herself, rocking back and forth.

Through the holes in the roof, she could see banks of black cloud rolling in and enveloping the city, sealing in the cold and grimness. Outside, she hailed a cab, and the driver recognised the destination and offered a lopsided smile. 'Good,' he said. 'That makes things easier.'

At first glance, nothing appeared to have changed. The old marble and grey stone buildings still stood as they had for hundreds of years and might for another couple of hundred, and their permanence fostered a sense of security, but the people were a precursor to what awaited. They appeared downtrodden and beaten. Even though the Nazi occupation had ended, there were few signs of confidence and no hint of a new beginning. As they sidled along the streets, they pulled their coats tight around them, heads down, unsmiling and not acknowledging each other.

'What brings you here?' The driver glanced over his shoulder.

'I lived here once.' But should she have admitted it?

'You'll ask yourself why you came back.' He nodded ahead as they turned a corner. 'It'll take years to fix. If ever.'

Disoriented and unable to find landmarks to get her bearings, panic rose in her breast. Mounds of rubble dominated the landscape, as even the inner city had sustained damage, and many streets were unrecognisable. But, as though it hadn't happened, the dirty yellow trams still weaved in and out of the destruction. Turning every corner revealed more devastation, and now she feared for her home.

'The Nazi occupation destroyed us,' the driver said. 'People disappeared. Evicted from their homes and interned. Jews were ostracised, refused jobs and schooling, deported to concentration camps and never came back. Everyone lived in fear. Years ago, it would've been unimaginable. We thought twice about what we were about to say, so we kept quiet. Germans in uniform were avoided because they held the power of life or death over you. They banned groups from gathering, and they stopped you and asked for your papers. And if you didn't have them, they took you away, never to be seen again.'

That resurrected memories of their abduction in the park, and she shuddered and wrapped her coat about her. Everywhere, there were uniforms which chilled her. Soldiers in fur hats, others in ill-fitting outfits. Some obviously French and, of course, Americans who looked as though they'd stepped out of a Hollywood movie. And the locals distrusted all of them.

The driver, sensing the shock in her silence, took his eyes off the road. 'It's not pretty,' he said, looking around. 'The Russians bombed us constantly for a year. By the time they invaded, we had no food or water and no gas or electricity. There were no police, so there was looting and the Russians were plundering and raping. You must have heard what happened here?' He watched her in the rearview mirror.

In Sweden, it had been difficult getting information about Vienna, and she felt guilty for not trying more, as though she'd turned her back on them.

'It was hell on earth. If the Nazis didn't get you, the Russians did. Every family lost loved ones. After the Nazis were driven out, the four powers—America, Britain, France and Russia—divided the city up into four zones…'

His voice faded into the background as she looked for anything she could remember, but recognised little. This was no longer her city, her home, just an alien landscape. She squirmed around in her seat, searching the skyline.

'Looking for something?'

'Yes.' Her voice lifted. 'It's still there.'

He slowed, following her gaze. 'Only just. It was destroyed during the war, but they rebuilt it with only half the gondolas.'

She counted the red wooden cabins to make sure. Only fifteen, but at least it had survived. High above the city, the Riesenrad Ferris wheel still turned slowly, and from two hundred feet up, you could follow the Danube meandering off into the distance. It had been a family ritual. None of the children's birthdays was complete without a ride on the big wheel. They all loved it, although at first only Willy's teasing forced Lily aboard. Afterwards, she was always first on. As soon as she could, she promised she'd take her father on a ride. With a flash of hope, she sighed and settled back in the seat. 'How can you tell which zone you're in?'

'Notice boards.' He pointed at one as they passed. 'If there are none, you can usually tell by the soldiers. Yanks are the best dressed and always smoking and surrounded by girls. The French have a certain style.' He shrugged. 'The British are down at heel as if wearing another's uniform. And the Russians? You'll recognise them when you see them. Avoid them at all costs. There are checkpoints everywhere. Where we're going, all four countries take their turn to be in charge for a month at a time.'

As they approached a group of soldiers, he swung into the kerb and brought the taxi squealing to a stop. A soldier sauntered over, stuck his head through the open window and winked at her and dropped a package onto the empty seat. Mumbled words were exchanged, and the soldier winked again and gave a low whistle, but the driver's look hardened, warning him off.

'American cigarettes,' the driver said, as though she deserved an explanation. 'They give me smokes and I see to their cultural needs.'

He rambled on, but she zoned him out, feeling more confident now and attempting to identify buildings. When they turned into Kumpfgasse—only a cobbled lane—a sense of normality returned. Despite the destruction, her apartment block rose out of the ashes like a phoenix.

She offered the driver the money the professor had given her, but he sighed almost in disbelief. She inspected the coins. Yes, they were Austrian schillings. Why wouldn't he take payment?

'Keep 'em.' As though ashamed to ask for money, he looked away. 'They're of no use to me. If you've got BAFS, I'll have 'em.'

Baffled, she screwed up her eyes.

'British Armed Forces pounds. Anything else is worthless.'

She put the money back in her pocket and thanked him, and as she climbed out of the taxi, he gave a wry smile as though sorry for her. 'Lucky you're staying here. It's relatively safe, but keep away from the Russian zone and don't go out on your own at night. There are a lot of kidnappings.'

The grey apartment block had been home for most of her life and appeared untouched and hope momentarily flared within her. Identifying the apartment's windows, she almost expected to see her family waving back at her, but the glass reflected only a cloudy sky.

'Miss, miss.' The driver ran after her, holding the violin case. 'Don't forget this. Looks like it's been in the wars.'

Although a reminder of the camp and all the bad things that had happened, it comforted her and she was glad she hadn't left it behind.

Her home hadn't appeared to have changed, she thought as her eyes swept from the lift to the stairs and back. After the journey, she didn't relish climbing two flights of stairs with a bag, and even the temperamental elevator was a better option. It lurched upwards, straining and creaking, and when it reached her floor, she opened the scissor gate, stepped out and put down the luggage. Hands on hips, she surveyed the area, remembering how she would race Lily and Willy up the stairs and burst through the apartment doors only for Mama to chide them with a smile. And their laughter echoed in her head.

39

The front door looked unfamiliar and, worried her appearance might surprise her father, she hesitated and pushed her hair into place and smoothed her clothes. Once reunited, there would be the inevitable questions and sad answers and she'd sit with him and explain what had happened and there would be grief and tears.

The bell also sounded unfamiliar, she thought as she waited for a response, but over the years, her father would have made changes. She paced back and forth before trying again. A chain rattled on the other side, and the door opened, and a crack of light escaped from the interior. A small face peered out at her. She pulled back before asking softly, not wishing to alarm the child, 'What's your name?'

The girl chewed on a finger and stared back at her.

'Please tell Max his daughter is home.'

The child closed the door.

After a few minutes, she rang again and, when the door opened wider this time, a plump woman, hair uncombed, stood with feet planted apart, as though ready to block the entrance. 'Yes?'

She repeated her father's name, but the woman didn't give even a flicker of recognition, only shaking her head. 'No one by that name here,' she said. 'We've been here for more than a year.'

'Oh.' Embarrassed, she checked again if she had the right address. 'Has he moved? Do you know—'

'Can't say.' As though she had better things to do, the woman

The VIOLINIST'S REVENGE

rubbed her hands together. 'Sorry. Must go.' The door slammed shut, trembling on its hinges.

Where was he? He must have left a message. What had happened? An unwelcome possibility increased her anxiety and her knees gave way and she slumped against the wall. She would go back outside and the fresh air would clear her head and she could gather her thoughts, but she'd taken only a couple of steps when a voice called her name in a querulous tone. 'Is it you?' Braced for another unpleasant surprise, she swung around.

She remembered the woman as elderly, but now she appeared younger, a nervous smile playing across her lips. Arms outstretched, Frau Strobl, the nosy neighbour, approached. 'Come here, child,' she said and wrapped her arms around her, and Anneliesa surrendered to her tears, the horrors of recent years rising like a flood overflowing a reservoir. 'Where's my father?' She looked back at the apartment door as though it had all been a mistake, and he would emerge.

'Come with me.' Frau Strobl took the violin case and ushered her down the corridor and into her apartment. In all the years she had lived here, she'd never been allowed across the threshold. To her surprise, it resembled a shrine, the walls adorned with crucifixes, although she couldn't recall her neighbour attending church. And that angered her. Religion didn't mean anything anymore to her. If there's a god, he didn't deserve her devotion, having let her and millions suffer in this way. The strain of the journey was telling, and she flopped into an armchair and dabbed at her face with a lace handkerchief. It was an old woman's room with many small tables laden with memories and, as if having stepped into an alien world, she was disoriented. It seemed familiar but different.

Frau Strobl disappeared into the kitchen and returned with two cups of steaming coffee and a plate of chocolate biscuits, then went back and brought a bottle of brandy and two glasses. She filled both and offered one and ordered, 'Drink.'

Taking a larger mouthful than intended, the warmth of the alcohol burned all the way down and made her cough, but brought her back to her senses. 'Where's my father?' She couldn't bear to hear the answer.

The old woman took a slow swallow of her brandy, staring at the window as rain smeared the panes, then turned back. 'Your father was a brave man. A very brave man. He never gave up looking for you.' Frau Strobl's voice softened. 'Went to the authorities and demanded information because he couldn't understand how all of you had vanished. The local police were useless, and the Germans were obstructive. He even confronted the Gestapo, but they wouldn't help and, when he continued searching for answers, they threatened to lock him up. But he wouldn't stop.'

She avoided eye contact and stared out at the rain. That would have been typical of her father. He was very determined. 'You must tell me what happened.' She dabbed at her face with a handkerchief, but the tears refused to come. 'Please tell me everything.'

To aid her memory, Frau Strobl rose and paced the room, her hands clasped in front of her before speaking. 'Several times he walked to the station, retracing your steps, but eventually he discovered what had happened.'

She imagined his despair and felt his pain.

As though considering how much she should tell her, Frau Strobl hesitated. 'Every day, he returned even more broken than before.' Her voice faltered and she had to compose herself.

The words echoed in her head, but they were scrambled, and a kaleidoscope of images of her despairing father searching the streets flashed before her.

'Your father always dressed smartly and took pride in his appearance,' Frau Strobl remembered with a smile. 'He'd always raise his hat and say good morning but, after a while, he stopped smiling and his hair grew long and unkempt and his face grey and gaunt. I don't think he changed his clothes for weeks on end. Once, I got into your apartment.' She raised both hands. 'Food and dirty dishes everywhere. Papers littered every top. Letters he'd received from official sources and those he'd failed to finish writing. Opened books lay where they fell. I tried cleaning it up, but it was pointless.'

'Where is he?'

Frau Strobl reached for a packet lying next to the coffee and extracted a cheroot. She lit up and inhaled deeply, then exhaled and watched the smoke spiralling up to the corniced ceiling.

'What happened to him?'

The VIOLINIST'S REVENGE

The old woman's eyes closed, as if coveting a secret that soon would no longer be hers. 'The dear man.' She hesitated before swallowing more brandy. 'The light had gone from his eyes.' She rose from her chair, ash from the cheroot falling on the carpet, and came over and took her hands. 'When I hadn't seen him for several days, I got into your home.' She paused. 'He was at peace. He died in his sleep. I think of a broken heart, believing he'd never see you again. Perhaps he just gave up as he'd have nothing to live for.'

As though another heavy door had slammed in her face, a sense of emptiness overcame her. Now there was no hope, and she'd face the future alone. 'Where is he?'

'He wished to be laid next to your grandparents.' Frau Strobl recalled the ceremony. 'We gave him a small funeral, and many came. People liked him, even Bishop Hudal said a few words.'

The brandy had cleared her head, and she got up from the chair, but not knowing what she should do.

Frau Strobl eased her back down. 'Tell me about Mama and Willy and Lily.'

She listened to herself recounting the events of the fateful day in Stadt Park, as if it had happened to someone else, and documenting her family's final days. And, in some way, it was cathartic, like putting them to rest.

When she finished, Frau Strobl mustered a sympathetic smile. 'You can stay here for as long as you wish.'

'No, I can't.' Panic surged within her as she looked about. 'I have things I must do.' But she was unsure what they were.

'Where will you go? I have a bedroom made up for you. I've been waiting for your return.'

The old lady's kindness saddened her.

'I insist,' Frau Strobl said. 'When you're ready, we can visit his grave. The lawyer will speak to you. Your father left money, not a lot, because after you vanished, he hadn't much work, but it can wait. You must be tired after your long journey and, once you're rested, together we'll tackle what needs to be done, but first…' She raised a hand and bustled through to her bedroom, returning with her hands behind her back and a secretive smile. 'After your Papa died, so-called friends sold off the contents of the apartment, but I saved one thing for you because I always believed you'd return.' From behind her back, the old lady revealed her surprise, and with a gasp, she snatched it from her and held it to her breast. And for a moment, her grief almost evaporated. As though new, the violin she'd played as a child gleamed in the low light.

'I kept dusting and polishing it, making sure it was ready for you.' Frau Strobl tutted and pointed to a smudge before erasing it with the cuff of her blouse.

She lifted the instrument, smooth and cool, to her cheek and memories of happier times flooded in. A little girl, her knees knocking with nerves, playing for an audience of the great and the good in the Sybaritic surroundings of the Metropole. Sobbing, she played the sad opening bars of Sibelius's violin concerto, then stopped.

'It's no use.' She threw down the instrument and collapsed into a chair. 'I can never play again.' And she fell into a deep sleep.

40

The next morning, lying in bed and uncertain of her surroundings, she pulled the bedclothes closer and smelled them. Was she safe? Frau Strobl had fussed around her and put her to bed like a child and, when she awoke, she had to convince herself her father's death wasn't just a nightmare. But the more she thought about it, the more she panicked and, unable to control her legs, they thrashed beneath the blankets. The noise brought the old woman running and, although Anneliesa didn't understand what she was saying, her presence calmed her.

She politely declined Frau Strobl's offer to accompany her to Vienna's Central Cemetery in the British zone and took a taxi. A city of the dead. It stretched as far as the eye could see. Graves ran along avenues and paths under a canopy of trees, and many were modest, but some, like those of Beethoven, Schubert and Strauss, were monuments to their genius. And there were others, especially the graves of Jewish citizens, damaged by the Nazis' vandalism on Kristallnacht, a year before the outbreak of war. They didn't confine their hatred to smashing the windows of Jewish shopkeepers. They dug up their graves, so even in death, they were targeted.

She skirted the white building of St Charles Borromeo Church, its dome dominating the cemetery like a gigantic green apple, but she didn't enter. Her faith was buried deeper than the brutalised dead of Auschwitz.

A white marble tombstone marked her father's grave, lying beside his parents and conspicuous by its newness and not yet stained by weather and time. She had imagined he might still materialise before her, but the finality of his name engraved in black on the stone removed any hope. Frozen in the moment, the fact that he lay alone and Mama, Willy and Lily weren't there with him hit her all the harder. Taking a deep breath, she laid on his grave a single red rose she'd bought at an old woman's stall at the entrance to the cemetery, and her fingers ran over the letters of his name as though reading braille. Her only consolation was that memories don't die—birthday parties, long walks with her father, afternoons cooking with her mother, their pride in her playing, Lily climbing into her bed in the mornings and demanding to be read a story.

But images of Wächter at the death march, laughing not only at the poor wretches waiting to die but at her as he enjoyed her despair, replaced those memories. Now she had to accept her role as the family's sole survivor, and the enormity of it frightened her. She wanted to cry, but still tears wouldn't come, increasing her guilt. Her duty now was to keep their story alive, only one of millions, and who would listen? Who would care? It might have been easier had she died with them.

As though distance might lessen the pain, she broke into a run, blundering into mourners with their embarrassed looks, and when her body gave up, she slumped to the ground and, as she lay there, a sense of resolve replaced her panic. She had survived the concentration camp, but had one more battle to win. And to succeed, she must stay alive.

She glanced back at the grave. This was not the end, only the beginning. Someone must pay for what had happened to them, and that meant revenge in whatever form it might take.

41

Family affairs took most of her time over the next few days and provided a respite from the grief. Hours were spent in meetings with lawyers, setting up bank accounts and organising another gravestone as a memorial to her mother and siblings and, out of necessity rather than vanity, she shopped for a new wardrobe.

No matter how bad the destruction during the Soviet offensive of 1945, she wanted to see it for herself and, only by walking the streets, could she grasp the reality of what had happened. The first time she entered Kärntner Strasse, the damage stopped her in her tracks as much of the shopping area was unrecognisable and finding something that had survived was a minor victory.

One afternoon in Kärntner Strasse, a tall, elegant woman with blonde, well-groomed hair attracted her attention. She wore a camel coat and low-heeled crocodile skin shoes and carried a matching handbag. A man, more a servant than a companion, followed two steps behind, and his eyes darted around and, like a lion about to pounce, he moved with an animal athleticism. This woman expected a path to be cleared for her. Famous? An actress? A singer? She had exited a store, and her bodyguard hurried ahead, leading her to a car parked at the kerb. A bystander with a scarf over her head blocked her. 'Nazi trash,' she spat at her. 'You should have died in the gas chambers, too.'

The woman's face contorted in panic, and, eyes wide and nostrils flaring like a spooked horse, she swivelled and brushed past Anneliesa. The bodyguard reached inside his jacket and stepped towards the assailant, then changed his mind and returned to his charge and, with a protective arm, ushered her into the safety of the car's back seat. As the car lurched away from the pavement— the woman protecting her face with a gloved hand—the assailant disappeared into the crowd.

The mention of gas chambers was like a punch in the stomach and Anneliesa lost focus and was back in the compound again, surrounded by barbed wire. On her way back to the apartment, she tried to dismiss the incident, but Frau Strobl realised something was wrong and brought her a coffee and poured a stiff brandy. In response to the old woman's gentle probing, she recounted her experience. Was the woman a local celebrity or perhaps the wife of a politician? But why did the assailant accuse her of being a Nazi?

With hands on her knees and a gleam in her eye, the old woman sat on the edge of her seat. She asked Anneliesa to describe the woman, and her tongue clicked several times as though forming a picture in her mind. Eventually, arms folded, she sat back with a sigh.

'You remember the trouble we had with the Nazis after the Anschluss?' she said. 'And not only the Germans but fellow Austrians as well. You were younger then and perhaps your parents shielded you from the harsh realities of life under the occupiers, but they were bad times. I had Jewish friends who suffered, especially once the war started.' Her eyes were full of memories, and she dropped her head. 'Most disappeared and were never seen again and we couldn't do anything, but some Austrians collaborated with the Nazis and we knew who they were.'

'Was she a collaborator?' she asked.

'If it's who I think it is, she's worse.'

'Why?'

As if lost in a memory, Frau Strobl stared at the window. 'Forgive me. A friend of your father would like to meet you. It's best he answers your questions.' She rose from the chair and went to replenish her coffee.

The following day, she met Albert, a small man, shorter than her, wearing a dark buttoned-up suit. He might have been a clerk, an accountant, or even a doctor and of her father's age, with wavy steel grey hair, a lined face and a hooked nose. He showed no emotion as they shook hands and never once changed his expression during their meeting, as though assessing her. He didn't offer a surname. First names were innocent, he said, surnames were incriminating. Despite his ordinary appearance, an authority emanated from him. He would go unnoticed in a crowded room, but in a room like this, he dominated it. Once seated, each with a glass of brandy, he spoke and his eyes never left her face. 'Your father was my friend.'

Eager to hear about his last days, she encouraged him to continue.

'A fine man.' Without waiting for her permission, he lit up. 'Don't mind if I...' He waved the cigarette in the air. 'I respected him, and I'm sorry for your loss.'

'How did you know him?' She turned away.

'We worked together.'

'You're an accountant, a businessman?'

'Not that kind of work.' He waited to see if she understood.

'How did you meet?'

'The war forged many alliances, partnerships of a kind.' He proffered his glass to his hostess, and she refilled it. 'Germany had its supporters, and you had to be careful what you said or did.'

When Frau Strobl offered to top up her drink, she covered the glass with a hand.

'The majority went along with the Nazi regime. We had little choice, but we didn't agree with them. To survive, we did things we'd be ashamed of now. Most of all, we couldn't stomach their inhumanity.'

He searched for an ashtray. 'But we opposed them in a small way.'

Frau Strobl smiled and nodded.

As though someone might be listening, he lowered his voice. 'Our resistance had successes. Not many, but enough to be an irritant. Like a mosquito that you know is there, but you can't find. We had to be careful because the more we did, the more our fellow citizens suffered. I like to think we did our bit, chipping away at the Nazi wall, and your father played his part, too. Unfortunately, some of us paid the ultimate price.' He hesitated, staring at the floor. 'But the work's not finished. Some still support the Nazi ideology even after everything that's happened. Like cockroaches, they've scuttled back under the floorboards, but give us time and we'll find them.' He went quiet again, remembering things he couldn't discuss.

She waited until Frau Strobl interrupted his reverie, then mentioned she'd seen a certain woman.

'I suggested you'd give Anneliesa more information about her.' The old woman frowned. 'You know who I mean.'

'Ah, yes.' Albert's mouth turned down with distaste, and he bridged his fingers together as he listened. Slow and deliberate, he struggled to keep hatred out of his voice. 'A living example of the injustices of war. She came through it unscathed and enriched and lives a life of impunity.'

When she finished her story, he got to his feet. 'With a man, you say? Tell me about him?' But he discounted the man as no more than a bodyguard. 'The woman should be reviled by anyone with a conscience.' He stared at the wall for so long she had to ask, 'Was she a collaborator?'

'Much worse.' He put his head back and stared at the ceiling. 'She was part of the cabal at the head of that evil movement. Her name is Charlotte Wächter, the wife of a Nazi SS general, a mass murderer—'

She put a hand to her mouth, stifling a gasp. How could it be? They slaughtered her family, and millions more, and yet Wächter's wife can shop protected by a bodyguard?

'And we believe Wächter is very much alive,' he added.

As though on the point of collapse, she leaned forward in her chair, remembering the screams of victims being gassed. 'Then why haven't they arrested him and hanged him for his war crimes like the others?'

'It's not that straightforward.' Albert searched for a cigarette. 'They must catch him first, and there are those helping him. Even Vienna's own dear Bishop Hudal is said to be one of them, but then he always sympathised with the Nazis.'

It depressed her that a member of her church, a man of God, could be involved.

'For some Nazis, the war isn't over,' Albert said. 'They regard it as merely a setback and believe they'll return and ultimately triumph.

The VIOLINIST'S REVENGE

Wächter—Gruppenführer Baron Otto Gustav von Wächter to give him his full title—was a member of the Nazi party years before the war and a particular favourite of Hitler's. He's an aristocrat and still regarded as a member of the ruling class here in Austria.'

As Albert's words seemed to echo around the room, she felt a slow paralysis creeping into her bones, and a toxic mix of anger, fear and revulsion made her gulp her drink. 'He's the monster who murdered my family.'

'My dear, don't—' Frau Strobl put a hand on her arm.

She shrugged her off and jumped to her feet. 'Where is he?'

'We don't know.' Albert looked resigned. 'Perhaps near here. American soldiers are searching the Alps for him.'

She recalled what the American soldiers had said on the train.

'It's as good a place as anywhere, I suppose,' Albert continued. 'As a boy, he knew the area well. And we believe Frau Wächter and maybe even Hudal know his whereabouts and help him with food and supplies.'

'Where is she?'

'Living an otherwise normal life in their house near Salzburg.'

'Can't they arrest her? Or Hudal? Make them reveal where he's hiding?'

To avoid the pain in her eyes, he averted his gaze. 'She claims she doesn't know whether he's dead or alive, and we have no proof she's helping him.'

'Unbelievable.' She paced the room, hands so clenched they were turning white. 'They're shielding a war criminal, and the authorities refuse to act. What about my mother and brother and sister and thousands more? I'd get the truth out of her. With my bare hands if necessary.'

Albert shook his head. 'You wouldn't get near her.' He raised his arms as if in defeat. 'She has a lot of protection.'

Her mind raced as she slumped back in the chair, and her words came out louder than she'd intended. 'We can't let this woman get away with it.'

'Believe me, we want justice as much as you,' Albert said. 'And we're doing what we can.' He almost spat out the words. 'How can the wife of a man responsible for the extermination of hundreds of thousands of Jews be innocent? She visited him many times and stayed at the camp for long periods, and must have known. Frau Wächter was a friend of Hans Frank, his superior and Hitler's lawyer, and helped herself to much of Poland's treasures and transported them to Austria for her collection.' He paused and, while his glass was refilled, his hand was shaking. 'That's why that woman shouted at her in the street. People despise what she and her husband did.'

She stopped listening, reliving the morning her family were marched to the gas chambers, and Wächter's presence was there in the room, smirking and mocking them, his laughter arriving in waves, such that she had to cover her ears. When it was too much, she slumped forward in her seat, and Frau Strobl encouraged her to take another sip of brandy. 'Have there been any sightings of Wächter?' she asked, her voice disembodied, almost calm.

'No,' Albert said. 'It's believed he's hiding with one of his SS lieutenants. If caught, the Allies will put him on trial, but we must get to him before they do. If we do, he won't be able to spout his poisoned ideologies in court or strike a deal as many war criminals have done. We'll make sure he dies a slow and painful death.'

'Let me help,' she said. 'What do you want from me? I'll do whatever I can because, beyond this, my life is meaningless.'

The news that Wächter lived sparked a mixture of emotions— anger, grief and even exultation. She could still avenge her family, and maybe he had news of Lily.

Later that night, a vivid nightmare dominated her sleep. She was back in the camp, and Wächter was forcing her into a gas chamber. And when the door slammed shut behind her and enveloped her in impenetrable darkness, his laughter boomed above the screaming of her fellow prisoners and didn't stop.

42

Two mornings after their first meeting, Albert visited Frau Strobl's apartment. 'You should see this,' he said. Despite the old woman's objections, he ushered Anneliesa down the stairs and out onto the lane and guided her to his battered grey Mercedes.

'Where are we going?' She removed his hand from her elbow.

'Please be patient,' he said.

Once inside the car, he raised his voice above the growl of the engine. 'I think you'll find this interesting.'

She put out her hands, palms up. 'Where are we going? I don't like mystery tours. I've had too many.'

'Sorry.' He placed a hand on her shoulder. 'Salzburg.' He pushed the car into gear and checked behind before moving off.

'What's there?'

'Wächter's home.'

She felt a sense of dread.

'We've been watching the house for some time.'

'Why if he's not there?' she said, but he concentrated on the road ahead. 'Will that awful woman be there?'

'That's why we're there, although it's unlikely Wächter will ever turn up. But one day we hope she'll slip up and lead us to him.'

'I'd like to confront her and tell her what a murderous bastard he is, although she probably knows.'

He shook his head. 'Don't even think about it.'

'Then what's the point of my going?'

'It might help you understand.' He shrugged.

'How?' She stared blindly out the window.

'Your father was a friend, but I couldn't help him in the end.' His mouth turned down. 'I want to help you if I can.'

'I'm sorry.' She touched his arm. 'I'm grateful. Really.'

'There's something I must tell you, but not in front of Frau Strobl. She means well, but sanitises everything.'

She raised her eyebrows in surprise.

'You've been through a lot.' He hesitated, his eyes searching her face. 'More than anyone should face in a lifetime. I don't want to add to your pain, but you deserve to know what happened.' He offered a half-smile and looked away. 'It might bring some sort of closure.'

'I don't understand,' she said, unsure she could face more revelations. 'What is it?'

He tightened his grip on the wheel. 'I'll tell you when we get there.'

Until a few miles from the destination, they kept their thoughts to themselves. Then Albert slowed the car and swerved off the road. Mounting a grass verge, they bumped to a halt, and he pulled on the handbrake and switched off the engine. For a moment, he stared at the dashboard, his hands still on the wheel. Under a lined forehead, his eyes were hooded. 'I'll tell you the truth about Max.' As if searching for the right words, he switched his gaze and stared out over a field. 'Frau Strobl didn't want you suffering more, but your father didn't die peacefully in his sleep.'

Heart racing, her body tightened, not sure she wanted to hear a painful truth, but knowing she must. The hope that at least one of her family had escaped the violence of war was fading fast.

'Max pined for you all and perhaps let himself go, but he didn't fade away,' he recalled. 'Far from it. A mounting anger supplanted his grief as the authorities put countless barriers in his way.'

He offered her a cigarette, but she declined, and he lit up, the warm smoke causing him to sigh, and he leaned back in the seat. Not wishing to interrupt him, she listened in silence.

Max had bombarded the authorities for information about his

family, Albert continued, but received no information from them. 'We had contacts inside the Gestapo headquarters. A cleaner read a report stating four Viennese citizens, a mother and three children, not Jews, had been by mistake transported to Poland.' She caught her breath while he waited for permission to continue.

'Perhaps we shouldn't have told your father. He went straight to the German embassy. Foolishly, we thought the Germans might admit their mistake and return you because if they hate anything, it's inefficiency. After all, you're an Austrian family of solid Aryan stock. At that time, we weren't aware of what the Nazis were doing, but they refused to investigate. What gave your father some hope was that Wächter controlled the area, and he knew him. He'd seen you play. But with each setback, Max became more withdrawn.' He waited for her reaction, but getting none, continued, 'I feared there was little hope for you and Max eventually believed it, too. I suspected he planned revenge, perhaps even on Wächter's wife or children.'

She shook her head vigorously. Her father would never do that.

'I did my best to dissuade him. Anyway, the Wächter family were well-guarded and an attack on them would have been suicidal. There would have been reprisals and many innocent people would have died.' Finishing his cigarette, he flicked the stub out the window and, for a moment, studied her, but she wouldn't meet his gaze.

'Your father became involved in our resistance work.' Albert's voice became more upbeat. 'We took small actions against the Krauts, like bombing petrol dumps. Anything that hindered them. And we kept a watch on Max because he had a gun. Once he almost got inside Wächter's house, but when he realised only the staff were there and one was the daughter of an acquaintance, he pulled out, not wishing her to suffer for his actions. But Max didn't give up, and his frustration made him angrier. One night, when drinking in a Vienna bar, he criticised the Nazis and claimed they were losing the war. We daren't talk openly about things like that. Unfortunately, he was overheard by someone he thought was a friend. In the middle of the night, a couple of policemen, accompanied by a plainclothes guy, probably Gestapo, smashed open the front door of the apartment.'

He waited for a response, but she turned away, the images

becoming too real. 'They arrested him.' Albert's voice almost broke. 'We believe they imprisoned him in the Metropole and tortured him for several days, but he never betrayed us.' He waited while she regained her composure. 'They left his body outside the apartment block.'

Although she wanted to cry, the tears wouldn't come, but she was proud that he went out with a fight. And only now could she accept his death.

'I'm sorry.' He rested a hand on her shoulder. 'You should know the truth. Your father was a very brave man.'

Up there, near the snow-covered summit of Untersberg, Wächter was hiding, and it increased her hatred of him so much that she wanted to go up and find him.

'Do you still want to visit the house?' he said.

She swept her hair back with both hands. 'More than anything.'

'Don't take matters into your own hands,' Albert warned. 'You wouldn't succeed, and it would ruin all our work. I understand what you're feeling, but you must be patient.' He waited for her agreement. 'Do only what I say. If we alert them, our work will have been wasted. Our time will come, but not today.'

He drove along the main road before forking right down a farm track, a cloud of dust following like a ship's wake. After a mile, they crested a rise at speed, and she gripped the sides of the seat as the car launched into the air and landed with a shuddering thud. As he switched off the engine, she exhaled in relief as they coasted to a stop in a copse. From there, they looked down on a large, square and solid building, set back from a lane and shielded by a line of trees. Its windows were shuttered, and on either end were brooding turrets like a castle.

He rummaged in the glove box, drew out a couple of objects and threw them over his shoulder before pulling out a pair of binoculars and handing them over. 'This is one of our vantage points. You can see all the comings and goings without them spotting you. The family spends most of their time at the back of the house, so you won't see much from here.'

A lush lawn ran around the side of the home to the back, and she glimpsed children playing, their shrieking and laughter carried on the morning air. 'Can I get a closer look?'

As if considering, he frowned at her, then relented. 'Okay.' He gestured for her to follow, and they picked their way down the hill. 'Keep behind me and do exactly as I say. They've got trigger-happy goons guarding them.' As they neared the house, he put a finger to his lips. They couldn't be seen from the house, but they had to be wary of guards patrolling the grounds. He crouched and beckoned for her to follow him, and together they ran across the road to the side of the house.

Double doors opened, and the woman she'd seen at the department store stepped out. Before, fashionable and confident, now her hair was tied back, and she wore jodhpurs and climbing boots and a heavy tweed jacket. As if expecting someone, she looked from side to side, and they shrank back against the wall. A car, the driver's face obscured, arrived and with another look around, she climbed in.

'Oh, that's bad luck,' she said in a broken whisper. 'You won't be able to follow her.'

'There's little point.' He shrugged. 'They'll bring up a second car and block anyone following.'

'So, they know they're being watched?'

Albert studied the house. 'They're experts, but we have people farther on who will attempt to track them.'

When he got no response, he turned around. She had disappeared and was striding across the lawn towards the back of the house, and he scrambled to catch up. 'What in hell's name are you doing?'

Ignoring him, she stopped at the corner of the house and looked around before edging to the rear of the property where the children had been playing. A blonde girl rode a bike and, briefly, her heart stopped. She stepped towards the child, who hesitated, surprised by the appearance of an intruder. From behind, footsteps made her wheel around. A woman, hair pulled tight into a bun and wearing a grey uniform and white apron, approached. 'Who are you? You shouldn't be here.' The woman grabbed the girl's arm, dragged her off the bike and marched her into the house. Although the child struggled, the woman was stronger, and bewilderment spread across the girl's face as she stared at her.

As her gut tightened, her heart raced and her head felt ready to explode. She remembered the way the girl tilted her head, but it couldn't be.

Although the maid slammed the French windows shut, she crept up and peered in. The children were playing in the room, and she tapped on the glass to attract the girl's attention, and she glanced back. Her mind reeled as she collapsed against the wall. She was hallucinating. Was she going mad? Every girl with blonde hair couldn't be her sister, who had died with her Mama and Willy in the camp. She must accept it. Coming here had been a mistake, only bringing up the nightmare of the concentration camp again.

From within, music played. Strauss. And instinctively, her fingers twitched, but she closed her eyes and covered her ears, blocking out the sound.

'What have you done?' Albert dragged her away. 'Get out of here.' He pushed her on, and men's raised voices and footsteps running towards them brought her to her senses. As they fled, she glimpsed a man watching before turning away and slipping deeper into the trees.

Why was she crying? Tears welled up and wouldn't stop as she pressed against the window. Her breath misted up the glass, and she left fingerprints and wiped them clear. Who was the woman? She seemed familiar.

That night, she lay in bed trying to remember, but her memory only went back so far, blocking what had gone before. Nightmares of horrific events, people tortured and killed, dominated her sleep and lingered during her waking hours. Traumatised and uncertain whether they were memories or just dreams, she sought a dark corner where they couldn't enter, but they kept returning. How could they be real? When she told Charlotte of her memories, the woman claimed she was making up hateful stories and, if she repeated them, would be sent away. Once, she was locked up for several days as punishment. She compared her reflection in the glass to the woman who had spoken to her, but she didn't understand what she said.

Tears caused her to blink, and she rubbed her eyes, and when she reopened them, the face was no longer there. Or had it been another dream?

43

Albert's knuckles whitened as he gripped the steering wheel and fixed his eyes on the road. He was driving faster than before, and she stared at him, but the set of his jaw suggested he was in no mood for talking. She dared not break the silence. Unable to contain his anger any longer, he swerved off the road and brought the car to an abrupt stop. His face flushed and eyes blazing, he bellowed, 'How could you be so stupid?' He slammed his hands down on the wheel, and it shuddered. 'What in the hell were you thinking of?'

Fearing he might hit her, she shrank away. 'I'm sorry,' she whispered.

'That's not good enough.'

'The girl—'

'You should have done as I told you.' He checked they weren't being followed. 'Why did you ignore my orders?'

'I wanted—'

He waved away her explanation. 'I was wrong to take you. Our work here is finished now. We've watched the house for a long time. They have a contact in the local police who feeds them information about raids, but they don't know about us. We hoped one day Wächter might break cover and visit the family, then we'd get him. There's no chance of that now. You've frightened him off.'

When he paused, she blurted, 'The girl looked like my sister.'

The VIOLINIST'S REVENGE

'Impossible.' He punched the wheel with his fist. 'You're imagining things.'

The blonde girl in Wächter's garden did resemble Lily, but years of war had twisted memories, and she couldn't be sure. Was her mind playing tricks? 'It triggered a memory,' she explained, bursting into tears. 'I only wanted to speak to her. I'm sorry.'

Albert nodded, and a sadness in his eyes reminded her of her father.

'You're mistaken.' His voice was softer now. 'How could a girl be in the home of the Nazi general who signed her death warrant? It doesn't make sense.'

Of course, he was right, but she persisted. 'I was told they drove a young girl out of the camp in Wächter's staff car after the death march.'

He drummed his fingers on the steering wheel and exhaled. 'It could have been anyone. Another officer's daughter, perhaps.' As if searching for the right words, he raised his eyes to the roof of the car. 'I wanted accountability for what the monster did, especially to you and your family. Now I doubt we'll ever get him.'

'I shouldn't have done it.' She bit her tongue. What a fool she'd been. 'But I had to try.'

'We must be rational.' His tone was more even now. 'If it was your sister—and it wasn't—we couldn't just walk in and take her.' His shoulders slumped as he stared at the road ahead.

He didn't speak until he started the engine. 'Let me explain,' he said. 'With the help of some in the Catholic Church, including Bishop Hudal, the Nazis operate an escape route for high-ranking officers. They call it aptly the Ratline. They hide war criminals in monasteries throughout Europe until they can escape. If Wächter is one of them— and I'm sure he is—he and his family will be spirited away and live the rest of their lives free in South America.' He waited to see if she understood. 'He'd be untouchable.'

'But what would happen to Lily?' Would she ever see her sister again?

'Our only is that he might slip up and we could get him.'

'How long will it take?'

'Who knows now?' He shrugged and reached for a cigarette.

She realised he now regarded her as a liability and wouldn't let her return to Wächter's house. As they left, somebody had watched from the shade of the trees. Was it him? If so, why had he broken cover now, but she daren't tell Albert. He wouldn't believe her.

That night, screams and the scratching of victims attempting to escape the locked buildings punctuated her dreams. Fellow prisoners arriving to drag out the corpses and remove the gold from their teeth with pliers before loading them onto carts to be transported to the ovens. She awoke, the screams deafening her irregular breathing.

44

Anneliesa's eyes were creased with sleep when Frau Strobl, wearing a floral dressing-gown, woke her the next morning. As the old lady pulled back the blinds, letting sunshine flood the bedroom, she said over her shoulder, 'Albert's here. You must get up. Hurry.'

Albert was pacing the sitting-room and didn't look up when she entered. 'Wächter will now run,' he said, thinking aloud. 'We must move before he disappears for good.' He raised his head and gave her a sidelong glance. 'A man was watching us. It might have been him.'

She was relieved he'd seen the figure, too, and it wasn't just her imagination.

'Come on.' He beckoned. 'This is our last chance.'

She hesitated. 'You're taking me with you, but yesterday—'

'Not to the house,' he said, understanding her disappointment. 'We need a driver. If the girl is there, whoever she is, we'll try to save her.' He offered a smile. 'But no promises.'

'She'll be terrified,' she said. 'If I go to the house, she's more likely to come with me.'

He stared at her, calculating his options. 'You will be our escape route, and you must follow my orders, or you'll put her in danger, too,' he said and waited for her agreement. 'Wächter is our priority, then perhaps the girl.'

Two thickset men sat in the back of Albert's Mercedes, and he introduced them, but her concentration was so intense she didn't hear their names.

'Is this all?' she said in disbelief.

'These men are worth half-a-dozen Nazis and we're fully armed.'

'So am I,' she said and held up Max's old revolver.

His voice hardened. 'You must stay out of it. We don't want any heroics.'

During the journey, no one spoke, and the men chain-smoked, so she opened a window to let the smoke escape. Albert drove slowly and parked in the same spot as the previous day and, when they got out, he came over and stood too close for comfort. 'Stay in the car. If there are gunshots or you see us coming, start up immediately.' He grabbed her, his fingers digging into her arm. 'Do you understand?'

She nodded.

'Our lives could depend on you.'

Albert's men huddled together in conversation and, with a backwards glance at her, set off down the hill. After scanning the house and its grounds through binoculars, he glowered at her. 'Remember what I said.' He drew a pistol and took a different route down towards the house.

After a while, she stuck her head out the window and listened for sounds, but it was too quiet. Was the girl still there? Perhaps the family had fled. She picked up the binoculars and scanned the area, but there was no movement, and she felt helpless. They were armed, and she had no weapon to defend herself, as there were no bullets in Max's old revolver. And when she searched the car, she found nothing useful, not even a starting handle.

An hour passed, and she considered going down, but pulled back when a car arrived at the house. The driver got out and opened the back door, and a tall, stooped man alighted and waved to Charlotte, who had opened the front door, then helped a younger woman out. Charlotte greeted them both with a kiss on each cheek.

Was Albert aware of this arrival? Were he and his men even safe, or had the guards found them? Surely she would have heard sounds of a struggle.

The door opened again and the tall man emerged from the house, instructed the driver to carry two suitcases to the car and then came back for a third bag. Dressed in a coat and hat, Charlotte reappeared and gave the woman an affectionate hug. Then, accompanied by the man, she got into the car and drove off with a farewell wave.

What in hell is happening?

The car door opening startled her. Gasping, Albert slid in. 'It's all going down,' he said. 'Yesterday's visit must have spooked them, and she's gone off to join him and left that woman to care for her children. By the amount of luggage she's taken, I don't think she's coming back.'

'What now?'

'Don't know.' Albert slammed a hand on the steering wheel and glared at her. 'If we've scared them off, we'll never find him.'

'But Lily's still down there.'

He ignored her and checked his watch. 'Where are they?' He tapped the wheel. 'My men should be back by now.' A fusillade of shots rang out, and he turned, eyes wide. 'Take the wheel and start it up. If we're not back in ten minutes, get out of here. Head for Vienna and keep going.'

If the worst had happened, it would have been her fault and, as time dragged, her anxiety increased. There was still no sign of them, but she wouldn't leave. And where was the girl? Her family had perished in the concentration camp, her father was dead and Jan, too. She couldn't turn her back on the girl.

Unwilling to wait any longer, she eased from behind the wheel and set off down the hill, picking her steps and listening as she went. Albert would be mad, but just waiting in the car would be worse. As she approached the house, she slowed. Using her knowledge of the layout, she found an observation point concealed by shrubbery, and only her rasping breath broke an eerie silence. Her stomach cramped, the pain spreading through her body, and she needed to stretch, even if it gave away her hiding place. As she rose, she heard the faint laughter of children, and that spurred her on. Where were Albert and his men? Were they being held at gunpoint, and was she walking into a trap? She crouched and listened. Again, it was too quiet. She had to get closer and ran across the lane into the shrubbery at the side of the house, from where she had a clear view of the back of the building.

About twenty yards away were the French windows, but it would be impossible to get closer without being exposed.

Above the noise of her heavy breathing, she could hear a girl's voice. Lily? With trepidation, she tiptoed across the open expanse, but the room was empty. Should she enter? But shouts and footsteps of men running hard made her swing around in alarm. There was only one way out.

She sprinted across the lawn and plunged into thick vegetation, and the razor-sharp needles of the black pines tore at her unprotected arms and legs, while the aroma of pine and the sweet honey fragrance of edelweiss overwhelmed her senses. The cracking and snapping of foliage would alert them, but she had no choice. How far back did the garden run? Would she come up against a stone wall and be trapped? Had Albert and his men made it back to the car and were waiting for her, and would they come back for her?

As they barged through the undergrowth, the guards shouted instructions and were getting closer. If she didn't keep moving, they'd shoot her on sight. Oblivious to the branches whipping at her arms and face, she pushed deeper into the ever-thickening vegetation, which had slowed her to walking pace, and underfoot, clumps of heather caused her to stumble. It was hopeless. It would be only a matter of minutes before they caught her.

She entered a small clearing and gulped in air, trying to get her bearings. As if waiting for her, a figure dressed in black and wearing a balaclava, showing only his eyes, stood nearby, and she slumped to the ground in defeat. She'd calculated her pursuers were behind her, but she must have been running around in circles. The figure moved closer and clasped a hand over her mouth, and his other arm lifted her and dragged her deeper into the vegetation. It was denser here, but he held back branches, allowing her to squeeze through as though knowing where he was going.

When she feared she couldn't carry on, the trees thinned, and they emerged onto a grassy ridge. Before them, a drop of twenty feet and, in the distance, the high walls she'd feared. She had no time to grasp the hopelessness of her predicament as he launched her out into space. Her arms and legs windmilling, she fell and bounced on hard mounds and cracked her head and rolled over several times, coming

The VIOLINIST'S REVENGE

to rest in long grasses. As she pulled the grass out of her mouth, he landed alongside her.

'Lie still,' he said. She did and dared not breathe as she listened to the man's heart thumping in his chest. 'With luck, the grasses will hide us,' he said and took a pistol from the holster on his hip.

45

Back in 1943, Captain Butch Hadron and the US Fifth Army, under the command of Lieutenant-General Mark W. Clark, had crossed the Strait of Messina from Sicily to Salerno on the Italian mainland. An invasion heralding the downfall of Italy. That was soldiering, not this. He would have preferred to be back home in Milwaukee rather than searching the Austrian Alps for a war criminal. And if they found the Nazi, he'd prefer to shoot the bastard between the eyes rather than arrest him to stand trial and provide him with a platform to spout his deranged ideology.

Hadron sat atop a rocky outcrop halfway up the Alps, scanning the terrain stretching before him. It only confirmed his belief that the mission was doomed. At least in the air up here, he could breathe, but the thinness made every exertion harder. He picked up a pebble and launched it down the slope and watched it run and bounce and gather speed until it disappeared. He had more chance of finding that pebble than any Nazi. His throat was dry and he craved a beer and his mood wasn't helped by a sleety rain sweeping in horizontally.

His Sergeant, an argumentative man who gave the impression he'd rather be anywhere but here, picked his way up the path and slid on the scree. His face framed the obvious question. 'How much longer, boss?' He pushed his helmet to the back of his head and wiped his forehead with a dirty rag.

Hadron threw another pebble.

'It's a waste of manpower.' The Sergeant pulled out a cigarette and lit it.

'Orders are orders.' Hadron was also convinced it was a wild goose chase. 'Until I tell you otherwise, we search.' He offered a rueful grin. 'Get on with it.'

After days on the mountainside, his men's moods were made no better by the rain's arrival, and they grumbled amongst themselves, wanting to be back in town near a bar and chasing women, not stuck up here looking for a general who may or may not be hiding around here.

'All this for one fucker.' The Sergeant kicked a pebble. 'If he's still alive.'

Hadron's bosses were certain Wächter was alive and hiding in the Alps, which he knew from boyhood as his family home was in the vicinity. To his knowledge, there had been no reported sightings of him and his companion, Lieutenant Jünger. But he was no ordinary general and reckoned to be one of Hitler's favourites, responsible for the execution of hundreds of thousands, and they had a noose measured and waiting for him.

His platoon was guided by a local who was as disenchanted as they were. He split his soldiers into teams, and they spread out across the mountainside. Unsure of what they expected to happen, they had to stay alert as their prey would be armed and dangerous and choose to die rather than surrender.

The number of people clinging to the mountainside like lichen to a rock hampered their search. Mostly families with unkempt children staring at them as if they'd materialised from another planet. They approached every shack, tent, or improvised living space with caution. Some didn't even have a shack and made do with a tent of sorts, a hole in the ground covered by a tarpaulin. Many had fled when the Russians invaded. And all that remained in the city for them were ruins and starvation.

Early in the search, when one of his men frightened children living in a hole in a cliff face, Hadron snapped and grabbed the soldier by the collar, slamming him against a rock. 'Don't threaten them. They're human beings and we're not Nazis.' The guide appeared bewildered as he watched the Captain make the soldier turn out his pockets and present the children with his rations. They were given chocolate and cigarettes for their parents. And he added his, too.

Wächter knew the terrain and would keep well clear of them, and it would be useless interrogating families who had seen nothing and would be unlikely to tell, even if they had.

He ordered his men to search higher up and, later in the day, when the altitude was multiplying their problems, the Sergeant ran down the slope towards him. 'Found something, sir. Looks promising.'

He was led upwards, and when he rounded a bluff, his men were spread out, lying on the ground, their weapons ready. The Sergeant passed him his binoculars. Close to the cliff face, an object lay on the ground by the entrance to a cleft in the rock big enough for a man to squeeze through. At first, it resembled a body, but he squinted harder. A discarded sleeping bag. And there were no signs of smoke or habitation, but they couldn't take risks.

If they captured them, they could get off this goddamned mountain. 'No one goes in until we're certain what's there.' He looked at his watch and up at the sky. With about an hour of light left, they must move before darkness. In the meantime, they'd hold back. It might just be another unfortunate refugee struggling for survival.

He sent one man to recce the entrance, but got no signal from him. While he considered his next move, he lit a cigarette. He'd prefer to chuck a grenade into the cave and blow them to pieces, but his orders were to bring them back alive.

Time was running out, so he ordered another two men to approach the hideout covered by the first soldier, but the rain made it difficult to determine what was happening.

A shot and a puff of smoke escaped from the cave.

'All clear.' One of the advance party waved.

Whoever had been hiding had left in a hurry, leaving two sleeping bags on the ground. There were the remains of a fire in the centre of the space, but it was cold. It was unlikely they'd return, but were they still on the mountain? A walkie-talkie crackled with a message to abort the mission and return to base. 'About time, too,' he said, and the Sergeant struggled to hide his relief.

46

Two men arrived at the top of the ridge, and one shielded his eyes against the sunlight and peered down the slope, scanning the area from left to right. His gaze rested on the stone wall bordering the property in the distance. 'She won't have made it that far,' he said.

His partner nodded towards their hiding place and waved his pistol at the long grasses swaying in the breeze. 'She's probably in there.'

The damp, musty grass made her nose twitch, and she panicked as she struggled to stifle a sneeze, but the noise was disguised by the snapping of branches and a cry of pain from someone running through the trees.

'How in the hell did she get there?' The guards swung around and turned back the way they'd come and disappeared into the trees.

Once sure they were clear, her rescuer jumped up and brushed off the dust and grass. 'We must be quick.' He offered a hand and pulled her upright. 'They'll be back.' Although the cloth of the balaclava muffled his voice, it seemed vaguely familiar. A pistol strapped to his waist and a lean, muscular build suggested she could rely on him. 'We'll need to return the way we came,' he said, glancing up the slope. 'If we headed for the wall and they returned, we'd be sitting ducks.' He turned his back to her and hesitated before pulling off his balaclava and running a hand through his dark, wavy hair.

As though the air had been sucked out of her, her knees buckled and everything whirled about like a fairground waltzer and she stepped forward, losing her balance and putting out a hand for support. He moved in and held her in his arms, and she buried her face in his chest. 'But you're dead.' Her voice was hoarse as she struggled for words. 'Am I going mad?'

'I'm not a ghost. At least, not yet.'

'Then how?' She touched his face. 'They arrested you and the Poles said you wouldn't survive the interrogation.'

What should she believe? For the first time in ages, she felt safe and traced his scar with a finger and reached up and kissed it, and suddenly he kissed her on the mouth.

'C'mon.' He let go of her hands. 'We must get out of here before those goons return.'

'How did you escape?'

Gunfire in the distance brought them back to the present, and he pushed her on. 'Time to go.'

'Why are you here?'

'Same reason as you.'

'This is Wächter's house, the monster from the camp. I think he's got my sister. You remember her?'

He nodded as he listened, calculating how close the gunfire was.

'Anything's possible.' He led her to the slope and pointed out a path winding upwards. 'Do you remember I told you they took a girl out of the camp in Wächter's car?'

She stopped and caught her breath and fell forward, grasping a clump of grass to avoid slipping back down. 'You only told me that to give me a reason for escaping because you reckoned I'd lost my nerve.'

'You had the nerve and guts all right.' He paused. 'It happened. Could have been Lily or maybe …'

'It's her. I'm sure.' Her words came out in staccato fashion as she scrambled upwards on her hands and knees. 'Why take a child from a death camp? It doesn't make sense…'

'Maybe the bastard had a conscience after all.'

'Can't believe that.' She gave a dismissive laugh.

The VIOLINIST'S REVENGE

'You and your family were abducted by mistake. You were fellow Austrians, and your sister was the perfect Aryan, with her blonde hair and blue eyes. Perhaps it's his way of righting a wrong.' He shrugged and almost lost his balance. 'Insurance for the afterlife, if you like.'

'But he still sent the rest of my family to the gas chambers.' She studied his face. 'Why are you here? The war's over.'

'Wächter and I have unfinished business.' He motioned for her to hurry.

Another fusillade of return fire rang out,

'We must get out of here,' he shouted as they reached the top and gave her no time to catch her breath and forced her through the trees. Now there was no reason to hide their progress. When they broke cover, there was no sign of the guards, and he took her hand and led her on a circuitous route away from the house.

'I know where Albert's car is.' She willed it to still be there. 'It's our only chance.' They pounded across the lane and started up the hill. Behind them, three armed guards were gaining on them. Jan was holding the pistol in both hands and dropped to one knee and fired, and one of the pursuers stumbled, holding his chest. The others gave their colleague a cursory glance and flattened themselves on the ground and returned fire.

'Get out of here. I'll hold them off.'

'No, I'm not leaving you.'

'Don't be bloody stupid,' he yelled. 'Run.'

She didn't run but walked backwards, reluctant to leave him now she'd found him again. Bullets gouged the earth around her. She couldn't help him. Sobbing, she made her way up the hill as the gunfire receded. Albert sat at the wheel of the car with the engine running and gesticulated at her. A small familiar face pressed up against the car window, and her lungs screamed for air as she ran flat out towards them. A back door opened, and she jumped into Lily's arms as the car lurched off, the door flapping open like the broken wing of a wounded bird before she reached out and pulled it shut. She took Lily's face in her hands, smothered her with kisses and cradled her so tight the girl wriggled to get free.

'How did you save Lily?'

'When they were chasing you through the trees, I realised she was unguarded.' His face turned grim. 'I took her. Poor thing was bewildered by it all, but she came with me.' He kept his foot flat to the floor as they bumped and swayed back to the track.

'Where are the other guys?' But she already suspected the answer and reached forward, putting a hand on his shoulder.

Two lives wasted, and she was to blame, and Jan would be next. He wouldn't make it back. The price of rescuing Lily had become too much to bear.

'They tried their best,' he said. 'They did it for Max.'

Lily trembled and burrowed into her and still hadn't uttered a word, but she managed a diffident smile now she was safe. She'd talk when ready. Eventually, the girl drifted into sleep, but on entering Vienna, she stirred and pushed away from her and pressed her face against the window. The magnificence of Schönbrunn Palace captivated her and her eyes and mouth were open in awe. 'Mama, Papa,' she whispered. And Anneliesa recalled the family visiting the palace and telling Lily that Mozart had played there at the age of six. Lily turned back to her and her face softened as memories returned and she giggled. She pulled her in close, and the child buried her face in her hair. 'You'll soon be home.'

But where was home now?

As though the intervening years had never happened, Frau Strobl welcomed Lily to her home and, after a meal and a bath, Anneliesa put the child to bed and stayed with her until she fell asleep. On returning to the sitting-room, Albert was pacing the carpet, drink in hand, and Frau Strobl was listening, her head in her hands. 'We must move Lily,' he said. 'I doubt she'll be safe here. They've eyes and ears everywhere.'

'But why would they want her now?' She frowned in bewilderment. 'I'm her sister. She should be with me.'

He nodded. 'We might be worrying needlessly. She won't be a problem for them as she knows nothing.'

The VIOLINIST'S REVENGE

'I hope you're right, but what if you're wrong?'

He lit a cigarette. 'Perhaps we should move on. We can't trust anyone.' He stared at her. 'Who was that with you at the house? Was he the one in the shadows the other day?'

Her smile confirmed it, and she briefly recounted their escape. 'Jan saved me from the concentration camp.'

'He's a brave man,' Albert nodded. 'We can take strength from the actions of others.' He poured another large drink without waiting for Frau Strobl to offer. 'We could have done with his help to get Lily out of the city, but…'

Her tears welled up. 'Yet again, he has risked his life for me. But this time he won't have got away.'

A scream startled her, and she jumped up with a worried look and ran to Lily's bedroom. Eyes closed, her sister was sitting upright, but her screams gave way to a low sobbing before slipping back into a deep sleep.

Frau Strobl offered a sympathetic smile on her return to the sitting-room and pushed a large brandy into her hand. 'You can stay here as long as you wish.'

A knock on the door made them stop and stare at each other, and Albert reached for his gun.

'Who's that?' She led the way and, holding their breath, they listened at the door, but heard nothing.

'Must have been another door,' Albert said. 'We're getting jumpy.'

When they returned to the sitting-room, there was another knock, louder this time. With a finger to his lips, he indicated they should move farther back into the room and, once sure they were out of the line of fire, he opened the door an inch or so but saw no one. A soft cough made him look down at a small boy, wearing clothes two sizes too big and holding a crumpled envelope. 'I'm to give this to Anneliesa,' he lisped through a gap in his teeth, rubbed his nose with the back of a hand and stuck out the other, palm upwards.

'Please give it to me.' Albert took a coin from his pocket. 'I'll make sure she gets it.'

After pocketing the coin, the boy handed it over and turned to leave.

'Who gave you this?'

Worried he might be in trouble, the boy shrank away. 'A man,' he said with a timid smile.

'What's his name? What did he look like?'

'I didn't see him.' The boy was ready to run. 'It was dark.' He edged away. 'But he had a foreign accent.'

47

A dingy city bar. Cigarette smoke drifting in clouds. The few remaining light bulbs revealed a cracked concrete floor and nicotine-stained walls. Sleeves rolled up, displaying unsavoury tattoos, the barman stared at his clients as though willing them to leave, and behind him, a cracked mirror reflected a sad panorama of drinkers.

Jan sat in a corner, his glass of whisky glinting gold in the dim light. Why here? There must be better places to meet. The contact had promised information on Wächter, but who was it, and why had he put himself in danger? Around him, fellow customers nursed drinks for as long as their money lasted and merged with the mundanity of their surroundings.

The bar was ideal for a clandestine meeting, and they would have reconnoitred the area. Easy access and, more importantly, an exit. From the entrance, they could walk straight through the room to a back door leading onto an alleyway. Perfect if planning a quick getaway. He'd chosen a corner table, as sitting anywhere else would have made him vulnerable. Someone could walk through and shoot him without breaking stride.

For the umpteenth time, he scanned the room, concentrating on certain individuals, but no one showed an interest in him. He checked his watch again and decided he'd give it five minutes more before leaving.

The creaking of the swing doors opening paused the conversations, and everyone scrutinised the entry of a man in a pinstriped suit. The newcomer's gaze roamed around the bar before dwelling on him in the corner, and he sauntered through the room to the exit. After studying the alley, he retraced his steps but didn't look at him again.

He relaxed. So that's who he was meeting, but why?

The man exited and returned minutes later, finding a table closer to the door, and pulled out a chair that scraped on the concrete floor. After a few minutes, a smaller man, whose ratlike features hadn't improved with time, entered and kept a hand on the door as he scanned the room with a scowl of distaste, a gold incisor glinting in the dim light like a beacon. As he approached his table, he dismissed the bartender's shout with a wave of a black-gloved hand.

'What's this all about?' Jan said.

An aura of foreboding sat on the man's shoulders like a bird of prey, but this time, they were on equal terms. Klebus sneered as he peeled off his gloves, lining them up on the table, and pulled out a pack of cigarettes and lit up. He exhaled, watching the smoke spiralling to the ceiling.

'What do you want?'

The Nazi chuckled. 'Still ungrateful, Mr Pastorek.' His tone was brusque. 'I saved your life in Prague. But for me, you'd have died in the siege with the rest of your men.'

'Get on with it.'

'We both want Wächter dead.'

'I'm no longer interested in your vendetta with him.'

Klebus sighed. 'Are you sure?'

'What's the point? The war's over.'

'Old scores must be settled, debts paid, otherwise they fester.' He signalled with a finger for his man to get him a drink. 'At one time, you were prepared to kill him.'

'Only because you'd have killed my parents if I hadn't.'

They had shown him a photograph of his father and mother sitting on a couch at their home, flanked by two SS guards, and Klebus was also in the picture. His father hated the Nazis with every

The VIOLINIST'S REVENGE

fibre of his being and in March 1939 watched as they marched into Prague. It was the first time he'd seen his father cry.

'We had a straightforward agreement.' Klebus studied his beer.

'It doesn't matter now.' He scanned the room, wondering how he could get out without being shot 'My parents are dead.'

After their first meeting, he had again met the Nazi, who had been more expansive, almost relaxed, but sweated so much the smell of garlic oozed from his pores. Although their assassination attempt contributed to Heydrich's death, he claimed the General's life could have been saved. The Führer's personal physician, Theodor Morell, had suggested a course of antibiotics, but Himmler refused. Within days, Heydrich died of sepsis.

Why would Himmler overrule an eminent physician? When he got no response, Klebus sighed, his eye flickering and roaming faster around the room. It might have been convenient for the Reichsführer, he suggested. Hitler was in ill health, and in secret, people were comparing likely successors.

While Himmler assumed himself to be the heir apparent, Hitler didn't. He disliked Himmler while he admired the ruthlessness of Heydrich, whom he called the man with the heart of iron. And many others agreed. In the past, Himmler had regarded each Heydrich success as another nail in his coffin. So, the attack was like a gift from the gods for Himmler. There before him in the hospital, his rival lay gravely ill. By refusing him the drugs, he eliminated his biggest threat. And his next step would be manoeuvring one of his men, Wächter, into Heydrich's position in the hierarchy on the back of his outstanding work in solving the Jewish problem.

Himmler and Wächter were friends and, on several occasions, the Reichsführer had stayed with the family in Austria. And they'd spoken before he visited the hospital. With Wächter in place, it made his position more secure and provided a buffer against other contenders.

Klebus had hesitated, checking he understood. This is what you will do, Mr Pastorek, he'd told him. Kill Wächter. Not an easy target. He doesn't flaunt himself like Heydrich. He's well-guarded and lives in the environs of Auschwitz, so that's where you will go.

Until then, he'd kept silent. It's crazy, he'd said. Do you expect me to break into Auschwitz and kill him?

No, not break in, Klebus had answered. You'll be there as a prisoner. But why couldn't his organisation do it? He explained there could be no suggestion of SD involvement. Jan would be the obvious suspect, having evaded capture after the attack on Heydrich. If successful—he had held up the photograph—his parents would be freed.

But that was in the past. What did he want now?

'You and Wächter share the blame for your parents' deaths,' Klebus took delight in reminding him after taking a sip of his drink.

'Not my doing.'

He hadn't intended to escape from the camp. He wanted to get her out of Junger's clutches by acting as a decoy and then hide in the camp until he found an opportunity to kill Wächter and free his parents. But once they started firing at her, he had no option but to get her to safety.

'I gave you a chance to save them, but you failed. I even promoted Heydrich's driver, Schmidt, and placed him in the camp to protect your back. You could've got to Wächter, but you were too interested in the woman. When you found out that Höss planned to kill her, you chose her over your parents. As they were no longer of use, I released them. Subsequently, they were rearrested, which wasn't my order, and interned in the camp.'

'Where they were executed,' he said.

Klebus shrugged. 'Wächter signed their death warrants as they were elderly and unfit for work.'

His guilt was always with him, and the commando knife tucked in his belt dug into his ribs. With both hands, he gripped the table until his knuckles whitened. An image of his parents marching to the gas chambers flashed before him, and the desire to reach across the table and rip open the man's throat was overpowering. He could do it before the bodyguard extracted his gun from its holster.

'I wouldn't try it,' Klebus said, studying his colleague, and settled back in the chair as though he'd won the argument.

'Anneliesa sought to avenge her family and was desperate to find out what happened to her sister,' he said. 'I wanted to help and protect her.'

'Ah, Mr Pastorek, revenge and lust are powerful bedmates.'

'As are greed and ambition. Why are you pursuing Wächter? Why now? It's all over for you. You lost the war.'

'You might think so.' Klebus sighed. 'Admiral Dönitz may have surrendered, but the war's not over. People like me still operate under the radar. You can't stop us, and many of your so-called war criminals escaped punishment as the Americans and the Allies are only too happy to use their unique skills. Our plans are far from dust. Many of our people have simply taken off one cap and replaced it with another for the time being. Our network is in place, ready to rise again one day. We in the SD swore an oath to the Führer, the Fatherland and to Heydrich. He was our leader, and we'll not rest until his murder has been avenged.' He took another drink but didn't enjoy it. 'At the moment, there are many factions in the Party vying for control. Some have escaped to South America through the so-called Ratline, organised by Bishop Hudal, a loyal friend of Wächter's.'

'Why should I care about their madcap plans?'

'I don't expect you to care, Mr Pastorek.' He took another sip of his drink and grimaced as though he wished he hadn't. 'Kill him. And by doing that, you'll help the woman and avenge your parents. And I can assist you.'

'If you know where he is, why don't you do it?'

'Nothing's changed.' As though speaking to a simpleton, Klebus glared at him with his one good eye. 'If we assassinate him, we'll draw attention to our continued existence. If you or the woman kill him, it will be seen as justifiable vengeance.'

It seemed to make sense. 'What stops me from informing whoever wishes to hang you for your crimes?'

'Simple. The woman and child wouldn't survive.' The German finished his drink, wiping his lips with the back of a hand and placed the empty glass on a beer mat. 'Anyway, in all this, I'm, how you say, small beer.' He chuckled as he rose. 'You'll find Wächter there.' He tapped the beer mat. 'Good luck.'

His henchman walked towards him, gesturing to the exit, but he ignored his advice and left the way he had entered.

48

She fidgeted and glanced at the door of the Kärntner Bar. She had been here too long. The message had indicated Jan would meet her here, but where was he? From her table, she had a clear view of the entrance and had watched everyone come and go. Where was he? Should she order another Riesling or leave?

A woman on her own attracts unwanted attention. She'd avoided eye contact with single males, and the bartender studied her as though calculating her intentions. He approached and asked if she'd like another drink. She declined, but as he turned away, she called him back.

'Yes, miss?' he asked, as though knowing what she would say.

'I'm meeting a friend.' She contrived a helpless look. 'Have there been any messages for me?'

'Don't think so.' Absentmindedly, he wiped the table with a cloth. 'What's your name?' He considered her answer before shaking his head.

Was Jan still coming? The note delivered to Frau Strobl's apartment puzzled her, but the signature, a familiar solitary sloping letter J, convinced her of its authenticity. It suggested they meet, and he would explain everything. At first, relieved he was okay, she set off in high spirits, eager to see him again, but now she wondered if he could have survived the gunfight. Wächter's people could have sent the note and even forced Jan to sign it to lure her away from the apartment. Not willing to waste any more time, she jumped up. As she hurried to the door, the bartender shouted across the room, 'Can I order you a cab, miss?' But she waved away the offer, and he shook his head.

A walk will clear my head. But she soon realised that was foolish. There were no streetlights, and clouds rolled across the moon, making a group of drunken soldiers blocking the pavement appear an impassable barrier. She should have listened to the bartender. A woman shouldn't be on the streets alone after dark. A soldier shouted and the others snickered, but she kept her head down. She'd survived much worse. To her relief, they parted, letting her pass, and she increased her pace. If Lily were awake, they'd have much to discuss and plan. She navigated another band of soldiers and night revellers and ruffians and the odd solitary woman, looking for something to happen.

As she approached the apartment block, the entrance was wide open, which was unusual as the concierge worked during the day and, after dark, residents locked the door. Perhaps someone was fetching an item from a car, but the street appeared deserted. She stepped into the foyer and closed the door behind her with a bang that echoed up to the high ceilings. Not wishing to disturb the sleeping, she ignored the clanking elevator and took the stairs.

On reaching their landing, she groped for the light switch, but it didn't come on, and she hesitated before creeping along the corridor to Frau Strobl's apartment. She rummaged in her bag for the key and, with difficulty, found the lock, and the door swung open at her touch. They must have left it ajar, believing she hadn't taken a key.

49

The silence magnified the ticking of the French Ormolu clock on the mantelpiece, but her heart beat louder. Thankfully, the hallway was lit. Before joining Lily, she would bid Frau Strobl and Albert goodnight if he was still here. She tiptoed past Lily's darkened room and knocked on the sitting-room door so as not to interrupt a private conversation but, getting no response, she pushed the door and it creaked open.

In the dim light from a table lamp on the other side of the room, she saw Frau Strobl sitting on a couch and she was leaning to one side on a cushion as if asleep. A sickness rose in her throat, and she swallowed hard. Disoriented, she rubbed her eyes before taking another couple of hesitant steps. The old woman's eyes were open, but unseeing, and from a throat wound, blood had poured down her dress and congealed in her lap.

She checked for a pulse and her touch caused the body to topple sideways and roll off the sofa, and she bent to help her. There was another person in the room. A pair of men's brogues were visible from behind another sofa.

Everything was happening in slow motion as she went over, ready to run if necessary. Surrounded by white feathers, Albert lay beside a cushion that had silenced a gunshot. She vomited and collapsed to her knees. *If I hadn't gone to find Jan, I might have stopped this*, she blamed herself.

'Lily?' she called as she got to her feet, and her heart raced and pounded so hard that it dominated her senses. What had they done to her? To have lost and found her again and now this, and tears overwhelmed her as she ran to her sister's room.

As she pushed open the door, her stomach cramped with fear, and she prepared for what she would find. She reached for the light switch and searched the far side of the bed and every corner of the room and wardrobes, but the room was empty. But was Lily still alive? Where had they taken her? The Wächter house? None of this made sense and, head in hands, she slumped on the bed. Was this the reason she'd been lured away from the apartment, and maybe Jan had walked into a trap, too?

Maybe I should call the police, she thought, but she couldn't muster the courage to re-enter the sitting-room with that sickly smell of death. Struggling to regain her feet, she slipped back like a newborn calf, and all her old fears resurfaced like a grainy black-and-white movie playing on an endless loop. The concentration camp and the stench of death and decay, and Wächter grinning at her. All so vivid, she was convinced he was nearby.

A muffled thud. A creak, a loose floorboard. Had she closed the door to the apartment when she entered? Another creak. Footsteps entering. They're back. Why had she left Lily alone? She should have protected her. What will become of her if she dies now? Ice-cold fingers ran down her spine, and she could almost smell the intruder. Will it be a bullet or a knife? Wächter's won again, and Frau Strobl was just collateral damage in the wrong place at the wrong time. But what has he done with Lily? The questions swirled around her skull. Once, she'd have regarded death as a welcome release from her pain, but now it terrified her as the footsteps grew closer. She picked up a brass candlestick and hefted it in her hand as she crouched behind the door.

Inch by inch, the door opened, and she heard irregular breathing on the other side. Praying the intruder couldn't hear her heart pumping, she pulled back and flattened against the wall. Perhaps they wouldn't realise she was hiding behind the door and leave after glancing into the empty room, but the door kept pushing against her, squeezing the air from her body.

A hand crept around the door, feeling its way towards her and, hoisting the candlestick above her head with both hands, she brought it down with all her strength. Yelping in pain as the door slammed into her, she dropped the weapon.

'Why did you do that?' Jan screamed through gritted teeth and waved his injured arm.

The shock of seeing him alive and realising she'd injured him brought her to her knees.

'Come with me,' he said and pulled her up. 'We must get away before they return, or they'll kill us.'

He bundled her out of the apartment and down the stairs, avoiding the lift which could trap them, and once outside, he took her arm and pulled her along as they ran. 'Keep going,' he encouraged her when she flagged. They sprinted down winding lanes until they were lost, all the time desperately glancing behind, checking if they were being followed. Between deep breaths, he apologised for not meeting her but explained he had information that could lead to Wächter, although she was no longer interested in Wächter, only what had happened to Lily.

When she could go no farther, he found a bench for her to rest, and she sat, head in hands, her eyes empty, as she stared into space. He put an arm around her and she leant into him, her head on his shoulder, and shuddered as waves of grief rippled through her.

PART V

50

The bride's beauty sparkled like a princess in a fairytale. A Hollywood fantasy. Designed by the fashion house, Sorelle Fontana, her gown of embroidered silk and satin and its train was so long that it took four helpers to bundle it through the throng surrounding the Church of Santa Francesca Romana.

Years of Nazi occupation had bullied and abused Rome, bringing the city to her knees. Now she was rising again, putting the grief and humiliation behind her. Everyone wanted to see the Wedding of the Century, and even Pope Pius XII would receive the couple after the wedding. Starved of glamour, the Romans clambered over the city's most venerable ruins for a vantage point where they could view the famous movie star couple, and photographers were in the vanguard, flash bulbs freezing their targets for posterity. And one risked all, balancing on a crane's gantry, swaying fifty feet above the crowd, to capture the moment.

When the bride, Linda Christian, arrived for her marriage to fellow movie star Tyrone Power, the paparazzi surged forward, trapping her, and police eventually extricated her and ushered her into the church decorated with two thousand carnations.

Paolo joined the crowd. Since losing Rachel, he had no interest in weddings and wished only to share his fellow citizens' excitement.

Hollywood's great and not necessarily good had flooded into the

Eternal City to join the dance of decadence, to be seen, to glow, to have love affairs. Ingrid Bergman took a lover in director Roberto Rossellini. Ava Gardner, Sophia Loren and Audrey Hepburn were among those whose beauty promoted the belief that the dark days were banished. And fans gravitated around the Excelsior Hotel, where most of the stars slept and some had sex.

Rome became Hollywood on the Tiber. It was the start of a golden age of neorealism and the Italian film industry was reborn. Famous faces were everywhere. They sipped drinks in the cafes on Via Veneto, shopped on Via Condotti at the bottom of the Spanish Steps, and used the Pantheon, the Forum and the Colosseum as backdrops for their photoshoots.

Paolo recognised Antonio in the crush, holding a cheap camera above his head as he attempted to snatch a photo. With luck, he could sell one to a magazine and it would earn more than his efforts as a *scattini*, taking photos of tourists or soldiers they sent back to families half a world away. Other times, he sold fake American cigarettes and, when those avenues of income dried up, there were other ways of earning a living. Like a brother, Paolo felt responsible for the orphaned youth, although he disapproved of the boy's pursuits. Like many, he was a product of the war.

The golden generation basked in the balmy glow of the spotlights illuminating Roman history. And the aroma of antiquity drifted on the night air, as if the ghosts of ancient citizens walked these streets alongside the luminaries, partying and indulging themselves to excess. Yet a darker world was always within arm's reach. While the stars dined on imported delicacies, most Romans struggled to find food. Antonio inhabited this world, always pulled back down, as if on the end of a chain. At the bottom of the Spanish Steps, where everything and anyone could be bought or sold, was where he spent most of his time amongst the tourists and soldiers.

Alfredo Reinhardt stood and watched from the fringe of the crowd. Also an actor, but unlike the Hollywood set, the only actor in Rome who didn't wish to be recognised or photographed. A tall, striking man, with fair hair and steely blue eyes, he savoured the atmosphere and the animal energy of the crowd reminded him of headier days. He remained until the bride entered the church, then turned away. His shadow stood nearby. Not close, but close enough to protect him.

51

Engrossed in their thoughts, they were silent as the battered yellow Fiat taxi battled through the chaos of Roman roads. The dry air blowing through the open windows aggravated Anneliesa's thirst, and the enormity of the task ahead overwhelmed her. Jan accepted what Klebus had written on the beer mat, but she believed they were on a wild goose chase. She had had Lily back for only a few hours before the killing of Albert and Frau Strobl, and now she doubted her sister could be alive.

Were they pursuing Wächter or being drawn into a trap? If Hudal was organising the escape of Nazi criminals to South America, he could help Wächter escape with his family and, perhaps Lily.

Klebus had provided an address—Vigna Pia, a monastery in Rome and a clerical institute, providing basic accommodation for students and scholars. And Hudal was also rector of the Teutonic College of Santa Maria dell'Anima and believed to be using the monastery to hide his Nazis until they fled the country.

As they pulled up outside a nondescript building, the street was deserted, and it worried him that it was so quiet. Had Klebus set this up, but what would he gain?

The driver drummed his fingers on the steering wheel and asked if they wanted to get out or go elsewhere.

'Okay, this is it,' he said and paid the driver. 'Let's check it out.'

Gloomy and cool, it appeared detached from the hustle of the world outside. A substantial staircase rose into darkness, and they waited and listened, but there were no sounds apart from the creaking of an elderly building.

'This way.' He led her down a long corridor, their footsteps clattering on the stone floors, but no one challenged them as if everyone had departed for the day.

A small, round woman with black hair tied up emerged from a door carrying a bundle of dirty sheets. On seeing them, she shrank back and dropped the bundle. He apologised for surprising her and asked about the monastery's guests, but she shook her head. When he enquired if there were any German guests, she pursed her lips as though she shouldn't be speaking to them.

Anneliesa touched the woman's arm. 'The war separated me from my family,' she said. 'My uncle lived here and it's my only chance of seeing him again.'

His translation relaxed the maid, who grasped her hands and explained that two German gentlemen were staying. One checked out several days ago, but the other was still here.

Footsteps running down the wooden staircase interrupted her. He headed back along the corridor towards the sound, and a figure brushed past him and the door rebounded in his face, knocking him off balance. The man ran towards a car sitting at the kerbside, its engine running. A back door opened, and he jumped in, and the car lurched away with the door flapping open.

'Wächter?' she asked as she followed him out.

He sighed. 'Maybe.'

He flagged down a passing cab. 'Follow that car.' He pointed to the yellow cab stationary at the traffic lights ahead. The driver hesitated, then gripped the steering wheel all the tighter.

'Try to get alongside.' But the cabbie scowled as if he wouldn't be told how to drive his taxi.

'Can you see anything?' She squinted at the car, but the passenger wore a cap pulled down over his eyes and a scarf covered the rest of his face.

He offered the driver more money if he kept the car in sight and the driver responded with a series of manoeuvres, several illegal. They exited a bend and swerved, avoiding an oncoming vehicle, and it flung her across the back seat, her face finishing inches from his, and he grasped her hand. Every time they attempted to draw alongside, another car squeezed between, blocking them. They were heading for the city centre, and the driver became more agitated as the traffic got busier.

At the Via Veneto, the man's taxi slowed and, while still moving, he jumped out and hurried away. Their driver stood on the brakes, and she got out and gave chase while he threw a bundle of lira onto the passenger seat. She was unsure what she would do if she confronted the man, but Jan sprinted past.

Head down, the man was walking fast, weaving in and out of the strolling pedestrians. He didn't look back but knew they were following. As they gained on him, their prey ducked down an alleyway, and he followed in, but she struggled to keep up. Every time she passed a pedestrian, another got in her way. A group of youths blocked her path and, as she darted for a gap, they closed it, laughing and shouting. She had to get past and kicked one in the shins, and as the victim hopped in pain, the others parted in surprise.

Jan was closing in on the man and brought him down with a flying rugby tackle. He tumbled face down and, for a moment, lay still. Catching up, she grabbed the man's cap and scarf and pulled them away. He was bald. 'Who are you?' she demanded.

Fearing he might be slapped, the man cowered and raised a protective hand. 'They offered me money if I got into the car,' he said.

'Who?' He grabbed his collar and pulled him closer.

'I don't know. I did it for the money.' On the verge of crying, the man's face crumpled. 'I don't want any trouble.'

'Why did you run away?' She felt sorry for him.

The man carefully considered his answer. 'The driver checked me out in his mirror and said we were being followed by your taxi. And I realised I was doing something wrong. So when I got out of the car, I panicked and ran.'

'Who paid you?'

'Never seen him before.' He looked around and reached for his hat. 'I've been there only one night.'

Jan let go of him and kicked the wall in frustration.

'He had a foreign accent.' The man mustered a diffident smile. 'He might have been German.'

52

The Spanish Steps flowing from Trinita dei Monti, the French church of almost white travertine stone, resembled a human staircase, with visitors continually climbing and descending. And many sat with a lover, often for hours, amongst the displays of pink and purple azaleas.

Nearby, Paolo sat at a table under an umbrella at a cafe on the edge of Piazza di Spagna. With him was Antonio, who was looking for wealthy targets. A waiter placed a jug of water and a basket of bread before them and waited for their orders, but he waved him away. He intended to speak to the boy and was in no mood for eating or listening to his friend's inane chatter.

Antonio wanted to impress him with the new gold bracelet dangling from his wrist, different from the gifts he usually received and meretriciously expensive and most likely from one of his new friends, who these days were predominantly American soldiers.

Seeing only disinterest in his eyes, Antonio crossed his legs and pouted. 'You're jealous because no one gives you gifts.' He waved his wrist in his face. 'Anyway, not like this.'

He ignored that. He enjoyed Antonio's company but disapproved of his behaviour. One day, the boy would realise they were merely dalliances and he'd spend the rest of his life regretting them.

'Shut up, Tony,' he slammed a hand on the table, rocking the glasses, 'and listen.'

The VIOLINIST'S REVENGE

'Only if you stop acting like a shit.' Antonio called for an expensive cocktail as he wouldn't have to pay for it and asked if he wanted one, but got no answer.

As his friend slurped his drink with one eye fixed on potential prospects, Paolo sighed. Why confide in him? But he must speak to someone and he was a good sounding board and the secret was burning through him. What had happened earlier made him question everything he believed in and now he was jumping at shadows. For all his silliness, Antonio listened, and his mix of ignorance and streetwise cunning often provided surprising answers, but if he shared his story, would he become a target, too?

As an employee of the Vatican, he must never divulge anything that happened in the city. But after losing Rachel, he questioned the Catholic Church and his religion, believing it was simply a business.

When he started work on the bottom rung, his mother believed him fortunate to have such a job. Every day you're closer to God, she would say. At first, his eagerness to learn impressed his superiors, and he excelled. Good-looking with an easy grin and dark wavy hair, he was popular in a place where the unusual proclivities of many were not appreciated outside the city.

Eventually, he was appointed as a clerk in the Camerlengo's department. The Pope's right-hand man and chamberlain controlled the finances of the Church and its business. Conscientious and hardworking, he graduated to work as a liaison to the Roman Curia.

Everything had been about forging a life with Rachel. Every day after work, she walked from her family home off Via Arenula and they met under the trees at Ponte Fabricio nearby, known to the Romans as the Bridge of the Jews. Although her parents disapproved of her seeing a Catholic boy, especially one working in the Vatican, they'd walk hand in hand across Tiber Island into Trastevere and find a quiet café and plan their future. Rachel was in demand as an accordionist and played at weddings, and often he'd accompany her and they'd dream of their own.

In 1943, the Nazis had demanded fifty kilos of gold from the Jewish community, or all family heads would be deported. A month later, they sealed off the Jewish ghetto, rounded up more than a thousand Jews and loaded them onto trains at Tiburtina

Station for deportation to Auschwitz. Rachel and her family were among them.

Pope Pius XII's meetings with Hitler's representatives were no secret. His supporters claimed the Holy Father was merely protecting the Church and its priests and followers in Germany. However, many in the Vatican were opponents of the Jewish faith and even Bishop Hudal was a self-declared Nazi.

His pleas to the Camerlengo's secretary for help were met with silence. Clerics brushed him off and suggested there were plenty more girls in Rome to pursue. But all he wanted was to find out what had happened to her, and his work suffered. And colleagues covered for him, although he doubted whether he could continue working there. After Rachel's disappearance, his two worlds drifted apart like planets in an expanding universe. Every time the Pope failed to condemn Hitler's mass murder of Jews, it reminded him of Rachel and burned like a red-hot poker twisting in his guts. Once he accepted he'd lost Rachel, it reinforced his desire to prove she and her family had existed. His disappointment with his church developed into anger, and instead of leaving a job he now detested, he believed he could do more to undermine the Church's authority if he stayed. He worked closely with Bishop Hudal's office, especially his secretary, and forged a relationship with several newspapers eager to receive information the Church preferred to keep secret.

'I have a story to tell you.' He reached over and placed a hand on Antonio's arm. 'It's important you listen until I'm finished.'

Such was the intensity of his friend's stare, Antonio's blood ran cold.

53

I was researching a project to be presented to the Camerlengo, Paolo told Antonio. They said it was an honour that I was given such a task.

I'm so immersed in my work in the library—not the main library, but the Apostolic Archive that houses all our secrets—I lose touch with the world around me, not realising how long I'd been there and how dark it had become outside. I didn't even notice the lights coming on. I'd found a quiet corner at a desk, allowing me to spread out my papers without being disturbed. When needed, I'd fetch another document and they piled up around me like a wall. The longer I worked, the more my concentration slipped, but I was determined to finish it.

Suddenly, I came to with a start. Must have nodded off. I'm yawning and stretching and checking my watch, wondering if I can slip away and finish it tomorrow, then I hear two people talking as though not wanting to be overheard. At first, it was a mumble, but you know how it is. If you concentrate, you can pick up a few words. The fact that they were speaking almost in a whisper gets my interest, and I recognise the voice of a guy who works as a clerk for one of Bishop Hudal's people. The other, a rougher voice, made the odd comment but was doing most of the listening. The clerk's man was giving the orders. It wasn't so much that it was hushed. Most people talk like that in a library, but it was their tone. Conspiratorial as if sharing a secret. The quieter they talk, the harder you strive to hear. It's only natural. Couldn't make out most of it. They thought they were alone. Well, they didn't notice me behind my wall of documents. I lowered my head until it was almost resting on the desk and tried to control my breathing. I feared they'd think I was eavesdropping.

The package is there, says the clerk.

I imagined the other man leaning in to hear. Where, he demands.

One of them mentioned a location. Couldn't make it out, but said close to the Vatican. Their voices became clearer and I'm thinking they've moved closer. He says we must be careful. No mistakes or there'll be serious implications. The rougher voice asks why they were moved. The answer mentioned their location being discovered by people looking for revenge. The clerk stresses they're not important, but if the information is revealed, Government agencies, the Americans, the British... I didn't hear the rest.

The rougher voice asks what's required of him.

You must discourage them, says the clerk, within reason, of course.

The other guy seems pleased.

Although the library is warm, I'm shivering and terrified that a slip, a rustle of papers, will give me away. Their voices are lower now and I'm struggling to hear.

Are you listening, Tony? This is important. If they find out about me, it'll be painful in more ways than one and I'll never work again in Rome. And the other guy's bad news.

I've almost slipped to the floor now and my heart's pounding and I want to run, but I daren't move as my legs are cramping, and I stop myself from crying out in pain.

The conversation fades and a door closes, but I wait until I'm sure I'm alone. Pulling myself up inch by inch, I creep away from the desk, glancing back, hoping my hiding place was as good as I hoped. My papers are spread over the desk, and I scoop them up and put them back into their folders. Now I must get away without being seen, so I head for a fire door at the back, but it won't open.

If they see me, they'll suspect I heard everything and know what they're planning. I'm sweating like a pig as I inch along the wall.

The VIOLINIST'S REVENGE

When I reach the entrance, I pause before stepping out into the fresh air. I hear the voices again, this time speaking normally, and I pull back into the building. My heart's racing and I'm panicking. You know what it's like when you want to run and get as far away as possible. Others are walking past. Perhaps I could join them. There's safety in numbers. About twenty yards away, the clerk is engaged in an animated conversation with a heavy-looking guy dressed in a brown cloak, a rope belt knotted three times at the waist like those Franciscan monks. I know who he is. Believe me, you don't mess with his kind. The cloak's cowl is down and he's got this shaven head on muscular shoulders. No neck. Hands as large as a leg of lamb and gold rings on every finger. His eyes are black and cold and I'm thinking, Christ, he's looking at me.

Didn't know what I should do. I'm shit scared and try to keep out of sight and wait, willing them to leave. The clerk makes his way back towards his office while the monk heads across St Peter's Square towards my house. I'm desperate to get away and I consider going the opposite way, but the Bishop's man might turn around and recognise me, so I head for home and try to appear like any other person out walking.

I'm convincing myself there's a rational reason for all this. Go to a bar, I tell myself. Have a drink. Relax. Forget about it. None of my business. The guy doesn't know me. But I've heard of him. Goes by the name of Enrico and he's a mad bastard. He's not a monk but wears the outfit, so he blends in. They say his eyes burn like coals on the blackest of nights and once he tore open a victim's chest and pulled out his heart while it was still beating.

Don't laugh, Tony, this is no joke.

Anyway, the monk isn't in a hurry. He's almost sauntering as if enjoying a stroll. Then, he stops to refresh his cigarette and lights up, turning and checking his surroundings and I dive into a doorway. We cross the square and, with every step, I feel even more guilty. Maybe he'll go off and I can go straight home and lock the door. But he doesn't. What if he knows I'm following and wants to see where I live? But then he stops at a house and raps on the door.

I'm craning to see without looking too obvious. The door opens enough to let out a crack of light. The monk is looking up and down the street. I squeeze into the brickwork. He enters the house and I hurry past, desperate to get home. There's an alleyway running down the side of the house, leading to a small courtyard at the back. A group of tourists are approaching, led by their guide, so I step out of their way and into the alleyway.

Why did I do it? Maybe it was all innocent, yet I couldn't get their words out of my head.

The darkness makes me bolder. The only light came from a lamp at the mouth of the alleyway and I can't be seen in the shadows. I move farther down and, as I enter the courtyard, I barge into one of those metal dustbins, knocking off the lid. It makes a hell of a noise and I freeze and my knees are trembling. This is crazy. I'm sweating so much that my shirt collar's damp and making me itch.

I hear Enrico's voice through an open window. Can't make out what he's saying, so I inch forward. He's talking to two men. An older guy with a full head of fair hair is sitting at a kitchen table with a bottle of red wine and two glasses in front of him. Standing behind him is a tall, younger man, blond and grey-eyed. His face is like stone. He's got a pistol on his hip and keeps his hand on it. Enrico is listening to the older man.

Couldn't hear much and couldn't get any closer without being discovered. The words were a jumble. 'Hiding' and the 'Vatican'. They sounded German.

Pay attention, Tony. This is the important part.

Enrico is listening, then says something like 'guarding you'. And then a name, General Wächter, I think.

Then the older guy loses it. I can hear it because he's now shouting. Never mention my name again, he says, in Rome, I'm known as Alfredo Reinhardt. Enrico says nothing and the younger guy steps forward and Wächter restrains him.

By now, I'm terrified. Why is Enrico hiding a couple of Germans and are they linked to Hudal? I'm feeling sick and I'm remembering Rachel and what the Nazi pigs did to her. You remember her sweet smile, Tony, and how she always had time for everyone? The day the Nazis rounded up her people was the worst of my life. Never saw her again and it took me years to find out they'd all died in the concentration camp.

After that, they got friendlier and drank beer together. I didn't know what I should do. If I hung around and got caught, it would be the end of me. What could I do?

It's wrong, but I can't tell anyone in the Vatican. It's a viper's nest. Step on one and the rest will turn on you. They wouldn't believe me and wouldn't trust me if I were eavesdropping on their conversations. The police would look the other way. And if Enrico and those Germans found out, I'd be in big danger and I'm too young to die.

54

Enrico had stepped out into the courtyard for a smoke and to plan a strategy for protecting the Germans. His presence intimidated most, but those Nazis were different. The way the younger German moved, he was a trained killer, and the older man, an aristocrat, was used to giving orders, not taking them. He would need to be wary of them.

Although he could handle it, he'd been given a poisoned chalice. Not only must he protect their lives, but he had to keep them out of the Allies' hands, and if it went wrong, it would be his neck on the line. He had no time for politics, preferring action rather than words, using his fists first and leaving negotiations to others, but like an animal, he had an instinctive sense of danger.

Footsteps interrupted his thoughts. Someone was picking their way, trying not to make a sound. He tensed for action and dropped the cigarette. The courtyard was clear, and he crept up the alleyway and out onto the street, but saw no one in either direction. As he turned away, a shadow slipped around the corner. Perhaps it was innocent, but he couldn't chance it, and they might have overheard. If so, who was it? Rome teemed with spooks. The Americans, British, Russians, and even the Italians were searching for fleeing war criminals and any suggestion that the men back in the house were being shielded by those related to the Vatican would be catastrophic for

The VIOLINIST'S REVENGE

everyone concerned. He took a deep breath before rounding the corner.

Ahead, a person was walking quickly and, as they crossed Ponte Cavour, the sweep of the Tiber curving away to Ponte Umberto, he had a clear view of his prey. A young man, looking like an office worker, appeared unaware he was being followed. Why would he spy on the Germans? He followed him down Via dei Condotti and stopped every so often to gaze in a shop window. Wearing his monk's cloak, he became a part of the furniture here. The young man turned left before the Spanish Steps, crossed Piazza di Spagna and joined a youth at a table outside a cafe.

He was relieved, but disappointed he'd wasted his time. The young man hadn't reported to anyone and he considered returning to the house, but his instinct told him to wait. If his prey told the youth, he'd have two to deal with.

He found a table on the other side of the cafe from where he could observe them without being seen. Everything was under control. His efficiency was legendary. Every large organisation needed someone like him. One who gets the job done without troubling their bosses with messy details. One who can turn an enemy into a useful supplicant or silence them.

ANTONIO TOOK one of his cigarettes and lit it and watched the match burn down, before placing another in his pocket. As he listened to his friend's story, his mouth dropped open and his eyes never left Paolo's as he fiddled with the gold bracelet.

When Paolo finished, they sat in silence for several minutes before Antonio gave a nervous laugh. 'Crazy, just crazy.' He flung an arm across the top of an adjoining chair to appear relaxed. 'Your imagination is running wild.' He glanced nervously about. 'Things like that don't happen here, especially not in the Vatican.' He hesitated, wide-eyed. 'Do they?'

Relieved to have unburdened himself, Paolo pulled his chair closer. 'I know what I saw. They were Germans and I can imagine them in uniform, but I don't know who they are. They must be important if they're being protected. Maybe war criminals. I've no idea.'

As though about to share a secret, Antonio opened his mouth but then clamped his lips tight.

Paolo recognised the look. 'Come on, Tony, out with it. Now's not the time for secrets.'

'My friend—'

'The American?'

Antonio rattled his bracelet.

'The Captain?' He disapproved of his dalliances.

'He tells me lots of things.' Antonio paused. 'Don't know why because I'm not interested.'

'Maybe he thinks it impresses you?'

'Doubt it,' Antonio replied. 'I think he wants to get things off his chest and I guess I'm the only one he can talk to.'

He urged him to get on with it.

'Before Butch came to Rome, he and his men were searching for a German general in the mountains near Salzburg,' Antonio continued. 'Apparently, he was wanted for war crimes. Had the deaths of about half a million Jews on his conscience.' He hesitated, as though trying to comprehend the enormity of it.

'Go on.' He grabbed his arm.

'They didn't find him, and he felt a failure. He believes the guy's in Italy and Nazi criminals are escaping by boat to South America.' He coughed. 'It's called the Ratline and a Catholic bishop is involved.'

'Bishop Hudal?'

'Might be.' Antonio scowled. 'He didn't mention names. We don't have much time together, so we don't waste it by talking about Germans.'

By the time he returned home, Paolo was convinced it wasn't his imagination. He poured a large glass of Barolo and replayed his meeting with Antonio. The men were Germans and, considering the allegiances in Vatican City, they might be Nazis. He flicked the top of the glass with a finger and the chime echoed around the room and added to his unease. Had he put Tony at risk by sharing his story? He extinguished all lights and sat with his back to the wall and felt safer in the darkness. Antonio liked to gossip, but none of this would interest his acquaintances. Maybe I should alert my newspaper contacts, he thought, but what could they do without more facts? He found it impossible to sit still and, as he crossed the living-room, a photograph in a silver frame caught his eye. Even in the gloom, the girl's self-conscious smile brightened the darkness. A beauty that wouldn't die. Sadness and anger welled up in him. He'd never forget Rachel.

He shouldn't have burdened Tony with his story. He often told him stuff about his work in the Vatican, confident it wouldn't go further because Tony regarded any mention of work as boring. Even if unreliable, he was still his best friend. Swayed by trinkets, he was a liability after a drink or two, but by now he'd have forgotten everything he'd told him.

He stopped in his tracks. If he went to the Americans claiming Nazis were hiding in the Vatican, they'd kick him out. But Tony could go straight to his captain.

55

Where was Klebus when you needed him? In the Vienna bar, the German had written the address of Wächter's hideout in Rome on the beer mat, knowing he would go after him. But if Klebus knew, he could also be here. If Jan had come alone, Anneliesa wouldn't be in danger, and her sister being involved complicated matters. Somewhere in this beehive of a city, Wächter was hiding.

As they walked up Via Veneto towards the Borghese Gardens, she took his arm and was more relaxed than he'd seen her. None of this was anybody's fault, but in quieter moments, she exuded guilt. They had discussed all eventualities. The worst being that Lily might be dead, or Wächter had fled the country and taken her with him.

To escape the confines of their hotel room, which had become claustrophobic as they bounced possibilities off each other, he encouraged her to go out for dinner, although she insisted she had no appetite. But as they strolled, she warmed to the idea. Anticipating danger, his eyes swept the area. A movement in a doorway, raised voices. A figure running would put him on edge. Now they could be targets, and he was fearful for her safety.

Under the old city walls at a table at Harry's Bar, he got her to eat, and a few glasses of Barolo relaxed her. He avoided talking about Wächter and Lily and attempted to distract her by commenting on the nightlife around them.

In party mood, the Romans were determined to put the privations of the occupation behind them, yet the city appeared to be still at war. Foreign soldiers in uniform were a reminder of what they had endured while in the darkness, spies filled the political vacuum. To America's dismay, Italy, freed from the clutches of one oppressor, could fall into the arms of another. Polls for upcoming elections showed the Communists were the likely winners, and America's agents were working to prevent that. For the black marketeers, it was business as usual and they were making deals around the clock. Women of all classes and ages connived to ensure their futures were secure, the arm that had been around a Nazi, now holding close an American. Former sworn enemies embraced and climbed into bed together. The new normal was no more stable than grains of sand in a tornado and trust lasted as long as it took to say the word. And amongst this, a man responsible for the deaths of hundreds of thousands was protected by those who should be above reproach.

For a city that had survived wars and political intrigue over thousands of years, this was but a blip and eternity drifted on the night air ruffling the tablecloths around which sat men and women who barely knew each other. She watched them drinking, chatting and laughing, amazed they could have forgotten the war she still endured. So different from Vienna, where the ruins were the people.

Over their meal, he refrained from discussing the task facing them. Where in a city like this could you find a man who didn't want to be found? He could be anywhere, perhaps hiding in plain sight. Somewhere they wouldn't expect a Nazi war criminal to hide. If the Austrian Bishop was helping him, he would be well protected, and their appearance at Vigna Pia had only alerted them to expediting his departure from the country.

Exercise would clear their heads and, encouraged by the surrounding grandeur, they walked farther than intended, crossing the Tiber and strolling along the riverside through the restaurants and stalls under a canopy of trees. As the magnificence of Castel Sant'Angelo loomed out of the night before them, drawing them onto St Peter's Square, he looked sideways at Anneliesa, in awe of the history around her. On entering the square, they made for the red granite obelisk in the centre and she slumped at its base, her face consumed by a mixture of conflicting emotions.

'It's hopeless, isn't it?' She pushed back her hair with a sigh. 'We might as well be looking for a ghost. By now, he's probably escaped and taken Lily with him.' She spread her arms wide, then dropped them by her side in resignation.

Why would Wächter want Lily? She would only slow him down.

'If there is a Ratline and Bishop Hudal is involved,' he said. 'It gives us a starting point.'

A light returned to her eyes. 'If we can't find Wächter and his people, let them find us. The best way to discover who set a trap is by walking into it.'

'It would get us killed.'

'If I spoke to the Bishop,' she persisted. 'I might persuade him we're not interested in Wächter and all we want is Lily.'

'And how would you do that?'

'He has an office here in Rome. I can contact them.'

He looked at the ground. 'They'll treat you as a crank and you won't get near him.'

'No. I know him, or at least he knew my father. We went to the same church in Vienna and he saw me play at the Metropole.'

'Even if he knows you, he won't say anything about Wächter.'

'I don't care.' She almost shouted. 'If they give me Lily, they can do whatever they want with the Germans.' She sprang to her feet and walked off, wheeling around, her arms wide, embracing the amazing panorama.

From across the square, the man watched the youth, hovering around a group of tourists, obviously looking for a bag to snatch, a pocket to pick.

And Jan had spotted him, too, lurking nearby, close enough to hear their conversation.

'Am I being stupid, Jan?' Her eyes were moist, and her mouth turned down in despair. 'How simple am I to think we'd find Wächter? Those Germans might be anywhere. If I continue, I'll put your life at risk, too.'

'Go away,' he warned the youth who was standing too close, and he put a protective arm around her.

'I can help you,' the youth said.

'We don't need a guide.'

The VIOLINIST'S REVENGE

'You mentioned Wächter and Germans—'

'What did you say?' Her heart jumped and she swung around, pulling Jan with her.

Fearing for her safety, he stepped between them.

'You're looking for Wächter here in Rome?' the boy said.

'What are you selling?'

'I know where Wächter is. Two Germans are hiding near here.' In sales mode, Antonio tried to embellish their value. 'Dangerous men.' His eyes locked onto them as he waited for a reaction.

'Clear off,' he warned him again.

But she smiled at the youth. 'He might have information.'

When he pulled her away, she resisted. 'Let me hear what he has to say.'

'They'll tell you anything if you pay them enough.'

'Maybe, but what have we to lose?'

Antonio stepped forward. 'The Vatican is protecting two Germans near here.' The boy bit his tongue, fearing he'd said too much, but he had their attention. 'My friend Paolo can lead you there.'

'How's he involved?'

'He works in the Vatican and has seen them. One who looks like a soldier and an older man.'

He was convinced it was a ruse to get their interest and lead them to where his accomplices would mug them.

'Paolo saw the Germans,' Antonio said. 'They're the ones you're after. The older man became angry when addressed as General Wächter because he was using another name.'

'Where are they?' Her eyes widened and she puffed out her cheeks, sending white clouds billowing around her face.

Antonio beckoned for them to follow and walked away, but then hesitated.

A shapeless mass barged into them, knocking her to the ground, and Jan sprang to her aid, believing the attacker to be the youth's accomplice. The man, dressed in a monk's habit, showed no interest in them, punching Antonio hard on the chin, and the youth collapsed like a demolished building. Before he hit the ground, the attacker pulled him back onto his feet and dragged him away.

He grabbed the monk around the neck, but was pushed away.

Surprised by the man's strength, he hesitated. A heavy body without a neck, like a bull and muscular tattooed forearms. Greasy black hair pulled back from his forehead and tied in a ponytail and gold glinting on his hands. A glancing blow knocked him off balance, and he staggered. Intent on finishing him, the monk moved in.

He readied for the incoming blow. Instead, the monk halted and put a hand to his neck. The heel of Anneliesa's shoe had pierced the skin, and blood spurted out of the wound, and a look of surprise rather than pain rippled across the man's face.

He expected another attack, but the monk scowled at him and turned away.

The youth mumbled through his tears, 'Enrico.'

'Okay, Enrico, take it easy.' She rushed over. 'Are you hurt?'

'I'm not Enrico. My name's Antonio. He's Enrico.' He pointed after the departing monk.

'The priest?'

'A priest of the Devil.'

'Why attack you? What have you done?'

'I told you,' Antonio said. 'My friend Paolo saw your Germans with him.' Fear made his face appear even more vulnerable. 'I must warn Paolo he's in danger.'

As they helped him up, they exchanged worried glances. 'We'll come with you,' Jan said.

If Paolo had information about the Germans, they must meet him.

'No.' The boy shrank away, brushing them off. 'I'll go alone.'

'Enrico will come after you again,' he said. 'You won't be safe. We can protect you.'

Although there was doubt in his eyes, he nodded.

Away from the square, the side streets narrowed, and the lighting was patchy, and they let Antonio lead. He became more anxious as they entered a labyrinth of lanes. Could he be lying to lure them away from the well-lit and crowded streets, then be ambushed and robbed or worse?

As they approached the dark doorway to a small house, the boy's pace quickened, and they hung back. 'In here,' Antonio said. 'Up the stairs.' He beckoned them forward.

The VIOLINIST'S REVENGE

Feet pounding on the wooden steps, Antonio ran ahead. Then silence.

Together, they held their breaths. Like a siren winding up, it started as a low wail until it reached a crescendo. He took two steps at a time and found a sobbing Antonio slumped to his knees. Paolo, he presumed, lay on a couch soaked in blood, his mouth wide open as if interrupted in mid-speech. There was no pulse, but the body was still warm, suggesting he had been killed not long before they arrived.

Ashen-faced, the youth trembled, not just for Paolo, but also for himself. Paolo's story wasn't the stuff of fantasy, and if Enrico had done this to his friend, he'd be next. Fear ageing his face, Antonio wailed, 'He's coming for me and no one can stop him.'

'Is this connected with Wächter?' she asked.

Antonio nodded.

'Is Enrico one of his protectors?' he said. 'Where are they hiding them?'

The youth appeared reluctant to give up his secret, but with his friend dead, he had no option. 'All I know is what Paolo told me, but I'm sure I can find it.'

'Near here?'

'Not far.' Antonio backed away. 'But there's no way I'm going there.'

She stepped forward to console him. 'We understand. You must leave the city, and we can help you.'

'I won't be safe anywhere,' Antonio said. 'The Church has a long reach.' He slumped in a seat, then brightened. With wide-open eyes, he gave a secretive smile that reminded her of her brother. 'I know where I'll be safe. Enrico won't dare look for me there.'

'Where?' she said.

'I have a friend.' Antonio held her gaze for a moment. 'A special friend. He'll protect me.'

She waited for an explanation.

'He's a Yank,' Antonio boasted. 'A captain in the army over here, searching for Nazis. I'll tell him about them in exchange for my safety. If they capture the Germans, maybe he'll take me to America.'

Telling the Americans would complicate matters. Wächter must pay for his crimes, but it would be taken out of their hands and many Nazis, whose skills were useful to the Allies, escaped punishment and were awarded new identities and given jobs. Even if they stood trial, a clever lawyer could get their sentence commuted to a prison term. Wächter didn't deserve to live a day longer. And what would happen to Lily? She glanced at Jan, but couldn't tell if he thought the same.

'You're in shock.' He put an arm around the shivering youth's shoulders. 'We'll get you food and drink and work out what to do next.'

They found a rundown cafe hidden away in a side street, took a table outside and watched Antonio devour two bowls of minestrone and a loaf of bread.

'If you tell your American friend about this, it will be tied up in red tape,' he said. 'Especially if influential members of the Church are protecting him. The Americans can't afford an international incident, and you'd still be in danger from Enrico.'

But the youth didn't want to believe it.

'He'll never take you to America,' he said. 'And you'll be on your own again.'

Seeing the disappointment on Antonio's face, she flashed him a warning look.

'You'll be back on the streets and fair game for Enrico,' he continued. 'Telling your friend only increases your danger.'

She reached forward and placed a hand on the boy's shoulder. 'We'll keep you safe,' she whispered, staring deep into his eyes.

'What can you do?'

'We can stop them,' he said, but Anneliesa wouldn't meet his gaze.

But the youth was tougher than he'd imagined and unconvinced. After another cup of coffee, Antonio asked to visit the bathroom.

Unwilling to share their thoughts, they sat in silence. If the US Army arrested Wächter, they'd try him in the courts and hang him if a cyanide capsule wasn't smuggled into his cell. But that wouldn't be enough. Wächter should endure the suffering of thousands in the camps and live with a death sentence, not knowing how and when it would come. Only then might they move on.

The VIOLINIST'S REVENGE

The boy was taking too long.

'I'll check him out.' He headed down a dark corridor leading to a single toilet. As he knocked, the door swung open. A gust of hot air wafted through the open window, and he climbed onto the toilet bowl and peered out onto a narrow alleyway.

She was so engrossed in a discarded newspaper, she didn't notice his return, but he coughed, and his grimace alerted her. 'Don't tell me you've lost him,' she said.

He nodded. 'We must get to him before Enrico does, or we'll never find Lily.'

A newspaper was spread out before her on the table and she pointed to a photograph as he sat beside her, craning his neck to see what had grabbed her attention. 'Let me contact him first,' she said. 'It's our only chance.'

He raised an eyebrow.

'There he is.' She jabbed a finger at the grainy image of a priest. 'That's Bishop Hudal and he's in Rome now.'

He raised his head, but she was already out of her seat and striding to the cafe's exit.

56

Feet up on a desk, Captain Butch Hadron stretched back in his chair. 'Rome's undoubtedly a magnificent city, but I've had my fill of pasta and wine,' he told his sergeant. 'Must get back home to Milwaukee. Walk along the riverside. Play pool and have an ice-cold Miller and a large burger. And listen to Louis Jordan's cool saxophone at Lakota's.'

The shrill ring of the phone startled him.

'A boy by the name of Antonio's asking to see you, sir.' He imagined the soldier questioning how the boy got hold of his name.

'What in the hell does he want?'

'He's rambling,' the soldier said. 'Talking about Nazis and information for your ears only.'

'Why me?'

'Should I send him packing, sir?'

'What else did he say?'

'It doesn't make sense. Sorry, I troubled you. I'll get rid of him.'

'Yes, do that,' he said. 'But where did he get my name?'

He replaced the phone and lit up a Lucky Strike. He'd told Tony never to come to his office, but information about Nazis intrigued him and, if Tony had broken their rules, it must be important. He didn't want the boy speaking to his men any longer than necessary. He picked up the phone. 'Bring him here.'

'Are you sure, sir?'

The VIOLINIST'S REVENGE

'Yes.'

Within minutes, there was a rap on the door and Antonio was ushered in with a sly grin, which didn't go unnoticed by the Sergeant. Nervous and gulping for air, he looked around.

'Leave this to me, Sergeant,' Hadron said.

The story was interesting but unbelievable, and he must be careful. Tony had a track record for telling lies, which made him question what he would gain from it, although his fear appeared genuine. He made him repeat the story and asked for more detail, trying to catch him out, but couldn't. Antonio told him everything, except for the fact that Jan and Anneliesa were with him when he found the body, believing it would dilute his ownership of the information.

He listened, his eyes clouded with suspicion, and Antonio shrank from his gaze as if at the mercy of a hunter. The boy hadn't seen him like this before, and the more he was questioned, the more he turned inwards.

Any trust they shared was evaporating, but the boy had nowhere to go. He was his only hope. Hadron offered the youth a cigarette, and Antonio took it with trembling hands. There was one way to confirm his story. He flung open his door and called for the Sergeant. 'Keep him here until I return. He has very important information.' And as an afterthought, 'Give him breakfast. Looks like he needs it.' As another soldier led the boy away, he pulled the Sergeant aside. 'Don't let him out of your sight.'

Antonio's information put him in a difficult position. He couldn't inform his superiors without confirmation and questions would follow about his relationship with the boy. If he ignored it and anything happened to Tony, the guilt would stay with him forever. It required good judgement. Accepting rumours as fact would harm any chance of promotion. Too many colleagues had been shot down in flames over a flight of fancy. Tony's story was fantastical, and making false accusations would have serious repercussions. Without proof, the response from his commanding officer would be cautious. Vatican City was a sovereign state. American soldiers barging into the city would be tantamount to an invasion. Instead of returning home in glory, they'd lock him away for the rest of his days. He paced his office. Until he had proof, he couldn't involve his men. But if it was as Tony claimed, it might be worth the risk and a deserved reward for his suffering in the numbing cold of the Austrian Alps, searching for Wächter and his sidekick. If only Tony had the address where the Nazis were hiding, but Paolo hadn't given it to him. Or was Tony withholding it as insurance? Everything about the boy was transactional—if you give me this, I'll give you that.

He had Paolo's address and would check the location and, if he found the body, part of Tony's story would stack up. Then he'd hand the case over to the Italian police. First, he must change. Wearing an American uniform would attract interest. After checking on Tony, ensconced in the canteen, regaling a couple of soldiers with his exploits and informing them of the best places to satisfy their desires, he made his way back to his billet and changed into street clothes.

As he needed to be careful, a taxi dropped him off a street away from Paolo's home. The Nazis and their people could still be in the area. The possibility that Tony was setting him up for blackmail crossed his mind, but he'd seen genuine fear in the boy's eyes.

No one gave him a second glance. Under his jacket, the presence of his Colt 1911 pistol reassured him and, as he approached the house, he dropped to one knee as if to tie his shoelace. At any minute, he expected to be accosted, but he went unchallenged.

As he raised a fist to knock, the door swung open. If Tony had fled in a panic, he wouldn't have closed it behind him. Or was somebody inside? Taking a deep breath, he stepped in and listened. Nothing. Steps led up a narrow stairway to the main floor of Paolo's apartment, where Tony claimed he'd found his friend's body. The stairs creaked beneath him and he paused on each step, expecting a reaction, then continued, wincing every time he made a sound. Near the top, he quickened his pace. The room was in darkness. He crept over to the window, pulled open the shutters and turned around, his teeth clamped together. Tony said the body had been lying on a couch. There was a couch, but no body and no sign of blood. Perhaps Paolo had crawled into another room? Three doors led off the main room. A kitchen and a bathroom yielded nothing, and a small bedroom hadn't been slept in.

Back in the main living space, he slumped on the sofa, cursing Tony, yet relieved he'd avoided a tricky situation. Once again, he'd been fooled by the boy's lies, but what would he gain from it, and what was he telling them back at HQ? He'd be the butt of his men's jokes and worse if his superiors learned of it. He must limit the damage and get the boy out of there and he'd end their relationship, once and for all.

As he rose, something on the floor beneath the window glinted in the morning sunlight. He picked up a fragment of broken glass with traces of what might be blood. Perhaps Paolo had trodden on it and cut his foot and gone for medical help. He placed it out of harm's way on a table. As he turned, he stumbled over the corner of a large floor rug and, attempting to straighten it, lifted it and turned it back.

He dropped the rug and reached for his pistol. The floor beneath was stained. Red wine from the glass Paolo had broken? He prodded it, then licked his finger. Blood. But cutting a foot on a glass wouldn't have caused this much. It was more like the contents of a body, and now flies were targeting it.

Tony hadn't lied this time. The killer must have returned to dispose of the evidence, and his friend would be next.

57

Every time Anneliesa went to the window, she banged her knees on the bed that dominated their hotel room. And when she looked out, she couldn't avoid seeing a young couple rowing in an apartment across the way. The woman, suspecting she was spying on them, scowled and pulled down the blind. She continued pacing the room, not improving the already threadbare carpet, and returned to the window and peered down on the lane below. It was impossible to identify anything in the shadows. Where's Jan?

Several times she approached the telephone, willing it to ring. What could she do, cooped up here, and the waiting only increased her anxiety? He'd gone looking for Antonio, the key to everything, knowing Wächter's hideout and perhaps where Lily was being held prisoner. But the longer they waited, the greater the possibility the youth might alert the Americans, and she'd lose any chance of finding her sister.

He had emphasised she should stay put and not answer the telephone or open the door to anyone, or she'd be risking her life. Naturally, he was thinking of her safety, but if she didn't take a risk, she could lose everything. She stopped pacing and pushed an errant lock of hair from her brow. Now or never. No going back. Her hand hovered over the telephone.

A woman's voice answered and she recognised the receptionist at the front desk and asked to be connected to The Vatican. Having received similar requests before, the receptionist thought about humouring her, but Anneliesa's insistence made her hesitate. She wanted to speak to Bishop Hudal or a colleague and mentioned that the Bishop was a friend of her father's. The receptionist agreed to call and, if successful, would connect them to her room.

As she replaced the receiver, Jan's notebook fell onto the floor, and something fluttered out. 'Sorry,' she muttered and studied a photograph, showing a fair-haired woman and a man wearing heavy-framed spectacles and, standing between them, a boy holding a tennis racquet, their smiles frozen in sepia. Embarrassed, as if she had spied on him, she returned it between the pages of the notebook.

When the phone rang, she snatched it up. The receptionist reported she'd been successful in contacting the Bishop's office and reached a man who claimed to be his secretary. She apologised for not getting his name.

At first, the receptionist reckoned they weren't interested, but on mentioning a friend from Vienna, the man enquired where she was calling from and, after another pause, said he would pass on the message.

'Didn't they say anything else?' She struggled to hide her disappointment. They'd regard it as a crank call, one of hundreds they received every day. She should have gone straight to the Vatican.

Almost immediately, the phone rang again.

'It's the Vatican for you.' The receptionist's voice rose. 'Didn't give a name.'

She waited, listening to the clicking while the woman made the connection. If it was the Bishop, she must be composed and not panic, and she conjured up a picture of him on the end of the line.

A man's voice. 'I'm calling on behalf of Bishop Hudal. I work in his office. Can I please ask why you wish to speak with him?'

'And you are?' she said.

'You must understand, he's very important—'

'It's vital I speak with him right away.'

A sharp intake of breath on the other end. 'It's not possible—'

Her chances of contacting Hudal were slipping away, and next, there would be an echoing click on the line and a deafening silence.

'Nazi war criminals are hiding in the Vatican.' She cursed herself for blurting it out.

The man, clearing his throat, broke a long silence. Then, as though he was holding a hand over the mouthpiece, she heard muffled voices on the line. She waited.

'Still there? His Excellency remembers your father with great fondness and would be happy to meet with you.'

Relief washed through her. Once she met him, it would all be sorted out.

'At the Vatican?' She wished she'd waited for Jan. He'd know what to do.

'That won't be possible, I'm afraid. The Bishop is elsewhere today, but I can take you to him.' The man's voice had taken on a kindlier tone. 'There's a public meeting point in St Peter's Square, which everyone uses.'

'Yes, I've been there.'

'Then we'll meet there. You can tell him everything and he'll help if he can.'

'When?'

'In fifteen minutes. He's very busy and this is the only time he has available.'

'How will I recognise you?'

'Don't worry, I'll find you.'

Although she wondered how he would recognise her, she dismissed it as meeting Hudal was all that mattered.

The line clicked dead, and the receptionist came on as if she'd been listening. 'Everything okay?'

She should have waited for Jan. But this was her only chance. She had no option.

58

Jan had to find Antonio before he got to his captain. If the Americans realised Wächter was in Rome, it would change everything, and, once involved, he wouldn't get near him, and he wanted him to himself. Confident she was safe if she stayed in the hotel, he headed to the cafe where Antonio had escaped through the toilet window. Although it was unlikely the boy would be there, someone might know his whereabouts. In Rome, as anywhere, loyalty lasted as long as it took to open a wallet.

A group of boys, who might have known Antonio, lounged on chairs around a table at the front of the cafe, and even though early, beer bottles littered the table like trophies. He walked past them and entered the cafe, but no one was inside apart from an elderly man sweeping the floor. He went back outside and, noticing they were watching him, approached their table.

'You lookin' for somethin', man?' A youth flicked cigarette ash in the air, and the others stopped talking and leered at him. Tourist or cop?

'I'm looking for a boy—'

'You're in the right place,' one said. The boys' laughter sent pigeons browsing nearby into the air in a flutter of fear. 'What are you after?'

'I must find Antonio.'

Unwilling to meet his gaze, they exchanged glances.

'Hey, man,' one broke the silence. 'I'm Luigi. Why bother with the no-good fucker? I'm not doin' anythin' at the moment.' The boys sniggered.

'It's got to be Antonio.'

'Waste of time, man,' another boy snorted. 'He's gone sort of exclusive.'

'What do you mean?'

'El Capitano takes up all his time nowadays,' said Luigi.

'Where is he?'

'Who knows? Who cares what the little shit is doin'.'

'Is he with the American?'

'Don't know.' Luigi pushed back, his chair screeching on the ground as he got to his feet. 'Come on, I'll show you where the Captain hangs out, then it's up to you.'

As they walked, Luigi relaxed in his company, swaggering and exchanging banter with passers-by, more confident away from the scrutiny of his friends, yet more vulnerable. 'Tony does what he does,' he said. 'Only way to get by, to eat, to survive. It's no big deal. Why are you lookin' for him anyway, mister? He in trouble?'

'Not with me.' He scratched his head. 'Bad people are looking for him and, if they find him, he will be in big trouble.'

The boy stopped to consider, then continued walking. 'So you tryin' to save his ass?'

'One way of putting it.'

'People don't care shit about us,' Luigi said. 'Why you?'

'He has important information that will save a person I care about.'

'Makes sense.' Luigi stopped again. 'It's always good to care about someone.'

When Jan didn't reply, just studied him, he said, 'Don't go all judgemental on me. People look down on us as if we're like the rats that are everywhere, but we're not. We're not lookin' for trouble. No one will help us. Eat when we can and sleep where we can. Tony's like the rest of us. When the Nazis came, we were fair game to them. Tony's mother became sick, and they locked her up in her house without food or medicine. She lasted only a couple of weeks. His father took to the bottle and hassled a couple of German soldiers,

The VIOLINIST'S REVENGE

who shot him in the street, and we weren't allowed to retrieve his body. It lay there and the rats and dogs all had a go. Not much left. That's when Tony became one of us. He had nowhere else to go, but he was lucky. He had Paolo, who was a real friend, a grande fratello, like a big brother, who helped him. People who come here do bad things they can't at home, anythin' they want and we don't matter.' He shrugged.

'Did that happen to you, Luigi?'

'The story's always the same and keeps repeating like a bad movie.' The boy turned his face away as though he'd said too much.

'Where are you taking me?'

'Palazzo Margherita.'

'What's there?'

'The American Embassy.'

They crossed the river and entered the Via Veneto, where the road opened out onto a magnificent ochre-coloured building with the Stars and Stripes fluttering over the entrance. 'You'll find el capitano in there.' Luigi gestured towards the building.

'Are you sure?'

'If Tony's not there, try Trastevere.' Luigi held out a hand for payment. 'When he's in trouble, he hides out there.'

As he scrambled in his pocket for lira, Luigi closed his hand and turned away. 'I don't want your money, mister. Just help Tony.'

'Take it.' He forced the notes on him, but the youth handed them back and left, waving a hand above his head and shouting, 'Good luck!'

'I'll need it,' he thought as he surveyed the building until the boy disappeared. He doubted Antonio would find sanctuary in an American establishment, but he'd wait in case he turned up.

Ornate iron railings protected the building and three armed American soldiers staffed the guard post inside the gates. 'Hey, you,' one called to him and approached, a hand on his holster. 'You wantin' something, buddy?'

'Just sightseeing,' he said.

'Do it someplace else.'

'I'm not looking for trouble.'

'You're not Italian.' The soldier glanced back at his fellow guards as though he might need reinforcements. 'Where are you from?'

'Just a tourist.' He chuckled.

Doubt spread across the soldier's face. 'Your English is good.' It sounded like an accusation, but Jan continued to smile.

The soldier's stare hardened. 'Get going.' He pulled out a pistol and prodded his chest. 'Move.'

He now doubted Tony would show up. He was too streetwise to be wandering around the streets in daylight, with Enrico looking for him. Perhaps Anneliesa had a point. Contact the Bishop and let them come to you. It would be walking into a trap, but what other options did they have? Annoyed he'd wasted the morning, he returned to the hotel to find the room empty. Had she left the hotel? He searched the hotel's public rooms but couldn't find her and, as he mounted the stairs to the room, the receptionist approached with a pleased smile. 'If you're looking for your friend, she went out about five minutes ago,' she said.

'Where did she go?'

'She had a call from the Vatican,' the woman replied with an apologetic shrug.

He groaned.

'She came rushing downstairs saying she had to meet somebody in St Peter's Square—'

He sprinted past her and out of the hotel. He had to find her before Enrico did.

ANNELIESA CAME to an abrupt stop when she entered St Peter's Square. Like a disturbed anthill, tourists milled about, gathering in groups, taking photographs, and being targeted by street urchins selling everything from postcards to sex. Locals were meeting up, groups of friends chatted and laughed, and old men played chess on makeshift boards. Were they supposed to meet by Caligula's Obelisk at the centre of the square? The man said he'd find her, but how would she know if it was the right person? As if waiting for friends, a few stood around on their own but showed no interest in her.

The VIOLINIST'S REVENGE

Colonnades lined either side of the square and whoever was meeting her could watch unseen from behind one of the many columns. On the far side of the square, she spotted a monk in a brown habit but discounted him. The man she'd spoken to could have been older, perhaps middle-aged. An office worker rather than a cleric.

She scanned the area, trying to make eye contact, but got no connection. She bit her lip. How could they recognise her in this mass of humanity? As if to show herself, she turned around, worried she'd misunderstood the instructions. Could she be in the wrong spot? It must be here. This was her only chance.

A man approached and, by the look in his eyes, wanted to speak to her and she relaxed. As he neared, he pulled a crumpled piece of paper from his pocket and shoved it into her hand. Written in an indecipherable scrawl was what she reckoned to be an address. He was only wanting directions.

The man stepped back, eyes flaring in fright, as from behind, two strong hands gripped her arms. She winced in shock and pain and tried to run, but she was held tight like in a vice and couldn't break away.

59

Trastevere provided the perfect haven for those not wanting to be found. A village within the oldest part of the city and a labyrinth of winding, arched lanes running between ochre-coloured buildings. If others couldn't find Antonio here, Jan doubted he would. Head down, he strode across Ponte Sisto deep into Trastevere, passing taverns and trattorias and through areas where trees grew out of the cobblestones. Consumed by anger, he questioned why Anneliesa had put her life in danger by leaving the hotel, despite his warning that she could be killed.

'Still angry with me?' she asked, hurrying to keep up.

He refused to look at her.

'Do you know where you're headed?'

'They didn't give me an address.' He couldn't avoid sarcasm. 'We walk around and, if we see a group of boys, we'll ask if they know Antonio or if they have seen him. It's a long shot, but it's our only option. Keep your eyes open.'

After marching her out of St Peter's Square, his anger had exploded when they got back to the hotel room, and he cornered her, his face only inches from hers. 'What in hell's name were you thinking of?'

'I wanted to see the Bishop…'

He backed away, shaking his head. It was pointless trying to

The VIOLINIST'S REVENGE

reason with her. 'Pack your bag. If Antonio's a target, then so are we. I've no idea how much they think we know, but they're taking care of all options. Thanks to your call, they now know where we are. We must leave. Now.'

'I'm not hiding away.' She pouted and dropped her bag. 'I want to find Lily. She's all that matters to me.'

'We might, but not if we're sitting targets for the mad monk and his friends.'

The next hotel was even more modest and smaller, the carpet more threadbare, the drapes struggling to meet in the middle, and the receptionist was offhand and disinclined to remember faces.

'We should go to the police?' she suggested.

'They wouldn't believe us,' he said. 'It would take a very brave policeman to investigate the Vatican.'

Tracking down Antonio was the key, as he could lead them to the Germans, or at least the area, if not the actual house.

'But Antonio might already be dead,' she said.

'It's a possibility. Only his street wiles are keeping him alive.'

'Do you think he's told his American captain?'

He shook his head.

'Why not?'

'He would have trouble getting past the guards.'

She'd done enough damage. He hadn't planned on taking her with him, but now she couldn't be trusted on her own. They wandered past restaurants and scanned the customers sitting outside and peered into the darkened recesses at their diners sheltering from the sun. They checked every road and alleyway for signs of Antonio and also watched for anyone who might be following them. After hours of searching, she was dragging her feet.

'It's hopeless,' she said, on the verge of tears. 'We'll never find him.'

Although he agreed, he wouldn't admit it. When they reached Piazza di Santa Maria, they took a table at a cafe across from the Basilica. 'This is reasonably central,' he said. 'While we have a drink, we can check out the area.' She ordered drinks and bread and ham, and he went inside and adjusted his eyes to the dark, shivering as he rubbed his arms for warmth. A couple of women were chatting, but gave him a cursory glance.

It was quieter than expected, and only a handful of tourists passed their way. Where would a youth in fear of his life hide? The map he'd picked up at the hotel couldn't provide an answer. He ordered more drinks. They could sit here for weeks and never see a familiar face.

'Do you think Hudal sent that person to meet me?'

'It could have been the others.' He hesitated. 'Why do you ask?'

'I can't believe he'd be involved in this. Maybe we could contact him in person and perhaps meet him?' Hope lingered in her stare.

'We don't know who we're dealing with. If it's Hudal, he might be the safer option. If it's Enrico, I wouldn't rate our chances.'

Her gaze dropped as she wrung her hands.

As the waitress arrived with more bread and ham, he leaned to his right, his eye catching a movement beyond the fountain, dominating the square. From a door in a building opposite, a youth emerged blinking in the sunlight and shouted to someone inside as he shut the door behind him. As Jan jumped up, he knocked over the chair and the noise attracted Antonio's attention. The boy stared at them, puzzlement rippling across his face, before a flash of recognition, and he sprinted away.

He called, but the boy had his head down and had no intention of stopping. He followed him down an alleyway, swerving past two women who stepped out of an open door, costing him valuable seconds. The gap increased between them and Antonio turned at a right angle and bounded up steps and, as the alley turned sharply left, disappeared out of sight.

Jan feared he'd ducked into a doorway and he'd lost him, but when he turned the corner, he glimpsed the boy. With spectators on balconies above shouting encouragement, Antonio took another turn and came back out on the other side of the square, and Jan saw Anneliesa, who watched with her mouth hanging open.

It was hopeless. Antonio would outrun him. He spied a bicycle leaning against a wall and pulled it away and mounted, wobbling, but got it moving. From behind, there was a shout, but he pedalled hard. If there were no other obstacles, he might catch him.

The VIOLINIST'S REVENGE

'Wait, Antonio, I want to talk to you.' Then louder. 'I mean you no harm. Stop.'

Determination shining from his eyes, the boy glanced back and found another gear and opened up more of a gap. He ran down another arched passageway and, to Jan's horror, a flight of stone steps led down into the gloom as the buildings leaned in towards them. Too late to stop, every bump reverberated through his body and rattled his teeth. Several times, he almost fell, but stayed in control as the alley opened out onto another square alongside the river. Without looking, the boy plunged into two lanes of fast-moving traffic to a cacophony of horns and shouts, causing vehicles to slew to a halt.

He hunched over the handlebars, trying to get more speed. Antonio was heading for the footbridge and, when he crossed it, he stopped at the apex and looked back, as if mocking him.

As he entered the bridge, a policeman stepped in front of him and grabbed the handlebars with both hands, ordering him to halt. Antonio had been swallowed up by the crowds, and he accepted he'd lost him. He dismounted, leaving the bicycle in the surprised policeman's hands, and retraced his steps to the piazza, hoping she'd waited for him.

The square was deserted, and their table had been cleared away. Expecting her to be enjoying the cool of the interior, he ducked inside. The waitress glowered at him. 'Her friends came,' she said, putting up both hands as if seeking an explanation. 'They went off together.'

Enrico and his men? Who else could it be? They'd abducted her, and if they were keeping her alive, where would they hold her? Probably where Paolo had seen Wächter, but only Antonio had the answer. He walked away slowly at first, his pace increasing with anxiety, but the waitress called him back and, thinking she might have information, he turned.

'Your lady, she didn't pay.' The waitress waved a slip of paper at him. 'Your bill, sir.' With a triumphant flourish, she handed it to him.

Only the faint hope Enrico and his friends weren't the culprits and she'd left and returned to the hotel kept him going. But back in the room, her open bag was where she'd left it, and the curtains were still closed. He was sinking in a quicksand of doubt and no longer cared about Wächter.

The harsh ring of the telephone filled the small room, and he snatched it up. 'Pronto?'

60

As Jan approached the embassy, the same soldier stood guard outside and, smirking in anticipation, marched over, and, legs apart and hands on hips, blocked his path. 'Told you yesterday, don't come back.'

He sidestepped him and carried on towards the gates, but the soldier followed and pulled on his shoulder, spinning him around, and he moved in close, pressing his face into his. 'What didn't you understand, buddy?'

The man's breath stank of onions and pasta, and his face reddened.

'I heard you.' He grinned at him and waited for the first blow. 'In my pocket is a gun and my finger is on the trigger.'

Wary now, the soldier's gaze switched to his jacket.

He moved the gun, and the man flinched at the sight of the barrel pushing through the thin stuff of his jacket. 'It's pointing straight at your belly button, and this gun can make quite a mess.'

With a hard swallow, the American stepped back, weighing up his options and calculating how serious he was. 'Come on, buddy, don't screw around.' He squared his shoulders. 'You haven't got the guts.' He held out a hand. 'Give it here before I take it from you and beat your ass with it.'

When he moved his hand in his pocket again, the soldier took another step backwards.

'Spill it. What do you want?'

He grinned again. 'To talk to your Captain. Do as I say and you won't get hurt. If you play the hero, I'll shoot you. I've killed more Nazis than you've had cold beers.'

The soldier laughed nervously and turned away, then reconsidered. 'Okay, okay, no big deal, but if you try anything, my men will shoot you.' He glanced at his colleagues at the guard post, who had been flirting with a group of girls, and motioned for him to follow. If they discovered he had a gun, they'd shoot both of them.

The American led him through the gates as the guards, now alert, tightened their trigger fingers. 'I'll go inside and see if the Captain will meet you,' he said.

'No.' He gestured. 'One of them can do it.'

The soldier called a guard. 'Ask the Captain if he'll see this guy.'

The guard sneered. 'Why doesn't he make an appointment?'

'Because he's got a fuckin' gun aimed at my balls, you dipshit.'

Their faces hardened as they trained their rifles on the visitor.

'He has important information for the Captain.' Now he was pleading.

'What's his name?' a guard asked.

'Just tell the Captain I saved Antonio's life,' he said.

'He saved Antonio's life, for fuck's sake. You know who we're talking about here.'

'Yeah, we know the boy.' The guard smirked at his mate as he picked up a phone.

Minutes later, Hadron emerged, putting on his cap while he looked around, appearing preoccupied. 'What's this all about?'

'Careful, sir, he's got a gun in his pocket,' the soldier said.

Hadron seemed more curious than surprised. 'You saved Antonio?'

He waited for the officer's reaction.

'Commendable, but why do you need to speak to me?'

'You know why.' What would a street boy and a US Army captain have in common? 'If you can't help, he and others will die.'

'What others?' The officer's eyes narrowed. 'Explain yourself.'

'Should I tell you out here?' He nodded at his men, who were listening to every word. 'It's for your ears only.'

The VIOLINIST'S REVENGE

Hadron understood. 'We'll talk in my office.' He waved at the guards to let him through, but one protested. 'He's got a gun, sir. We can't let him in.'

'Don't worry,' Hadron said. 'He's on our side.' And he turned to him. 'Please give us your gun.'

Without the gun, he felt naked and vulnerable, but had no choice. He pulled it out of his pocket. With a scowl, the soldier snatched it from him, pushed him to the ground and shoved his face into the dirt. The soldier twisted an arm up his back, and a knee slammed into the base of his spine.

'Let him up for Chrissake,' Hadron said. 'He's not the enemy.'

With a gleam in his eye, the soldier pulled him up and made a show of dusting him down.

'Give me back the gun when I leave,' he insisted. 'Fully loaded.'

Once they entered the building, a sergeant led him to Hadron's office and, when they were alone, the Captain relaxed. 'They're still edgy.' He gestured to a seat and offered him a Lucky Strike, lit up, exhaled and waited for an explanation.

He recounted Paolo's story via Antonio. 'Although I have only his word for it,' he admitted. And he told how, together with Anneliesa, they found Paolo's body. As he spoke, Hadron nodded as if ticking off the points one by one, as though he already knew.

Hadron exhaled and stood up and stretched, and offered him the cigarette packet. 'Unfortunately, I know a bit of the story.' He frowned. 'I went to Paolo's house. The killer must have disposed of the body, but I found evidence that backed up Tony's story.'

'But now they've taken it to a whole new level. They've got Anneliesa.'

Hadron gasped and put a hand over his face.

'You've got the power to arrest the Germans.'

'If they are Germans,' Hadron corrected him.

'What do you mean?'

'We have only Tony's word, and he's not a very reliable witness. You could say he's a stranger to the truth.'

'But you must investigate it?'

'Don't misunderstand. I want Wächter.' Hadron put his feet up on the desk and leaned back in his chair. 'My men and I spent months in the Austrian Alps looking for the bastard.' He paused and stared out the window. 'Even if there are Nazis in the house, it's difficult. Certainly, Paolo's death was suspicious and should be investigated by the local police. Nazi criminals? They're a different caboodle.'

'Surely, you must act on reports of Nazi criminals hiding in Rome?' He took another cigarette.

'Where do you want to start?' Hadron ran a hand through his crewcut. 'First, there isn't a body and where are the witnesses who have seen the alleged Nazis?'

'They gave me an ultimatum,' he said. 'Stop the boy talking or we'll find her floating in the Tiber. Both are in danger, and the longer we delay, the greater that danger.'

Hadron lifted his feet off the desk. 'We can't just march into Vatican City,' he said, his voice almost apologetic as he studied the ceiling. 'It would be like invading a sovereign state, even if a Catholic bishop is involved in facilitating Wächter's escape.' He tapped on the desk. 'It's a fucking can of worms.' He slammed it with the flat of his hand. 'I've spoken to my superiors. They've washed their hands of it, saying it's for the local authorities to deal with. They don't want any part of it and warned me not to go freelance. For the moment, my hands are tied. I'd advise you to go to the police.'

He jumped to his feet. 'I don't care what your bosses say. I've got to stop the Nazis before they kill her and I need Antonio's help to find the house.'

Hadron frowned. 'The problem is, I don't know where it is. I told my men to keep Tony here while I checked out his story. When I returned, he'd left and I haven't seen him since.'

61

The ceiling was grey and cracked with a hole where there should have been a lightbulb. Trying to focus, she rubbed her eyes as she looked around. The walls were rough brickwork. Across the room, a closed, heavy metal door had no handle. Lying on her back on a bare wooden bench, her shoulder blades ached, and her hands and feet were numb with cold. She recalled sitting at a table in Trastevere and two men approaching with a smile. Before she could move, a hypodermic needle slammed into the side of her neck and everything turned black. Now, when she touched the wound, it hurt.

The bench was bolted to the wall and, when she swung her legs around and put them on the ground, she wobbled. She crossed the stone-paved floor and pushed the door, but it didn't budge. She tried to force her fingers into the edges, but it was sealed. High up, iron bars on the outside protected a slit of a window, its tinted glass softening the daylight but too thick to break with her hands. She attempted to get a grip to pull herself up by jumping, but each time slid back down.

This must have been where Paolo saw the Germans. If so, her chances of escaping were slim. When abducted by the Nazis before, she had panicked, not understanding, but this time, she stayed calm. Once again, she was a prisoner and vulnerable. Shouting would waste her breath and she must preserve her strength. How could she have been so stupid, ignoring Jan's advice and not staying alert? It was light outside. How long had she been here? She tiptoed back to the door and put an ear to the cold metal, but there were no sounds. Had they fled and left her here to starve to death? Why hadn't they just killed her? Her life was of no value to them. If Enrico was intent on killing all witnesses, what had stopped him?

Footsteps.

As sounds emanated from a room above, she relaxed. At least she wasn't alone in the house. What did they want from her? Scanning the cell for anything that might serve as a weapon, there was only a porcelain chamberpot in the corner. She concentrated on lowering her heart rate and circled the room. What could she do to prolong her life? Bolts being drawn back alerted her to retreat to the bench, and she lay down and feigned sleep.

Enrico's malevolent presence filled the frame. 'Come.'

Relieved to leave the cell, she breathed deeply. He led her up wooden steps and along a windowless corridor without doors and, in control, he swaggered, unconcerned that she might attempt to escape. They climbed another short flight of steps and stopped before a closed door, and he stared at her. 'One wrong move and—' He slammed a fist into the palm of his hand.

Enrico opened the door and stood aside for her to squeeze past. Two men were sitting at a table. The younger stiffened like an animal ready to pounce, while the older man lifted his head from papers before him and studied her. 'We meet again, fräulein,' he said, his voice brusque, but with the hint of a smile. 'Perhaps not in such auspicious circumstances.'

She showed no surprise. 'The last time was in a death camp, and you were doing the killing. What's changed?'

He ignored the remark. 'Apologies, but you and your friend have only yourselves to blame for interfering in matters that shouldn't concern you.'

With a look of distaste, her eyes searched the room. 'The great General Wächter hiding like a rat in a hole. A fitting end for an evil man.'

Jünger moved towards her, but Wächter restrained him with a hand on his arm. 'I go by the name of Alfredo Reinhardt these days.'

'Reinhardt?'

'It's my little joke, but now I'm just a simple actor, getting a few bit parts, but it fills my time. Can't spend all day swimming in the Tiber.' He laughed, and the others joined in.

'Where is she?' She stepped forward, but the younger man blocked her path.

'First, let me introduce my friend, Obersturmführer Jünger.' Wächter waved a hand at the younger man. 'We've been through much these last few years. Once my junior officer, but now we're partners, and I wouldn't have survived, but for him. There's nothing he wouldn't do for me and I for him.'

His eyes veiled, Jünger appeared less enthusiastic.

Wächter had aged since she last saw him, but he still had a powerful presence and a full head of hair that he kept pushing off his brow, and the aristocratic air of one not concerned with the realities of life.

Being in the same room with him made her want to vomit. He had destroyed her life, and she'd walked into his trap like a lamb to the slaughter. She'd imagined killing him in many ways. Now it wouldn't happen. 'Where's my sister, Lily?' She managed to keep her tone even.

Across the table, Jünger tensed.

'Is she—' she hesitated '—dead?' This was crueller than anything she'd endured. To have lost her family to this man was one thing, but his taking Lily away a second time had turned the knife into a deep wound. And he enjoyed it.

'She's safe for the moment.' Wächter picked up a cigarette burning in an ashtray on the table and drew on it, savouring the warmth in his lungs.

'Why should I believe you?' she asked, relieved she was alive.

'That's your decision. You should be grateful I spared her life. On my orders, the guards took her out of the queue to the gas chambers.'

'Why? Did it make you feel like a human being?' She flashed a sneer of disbelief. 'Did it salve your conscience for killing my mother and brother and thousands of others? Who gave you the right to decide who lives or dies?'

'Unfortunate,' Wächter said without a trace of remorse. 'I knew your family. I saw you play at the Metropole.' His eyes drifted to the ceiling as if recalling better days that could never be repeated. 'The camps were not intended for people like you. You are of Aryan stock, the people we built the Third Reich on.' He shook his head. 'Mistakes were made, and you got caught up in it. Unfortunately, you were where you shouldn't have been, and our soldiers were overzealous.'

'You could have stopped the executions,' she said. 'After all, you ordered them in the first place.'

He lifted the cigarette to his lips, then hesitated. 'You played several times at the camp, but at first, I didn't recognise you. It brought back happy memories of you playing beautifully. I wasn't sure it was you until an old friend, Bishop Hudal, informed me.' Wächter observed the end of the cigarette. 'You remember him?' He paused. 'Of course you do. We were all members of the same church.'

Annoyingly, she couldn't stop herself from nodding.

'Your father, a good man as I remember, contacted the Bishop for his help, claiming his family had been abducted in error and had been transported to a camp in Poland. I made the necessary enquiries. Only when you played for the march did I realise it was you.'

'Then why didn't you do something?'

'It would have been harder than you can imagine. We removed the girl, your sister, from the procession, but it would have been impossible to do that for your mother and brother without causing a stampede amongst the prisoners.'

'And the hundreds of thousands you consigned to the gas chambers? Didn't they deserve to live? Or were you keeping up the numbers to curry favour with the maniac you worshipped?'

'Enough.' Wächter winced and a nerve twitched on the right side of his mouth. 'You're ignorant of the real world. The Jews deserved everything that happened to them. It was our duty to rid the world of them. Reichsführer Himmler said, and I agree, Jewish influence cost us the First World War. We were merely balancing the books. Auschwitz wasn't a concentration camp, as it's claimed now, but merely a re-education camp.'

'Then why were the prisoners exterminated?'

'Infection control.' He waved a hand.

'Why didn't you kill me?'

He hesitated. 'You were too valuable.'

'As a member of your orchestra?'

'If we'd lost you, it would have ruined the orchestra and been bad for morale.' He ran a hand through his hair.

'Morale?'

'My men's.'

Her look of disgust didn't receive a response.

'Where's Lily?'

'You have my word she's safe and with a friend who's looking after her.'

As she stared past Wächter's attempt at a smile and through the window at the rippling sunlight changing the colours of the facades of neighbouring houses, she experienced a flutter of hope. At least Lily was alive. 'How can I believe you? You killed Frau Strobl and Albert.'

'A mistake,' he admitted. 'We only intended to recover the child—'

Jünger interrupted, 'Those people were members of the Resistance.'

'You were tying up loose ends?'

'In a way,' Jünger smirked.

Wächter sighed and waved it away. 'It's of no account.'

'What happens now?' But she'd already guessed the answer and glanced at the hulking presence of Enrico, whose black eyes bored through her.

'Soon, I'll be leaving,' Wächter said, 'and I owe a debt of gratitude to Enrico and his friends.'

'Where are you going?'

'To Genoa and a ship to freedom—' Jünger flashed him a look as if he shouldn't say any more '—and once settled, I'll send for my family.'

It deflated her, emptied her. Wächter was convinced he was a good soldier following orders for the good of his country and cause, but how could he slaughter thousands of innocents and believe he deserved a life of safety thereafter? 'What happens now?'

He gestured with a finger for Jünger to prepare another cigarette. 'You and your friend and the boy—' he searched for a name '—Antonio, have given us problems. I believe the boy has a friend, an officer in the American Army.' He looked up. 'It could cause us and the Church problems. At the moment, your friend is searching for him, but we're following him. When he finds the boy, we'll bring this to a swift conclusion.' He paused. 'As for you, it's in our friend's capable hands.' He nodded towards Enrico.

'It's not you we want,' she said. 'Go wherever you like. I only want Lily back.'

Enrico moved closer. 'Not possible.'

Jünger walked around the table and whispered to Wächter, who nodded and turned to her. 'I will give you one last chance to save your sister.'

'How?'

'These are difficult times.'

Her stomach cramped as she stared at him.

'It's simple. You need your sister. We want your friend.'

She'd dreaded it would come to this.

'Call him and ask for his help.'

'But that would—' She tried to rise from the seat, but Enrico clamped a hand on her shoulder and forced her down. 'No, never, he'd be walking into a trap.'

'If you refuse,' Wächter shrugged, 'you will never see her again, and our people will eventually catch up with him.'

Unwanted thoughts flooded her mind. Somebody would die, whatever she decided. 'First, you must prove to me that she's alive.'

'That can be arranged. I knew you'd see sense.' He dismissed her with a wave of an arm.

Back in the cell, she ran through her options. If Lily were alive, Jan and the Americans could rescue her if Antonio lived long enough to give them the address. But they were running out of time. If she agreed to Wächter's demand and betrayed Jan, could she trust the Nazis to keep their word?

She punched the wall in frustration. Again. And again. And again. Until her knuckles bled. And, sobbing, she collapsed against the wall.

62

Without Antonio's information, they had reached a dead end. The Embassy visit had been fruitless, and not knowing where the boy was hiding confirmed the hopelessness of Hadron's task. And his superiors were preventing him from taking action.

The message in the telephone call was implicit. Stop Antonio talking, which meant killing him. If he couldn't find the boy, he must find the house, which could be nigh on impossible. Paolo claimed it to be within walking distance of the Vatican, in an area of nondescript houses and narrow lanes. A small house with an alleyway running down one side to a small courtyard at the back. There were too many like that.

It was a desperate hope, but he would walk the streets around the Vatican and search for a house matching the description. Perhaps he'd glimpse Enrico. Better than sitting and worrying in a room. He headed for the Prati area and moved on to the Borgo district, a more likely location, as the houses resembled Paolo's description. Enrico's people would have eyes everywhere, so he attempted to blend in with the locals and, having bought apples from a street vendor, sat on a wall, observing while he ate them.

Doors opened in houses. Customers sat outside street cafes. Crowds walked towards him until they were a kaleidoscope of faces. All received his scrutiny. When he discovered a likely house, he loitered, only to be disappointed by families leaving or entering.

Monks in brown robes mixed with the crowds, and he followed them, but they were half the size of Enrico. He began to lose hope. He imagined Paolo's journey that night, following Enrico across St Peter's Square, but the image was supplanted by one of Anneliesa dead.

After hours of fruitless searching, he slumped on a bench at a crossroads, ready to admit defeat and frustrated by the knowledge that she might be close by. Why had he left her on her own while he scoured Trastevere for the boy?

Wandering without direction, he arrived at the bottom of the Spanish Steps and got caught up in the crowd. He climbed, paying no attention to a wedding party, a bride in white and her new husband in a cheap suit, taking photographs halfway up. As the steps became more crowded, his progress slowed and, around him, tourists complained as they were pressed from behind and blocked by those descending. They panicked. To his left, a woman shrugged an apology as she stumbled into him and clutched his arm for support, her fingers closing on his wrist. As the crowd wrenched him around, the woman was swept away, holding her arm above her head like a salute.

'Hey, my watch.' But the clamour of the tourists drowned out his protest.

A youth wearing a cap pulled down over his eyes and a muffler around his face pressed against him. As the crowd surged, he felt a hand in his pocket and tried to turn, but the crowd held him as if in a vice. 'My wallet,' he cried.

Gaps opened as the wedding party dispersed and, freeing his arms, he checked his pocket. Up the steps, the youth weaved around those descending and hurdled couples sitting on the steps, but he wasn't increasing the gap and looked back to see if he was being followed.

He gave chase along winding streets and across junctions, confident he'd catch him. With another backwards glance, the youth dived into an alleyway, and he followed into the shade and adjusted his eyes. There was no way out. The thief was cornered. 'Give me my wallet.' He stuck out a hand.

The youth turned and lowered his scarf and, as he stepped

forward, footsteps behind made him pause. He swivelled and recognised the face before a blow knocked him off his feet.

Eight steps long and six steps wide, her cell was now hot, adding to her claustrophobia, but she walked around and around, questioning her options and getting the same depressing answer.

Although she didn't hear footsteps, the door opened and Enrico, wearing a vest revealing his intimidating muscular arms and tattoos, entered, carrying a glass of water and bread and ham on a tray.

'Don't want it,' she said. 'You'll poison me.'

'Your choice.' He shrugged and placed it on the floor. 'Just make the telephone call.'

Uncertain, she looked away.

'The boy or your sister,' he said. 'It's a simple choice.' His laugh reverberated around the cell. 'Blood's thicker than water.'

She gauged the distance to the door. Could she make it? 'Once Wächter leaves, you'll have no worries,' she said. 'He'll be out of reach.'

'Maybe,' Enrico said. 'But my people could still be implicated.'

'What happens if I don't call Jan?'

He emitted a low, guttural laugh. 'You and I could spend a couple of hours together.'

'Aren't priests celibate?' She edged closer to the door.

He sneered. 'Don't even think about it because you won't make it. Call him while you can.'

'Or what?'

His eyes contemplated the eventuality. 'Once it's dark, we'll take you for a swim in the Tiber. You would be surprised how many suicides there are. Your body will wash up miles from here and will be just another statistic. Another love affair gone wrong.' He drywashed his hands. 'Enjoy the food and drink.' He stepped on the ham and bread, grinding them with his heel, and slammed the door behind him, double-bolting it, and his footsteps receded up the stairs.

Avoiding the tray of food and drink, she paced the cell. The food she ignored, but the water enticed her and, with every pass, her thirst increased. Could the water be laced with drugs? She slumped on the bed and rolled over and, so as not to be tempted, faced the wall.

A tinkling like running water splashing into a basin, and she imagined droplets sparkling like diamonds bouncing on the stone floor. Cool, cold water. Her thirst grew, and she rolled back over. The glass was inviting. She tried averting her gaze. They were playing with her mind. Like a wary animal, she moved off the bed and approached, intending to kick it over so the water and temptation disappeared between the cracks in the floor.

With both hands, she lifted the glass and studied it. Just one sip. The water ran over her tongue and down the back of her throat and made her gag. Another sip. And another. Then a mouthful. She drained the glass, and it fell from her grasp and smashed into pieces on the floor.

WHEN JAN REGAINED CONSCIOUSNESS, a grey dawn was awakening. He was lying face down in the cobbled alley, his head resting in a puddle. Was it water? It smelled much worse. His head ached and the memory of being hit hard returned. He got back onto his feet and leaned against the wall, and felt where he'd been hit, then inspected his fingers. No blood. He retched.

He hadn't believed Luigi capable of it. Theft, yes, but not violence. When he dusted himself down and searched his pockets, something was there. Why hit him if they were returning his wallet? He opened it, checked the contents, and chuckled. As expected, his lira notes had been taken. Old habits die hard. Something else was there, a folded slip of paper. He opened the note, peering at it in the gloom. Unable to decipher the childish scrawl, he went out of the alleyway to read it under a street lamp.

63

'Not long, Kurt.' Wächter scanned the small bedroom before concentrating on his two packed bags. 'Our departure has been brought forward. We're leaving later today.' And when his colleague showed surprise, he added, 'They're worried I'm attracting attention to the escape route.'

He lifted a bag, testing its weight. 'Can't say I'll miss it.' He slapped Jünger on the back. 'A road journey, then a voyage to safety.' He ushered him towards the door. 'Don't regard this as exile. It doesn't end here. In South America, we'll plan for the Reich to rise anew.'

Junger's grey eyes were emotionless as he grimaced. 'There are too many loose ends,' he complained. And before Wächter could answer, he raised a hand. 'What will we do with the woman in the basement and the others—the man, the boy, the American?'

Wächter patted his shoulder. 'All will be taken care of.'

'You make it sound simple, Herr General, but the change of circumstances is a problem. The Church will do anything to hide its involvement. And how safe will we be?'

'Enrico will handle everything,' Wächter said. 'Anyway, who would believe a Nazi general could be hiding here?' He snorted. 'It can't go wrong now.'

'Will Enrico dispose of them?'

'Why? Do you want to?'

Absent-mindedly wiping dust off a bedside cabinet, Jünger ignored the remark. 'Do you trust him?'

'Of course not, he's a barbarian.' Wächter regarded him with detached amusement. 'And like such people, he has to be handled with extreme caution.'

'You're not on the boat yet. He could still double-cross you.'

'Don't worry, my friend, I'm confident Enrico will tie up all those loose ends of yours.'

Jünger kept quiet.

'Come on, man,' Wächter said. 'Spit it out. What's troubling you?'

'One minute we're hiding, the next running again,' Jünger said. 'We're reliant on others, and they're not Germans. They don't have our attention to detail or our discipline. And I still haven't had a guarantee I'll be on the ship.'

'Ah,' Wächter said. 'But you'll soon join us in Argentina.'

Jünger stopped in his tracks as a coldness crept through him. 'Are you saying I'm not going on this boat? But you promised.'

Lips pursed, Wächter attempted to clap him on the back, but he shrugged away the touch. 'You've done your duty and more. You will go to Argentina, but there are only a limited number of berths. It's decided by rank.'

'When?'

'I can't give you a date. That's not my decision to make. You'll be informed in due course.' Wächter delivered it with an air of detachment he'd often seen him use when dismissing others.

'But you—' He now realised he'd been double-crossed, betrayed. His path to freedom had been through Wächter, but the General had never intended he should escape with him. He was becalmed. Used to working to a plan, that had been taken from him and he couldn't see a way ahead.

Wächter mistook his silence for acceptance and consulted his watch. 'I leave in three hours and then it'll be farewell, Rome.'

Jünger stared at him and Wächter, seeing a slow smile, relaxed.

'Farewell, Rome, indeed.' Jünger smoothed the lapels of his jacket. 'If I might suggest, Herr General?'

Intrigued, he replied, 'Of course, what is it?'

'As you know, my concern has always been for your well-being.'

The VIOLINIST'S REVENGE

'Indeed, Kurt.' Wächter looked around the small room and laid a hand on his arm. 'We should go out and get some fresh air.'

At the door, Jünger said, 'As this is a victory of sorts, you should mark your departure accordingly.'

'How on earth can I do that?'

'What you've done every day since we've been here.'

Wächter's face lit up, but he checked his watch. 'I don't think—'

Jünger persevered. 'Why not? A farewell salute to the Eternal City. Like all the great generals in history. If you like, it's your Rubicon.'

Nodding with a gleam in his eye, Wächter mulled it over and squared his shoulders. 'Yes, my Rubicon,' he said. 'Just like Caesar.' Then he remembered Caesar had been assassinated.

64

Captain Butch Hadron lit a Lucky Strike, put his boots up on the desk and leant back in his squeaking chair. Having information about one of the most wanted Nazi war criminals hiding in Rome, shielded by people connected to the Vatican, was like winning a lottery but losing the ticket. A triumph for America and the Allies, and a feather in his cap. Medals, promotion, more money and a visit to the White House, but the political ramifications could be immense. Tony remained the key to it all and the problem. The boy had gone to ground in this vast city teeming with those in search of their salvation, but after all the money he'd blown on him, he deserved payback. Big time.

His hands were tied. Anyone who had witnessed the atrocities of the Nazis knew what he should do, but his superiors were reluctant to be dragged into it. They'd made it clear that if he ignored orders, they'd incarcerate him in Leavenworth, but if he did nothing, it would be on his conscience forever.

The phone ringing on his desk made him jump.

'Sorry to bother you, sir.' The Sergeant sounded perplexed. 'Didn't know what I should do.'

'What in God's name is it, man?'

'There's a woman here asking to speak to someone in authority.'

He chuckled. 'So why bother me?'

'She's strange, saying wacky things.'

'You deal with her. I've got enough on my plate.' He cut off the Sergeant and returned to his problem, finding it difficult to think straight as there were too many imponderables.

The phone rang again. 'What now?'

Fearing the call would be terminated before he got to the important part, the man babbled.

As Hadron listened, he removed his feet from the desk and sat upright. 'Bring her through,' he said.

A single knock and a tired middle-aged woman entered, glancing about as though expecting to meet someone she wanted to avoid. Her dark hair, flecked with grey at the temples and parted in the middle, was pulled back into a tight bun. A prominent nose and dark, frightened eyes dominated her face.

He directed her to the chair opposite and waited while she composed herself, but she didn't speak. 'Please tell me what you told my Sergeant,' he said with a look of encouragement.

He lit a cigarette and offered her one, which she refused with a curl of the lip. She resembled an unhappy schoolmistress about to address an unruly class, and she took a deep breath. 'I have information that'll interest you.' Her voice accented, perhaps mid-European. 'I was a nurse in Poland when they invaded, and they placed me in service with a German family. I didn't want to do it. The Nazis killed all my family, and I survived only because I was working in a hospital.' She hesitated, her eyes clouded with memories. 'They gave me no choice. It was that or the firing squad. Anyway, the children were innocents. They weren't responsible for their father's sins.'

'I see.' Why is she here, he thought. 'Please continue.'

'Their father, a German, an SS general.'

Had he heard right? He paused. 'What's his name?'

Fear showed in her dark eyes and she hesitated. 'I shouldn't have come.' She glanced towards the door as though planning to flee.

'Don't worry, you're safe here. Please tell me his name.'

'I daren't.' Tears welled up. 'Unless you can guarantee our safety?'

'You'll have the full protection of the United States, I promise you.'

As if an obstacle had been removed, she relaxed. 'His name is

Gruppenführer Otto von Wächter.' Her lips pursed as if about to spit. 'And he's in Rome—'

He jumped to his feet. 'Where?'

'I don't know.'

Deflated, he sat down again.

'His family are living outside the city, but he's not with them. They're planning to travel abroad, but I don't know where. We're not sure what will happen to us or even if we'll survive, so when they let us walk in the park this morning, we escaped and came here.'

'We?' he said. 'Who else—'

The telephone rang again and he snatched it up. 'Who?' He ran a hand through his crewcut and studied his visitor without seeing her. 'Yes, yes, okay, I'll be right there.' With a preoccupied expression, he pushed up from the desk. 'Please wait here until I return.'

Outside his office, he ordered a soldier to get the woman a coffee and on no account let her leave.

With a mixture of relief and trepidation, he recognised the slight figure held at gunpoint by one of his soldiers in the hallway.

'Antonio.' He stopped himself from running to him. 'Where have you been? There are people out there who want to kill you.'

Open-mouthed, the soldier glanced at him and then at the boy, and Antonio cowered, staring at his rifle.

'I've just seen them,' Antonio said. 'I didn't know who else to tell.'

'Seen who?'

'The Nazis I told you about.'

'At the house?'

'No, no,' the boy insisted. 'They were walking in the street.'

'Don't, Antonio, no more.' He raised his arms, finding it hard to suppress his anger. 'I've had enough of your lies.'

'I'm not lying.'

'Your friend Paolo saw the Nazis, not you.'

'Yes, but from what he told me about the house, it was easy to find,' the boy said. 'I watched it for hours before two men came out. They spoke German, and they matched Paolo's description.'

Could he afford not to believe him? 'Where were they headed?'

'I don't know,' Antonio said. 'Maybe the river.'

He tried not to show his disbelief.

'Sant'Angelo, maybe. I dunno.'

It made little sense.

'They were strolling along, laughing and relaxed.' The boy's eyes implored him to believe.

'Did they look as if they were running away?'

'No, but the older one carried an object under his arm.'

'Are you sure?' He grabbed him by the collar.

Antonio recoiled but nodded.

He wheeled around. 'Sergeant. Six men. Fully armed. At the double.'

As the boy watched wide-eyed, the Sergeant strode away, his shouted orders echoing down the corridor.

65

Jan recognised the house from the day before when he had scouted the area. It fronted onto a narrow lane with paint peeling on the front door and weeds growing beneath its ground-floor windows. Without breaking stride, he walked on and found a vacant table at a street cafe on the corner and ordered a black coffee. He checked the address Antonio had scribbled on the scrap of paper, and the same house number was written in white on a blue porcelain plaque on the wall by the door. It was hardly befitting of Wächter's status, but it was perfect as no one would expect an Austrian aristocrat to be staying there.

Antonio had done well. Knowing people were looking for him, he'd engineered the pick-pocketing situation to get him away from those who might be tailing them. But Luigi shouldn't have hit him so hard.

While he drank his coffee, he studied the house and tried formulating a plan of action. Shutters covered the windows, and no lights showed, and there was no sign of life. Wächter and Jünger must be inside, plus Enrico and a few heavies, and she must be there, too.

There was no way in at the front, but Paolo had mentioned an alley leading to a small courtyard at the back of the house, which could have possibilities. Unhurried, he rose and stretched and surveyed the area like a tourist taking in his surroundings, and he checked the pistol in his pocket. He sauntered along the lane and, at the mouth of the alley, paused and squinted in. Deserted. After a glance around to check if his presence had alerted anyone, he stepped in and walked carefully down to the courtyard.

At the back of the building, there was a single window on the ground floor through which Paolo must have seen the Nazis. Below the window, at ground level, was an opening, a slit protected by iron bars, that could be a basement. If they were keeping her prisoner here, it would be the likely place. Unable to see in, he rapped on the opaque glass with his knuckles but got no reaction. Nausea swept through him. Was he too late?

He peered into what appeared to be a normal kitchen with a table surrounded by chairs in the middle of the room. Putting an ear to the glass, he listened, but heard nothing. The window's wooden frame had warped, leaving a slight gap, and he slid the blade of his commando knife into the space and moved it in and out and from side to side to loosen it. With a little pressure, the window sprang open.

To ensure no one was watching, he looked around before stepping up onto the windowsill and climbing in. Stumbling down to the floor, he waited for a reaction. In a sitting room at the front of the house, he found evidence of recent activity—a half-empty beer bottle on a coffee table and half-smoked cigarettes were stubbed out in an ashtray as though they'd left in a hurry.

A noise stopped him.

Could it be inside, or people passing by in the lane? He paused before climbing the stairs, willing them not to creak. In the two bedrooms, the beds were made and baggage packed as though ready for removal, but where were they? Had they fled without their bags?

The basement was where she'd be held. A door in the hallway led down to another level, and he removed the gun from his pocket and took care to muffle his footsteps on the wooden steps. At the end of a narrow, white-washed corridor was a metal door bolted top and bottom. He braced before slipping back the bolts and, with both hands, opened the door. What little light there was came from the slit of a window and it took minutes for his eyes to adjust. Remnants of bread and ham lay alongside broken glass on the floor and, against the far wall, a body lay in a foetal position on a low bench.

He put down the gun and, taking Anneliesa by the shoulders, shook her, but there was no response.

'Anneliesa, it's Jan.' His voice rose. 'Wake up.' He couldn't find a pulse and, in panic, pulled her up again and brushed the hair from her face. He beat on her chest and slapped her face harder than he wanted to, but got no response.

JÜNGER HAD MARCHED AHEAD, and Wächter found it hard to keep up. 'What's your hurry, man? We've got hours yet and I don't want to tire myself before my swim.'

'Apologies, Herr General.' The young officer paused, allowing his superior to catch up. 'You've enjoyed swimming in the river every day since you've been in Rome. You deserve one last swim before your departure.'

Wächter also wished to savour his last stroll in the city. He'd enjoyed his exile in Rome and felt freer than he'd done for years, but everything must end. He was looking forward to a new life in South America with his family, without continually looking over his shoulder. Under his arm, he carried a rolled-up towel and had already put on his swimming trunks under his trousers. His last chance to luxuriate in the waters of the Tiber, no matter how dangerous and dirty everyone said they were. Every time, it was like being re-christened, and he emerged with an aura of invincibility.

As they approached the river, Borgo's narrow streets opened out onto an amazing vista with the awe-inspiring enormity of Castel Sant'Angelo to his left—the castle Emperor Hadrian had built for his mausoleum—and before them Ponte Sant'Angelo, the footbridge lined with marble statues of angels.

Jünger hurried on ahead and almost ran down the steps to the embankment, a hand feeling for the comfort of the pistol in his pocket.

Wächter followed and, halfway down, stopped. Jünger was

already at the bottom and waved, but Wächter ignored him and stared up at the bridge and, with a shake of his head, turned and climbed back up the steps.

'Herr General, where are you going?'

'You know, Kurt, every January, the Romans celebrate the New Year by diving into the Tiber from these bridges,' he said over his shoulder. 'Like a true Roman, I'll celebrate in the same way.'

Unable to contain his disbelief, Junger pointed to the river. 'It's safer down here where no one will notice you,' he said. 'If you jump from the bridge, you'll attract attention. Why take the risk when you're so close to freedom?'

Wächter grinned as he mounted the steps, stamping his feet as he went.

'Jumping off a bridge is dangerous,' Jünger pleaded. 'You could die.'

A BLOW with the force of a sledgehammer almost dislocated his shoulder, and he fell face-first into the wall, grazing his forehead. Before he grasped what had happened, a hand wrenched him back by the hair into the path of a massive fist. For a moment, he blacked out.

His black eyes glinting in the dim light, Enrico grinned as he launched the next blow. It loosened a tooth and, as Jan slid to the ground, the monk stepped in and pinned him to the flagstone floor with a knee on his chest. The monk grabbed him by the collar and pulled him into a sitting position, his face so close that the smell of sweat overwhelmed him.

'Go on, do your worst.' The words came out in a mix of blood and spit. 'But let her go. She can't hurt you.'

Enrico's presence filled the room, and his eyes showed as much compassion as a scientist about to dissect a rare specimen. 'Save your breath.' He glanced at her lying on the bench. 'She won't wake and, after dark, I'll take her for a swim and dispose of her body.' The monk cleared his throat.

He attempted to get enough purchase to charge at the monk, but his legs weren't responding. 'Where's Wächter?' His voice sounded disembodied.

'It's no longer your problem.'

'I always like to hear how a story ends.'

Enrico bellowed like a rutting bull and let go of him and stepped back, his ponytail swinging like a predatory snake. 'Wächter's gone for one last swim.'

'Why would he?' He had to keep Enrico talking while he figured out what to do.

'Arrogant fuckin' Nazis,' Enrico shouted. 'He'll soon be out of here and good riddance. Caused me enough problems.'

He felt for the knife in his pocket and, moving his fingers, could almost reach it, but got no leverage. 'What have you planned for me?' he said.

For a moment, the monk studied him as though considering whether it was worth the trouble to explain. 'Killing you is easy. It's the disposal that's the problem. I could do it here now, but in this heat, you'd rot and start to stink.'

He couldn't think of an appropriate answer.

'We can't have two of you floating in the Tiber tonight. It would attract attention.'

'Look,' he said, the wall giving his back support. 'I won't cause you any problems.' He tried pushing against it. 'I'm just a mercenary.' He offered an apologetic expression. 'Don't care what happens to the woman or your Nazis. I'll leave Rome and be no further trouble to you.'

'I understand,' Enrico said. 'I can be reasonable, but you know too much. As they say, a simpleton isn't a problem, but a man with a little knowledge is a threat.' He frowned. 'Your time has come, and it will be easier for you if you accept it.' His raucous laugh reverberated around the room, then transformed into a gasp, and he put a hand to the back of his head. Blood bubbled through his splayed fingers, and his eyes flashed wide as he pulled a shard of glass out of a widening wound, causing the blood to flow more freely. He stared at it in disbelief and turned and took a faltering step towards her before collapsing.

The VIOLINIST'S REVENGE

It displeased Wächter that a junior officer had the temerity to question his decision, no matter how close their relationship. A strong swimmer and a confident diver, he'd dived many times from comparable heights. It amused him that Jünger had to run. By the time he reached the apex of the bridge, Jünger caught up and looked around, his face full of concern. 'Sir, please don't jump from here. It's dangerous. Why take the chance?'

'Listen to me, Obersturmführer. This is an order. I will jump and you will not say a word more.' He removed his shirt and handed it to him before struggling out of his trousers. 'Do you understand?'

Jünger turned away. 'You'll draw attention to yourself.'

Wächter held onto one of the marble angels, lining the bridge, and climbed onto the balustrade and stared down at the roiling waters. The skies had turned grey and the wind ruffled his hair and, brushing it off his brow, he harboured a brief doubt. Towering above him, the statue of the angel held out a hand as if in salvation. The dive would have to be clean, so he didn't swallow a mouthful of the yellowish waters. He glanced at the castle where an angel reputedly appeared overhead, signalling the end of an epidemic in ancient Rome. No matter what Jünger believed, this wouldn't be a triumphal withdrawal. More slinking away, and when he raised his eyes to the angel again, the hand was more like a warning.

'One last point before you dive, Herr General.'

'What now?' Irritated, he swung around and clutched at the statue to stop losing his balance.

'I'm sorry.' Jünger was pointing a Luger at his midriff.

'What are you doing, Kurt?' His face was twisted in shock.

'I'm a soldier and I obey orders, but you give me no option.' With both hands, Jünger held the pistol steady and stepped closer. 'I would have served you to the very end, but you have betrayed me.'

'You will be on the next boat, I promise.'

Looking around, Jünger said, 'You've cut me adrift. You put yourself first, although you know that without the help of your influential friends, I cannot survive.'

'That's not true.'

Jünger shook his head. 'Your colleagues in South America will have to survive without you.'

'On whose authority do you presume to stop me?' Wächter drew up his shoulders and let go of his hold on the statue. 'As your superior officer, I command you to put down your gun.'

Jünger took a step forward.

'I demand you stop this nonsense.' His face reddened, then, realising his junior had no intention of backing down, he became more conciliatory. 'Now, Kurt, we can sort this out. We've been together for years. We're friends. On first-name terms. Why would you do this to your friend? Think of my family.'

His face as impassive as stone, Jünger didn't answer, and that annoyed him more.

'This is an outrage, do you hear? You will be stripped of your commission and face a firing squad. You, a mere obersturmführer, can't execute a hero of the Reich.'

Jünger just stared at him, his lips tight.

'The Führer always speaks highly of me, and Reichsführer Himmler has promised I'll go on to even higher office. My record of service is impeccable. My work in controlling the Jewish problem is much admired by all my peers.' His rant tailed off as Jünger's expression didn't change.

'They can't help you now.' Jünger could not resist a smirk. 'Just like me, you are alone.'

'If you kill me, it will bring attention to the Ratline.' He stole a glance below. If he jumped now, he might avoid the bullet. 'And you'll never get away.'

'I said I'd shoot you,' Jünger lowered the gun as a man cycled past. 'Not that I'd kill you.'

'Good man.' Although he relaxed, he was puzzled.

'As you know, Herr General, I'm an excellent shot. I can hit a pfennig at 50 paces. The bullet will crease the side of your head, concussing you.' He scanned the area before taking aim. 'You'll fall into the river, unconscious, and drown within minutes. In a few days, your body will be found miles downstream. They won't be able to identify you. It won't be a suspicious death and will be dismissed as another vagrant who has fallen into the river.'

Panic overwhelmed him. His family would never know what had happened, and he'd face the unforgivable sin of dying unrepentant and being buried in a pauper's grave.

66

She stared at Enrico's body in bewilderment. 'What have I done?'
Jan fetched a glass and a jug of water from the kitchen and made her drink, then upended the remains over her head, receiving a glare in exchange as she shook away the water.

'I can't believe I did that.' Her eyes were wide open. 'Didn't mean to kill him. It means I'm no better than them.' She frowned in disgust and tried to stand, but staggered and held onto him.

'We must get away from here,' he said.

She observed him bleakly. 'Where's Wächter?'

'Gone.'

Her voice was high-pitched and trembling as she replied, 'Oh no, we've lost him. I'll never find her now.'

'Not exactly, Enrico said Wächter and Jünger had gone for a swim in the Tiber.'

Bemused, she shook her head. 'Why would he?'

'Because he's arrogant, but he'll come back and, when they do, you mustn't be here.'

He put a finger to her lips to silence her protests. 'Go to the American Embassy, you'll be safe there, and tell Hadron to send the cavalry.'

'And what will you be doing?'

'I'll wait here for them.'

The VIOLINIST'S REVENGE

'You can't,' she said, putting a hand to her mouth. 'They're armed. I don't want to lose you, too.'

He grinned and placed a reassuring arm around her. 'Don't worry, I'll be ready for them.' He waved his gun in the air. 'And they won't be expecting me to be here.'

'No.' She staggered again before slumping on the bench. 'And what if they don't return? I'll have lost Lily.'

'Just do as I say. I'm not putting you in more danger.'

'It's my only hope.' She rose to her feet. 'I have to confront Wächter before he disappears again, or it will all have been worthless. We can go down to the river together?'

'It's not safe.'

'I'm going, anyway.'

As she made for the door, he grabbed at her arm, but she pushed him away.

'This is madness,' he called as he followed her up to the street.

She was unsteady on her feet, and he had to support her, attracting a mix of amused and questioning glances from passers-by, but she was determined. If Lily were alive, she'd find her.

When they arrived at the river, they scanned up and downstream. 'It's hopeless,' he said. 'They could be anywhere.'

She wandered along the embankment and turned around and around, eyes searching everywhere. When she reached the steps leading up to Sant'Angelo Bridge, there were people on it, and she shouted over her shoulder. 'We'll have a better view of the river from up there.' The effects of the drug were making it difficult for her to focus, and she clutched at the steps as she clambered up. A movement caught her attention and she broke into a run, weaving in and out, fearing she'd stumble. Wächter and Jünger were there and appeared to be arguing. She thought she was hallucinating and rubbed her eyes to be sure. Jünger was pointing a gun at Wächter and, if he fired, her hopes of finding Lily would die with him. 'Stop,' she shouted.

Weapon in hand, Jan sprinted past. 'Put down your gun,' he shouted. 'It's over.'

'Don't shoot,' she implored him, but doubted he'd heard. Tears and sweat were blinding her, and everything appeared to be happening in slow motion.

Wächter was standing on the balustrade and, as Jünger stepped closer, she heard a shot. But who had pulled the trigger? Wächter, holding the side of his head, wheeled around and, losing his balance, tumbled head over heels into the churning waters below.

'No, no.' She ran to look over the edge, but there was no sight of him, and she dropped to her knees as hope drained away.

As Jünger turned, pointing his Luger, an American army jeep skidded to a halt at the far end of the bridge. Six soldiers carrying rifles were shouting to each other as they jumped out of the back. A sergeant climbed down from behind the wheel, and Jan also recognised Hadron, who shouted, 'Put down your gun now.' His command coincided with Jünger firing again, the bullet kicking up dust and fragments of brick ricocheting into Jan's knee and bringing him down. As they were in the line of fire, the Americans held their fire but advanced along the bridge.

Jünger strode over to where Jan lay helpless and held the pistol to his head. And she closed her eyes, waiting for the flash that would signal the end of his life.

Hadron again called on the German to put down his weapon and, while Jünger was distracted, Jan struggled to his feet and knocked the gun from the German's grasp, sending it skittering out of reach across the bridge. The Americans opened fire, but Jünger grabbed him around the neck and kicked away his good leg, using him as a shield, and Hadron ordered his men to stop firing.

From his left wrist, the German extracted a length of wire and tightened it around his neck, cutting off his air supply and slicing into his flesh. His eyes bulged and his face reddened as he battled to get his fingers under the wire. But Jünger's grip tightened until Jan's arms flapped by his side like a bird with a broken wing.

A puff of smoke and the crack of a rifle, and Jünger's eyes widened and his hands went to his side where a large red stain spread like a blooming rose. Yet, he still had the strength to pull Jan back onto his feet.

'Stay where you are,' Jünger warned the soldiers, 'or I'll kill him.'

Hadron ordered his men to lower their weapons, while Jünger

inched back, dragging Jan with him and, when level with the steps leading down to the embankment, pushed him away.

Showing no regard for her safety, she ran to Jan and knelt and cradled him in her arms, her tears falling on his face and, when she looked up, Jünger had disappeared.

JÜNGER STUMBLED and held on to prevent tumbling down the stone steps, every movement like a hot poker piercing his side and the white handkerchief he'd stuffed into the open wound saturated. He was losing blood fast. The berth to Argentina had gone, but he clung to the hope he might still escape, although he realised he was deluded.

The American voices were drawing closer. At first, there appeared to be nowhere to hide, but he'd rather shoot himself than surrender. As he moved along the embankment, every step draining what remained of his strength, he spied a couple of large rubbish bins fronting what appeared to be a break in the stonework. The clatter of the soldiers' footsteps descending from the bridge decided him, and he squeezed in behind the bins and discovered it opened into a large drain, smelling of something he'd rather not confront. In the darkness, the ominous, slow drip of water counted down what remained of his life, and he crawled into the farthest corner and pulled his jacket close. He had wanted a more heroic death, not lying in his own blood and dirt like a rat in a sewer.

Outside, the questioning voices of the soldiers were louder and more urgent as they headed upstream, others downstream. It would be only a matter of time before they found his hiding place. He had bled so much that he must have left a trail. He struggled into a sitting position and held the Luger with both hands, pointing at the opening to the drain. Whatever else, he'd take a few of them with him.

But he couldn't concentrate and shook so much from the pain and cold that he doubted he could hit anyone. It was an effort to lift his head, and he was losing consciousness.

He snapped awake.

Had he passed out? He was lying on the cold concrete floor and searched for the pistol in the dark. How long had he lain here? He rubbed his eyes as he struggled to sit up, his gasp of pain echoing around him. He couldn't keep his eyes open, and his head kept falling onto his chest. It wouldn't be long. He almost willed his pursuers to find him and end his suffering. If he could get to his feet, he'd gladly confront them.

His nostrils twitch. A smell of garlic that wasn't there before. Close by, but it's too dark to see. The smell is stronger now. Cold steel on the side of his head. A gun barrel. His eyes open wide. And in the milliseconds between a flash of blue light and the explosion, a glint of gold.

67

'Where's Wächter?' she asked as she paced up and down the bridge. 'Has he surfaced?' Hadron joined her, and together they leant out and peered down into the Tiber's turbulent waters and scanned both sides of the riverbank and the pathways. But there was no sign of him. The unrelenting flow of the river might have carried him under the bridge, and she ran over to check the other side. She saw a clump of flotsam caught up on the riverbank, and she leant over the balustrade, straining her eyes. An object surfaced, bobbing and turning in the current, and separated from what appeared to be a tree branch. It resembled a body, but before she could be sure, it went under. It couldn't end like this. Wächter had been within their grasp and had slithered away like a slippery fish.

Without hesitation, she ignored Hadron's shouted warnings and climbed onto the balustrade and plunged into the river. The impact of hitting the water was greater than she could have imagined, squeezing all the air out of her. Within seconds, she lost control and sank deeper into the cold blackness until her lungs burned before a feeling of serenity replaced her panic and she relaxed, drifting weightless.

Something moved against her. She reached out and, realising it was Wächter, pushed him away. The current brought him back, unconscious, and she wrapped her arms around him, wanting to pull him deeper, but an inner voice reminded her that if she did, she'd never learn what had become of Lily. When on the verge of blacking out, adrenaline surged through her and, with every ounce of her remaining strength, she drove upwards and broke the surface, spluttering and gasping for air. And, like a cork, Wächter bobbed up alongside, but he was close to death. In a moment of compassion, she held out a hand to him, and, after a moment's doubt, he grasped it, almost pulling her under in his desperation. As they drifted close to the bank, an American soldier jumped in and swam towards them.

'I'm okay,' she called. 'Save him.'

With the help of two colleagues, the soldier hauled Wächter out of the water and dragged him to safety. On the riverbank, they stretched Wächter out, working to revive him and, after several attempts, he coughed and spat out foul water.

Numb with cold, she shivered and was on the point of collapse when Hadron approached and wrapped his jacket around her, and she welcomed its warmth.

'We've got the bastard at last,' he said with grim satisfaction.

She responded with a thumbs-up. 'How's Jan?' She feared his response.

'He'll live.' Hadron returned the thumbs-up with a grin. 'Only a flesh wound and he's got an ugly red weal on his neck.' He winked. 'Will need a couple of days' R and R.'

When she studied Wächter, there was no emotion, not even hatred. He was alive, although his chest heaved with the effort. His eyes fluttered open and glowed with contempt before he turned onto his side and vomited more dirty water. So many times, she'd imagined having Wächter at her mercy and how she'd make him pay for the agony he'd inflicted on her family. Yet now there was only an emptiness as he lay defenceless, like a beached whale.

Hadron spoke, but she didn't hear a word. She shook, not from the cold but because of memories replaying in her head like a film on an endless loop, and she whispered the names of her family over and over as if summoning them to witness his downfall. All those lives were wasted for this.

A figure emerged from the bushes on the riverbank and walked towards them with a limp, and her heart jumped as Jan acknowledged her. As he approached, his face appeared set and he veered off, heading for Wächter, who also had noticed and turned his head with fear in his eyes.

Carrying a boulder, green with moss, he neared his target and hefted it above his head. In alarm, Wächter stuck up an arm as a shield, but she got to her feet, and the impact of their bodies and the weight of the boulder threw him off balance. They fell in a pile together, and the stone landed in the mud with a dull thud.

'Why did you stop me?' He turned on her. 'You wanted him dead as much as me.'

'That's why I saved him. We must make him pay for his crimes. They'll execute him, then it'll be legal. If you'd killed him, you'd be no better than the Nazis and you'd hate yourself for the rest of your life.' She pulled him close and felt his tears on her cheek.

As though time had stopped and restarted, a cacophony of sirens and voices resumed. Soldiers, armed police, and ambulance men were milling about, gesticulating and shouting in several languages, the police attempting to lock up everyone, and Hadron endeavouring to calm the situation. After treatment, Wächter was strapped onto a stretcher and carried to an ambulance, guarded by two policemen and two of Hadron's men.

Hadron reassured her, 'We'll guard him night and day in the hospital. He won't get away now.'

An Army medic took Jan's arm and led him to a second ambulance, and he blew her a kiss as he departed. Now, as the realisation of what had happened sank in, she collapsed and sobbed into the dirt. They had Wächter at last, but they should have killed him while they had the chance.

68

Doctors ordered Jan to rest and, for a couple of days, it took her mind off Wächter, although Lily was never far from her thoughts. Whatever the authorities had planned, she wanted five minutes with him to learn her sister's whereabouts. Hadron owed it to her, she reckoned. He updated them daily but was basking in the glory of finding Wächter and had warned her not to visit the San Spirito Hospital, which was close to the Vatican. To her annoyance, he informed them that Bishop Hudal was granted regular access as Wächter's priest.

After days, when she was almost punching the walls in frustration, Hadron came to the hotel, and she sensed a change. As if planning a quick exit, he refused the offer of a seat.

'Oh, no, he's escaped, hasn't he?' she said.

'You could say that, I suppose.'

Her arms crossed, she blocked his exit and demanded an explanation.

'Wächter's dead,' he said and hesitated while he studied her face. 'Hudal gave him the last rites and was with him at the end.'

Anger threatened to engulf her as she wiped away tears of frustration. 'I don't believe it.' Yet again, he had evaded punishment. There would be no trial and the agonising wait to be executed. More importantly, he'd taken the secret of what had happened to Lily to his grave. Unable to speak, she flopped on the bed, shaking her head.

'It's true, I'm sorry,' Hadron said and lit a cigarette and exhaled.

'What caused his death?' Jan asked.

'Bit of a mystery.' Hadron spread his arms. 'The medics aren't saying at the moment. To be honest, I don't think they're sure.'

She stared at the ceiling. 'Could he have been poisoned?'

'Anything's possible,' Hadron admitted. 'You're not the only one who wished him dead.'

'I had hoped he'd tell me where Lily was.'

Hadron turned away.

'Is that all?' She sat up, exasperation creeping into her voice. 'Surely, you've interviewed Hudal?'

'The Bishop's off limits.' Hadron sucked in as he stared out the window. 'A man who supposedly has the ear of the Pope is untouchable in this city. I've strict orders …' He kept his back to them. 'My hands are tied. As far as the politicians are concerned, it's another war criminal ticked off the list. Case closed. I'm sorry it's not the end you wanted.'

Her mind battled with possibilities as she paced the room. 'Are you sure he's dead?'

'Yes, I've seen the body.' He frowned, confused and annoyed at the same time. 'I've seen enough dead bodies to know.'

'Who identified the body?' she asked.

Jan rubbed his chin and gave a half-smile, suspecting her intentions, but Hadron looked away.

'Who?'

'His wife visited the hospital,' Hadron replied, 'but…'

'What?'

'At first, she claimed it didn't look like him. Said the body appeared to be blackened like burnt wood.'

With her arms crossed, she questioned him in silence. 'So not a positive identification? Could Hudal have helped him escape, and he's on a boat heading for South America?'

'You think they switched his body?' Hadron looked bewildered.

'I must see him.'

'What good will that do?'

'Anneliesa could identify the body,' Jan interjected, and she flashed him a smile of thanks.

'Whoah, hold on a minute,' Hadron said, raising both hands, his face creased in doubt. 'I must be careful. My orders are to back off.'

'All I ask is a few minutes to check him out.' She moved towards him with a smile. 'Then I'll know for sure.'

'Impossible.' The Captain replaced his cap as he backed towards the door. 'Can't allow it.'

'If he's dead, what damage will it do?'

'Let me be clear, my men are watching you, and if you go anywhere near the hospital, they'll arrest you.'

'On what charge?' Jan said.

'We'll think of one.' Hadron slipped out the door and slammed it behind him, but within seconds, there was another knock and he re-entered. 'I almost forgot.' He offered a lopsided smile. 'I'll see you later.'

'Why?'

'Later.' He gave a quick wave and departed.

'It's no use,' she said, tears now flowing. 'I'll never find Lily. We've lost her.' With an anguished cry, she dashed for the door and wrenched it open.

Alarmed, he shouted, 'Where are you going?'

There was no answer.

'Come back, there's nothing we can do.'

He grabbed her arm, but she shook him off, her words punctuated by sobs. 'Got to. Find. Lily. She's alive. I know it.' She fell against the wall and slid to the ground, her body convulsing. 'It's all that matters. Please, someone, help.'

He lifted her and coaxed her back into the room. 'We'll work it out.' But he didn't know what they could do.

Defeated, she slumped on the bed and stretched out, and he lay beside her, cradling her in the crook of his arm, holding her as if he feared she might break and wiped away her tears with a finger. She sighed and, as they moved closer, he went to kiss her.

'No.' She put a finger on his lips and, relaxing into him, moved slowly, rhythmically, her body rippling like the still waters of a lake caressed by a sudden breeze. 'Now.' Her voice was almost inaudible. Trembling and smiling, she lifted her head, and a vibrancy flowed between them, infusing their being as if they were one.

69

She had to see the body before she could accept Wächter had died, but how could they get past the soldiers guarding the hotel? The confines of the room were oppressive, and she seemed to be on the point of exploding with frustration as she paced the room. And every time Jan tried to speak, she raised a hand, silencing him. Eventually, an idea came to her and, with a sly smile, she picked up his walking stick. 'Take this and wear your cap,' she said.

She fashioned a headscarf from a pillowslip and removed the runner from the dressing-table. Wrapping it around her shoulders like a shawl, she glanced in the wardrobe mirror. 'That'll do. Come on, let's go.'

Downstairs in the bar, the soldiers lounged on couches, smoking and drinking and chatting to the hotel's female staff and showed no interest in the elderly couple, one bent over, leaning on a stick and limping, as they left the hotel.

Once outside, they disposed of their disguise and headed for Santo Spirito Hospital, which overlooks the Tiber in the Borgo district. An imposing ochre-coloured edifice crowned by an octagonal tower, its size intimidates everyone entering. They pushed through large double doors and walked through a loggia without attracting attention.

'You've been here before,' she said. 'Where do we go?'

'I didn't pay attention. I didn't expect to be coming back.'

A nurse passed with a cursory glance, and he asked, 'Mortuaria?'

She pointed and gave directions.

'Follow me,' he said.

Only the occasional cough or sniffle broke the uncomfortable silence of a reception area, lined with patients, and even a child crying nearby didn't disturb an old man asleep on a bench. Behind a counter, an officious-looking receptionist glowered at the congregation.

'Keep walking or she'll tie us up in red tape,' he said, pulling her aside. 'Let's go in here.'

The sign on the swing door said *Non entrare*, but he pushed it open and she followed with a glance behind. A white-tiled corridor wound around a right-angled turn and led to the mortuary, where the temperature was cooler and the pungent odour of formaldehyde almost overpowering. An assistant wearing green scrubs sat at a large embalming table and jumped to his feet, surprised at their entry, scattering the remains of his lunch of bread and cheese.

Before the assistant could protest, he raised a hand. 'We need your help. My friend has travelled far to see her father.' He gestured to her and nodded towards the rows of refrigerated cabinets, and the man followed his gaze. 'She wants a last moment with him.'

The assistant, a slight man with a long face, sad eyes, untidy hair and a wispy moustache, shook his head and dandruff showered his shoulders. 'This is very irregular.'

He ignored that. 'We're looking for Otto Wächter,' he said as the assistant shifted on his feet.

'Or Alfredo Reinhardt,' she said. 'They took him from the river.'

'Aah.' As if remembering, the assistant approached a bank of cabinets. 'The one the Americans brought in,' he said over his shoulder.

She let out a gasp and held her head in her hands. 'Please, sir, I should have been here when my mother visited, but my train was delayed. Just want to say goodbye. Please?' Her tears embarrassed him.

'It won't do any harm.' He put an arm on the assistant's shoulder. 'No one will know.'

'It's more than my job's worth.' With a smirk, the assistant reached for a phone on the wall. 'I must report this to my superior.'

The VIOLINIST'S REVENGE

He grabbed the man's wrist, forcing it down on the table, and pulled him close. 'Open it now. We don't want any accidents, especially here in the mortuary.' He stuffed a wad of banknotes into the assistant's breast pocket. 'For you.' He smiled. 'If you call your superior after we've left, we'll claim you demanded payment.'

The assistant raised both hands, then patted his pocket. 'Okay, okay. As long as no one else knows.' He consulted a clipboard. 'The corpse, I'm sorry, your father, is on the list.' With a flourish, he pulled out a drawer. 'Alfredo Reinhardt aka Otto Wächter,' he announced and stood back, observing.

'Give me a moment alone with him,' she said.

'You've got five minutes.' The assistant stepped away. 'I'll be outside in the corridor to ensure no one disturbs you.'

As Jan turned away, she moved in and peered down at the body, which looked different. Puzzled, she stared at him and then at Wächter and lifted the corpse's hand and studied its fingernails. She let the hand drop and raised the left arm, inspecting the underside of the upper arm and rubbed the skin. After a few minutes, she straightened up and stepped away. 'I've seen enough.' She sighed.

When the assistant returned, she rounded on him. 'Are you sure this is Otto Wächter? You must have made a mistake.'

'It's just a body.' The assistant waved at the name printed on a card at the end of the drawer. 'After a time, they all look alike.'

Her scowl forced him to gulp and consult his clipboard again. He ran a finger down a list of names, then checked the tags on the corpse's toes. 'Yes,' he said, haltingly. 'It's him.'

She sighed. 'Wächter may have been in the hospital bed, but that's not him.'

'Are you sure?' Jan asked. 'After death, bodies can change.'

'The Waffen-SS tattooed every member's left arm with their blood group,' she said. 'There is no tattoo. They must have substituted another body for him, which means he could still be alive.'

After walking away, she returned to the corpse. 'Give me something to clean him up,' she instructed the assistant over her shoulder. He handed her a container containing a clear liquid and a cloth, and she bent over, dabbing the inside of the left arm with the liquid and feverishly rubbing the skin.

After several attempts, she put down the cloth and glanced at the ceiling and stepped back, a numbness crawling through her body. Any shred of hope had evaporated, and she felt empty, drained. He moved closer, but she shrugged him off and ran for the door and was halfway down the corridor before he caught up.

'There could have been a mix-up,' he suggested. 'Maybe Wächter's lying dead elsewhere in the hospital.'

It wasn't until they were outside the building that she stopped and put a hand on his arm. 'When I cleaned away the dirt, I saw a faint tattoo of his blood group. It's Wächter. Now there can be no reckoning, no justice, no humiliation for him. Once again, he's escaped.'

A look of defeat clouded her face, and she glanced back at the hospital as if intent on going back in to check again.

But she shook her head. 'It's over,' she said as tears welled up. 'I'll never see Lily again. Now I'll never know what happened to her.'

BEFORE HE COULD CONSOLE HER, the soldiers from the hotel arrived and blocked their path. 'Ma'am, sir.' One touched his helmet to each of them. 'You must come with us.'

Defiantly, she stood her ground as the soldier reached for her arm. 'Why? Are you arresting me?'

'I'm to take you to the Captain,' the soldier sighed. 'Just doing as I'm told.'

'Well, I don't.'

'He wants to speak with you,' the soldier said. 'Now, it's important.'

And when she flashed him a look of defiance, he quickly added, 'We'll meet him on Sant'Angelo Bridge, which is only a short walk from here.'

'I know it.' The mention of the bridge chilled her, filling her with foreboding, but the meeting would allow her to press Hadron for news about Lily.

Jan struggled as the soldiers marched ahead, and she waited for him, and each time he apologised. They turned onto the bridge, past the statues from where she'd dived into the Tiber. Below, the waters continued their eternal rush to the sea, and although the midday sun bathed the city in gold, she was shivering. Why was she doing this? It was a forlorn hope that Hadron knew anything more about Lily.

Tourists and Romans thronged the bridge. The women in thin summer dresses and the men in shorts and sandals were enjoying a warm July day, and they had to battle to get through.

When he slumped to the ground, she called to the soldiers. 'He can't go on, he must rest.'

'It's not far.' The soldier checked his watch.

'Your Captain must come to us,' she insisted.

Jan got to his feet, and she supported him, or he'd have fallen.

With a look of annoyance, the soldier appraised them and again checked his watch before barking into his radio and garbled voices echoed around them. 'Okay. He's approaching the bridge now.'

Standing on her toes, she peered towards the end of the bridge, trying to spot Hadron. At first, she didn't recognise anyone, then she glimpsed him picking his way through the crowd. To his right was a woman with a severe, determined face, and he was talking to someone on his left, although fellow pedestrians blocked her view.

Moving to the side of the bridge was no better, and she climbed onto the balustrade, ignoring the hypnotic, churning waters beckoning her. The crowd parted briefly, and a mixture of emotions engulfed her as she jumped down onto the bridge.

As if in a dream, she hears Jan's voice. 'What's happening?'

She walks hesitantly, then breaks into an uncertain trot. Then runs, weaving in and out of the crowds with such determination that they pull back out of her way. Now she is sprinting, her head up and shoulders back, hair streaming around her face, tears cascading down her cheeks, and her heart pounding as her feet slap the ground and she feels like a bird soaring above everyone. Hadron is holding a girl's hand and talking to her, and she recognises that cheeky smile.

'Vögelchen,' she cries.

ALSO BY VIC ROBBIE

IN PURSUIT OF PLATINUM

Book 1 of the Ben Peters WWII thriller series

'Brilliant! Exciting! Suspenseful! An action-packed thriller that keeps you wondering right to the end. As Nazis invade Paris in 1940 American Ben Peters attempts to smuggle a fortune in platinum out of the city in the legendary Bullion Bentley. But the Bentley is carrying a more valuable cargo, a mysterious Frenchwoman escaping with her son and a secret that could change the course of the Second World War. Why do the Germans want the boy and what is Alena's secret that could destroy everything Adolf Hitler and the Nazis stand for?

PARADISE GOLD

Book 2 of the Ben Peters WWII thriller series

America is facing its biggest threat.

Nazi U-boats are dominating the Atlantic from their base in the Caribbean. And the US government has joined forces with the Mafia to stop Germany from stealing a fortune in gold. Caught between ruthless Germans and Mafia assassins, only American agent Ben Peters knows the Nazis' terrifying plans for America, but first, he has to deal with two beautiful and dangerous women who will do anything to achieve their goals. Award-winning author Vic Robbie continues with his blend of fact and fiction. A pulsating spy thriller that is a roller-coaster read. If you enjoyed *In Pursuit Of Platinum*, you won't be able to put this one down.

THE GIRL with the SILVER STILETTO

Book 3 of the Ben Peters WWII thriller series

Could you murder a child to save your own life?

At the end of World War II, Natalie is given an ultimatum. Execute the boy or die. Her only alternative is to hand him over to the Nazis. Why do the Nazis want the boy and who is he? As the suspense builds, the action races across three continents, from London to New York to California to Buenos Aires, and American agent Ben Peters stands alone against evil and his former lover.

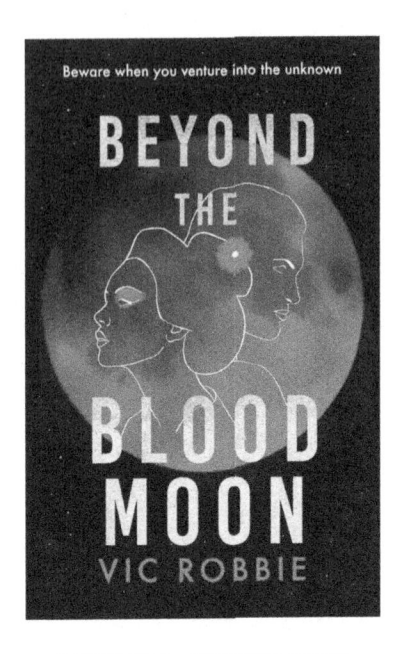

BEYOND the BLOOD MOON

Headlock Hartington is keeping a low profile, hiding away from those who want him to pay for killing their friend in the ring. Then he meets a beautiful and mysterious woman from a different place, a different time and a different world. And nothing will ever be the same again.

ABOUT THE AUTHOR

Vic Robbie lives in England and spends time in California. An author of fiction and non-fiction, his work as a journalist has been published worldwide. He has worked as a writer, columnist and editor for newspapers and magazines in the UK, US and Australia. His first book in the Ben Peters thriller series, *In Pursuit Of Platinum*, reached #2 on Amazon's best sellers list for War stories and #3 for Spy stories. He also founded and edited *Golf & Travel* magazine and the *PGA Official Yearbook*. A golfer of little skill, he has also run several marathons, including New York and London, for charity.

Find out more at
www.vicrobbie.com
vic@vicrobbie.com

ACKNOWLEDGEMENTS

Part of the enjoyment in writing a book is the amount of research that it entails and the various, often surprising, paths it can lead you down. My thanks to the many sources who have contributed by supplying information and knowledge, and advice.

Thanks in particular to Christine for her never-ending support, and Sandie and John for being invaluable sounding boards. Also, Gaby, Kirstie, Nick, Maia, Jed, Archie and Isla for their enthusiasm and encouragement. Their support and inspiration is more valuable than they realise. Isabella is the latest addition to the family, and this one is for her.

Made in the USA
Las Vegas, NV
08 July 2025